Praise for *Fears: Tales of Psychological Horror*

"For decades, Ellen Datlow has set the bar. One of the most influential editors in the history of genre fiction, the gold standard of anthologists, and the ultimate tastemaker for horror stories. Datlow's career and reputation are entirely unique—there's only one Ellen."
—Christopher Golden, author of *Ararat*

"Ellen Datlow has long ago earned her place as the premier anthologist of fantasy and horror. Appearing in one of her unique volumes is recognized as a significant honor, and *Fears: Tales of Psychological Horror* is no different."
—Joe R. Lansdale, author of *In the Mad Mountains*

"Ellen Datlow has a supernatural talent for assembling fantastic stories into must-read anthologies, and *Fears* is another extraordinary example of that talent. There are no ghosts here, no monsters. Just some of the most terrifying people you're likely to meet. *Fears* is filled with deeply unsettling stories of psychological horror that will continue to haunt you long after the book is closed."
—Josh Rountree, author of *The Legend of Charlie Fish*

"Ellen Datlow has expertly gathered stories that surprise by enticing us down one path and then morph, unexpectedly, into a deeper level of anxiety and dread. Here we discover the most creative creatures of terror are human beings, who wear masks of normality to hide monstrous desires and actions. Each author skillfully finds different ways to lead us one step deeper into their flavor of mental, emotional, psychological horror."
—Linda D. Addison, author of *How to Recognize a Demon Has Become Your Friend*

"Ellen Datlow, literature's mistress of darkness, has an unflinching eye for the glorious and the grotesque and an unerring ear for the voices that define and illuminate our genre. With *Fears*, the latest addition to her

already remarkable bibliography, she proves yet again that she is one of the premier anthologists of her—or any other—generation."
—Pete Atkins, author of *Hellraiser: Bloodline*

Praise for *Body Shocks*

★"Hugo Award–winning editor Datlow (*Edited By*) brings together 29 spine-tingling tales of body horror to terrify even the most seasoned horror reader. These visceral works take myriad approaches to the genre, but all revel in the grotesque possibilities of the human body. 'The Old Women Who Were Skinned' by Carmen Maria Machado is an eerie, cautionary fable about the pitfalls of vanity. Terry Dowling's stomach-churning 'Toother' follows the grim exploits of a serial killer who collects the teeth of his victims. The woman in Kirstyn McDermott's 'Painlessness' feels no pain when injured and makes her living giving men an outlet for their violent fantasies. In 'The Lake' by Tananarive Due, a woman metamorphoses into a predatory sea creature. A confectioner transforms his fiancée's ghost into delectable treats enjoyed by the Parisian elite in Lisa L. Hannett's grossly gluttonous and deliciously weird 'Sweet Subtleties.' Cassandra Khaw's intense 'The Truth That Lies Under Skin and Meat' follows a werewolf who takes distinct pleasure in devouring her victims, much to the dismay of her handler. And Simon Bestwick's bizarre alternate history 'Welcome to Mengele's' takes readers into a Nazi doctor's movie theater where patrons watch their sickest fantasies play out on screen. These wholly original and truly chilling tales are not for the faint of heart."
—*Publishers Weekly*, starred review

"Ellen Datlow is the undisputed queen of horror anthologies, and with *Body Shocks* her crown remains untarnished."
—David J. Schow, author of *Suite 13*

"So vivid and intense as to result as a slap in the reader's face."
—*Hellnotes*

"Ellen Datlow doesn't just have her thumb on the pulse of horror, she *is* the pulse of horror."
—Stephen Graham Jones, author of *The Only Good Indians*

"Ellen Datlow is the empress of the horror anthology—enviably well-read, eagle-eyed for talent, eager for originality, she's one of the glories of the field. Nobody who loves horror should lack any of her books. They're a crucial shelf all by themselves, and something of a history of modern horror."
—Ramsey Campbell, author of *The Searching Dead*

"I have a short list of editors that I will buy an anthology of, regardless of whether or not I have even heard of the writers it contains, and Ellen Datlow is at the top of that list."
—*Horror Talk*

"The field's leading anthologist."
—*Washington Post*

"To produce an excellent horror anthology that will endure, it takes an editor with the knowledge of the history of horror and a genuine feel for the delightfully grisly genre. It is a high bar to obtain. Only the best reach it and produce a book that is gilt-edged. Ellen Datlow's books are the gold standard."
—Del Howison, author of *The Survival of Margaret Thomas*

"There are certain brand names that imply undeniable quality, and when I see Ellen Datlow as editor on an anthology, my first thought is always *That's a must-buy.* She's such a knowledgeable editor, with a sharp eye and a long-standing love of the genre that leaps from every page."
—Tim Lebbon, author of *The Silence*

ALSO EDITED BY ELLEN DATLOW

A Whisper of Blood
A Wolf at the Door and Other Retold Fairy Tales (with Terri Windling)
After: Nineteen Stories of Apocalypse and Dystopia (with Terri Windling)
Alien Sex
Black Feathers: Dark Avian Tales
Black Heart, Ivory Bones (with Terri Windling)
Black Swan, White Raven (with Terri Windling)
Black Thorn, White Rose (with Terri Windling)
Blood Is Not Enough: 17 Stories of Vampirism
Blood and Other Cravings
Body Shocks: Extreme Tales of Body Horror
Children of Lovecraft
Christmas and Other Horrors
Darkness: Two Decades of Modern Horror
Digital Domains: A Decade of Science Fiction & Fantasy
Echoes: The Saga Anthology of Ghost Stories
Edited By
Fearful Symmetries
Final Cuts: New Tales of Hollywood Horror and Other Spectacles
Haunted Legends (with Nick Mamatas)
Haunted Nights (with Lisa Morton)
Hauntings
Inferno: New Tales of Terror and the Supernatural
Lethal Kisses
Little Deaths
Lovecraft Unbound
Lovecraft's Monsters
Mad Hatters and March Hares
Naked City: Tales of Urban Fantasy
Nebula Awards Showcase 2009
Nightmare Carnival
Nightmares: A New Decade of Modern Horror
Off Limits: Tales of Alien Sex
Omni Best Science Fiction: Volumes One through Three
The Omni Books of Science Fiction: Volumes One through Seven
Omni Visions One and Two
Poe: 19 New Tales Inspired by Edgar Allan Poe
Queen Victoria's Book of Spells (with Terri Windling)
Ruby Slippers, Golden Tears (with Terri Windling)
Salon Fantastique: Fifteen Original Tales of Fantasy (with Terri Windling)
Screams from the Dark: 29 Tales of Monsters and the Monstrous
Silver Birch, Blood Moon (with Terri Windling)
Sirens and Other Daemon Lovers (with Terri Windling)
Snow White, Blood Red (with Terri Windling)
Supernatural Noir
Swan Sister (with Terri Windling)
Tails of Wonder and Imagination: Cat Stories
Teeth: Vampire Tales (with Terri Windling)
Telling Tales: The Clarion West 30th Anniversary Anthology
The Beastly Bride: And Other Tales of the Animal People (with Terri Windling)
The Best Horror of the Year: Volumes One through Sixteen
The Coyote Road: Trickster Tales (with Terri Windling)
The Cutting Room: Dark Reflections of the Silver Screen
The Dark: New Ghost Stories
The Del Rey Book of Science Fiction and Fantasy
The Devil and the Deep: Horror Stories of the Sea
The Doll Collection
The Faery Reel: Tales from the Twilight Realm (with Terri Windling)
The Green Man: Tales from the Mythic Forest (with Terri Windling)
The Monstrous
Troll's-Eye View: A Book of Villainous Tales (with Terri Windling)
Twists of the Tale
Vanishing Acts
When Things Get Dark: Stories Inspired by Shirley Jackson
The Year's Best Fantasy and Horror (with Terri Windling, and with Gavin J. Grant and Kelly Link) *Volumes One through Twenty-one*

FEARS

TALES OF PSYCHOLOGICAL HORROR

EDITED BY

ELLEN DATLOW

TACHYON • SAN FRANCISCO

Fears: Tales of Psychological Horror

Cover and interior design by Elizabeth Story

Tachyon Publications LLC
1459 18th Street #139
San Francisco, CA 94107
415.285.5615
www.tachyonpublications.com
tachyon@tachyonpublications.com

Series editor: Jacob Weisman
Project editor: Jaymee Goh

Print ISBN: 978-1-61696-422-1
Digital ISBN: 978-1-61696-423-8

Printed in the United States by Versa Press, Inc.

First Edition: 2024
9 8 7 6 5 4 3 2 1

CONTENTS

i. **INTRODUCTION**
ELLEN DATLOW

1. **BAIT**
SIMON BESTWICK

15. **THE PELT**
ANNIE NEUGEBAUER

26. **A SUNNY DISPOSITION**
JOSH MALERMAN

37. **THE DONNER PARTY**
DALE BAILEY

68. **WHITE NOISE IN A WHITE ROOM**
STEVE DUFFY

87. **SINGING MY SISTER DOWN**
MARGO LANAGAN

98. **BACK SEAT**
BRACKEN MacLEOD

112. **ENGLAND AND NOWHERE**
TIM NICKELS

131. **ENDLESS SUMMER**
STEWART O'NAN

136. **MY MOTHER'S GHOSTS**
PRIYA SHARMA

154. **THE WINK AND THE GUN**
JOHN PATRICK HIGGINS

164. **ONE OF THESE NIGHTS**
LIVIA LLEWELLYN

177. **LD50**
LAIRD BARRON

198. **CAVITY**
THERESA DeLUCCI

208. **SOUVENIRS**
SHARON GOSLING

219. **WHERE ARE YOU GOING, WHERE HAVE YOU BEEN?**
JOYCE CAROL OATES

237. **THE WRONG SHARK**
RAY CLULEY

262. **21 BROOKLANDS:
NEXT TO OLD WESTERN,
OPPOSITE THE BURNT OUT RED LION**
CAROLE JOHNSTONE

281. **UNKINDLY GIRLS**
HAILEY PIPER

292. **A LOVELY BUNCH OF COCONUTS**
CHARLES BIRKIN

306. **TEETH**
STEPHEN GRAHAM JONES

340. **ABOUT THE EDITOR**

INTRODUCTION

ELLEN DATLOW

FEARS, as its subtitle expresses, is an anthology of stories focused on psychological horror. There might be a slight supernatural aspect to a few of the included works, but if it does exist, it is not the main thrust of the story.

Some misguided connoisseurs of horror refuse to accept a story without supernatural elements as horror. This to me is short sighted. The horror umbrella is large enough to encompass all sorts of sub-genres. Take science fictional horror like John W. Campbell's great novella *Who Goes There?* And George Langelaan's "The Fly," and Jack Finney's *The Body Snatchers*. The conte cruel is generally considered a tale of gruesome horror that ends in a cruel twist of fate. Charles Birkin (with a story included herein), Edgar Allan Poe, and Roald Dahl are important practitioners of this usually not supernatural type of fiction. A subset of crime fiction—the deeply disturbed serial killers such as Hannibal Lector in Thomas Harris's *The Silence of the Lambs* and Gretchen Lowell, the viciously sadistic killer of Chelsea Cain's *Heartsick* series—creates the same feeling in me as the best supernatural horror does—dread.

For me, it comes down to how the material makes me feel as I read it.

So where does "fear" come in? Well, as Bracken MacLeod has said: "I think of fear as the precursor to terror—an anticipation of emergent or imminent harm that can start small like an unseen virus that eventually spreads until it's taken over. Where terror, being the reaction to violence (let's say) witnessed or experienced in the present moment, always seems large. I think the two (along with horror and disgust) are related. Fear transforms into terror. Terror leaves us with lingering fear. But one's germinating while the other is cascading."

The stories included were all written between 1964 and 2022. They're about serial killers, hunters of murderers and the blowback this can cause in the hunter, about cruel traditions, horrific appetites, toxic friendships, dysfunctional intimate relationships, revenge for real and imagined slights. Hopefully, they will instill a frisson of fear in the reader.

*The ruminations by Bracken MacLeod came about from a conversation he and I had during Storyfest 2022.

BAIT

SIMON BESTWICK

Simon Bestwick's short fiction has appeared in *Shakespeare Unleashed* and *Par-Sec* magazine and has been reprinted in *The Best Horror of the Year.* His latest novel, *The Hollows*, published under the name Daniel Church, was shortlisted for 2023 British Fantasy Award for Best Horror Novel, his fifth nomination in all. He lives on the Wirral with fellow author Cate Gardner and loves dogs, tea, and Pepsi Max. He also (to the dismay of editors everywhere) loves semicolons. *Lots* of semicolons.

LATE NIGHT, in a bar where you couldn't smoke anymore but where the memory of stale tobacco hung in the air like a ghost. I was nursing a double Black Bush against the evil hour of having to go out into the cold when the door flapped open and in she came, chased by a flurry of snow and a gust of bitter wind.

She barely looked old enough to drink, but the barmaid didn't bother her for details like ID; Mulligan's wasn't that sort of bar, or the kind that can afford to turn away paying custom. So she served the girl—a pale slip of a thing, flower-pretty and flower-fragile to look at, dark-haired and white-faced—a beer, then went back to polishing glasses while the girl sat at a table and drank.

With its old worn carpets, padded bench seats, and faded flock wallpaper, Mulligan's isn't the kind of bar that pretty, innocent-looking girls like this one came into either, as a rule, and while my normal tendency's to mind my own business, I found myself keeping an eye on her as I nursed my drink. Some of it might have been out of a vestigial sense of chivalry or paternal instinct, but—at least to start with—it was probably the kind of fascination that draws the eye to a car wreck as it happens.

There were three or four other customers in the bar, none of whom I knew by name and a couple of whom I knew by sight; I'd never exchanged more than a dozen words with any of them. Because—all together now—Mulligan's isn't that kind of place. You don't go there to socialise or get lucky, except maybe on the rare occasions one of the working girls from Becker's Lane comes in to warm her bones between customers. You go there to drink and either brood on, or temporarily blot out, any recollection of the circumstances that had made you the kind of person who spent their nights drinking at Mulligan's.

That, and occasionally you'd put something on the jukebox. They had a good selection—Pink Floyd, Sisters of Mercy, Leonard Cohen—along with the usual crowd-pleasers. Just then it was playing "Shine On You Crazy Diamond," all thirteen or fourteen minutes of it. That's what's known as value for money. The song was still on the intro, where the opening G-Minor chord's giving way to Wright's low, mournful Minimoog solo but Gilmour hasn't come into on the guitar yet, all of which suited the mood of painless melancholy I'd been sinking into throughout the night.

And then the prick in the corner had to spoil it all.

He didn't do anything—not there, not then—but I'd seen him in Mulligan's a couple of times before. He wasn't big, but he was wiry, with scrubby gingery hair and an equally scrubby ginger beard. There was an eerie stillness about him: I'd never seen him move except to drink. The rest of the time he'd just sit, staring blankly ahead, until it was time to get another vodka and Coke or to leave.

Except this one time; the last time there'd been a pretty woman in the bar at the same time as him. Ginger's head had swivelled 'round like part of a machine, and he'd hunched forward, staring at her. It was the only time I'd ever seen anything resembling emotion on his face. It had looked like hunger. When the girl had gone out—maybe because his scrutiny had started to disturb her—Ginger'd sat in silence for a count of five, then got up and followed her out, leaving his drink half-finished on the table. I hadn't gone after them, and I'd purposely avoided reading the papers or looking at the news for several days afterwards. I'd done my best to screen out the bar gossip, which I normally liked to eavesdrop on. But I didn't want to know. I knew enough. And while not much bothers me these days, that did.

And so I wasn't surprised to see Ginger looking at the girl, the same way he had the other one. Nor was I at all surprised when, after the girl finished her beer—tapping the base of the bottle to coax the last few suds into her mouth—got up and went out, Ginger sat still for a mental count of five before getting up and going out too. The only surprise was the one I gave myself, when I knocked back the last of the Black Bush and went across the bar, pulling my parka on as I went.

I had no real idea what I was going to do beyond not letting history repeat itself, and I had even less of a clue once I made it out onto Cairn Street, because there was no one in sight—not the girl, and not Ginger. A car swished by, wheels churning at the slush on the tarmac and headlights trapping swirls of snow, but the only person in it was an old man with white hair and thick moustache.

I spun first one way and then the other, but all I saw was the light shining on wet, empty pavement and grey slush. Cairn Street cuts a pretty straight line through downtown, linking two other main roads, and there's little or nothing branching off.

Other, I remembered then, than the side alleys that connect it to China Row, a narrow, cobbled backstreet that runs behind the buildings on this side of the road, where the various businesses put out their garbage. One of those side alleys was three or four yards ahead, and now I could see what'd happened very clearly, projected onto the screen on the back of my skull: Ginger coming out of Mulligan's, seeing the girl, and then accelerating after her with a cat's speed and silence.

I went towards the alley, converting my normal shuffle into something like a shambling trot, and I was almost there when I heard the scream.

I did the only thing I could think of and blundered down the alley onto the backstreet with a bellow. "Get off her, you bastard" were, I think, my exact words. Definitely something along those lines, anyway. Something that would have immediately made clear why I was there; I know that much, because I left China Row alive.

I caught a glimpsed blur of motion darting into the shadows, but my main focus was the small thin body lying on the ground and the blood shining black around it in the reflected light pollution from the snow clouds above. "Fuck," I said, and then "Fuck," once again. I dropped into a crouch by the body, although I could already guess from its stillness and the amount of blood that there wasn't much point. Maybe I was just glad of the excuse not to try and chase Ginger and risk serious injury even if I caught the bastard.

I genuinely thought the body was her, though—I'll blame the dim light and the influence of several Black Bushes for that—until I flipped it over and saw who it really was.

Ginger was actually still alive, if only just. His eyes were staring up at the falling snow and his lips were twitching. If I had to guess, I think he was trying to say something along the lines of *What just happened?*

A switchblade lay in the snow beside him, but there was no blood on the blade: his weapon, not hers, so I guessed I'd read his intentions correctly. There was a stab wound in his throat, but it wasn't a cut. I felt a little sick when I realised what she'd done: her knife had both a cutting edge and a sharp point, and she'd used the point to puncture his voicebox, so that after the initial scream all he'd been able to manage were the thin whistling sounds I finally registered he was making.

As for the rest of the wounds: he'd been cut up badly, and in what could only have been seconds, given the time it'd taken me to get down the alley. But I could see, too, that it hadn't been a frenzied act; madness might or might not have been involved, but a method of some kind certainly had been. One of the wounds, for instance, ran down his right arm from the shoulder to the elbow, slicing through coat, clothing, and muscle like warmed-up butter. Bone gleamed white through the red. That would've been when he'd screamed, at a guess: when she'd turned on him and turned the tables. Then the stab to the throat, silencing him. And then, the rest of the damage.

The crotch of his jeans was a sodden, ragged hole, and the source of most of the blood, although he was leaking from a couple of torso wounds too. When I looked across the alley, I could see something else lying wet and steaming in the snow. A chunk of blood-soaked denim, and something else. It was too shadowy to see it in any more detail, thankfully, but lying a few inches from it was something small and egg-shaped, and I quickly looked away.

A *very* sharp blade, indeed. She'd grabbed his groin and sliced—quickly and surely, presumably without injuring herself—then stabbed him and run. If I hadn't turned up, I suspected she'd have taken a lot more time and been considerably more inventive. What she'd done to Ginger hadn't been about self-defence. It had been punishment.

Boots clicked on the cobbles, down in the shadows she'd run into. I could hear the sound of cars up on Cairn Street, the hiss and swish of their tyres on the road, but it seemed very distant suddenly, and China Row seemed far colder and lonelier than it usually did.

She was holding two knives when she came out of the darkness. Both had long, thin, black triangular blades. Old-style commando knives, I guessed. One glistened and dripped.

I stood up and stepped back from Ginger, who let out a last whistling breath which then rattled in his ruined throat. I hadn't realised how much noise he'd been making—relatively, at least—until he stopped and the alley was silent.

She stood there, very still. There wasn't, as far as I could see, a drop of blood on her, not counting the knife and the fingers of one preternaturally white—latex-gloved, I realised—hand. Her face was very pale, haloed by her dark hair, and utterly calm, almost like a Madonna. Dark eyes, studying me.

She cocked her head, lips pursed. I was a problem: not a threat, because she clearly knew how to deal with one of those and could have caught and finished me long before I reached the alley, but a puzzle, a conundrum. I'd come to help her, after all. And I wasn't trying to run, or screaming for help or cops (which, in my experience, are rarely the same thing). All that, I suppose, is why she hesitated; for a few seconds, she had as little idea as me what to do next.

And so I said: "Fancy a drink?"

The corner of her mouth went up; then she showed her teeth in a small laugh, and nodded. "All right," she said, then motioned with her blade in the general direction of Mulligan's. "Not there, though."

"Obviously."

She moved across the alley, moved one of the bins aside, and took out a rucksack, shrugging it on. "Know anywhere near the bus station?"

"Yeah."

"Lead on, then."

But not from too great a distance, she added without actually saying it aloud. She was no more than a couple of paces behind me when we came out onto one of the city's more populated streets, the knives out of sight but no doubt ready to be deployed at a second's notice.

"You broad-minded?" I said, nodding in the direction of the Black Swan.

"Take a guess."

I guessed she was, and led the way into the bar.

Once upon a time, the Swan had been the hub of the city's queer community; these days it was more of an outlier, although it still had a loyal, if aging, clientele of the drag queens who'd frequented it in its heyday. But when they'd built the new coach station—twenty years ago now, so not really so new—the Black Swan had had the good luck to be on the corner beside it, giving it a new lease of life from people just arriving or departing who wanted the permanent chill chased out of their bones.

"Get us a drink," she said. "Bottle of Beck's for me."

I did as she told me to, plus a double Jameson for myself—the Swan sadly didn't run to Bushmills—and joined her at the out-of-the-way corner table she'd selected. I didn't sit too close; I didn't want to crowd her, having seen how swiftly and decisively she reacted to anything she interpreted as a threat. Not to mention gruesomely. I had a mental flash of the dark, clotted thing lying in the alley a few yards from Ginger, and that little egg-shaped object beside it. I took a larger sip than I usually manage of the Jameson, and wished I'd ordered a triple.

The girl, meanwhile, had picked up her beer. She'd scooped up a couple of the paper napkins the Black Swan's staff left on their tables—they serve food within certain hours—and wrapped it 'round the bottle's neck. No fingerprints that way. Good at covering her tracks, this one.

"You've done this before, haven't you?" I said.

She raised an eyebrow. "Done what? Gone for a drink with a strange man in a gay bar?"

"What you did in the alley back there."

"Keep your voice down." She wasn't even looking at me while she said it, but scanning the bar; even so, and despite the lack of volume or inflection, I knew that was a threat. She spent a little longer taking in her surroundings, then returned her attention to me. "You only just realised that?"

I sighed. "Suppose I always knew it. Ginger didn't stand a chance, did he?"

"You're sorry for him now?"

I suppose a part of me was, having seen how thoroughly and brutally she'd dealt with him; besides, anyone dying like that is going to look so lost and alone in those last few seconds it's hard not to feel a glimmer of pity, whatever they've done. But I shook my head. "He got what he paid for," I said, which was just as true.

"That he did." She smiled for the first time, and there was something oddly genuine and warm about it; in that moment she just looked like a girl, barely old enough to drink legally, who'd just heard a joke she liked. "They always do."

"Right."

I hadn't meant to sound sceptical, but her smile faded. "Hey. You saw what happened. You didn't come chasing after us for *his* sake, did you?"

"No, I didn't."

"Well, then." Another swig of Beck's, and she leant back in her seat. "This is nice."

"Really?" I've heard the Swan called a lot of things over the years, but never that.

"Mm." She closed her eyes. "Actually being able to relax in someone's company—'specially a man's. Don't think I've ever done that bef—"

I only moved to pick up my drink, but that was enough; her eyes snapped open and she sat up straight, one hand in her pocket where her knife lived. After a moment she breathed out and settled back again. "Sorry," I muttered.

"Forget it." A sigh. "Force of habit, I suppose. I'm out of practice relaxing. But it's nice, all the same. Nice to be honest with someone for once."

"Yeah, I can see that wouldn't be an option."

"It's easier with women," she said. "You can tell some of the truth. Cry them a river about abuse or whatever. But even then—it tends to mean having to play the victim." When she looked at me this time, all the warmth that had seemed to accumulate between us was gone; I think I actually drew back from her a tiny bit, hunched inside my parka against the sudden chill. "And I don't like that."

Sometimes it's better to say nothing; I couldn't think of any response that wouldn't have sounded either fatuous or like clumsy, unsubtle probing. So I waited instead; if she wanted to talk, she would.

"I never do anything," she said. "Well, you saw that yourself, back in that shithole bar."

"Hey," I said. "That shithole bar's my local."

She gave me a look that rendered words superfluous. "I just need to go in and have a drink. That's all I ever seem to need do. Have a drink and look halfway pretty—that's all any girl needs to do in the right place, right time of night. Sometimes you don't even need that. And they come trotting after you. Just like that little creep did tonight." She smiled now; it would have been warm and welcoming if not for the context. "They think they're going to have their fun with you."

"And you disabuse them."

She nodded. "Pretty much, yeah." She looked mildly impressed that I knew a fancy word like *disabuse*. Well, as she'd said, opportunities for this kind of conversation couldn't be common, so it must be nice to feel as though you were talking to someone with half a brain. "It's very easy," she said. "Because they think it will be. They think it's going to play out one way, and before they know it, it's playing out the other. That's half the battle right there; by the time they even realise they're in trouble —"

"Their knackers are lying on the floor," I said.

She actually laughed out loud at that—a genuine laugh, like her smile a minute ago. "You're funny," she said, with what sounded like real—affection? No, that would be going too far. Warmth, anyway. "But yeah. I mean, not that I can't handle myself in a fight, if one of them *did* know what'd hit him. I know that because I *have*. But nine times out of ten—ninety-nine out of a hundred, really—they never get that far."

"Ninety-nine out of a hundred?" I said. "You've done that many?"

The smile faded. "I've actually lost count," she said. "I'll go somewhere new, enjoy myself for a bit, then catch the bus or the train or whatever before anyone starts asking questions. You've just got to keep moving."

"Like a shark?" I heard myself say. "If you stop moving, you die?"

"That's a myth," she said. "About sharks. But—" Another smile. "I suppose, yeah. I kinda like that idea. And if you think about it, it's a kind of public service. Cleaning up the streets."

"How long have you been—"

"No idea. Feels like forever. Next question." There was a sudden, brittle coldness in her voice: I don't want to explore that topic, it said. Move on if you know what's good for you.

"All right," I said. "Why, then?"

She gave me a long, cold look: I guessed—and it shouldn't have been hard to—she found this question no less intrusive than the one before it. I remembered the knives and sat very still; I wanted to look around for potential escape routes if she went for me, but I was afraid to break eye contact. It was hard to gauge how long that moment lasted, but in the end she reached for her beer, picked it up again and took a swig. "A man raped me," she said. "He raped me and he got away with it. So I went after him and I punished him myself, and then I ran away, so that the police couldn't get me. And since then I've got by by doing the same thing over and over again. Your friend, back in the alley there?"

"He wasn't my friend —"

"Emptied his wallet out first. That's how I do it. Revenge and money." She finished her beer and put the empty bottle down. "No?"

"What do you mean, no?"

"Is that a neat enough explanation or not? How about this? It was my daddy. He used to molest me when I was a little girl. Died before I ever got the chance to do anything about him. So now I'm getting my own back. Again: plenty of men like that out there, and there's nowhere near enough being done about them. Which works better for you? Both are pretty clichéd, I know. The childhood trauma angle makes me more sympathetic, doesn't it?"

"I just asked why."

"You did, yes. But those were the answers you were expecting, weren't they? I was a victim, so now I'm a monster. I told you before—I don't play the victim. I hate that. That isn't why I do this."

"So what is?"

"Does it matter? You want an explanation. X happened, therefore Y. It isn't like that." She leant forward. "There was somebody I thought was the one I'd marry, and he dumped me. Or ghosted me after one date. You wouldn't feel so sorry for me then, would you? And you'd be a lot more scared of me."

I wasn't exactly feeling free of fear just then as it was. "Is *that* true?" I said. But she just smiled.

"Maybe," she said, "there *isn't* any explanation. Maybe I just do it because I like it."

I think—I can never be sure, of course—but I think that she didn't know, herself. Or she'd forgotten, along with how long she'd been doing it. I wondered how old she was; even under the lights in the Black Swan, which were brighter than those in Mulligan's, she looked no older than her early twenties. How many Gingers could there have been for her? Maybe she didn't get old: maybe she was a kind of Flying Dutchwoman, condemned to walk the earth eternally luring predators to their doom, like a landbound siren with a sharp knife. Too many whiskies talking, there: I shook my head.

"What?" she demanded.

"Nothing," I said. "Just . . . I suppose you're right. It doesn't really matter why."

"That's right," she said. "This is what I do. It's what I am."

I thought, again, of sharks; moving, killing, and moving on. Or maybe it wasn't even that. *It's what I am*, she'd said. She was a function; she was what she did. Like a machine. This little encounter was an aberration: what had happened in the alley was the norm.

"So what happens now?" I said at last.

She shrugged. "Are you going to go to the police?"

"I don't think we'd be here if I was, would we?"

"Do you not think so?"

"It's a bit of a public place for a murder," I said.

"It wouldn't be murder. It'd be simple self-preservation on my part."

"The police wouldn't agree."

"The police." She gave a short laugh. "Yeah, well. They've never been a problem in the past." She settled back in her chair and gave me a calculating look. "You've seen how fast I work. And I didn't pick this seat by accident. We're tucked away, out of sight. And you're the one who went to the bar. How many people here do you think would remember my face?"

Under the parka, under the sweater, under the shirt, under the vest, I felt sweat run down my spine.

"You're thinking you could call out for help. And I mean, yeah, you could try. You could definitely *try*. Like I just said, you've seen how fast I am."

I licked my lips, which were very dry. I badly wanted to take a sip of my drink, but I was afraid to move. She was right. It had taken her seconds to practically dismantle Ginger. She wouldn't need anywhere near as much time for me.

"Oh, it'll be a quicker death than *he* got," she said. "You're not like him. You're just a loose end. Nothing personal. Just covering my tracks. You've got a few layers on there, but . . ." She shook her head. "My knives are good. Very sharp, very strong. And I know exactly where to slide it in.

Straight into your heart. You wouldn't make a sound. It would look like a quick hug, if anyone even bothered glancing our way."

She settled back and added, distantly: "And then I get up and walk out, get the first coach to somewhere else. I get off, somewhere along the way, find a place with a bathroom and make a few quick changes." She tapped the rucksack beside her. "Makeup. Hair dye. A change of clothes. And then go back to wait for the next coach. Everyone's looking for a brunette in a long coat, but I'll be a blonde in leather, or a redhead in a hiking jacket by then. Or . . ." She shrugged. "You can take your pick. That's if anyone here's even noticed you by that point. But none of that'll matter to you, will it?"

A shark. A machine. A process, repeated over and over again, and she didn't even know why. Despite everything, I almost felt sorry for her, but I didn't say that and hoped to God she couldn't see any sign of pity on my face. I was pretty sure she *would* kill me if she did.

"Will it?" she said.

"No," I said. "I suppose not."

She looked at me for a few seconds, toying with her beer bottle (still keeping that paper napkin between her fingers and the glass); I felt more sweat trickling down my spine and wondered what she expected to see in my face and what she'd do about it if she did. I tried to keep my expression blank, but in the end she smiled. "You *are* a cool one," she said. "Especially for a drunk."

I shrugged. It seemed safest.

"That, or you've just got a good poker face."

I shrugged again, for the same reason.

"I don't want to kill you," she went on, "but I'm struggling to find a good argument why I shouldn't."

"Still very public out here," I said. "Still a risk you'd be seen."

"True," she said. "But we could walk out of here, then down an alleyway. Plenty of them around the coach station. Two minutes' work before I get the coach."

"And you think I'd go with you? When staying put's my best chance?"

"I can be very persuasive."

"I bet." I reached for my whisky, very slowly. I couldn't wait any longer for another sip. "I've already said I'm not gonna go to the police."

"And why should I believe that?"

"Because he deserved it. Ginger did."

"Come on. Can't you do better than that?"

"Maybe I lost someone to a scumbag like him," I said. "How's that? Maybe that's why I'm drinking myself to death in shitholes like Mulligan's."

"I thought you said it wasn't a shithole."

"I said it was my local," I said. "Not the same thing. It's different when I call it that. So there's one reason. Or, hang on, here's another—maybe I've got a daughter I haven't seen in years and you're the right age and you remind me of her. How would that be?"

That got me an eye roll by way of a response.

"Or how about this one?" I said. "I just don't give a shit."

She laughed. "That's a good one. *But*—" She pointed the bottle at me. "—if you really didn't give a shit, you wouldn't have gone chasing after Ginger in the first place."

She had a point.

"Not looking good for you, is it?" she said.

"Suppose not," I admitted. "But what's it to you if I *did* go to them? You said yourself, they've never been a problem."

"I don't like tempting fate," she said. "Hm. What to do? What to do?" She extended a forefinger and began tick-tocking it back and forth from side to side. "Ip, dip, sky, blue, who's it? Not you." She pursed her lips and cocked her head, looking over my shoulder. I had a brief, momentary fear there was someone behind me, an accomplice, and that in a second the edge of a knife would slide across my throat.

Then she grinned. Suddenly, she was just a young girl again, and the idea of her being any harm to anybody was ridiculous. "Oh, what the hell," she said. "Go on. You can live."

"Thanks."

"You're funny. I don't get to have a proper break very often. This has been nice. Better get on, though."

She stood up, then hesitated. She rummaged in her pocket, took out a couple of high-denomination notes, and dropped them on the table. "You're a lucky man," she said, then leant over and kissed my cheek. It was like ice, and I tensed up, convinced that the knife was going to slide between my ribs after all, but it didn't, and she straightened up. "Have a drink on me," she said, "lucky man."

And that was it. She turned away and walked out of the Black Swan, into the night, and (presumably) towards the coach station, and I never even got her name. I don't suppose it would have been her real one, anyway, even if she still remembered what that was. No one else in the bar even looked up to see her go.

As for me, I finished the rest of the Jameson, then went on out in search of another bar that served Black Bush. *Have a drink on me, lucky man*, she'd said. So I did.

THE PELT

ANNIE NEUGEBAUER

Annie Neugebauer is a novelist, blogger, nationally award-winning poet, and two-time Bram Stoker Award–nominated short story author with work appearing in more than a hundred publications, including *Cemetery Dance*, *Apex*, *Black Static*, and *Year's Best Hardcore Horror* volumes 3, 4, and 5.

You can visit her at www.AnnieNeugebauer.com.

The dogs hadn't barked.

Debra knew because she'd been up all night fuming about the fight she'd had with Mike. Even if she had caught a few minutes of sleep here and there, she still would've woken up. A little whining or whimpering would've done it, but the dogs hadn't made a sniff. As she stared at the strange animal shape on the electric fence, she wondered why.

When she came out to the porch in the predawn dim with a mug of coffee so hot she had to hold it by the handle, she thought at first that a calf had gotten stuck on the fence somehow. It wasn't surprising that the fence's charge was down. They were constantly behind on something, and the fence was as finicky as a housecat in the barn. Truth be told, the place was too big for the two of them. A hundred and thirty acres for two people with no kids was ludicrous, but when the love of your life tells you this is his dream, you make it work.

And so they'd bought a gorgeous house on some land in Anderson, Texas—a town so tiny Debra instead called it by the nearest small town's name: Navasota, ten miles southwest and still in the boonies. It was the type of property people called "land," not a ranch or a farm. It was the lifestyle of those wealthy enough to be nostalgic for the good old days they'd never experienced.

They'd stocked it with cattle, a chicken coop, a few horses, two dogs, innumerable cats, and even some fish for the little pond. With two people to maintain everything, and Mike still working as a vet, it was no wonder the fence was dead as often as it was charged.

The dark shape against the fence didn't move. Debra stared, trying to force it into a recognizable form. After a few moments, she began to think it had no head. She went back inside to grab a flashlight. She shucked her flip-flops, got a pair of socks, and shook out her boots before sliding them on.

Grasshoppers vaulted as she walked through the yard. Her flashlight beam caught their movement like the backsides of tiny fleeing ghosts. The most persistent crickets of the night creaked out their cryptograms, and the air was ripe with the scent of sulfuric water but no under-notes of manure. The cattle hadn't been up to the house in a while. So what was this thing without a head?

Her light traced it, and soon she realized it wasn't actually an animal but a pelt draped over the fence. In the off-yellow beam of her flashlight she couldn't determine a color. Something middling, probably, not black or white. It was large but not overwhelmingly so. It was the pelt only. The feet, head, and tail had been detached, so Debra couldn't pose a guess at what type of animal it had come from. Why was it here?

Debra reached out to touch the fur but hesitated. Was it drying, or curing, or whatever the process of preserving an animal hide might need? And if so, why on their property? Neither she nor Mike hunted. Was it a message of some kind? Someone had to have placed it here, which meant that someone had walked over a mile from the road and their gated drive. And she'd looked out at this portion of the property last night, from their bedroom's French doors. Wouldn't she have seen it then? Had someone hung it here in the middle of the night?

She saw the random, vivid image of the animal, whatever it might be, still out there running around without its fur or skin. An unidentifiable living hunk of muscle, fat, and veins. A sound escaped her, something she'd intended to be a word that instead came out formless. She felt suddenly worried, threatened, and lifted her light.

The fence looked whole, wooden posts of about chest height holding up the four lengths of wire. She didn't see any obvious downed spots or gaps, but that didn't mean anything. It was obviously off or the pelt would've caught fire. Beyond it the land sloped gently downward to clusters of oaks. As she moved her light to the right, she saw the dark silhouette of the pond, the pale length of the drive, more trees, and then back to the house behind her, sweeping over the concrete portion of the drive and their truck parked there, the garage and its swell into the two stories of the actual house. The kitchen light was on, but the bedroom was dark, quiet. Mike was still asleep.

Should she wake him? He had work today. With their squabble last night, Debra didn't feel like begging any favors. He'd be up soon to feed the horses before driving into town. She left the pelt where it was and went inside.

Debra stared blankly out the window over her kitchen sink. From this spot she could see the back of their yard from the vegetable garden to the dog runs, but her eyes didn't focus on any of it. She was slumped in contemplation, a swirl of thoughts that didn't connect: the pelt, the fight, the dawn breaking.

"HELLO?"

Debra gasped, whirling. She brought her hand to her chest and forced a laugh, staring at the parrot in his cage next to the dining room table. "Shakes, you scared the crap out of me."

"HELLO?" he squawked again. Then he paused. "Oh, hiiiiiii."

She shook her head hard enough for the tip of her short ponytail to brush her cheek. She walked over to his large wire cage that had its own stand and bent to look at him. Shakespeare danced on his perch, little head bobbing. "I've got the spooks," she told him.

"Okay, talk to you later," he said. "Bye-bye now."

"It's that damn pelt."

"What pelt?"

Again, Debra whirled. This time it was Mike standing in the doorway from the living room. He looked all sexy-sleepy with his sweats hanging low on his hips and his dark chest hair ruffled and gleaming. She had a compulsion to say something. Anything. Just enough to dissolve their argument and let them move on today without the cold shoulders. It had been a misunderstanding, that was all. A poor choice of words that had blown out of proportion and left her confused all night.

Instead, she said, "I'll show you. You'll want to put some shoes on."

It looked different in the sunlight. It seemed larger. It hung symmetrically, spine aligned with the top fence wire, and the lowest dip in its belly almost reached the third wire. The ends of the legs, cut before they would become paws or hooves, nearly reached the ground.

"What is it?" Debra asked.

Mike shook his head. He didn't seem surprised or half as concerned as she was.

"Could it be a deer pelt?"

"Nah. The fur's too long."

"A bobcat?"

"Not the right patterning."

"Coyote?"

Mike shook his head. "Too big."

"Mountain lion?"

"Not the right color. Cougars around here are tawny. This is gray, and too patchy."

Debra made a sound of dismay in her throat. He was the vet. Shouldn't he know what animal it came from? "Then what the hell is it? A horse? A buffalo calf? A bear?"

He quirked a smile at the bear option, but still he shook his head. "No, I don't think so. I don't know what it was."

Neither of them had touched it yet. The morning sun was already gaining steam, and Mike's lack of emotion over this odd intrusion bothered her. "Well who left it here? Someone had to come onto our property for this."

"It's probably a gift. I'll ask around today at work. Maybe one of my clients thought it would be nice."

Debra restrained a scoff. *Hey, I brought you part of this dead animal* didn't seem like much of a gift to her. The anonymity of it was baffling. Why wouldn't they leave a note? Why not tell them what it was?

From the corner of her eye, she saw Mike smirk. An unexpected rush of anger spiked through her. "Did you do this? Is this some kind of a joke?" she accused.

"No."

"Really?"

"Yes."

Was he lying? The thought bothered her, especially on the tail of last night's fight. He almost seemed like a stranger, standing there in his work clothes, simpering in the sunlight. She had a strong and sudden urge to slap him into a reaction she could recognize, but the thought shocked her into guilt.

Sugar meowed at them from the corner of the house, where she rubbed against the brick. Debra shook her head, walking toward her. She'd already fed the cats this morning.

Over her shoulder she said, "I would appreciate if you moved that thing before you leave. And we need to get the fence back up and running soon."

Her only answer was Sugar's erratic little mewings—something wrong that couldn't be told.

In this part of Texas the sun sunk tiredly, slipping below the high points of their land as if relieved. Dusk found Debra pacing the kitchen, circling the large center island countless times, talking to Shakes. By the time Mike got home she had all but convinced herself the pelt came from a wild hog. They were quite the nuisance and could be shot any time as vermin.

Mike walked in from the garage through the short utility hallway that led to both the walk-in pantry and the powder room, and hung his Stetson on the hook in the kitchen. There was a crease around his sweaty forehead from the hat band.

"It's hot as balls out there," he said, grinning.

Half of Debra's anxiety slipped away. He certainly had a way with words. He used "what the crap" so much it had been the parrot's first phrase. Mike had said, "He's a regular Shakespeare, ain't he?" and from then on that had been his name.

Debra felt a return grin tugging at her lips, but she was still mad. She bit her cheek to hold it back and turned toward the island. "Did you find out who left the pelt?"

"Well hello to you too."

"Wild hog!" Shakespeare screeched. "Wild hog! Itza wild hog!"

Debra turned in time to see Mike raise an eyebrow. Had she said it aloud so often today?

"Could it be?" she asked, voice softened.

"Wildhog!"

Mike shook his head, wiping his eyebrows with the backs of his hands. "It's about the right size for some of the big bastards, but the legs're too long to be a hog."

Debra's stomach clenched. "God, Mike. What is it? Did you find out who put it there?" Why wasn't he as worried about this as she was?

"Wild!"

"If someone had left it as a gift early in the morning, they probably would of called during the day to let me know. I didn't hear from anyone. I asked around a bit, but I just can't figure out what kind of critter it was."

Debra pulled her ponytail down then put it back up.

Shakes began to do the bouncing lurch he sometimes did when he got worked up. His voice could be ear-splittingly loud in their tiled kitchen and dining room. "Wild-wild! Wild-wild!"

"All I can think," Mike continued, "is that it's something not from around here. Maybe a kind of deer or gazelle or something from a colder climate with the longer fur. Or a small moose. A feral dog? I don't know. But whatever it is, it's something boring, not exotic, or we'd recognize the coat pattern. It's probably some sort of herbivore."

"Wwwwwwwwwwi-uld!"

"But why was it left on our fence?"

"WwwwwwwwI-ULD!"

"I don't know," he said. "But it seems well cured, no gashes or anything. Whoever skinned it must have known what they were doing. Anyway, I'm gonna go hop in the shower."

Debra watched Shakes churn and bob on his perch, pausing occasionally to preen. What would he look like without his skin and feathers? She supposed that underneath, everything pretty much looked like so much meat.

"Wwwwwwwww-aiy-o! Why-o!"

Mike slept. How? How could he sleep amidst this? Didn't he have dozens of questions swarming his head like she did? Didn't he care at all? It infuriated her.

It had been the same last night. Debra had stayed up in a roil of emotions, and he had snored peacefully. He didn't used to snore.

The fight was stupid. She knew this, but it didn't change the reality of her feelings. Her casual "Ready to watch the show?"—so ordinary, so habitual—had been met instead with "I don't even *like* that show."

Debra had laughed. His response was so ridiculous that laughter was her only option. Of course he liked it. They'd been watching it almost every week for three years now.

"Come on," she urged. "I know you're tired, but it's only an hour. Forty-five minutes if we fast-forward through the commercials."

"No, I'm serious."

Her smile died, because she could see on his face that he was telling the truth. "What do you mean?"

He'd gone on a tirade about the show and all its flaws.

She was stunned by how badly it hurt her. It wasn't about the show. Debra didn't care about TV, not really. It was the dishonesty. How could he have misled her for so many years? What was the point of sitting on the couch with her week after week to laugh and discuss it if he secretly thought it was crap? Why not just suggest a new show? And if he had some good reason for the deceit, why tell her the truth now?

Perhaps most startlingly, how could she not have known?

The sound of cattle mooing in the distance brought her back to the present. Their calls were low and urgent. Was there something wrong with the cows?

Debra climbed out of bed and padded to the French doors. The cattle weren't near enough to the house to see from here, but nothing appeared to be wrong nearby. The fence where the pelt had hung was empty. She wondered where Mike put it. What animal had it come from? Were there more of them out there, lurking in the darkness, stalking over their land? Was some mysterious beast upsetting the cattle?

Or was it whoever had brought the pelt? Some*one* on their property?

Debra turned away from the glass to see Mike on his side facing her, still snoring. In the shadows she couldn't make out his features, the familiar jaw line or the dark arches of his brows. He could be anyone, lying there. He could be a complete stranger who vaguely resembled her husband in shape and form.

Could Mike have left the pelt? She'd never known him to hunt or skin an animal, but then again for three years she hadn't known he was humoring her by doing something he detested. Maybe Mike didn't go to work some days. Maybe he went out and hunted, field dressing animals before spreading and curing their hides to keep the fur as some sort of trophy. Were his veterinary skills enough to account for that?

How hard was it?

Without looking again at Mike's silhouette, Debra left to turn on the computer in the back office. From there his snoring blurred with the distant lowing until both were indecipherable. She spent the entire night researching how to make a pelt. The whole time she pictured Mike's strong hands doing these things, but she didn't know why.

"Gooooood morning!" Shakespeare sang.

Debra stood from behind the lower cabinets to see Mike walk into the kitchen, already dressed for work.

"Morning, buddy," he said to the bird. Shakes bobbed his head. Mike turned to her. "You making something?" He eyed the knife drawer, which sat on top of the counter.

"Just time for them to be sharpened and oiled."

He moved toward his hat on the hook, so she stopped him with a question.

"Mike, have you ever been hunting?"

He cocked his head at her. "You know I don't hunt."

"But even once? Maybe as a kid?"

He shook his head. "Only quail."

"Quail!" Shakes belted. Debra and Mike both jumped. "Quail!"

"Where'd you put the pelt?"

He squinted at her. "I hung it in the stable."

The answer seemed canned, meaningless, almost anonymous. It was like he wasn't even Mike at all, just some stranger borrowing his skin.

Shakespeare started to rock back and forth.

"I made you some coffee," Debra said on a whim. She pushed her travel mug, which she had taken earlier to check on the cattle, toward him. All of them were fine.

Mike picked up the mug. "Thanks."

"No problem," Shakes chirped. "Gotta go into town."

"I put some sugar in it this time," she said. "For a nice little change."

Mike paused. He always drank his coffee black. "Oh." How odd, the small disruptions. How unsettling. How would this stranger reply? "Well thanks, I guess."

Debra nodded. It wasn't Mike. She was sure of it.

He took the hat and left.

Shakespeare was silent.

The pelt hung from a nail in the stable the way a robe hangs from a hook on the back of a door. Debra examined it, studying it for clues, but it gave up nothing. It smelled similar to leather, but mustier and sharp enough to taste in the air.

Mysterious, maddening, ineffable. But not meaningless.

Try as she may, she couldn't picture the animal that fit this pelt, exotic or not. The fur was thick, a mixture of soft undercoat and coarse longer hair. The hide on the inside was indeed smooth and free of nicks. She ran one finger along the edge, where the blade had separated the flesh.

The horses whinnied and hooved the ground. Debra fed them, but they did not quiet.

She studied the pelt from every angle.

When he finally woke up, his eyes opened very wide. They roved to look at the restraints holding him to the bed, then stopped on her. "What is this?" he asked. "Did you . . . slip me something?"

"Slip me something?" she repeated. The shape of the words was strange in her mouth. "I slipped you something."

He pulled at his arms and legs, but he wouldn't be able to get loose. She'd tied him securely. "Why?"

She sat beside him, on the edge of the bed. He wore only the sweats he went to sleep in. The dark patch of fur on his chest shone dully from the moonlight streaming in the French doors. She wanted to run her fingers through it, but didn't.

"Say something Mike would say," she commanded.

"Say some—huh? Debra, what? I am Mike! What the hell is going on?"

That wasn't what Mike would have said. Mike would have said "what the crap" or "come on, baby." This was someone else. A stranger. Who?

Was it the person who left the pelt? Had they taken Mike's skin? Was Mike out there, hideless, wandering around?

And what in God's name had the pelt come from?

The stranger in Mike's skin continued to thrash. "Look, Debra. I know you're mad, but this isn't funny. I don't know what you're trying to prove here, but this is too far."

"This is too far," she echoed. The words didn't even mean anything. There was nothing behind them.

She pulled out the gloves and the butcher knife. It wasn't quite the right kind, but it would have to do.

The person on the bed started to cry.

When she began her process of field dressing, starting with a careful incision near the pelvis, the crying turned to screams. Blathering. Phrases, words, incoherent sentences. Complete gibberish.

Finally, when she got to the ribcage and split it open like she'd learned, the noises stopped and she was able to work in peace.

It was her first time to skin anything, but she thought she did pretty well. She didn't have to worry overmuch about tainting the muscle, since she wasn't going to eat it, nor tearing the hide, since she didn't care to keep it. All she wanted was to see inside—to see what had been wearing her husband's skin.

When she was through, the pelt, organs, head, and extremities sat in a steaming pile on the tarp on the floor. The room smelled raw and metallic. She stood, removing her gloves, and looked down at what remained on the bed.

It was acutely indistinct. Meaty. Still. Not her Mike. She'd been right. She didn't recognize what was underneath at all.

A SUNNY DISPOSITION

JOSH MALERMAN

Josh Malerman is the *New York Times*–bestselling author of *Bird Box* and *Spin a Black Yarn.* He's also one of two singer-songwriters for the Michigan band the High Strung. He lives in Michigan with the artist and musician Allison Laakko.

THE OLD, dying living room still smelled of butterscotch candies because Grandma Meryl had always had a bowl of them out, unwrapped, with the intention of scenting the space, an air-freshener before such things were invented, a custom kept till her death. Having died only a month ago, the candies were a custom unchanged by Grandpa Ray, who hadn't swapped out the very butterscotch cubes she'd left behind—Grandpa who at this very moment sat erect and still in his long lived-in easy chair. It was a chair his grandson Benji didn't like the smell of, an admission that angered Benji's mother and caused Benji's father to snicker, the way the boy complained of the smell of that chair and the eeriness of sitting alone with Grandpa Ray as if the old man was a monster.

Benji sat alone with him now.

Grandpa wore a sleep mask, like a signature blindfold, a thing he'd worn since having his eye trouble about the same exact time Grandma Meryl passed. Grandpa Ray didn't die, no, no lover's broken heart to kill him, but eye trouble all the same, as if he could no longer stand to see the world without his wife of fifty-five years beside him. Both eyes did die, and as much as Benji didn't like the mask, at least Grandpa wasn't sitting in the easy chair with two huge holes in his face as the radiator whirred and trucks passed on Dillon Street here in Chaps, Michigan, in the year 2022.

Benji sat on the couch. And while the couch didn't smell much better, at least it smacked more of Grandma, that sweet, smiling woman who always seemed to Benji like the living color blue, while Grandpa was like a deep brown or dark green. Grandma was always the daytime sky above Grandpa's dark woods.

Grandpa hadn't moved since Mom and Dad left for the afternoon movie and he hadn't said farewell to them when they left. Benji was used to this. He'd spent many afternoons and evenings at his grandparents' house, when Mom and Dad went to a movie or to the store or, as Grandpa one time joked but also maybe didn't joke, to a hotel. But any good cheer in this house had died with Grandma, even a kid like Benji could sense that much, and staying put with Grandpa didn't mean what it meant to other kids at school, those who spoke of puzzles and playing catch in the yard and long, interesting stories. These days, Benji just sat on the couch and waited for Mom and Dad to return.

Just like he waited now, Benji himself also still, inert on the couch, his shoes not quite reaching the carpeted floor, as Grandpa remained erect in his flannel shirt and dark jeans, his body seemingly melded to that easy chair, that shirt and those pants in the crook-and-cranny shadows of that chair, Grandpa Ray's head set upon those shadows and that cloth like a bust, the sockets of his eyes hidden well behind the black sleep mask with the tiny lettering at the bottom corner:

LUCILLE CHAPS HOSPITAL

Benji tried not to look at him. But how? It was either the old man in the mask or the slim, chipped doorway that led in and out of this living room or the radiator. The old man might as well have been a statue, stoic as the ones at the foot of the steps of the Cyril Museum downtown. Best not to check the shadows for Grandpa Ray's breathing, better to eye the old television on the old dresser across the carpeted living room. Benji knew how to turn the thing on, how to turn the volume quiet enough not to disturb Grandpa Ray. The set was old, ancient for modern sensibilities, but Benji had seen it done, done it himself many times.

He slid off the couch, felt the soft cushion of the carpet, crossed the space, and got on his knees before the black screen. He was quiet as he knew to be, which was both considerable and also prone to mistakes. He was a kid, after all.

His finger upon the button, he saw himself reflected in the glass. Saw Grandpa Ray lean forward in the reflection, too.

"Benji, grandson. You wanna see something?"

Benji turned quick to face him.

"I thought . . ."

"I'll show you something," Grandpa Ray said. "Because if I don't show someone, I'll go mad."

Benji had seen Grandpa get mad before. There used to be some yelling in this house.

"Sure, Grandpa Ray."

"Alright, but don't yell about it," Grandpa said. "Don't start crying."

His hand rose quick then from those ink-like shadows and his big, discolored fingers removed the sleep mask from his face.

Instinctively, Benji closed his eyes.

"Look!" Grandpa Ray said.

Benji looked.

There were no empty sockets bored into Grandpa Ray's face.

"What do you think?" Grandpa said.

Benji couldn't bring himself to think. For a confusing second, he almost smiled. Almost said, *Grandpa! You can still see!* But something was off. As if Benji wasn't looking at Grandpa Ray exactly. It was more like a living cartoon sitting in that smelly old easy chair. With wrinkles too deep to be real. And eyes too big—

"They aren't mine," Grandpa Ray said, his voice suddenly too loud, too creaky, too close. "And they're a little too big, aren't they?"

Benji only nodded, despite being unsure if Grandpa could see him or not. *Too big* was the right way to say it. Yes. The eyes were too big for Grandpa Ray's face. Too big and too blue.

"You're not saying anything," Grandpa Ray said, his ear cocked, as if listening for Benji. And Benji understood these eyes could not see.

"It's just as well," Grandpa said. He tilted his head, and the eyes remained unblinking, fixed. Like the eyes of a statue. Or a drawing. Unchanging. And thick folds of skin circled the eyes, like the eyes had been forced into those sockets. "I think it's the preservation method. The lamination was too thick. Still . . . they're mine now." Then, "Come on, Benji. Sit on the couch. Let me tell you a story."

Benji was a little too afraid to move. Grandpa Ray turned his face from side to side, and those big, blue orbs acted like headlights, unused, unilluminating.

"*Do it*," Grandpa said, his voice solid wood then. And Benji, hot, embarrassed, got up and crossed the space, giving Grandpa Ray a wider berth on that easy chair. He had to climb up the couch to get to sitting again.

Grandpa Ray turned his face Benji's way.

"You can't tell your father what I'm about to say. And you sure as hell can't tell your mother. Do you understand, Benji? Answer me or you're gonna make Grandpa mad."

"Yeah," Benji said.

"Yeah what?"

"Yeah."

"Yeah what, Benji?"

"I won't tell."

Grandpa nodded. And those big, lifeless eyes moved in step with his head.

"That's good. Because I'm too old to go to prison. I wouldn't survive the drive there, I don't think." He brought those fingers to his face and Benji saw the mask still hung from them by the thin string strap. "I spent time in prison before. Did you know that, Benji?"

"No."

"Well, you should. There's a lot you should know about your grandparents because it's the kind of stuff that leaks out and becomes mystery, and when mysteries can't be solved, when the main players aren't alive anymore to tell you the answers, those mysteries start to haunt you. You ever feel haunted, Benji?"

Those blue eyes. Unblinking. Aimed at the carpet at the base of the couch now.

Benji moved his legs a little farther away.

"No," Benji said.

"That's good. But that won't last. You'll come to be haunted by a lot of things. The older you get. Each year brings another haunting. Until you got forty, fifty, sixty, seventy, a hundred things you try not to think about." He leaned forward, more of him emerging from the easy chair shadows. More of that easy chair smell, too. "But it's never a ghost that haunts you, Benji. It's other people and your relationship to them and how they saw the world and how you didn't. You know anything about perception?"

Benji only shook his head no. The word was too big for him.

"Do you?" Grandpa asked. Anger in the two syllables. Benji imagined Grandpa, as he was now, but in prison. Imagined those eyes behind bars.

"No, I don't," Benji said.

"That's the fault of your shortsighted parents. I'd expect as much from Steve, but not my own daughter. Your mother should know better. Perception is king. Your worldview and how you think about yourself is how your life goes. You ever think about yourself?"

Grandpa tilted his head at an up angle, waiting for an answer.

"No."

"Come again?"

"Yes."

"Well, which is it."

"I don't know."

Grandpa Ray grunted and Benji knew he hadn't answered correctly. But the truth was, he *did* think about himself. All the time.

"Yes," he said. "I think about myself all the time."

"Course you do. Everybody does. And if you're the kind of person who likes what he sees, if you like yourself, if you give yourself the benefit of the doubt, you're less likely to get angry at the world around you. You're less likely to blame."

A noisy truck passed on Dillon Street, striking the uneven concrete Benji knew well from coming and going to Grandpa and Grandma's house through the years. Only Grandpa's house now.

"I've never liked myself," Grandpa Ray said. The words made Benji uneasy. What did this mean? "From back when I was your age, I liked nothing about myself because I saw I didn't have anything special to offer. Now, there are friends and family who will tell a person like me that he is wrong in coming to this conclusion, that he is being hard on himself, that he *is* special. But I knew then and I know now: if there are going to be extraordinary people in this world, there must be ordinary people, too. Lots of them. Are you special, Benji?"

Grandpa Ray turned his face toward Benji in full and the dead eyes seemed to be looking at the windows, the lowered blinds, as if he was finally reacting to the truck of moments ago.

"I don't know," Benji said.

"Your Grandma. Meryl. *She* was extraordinary."

Grandpa Ray lifted his head toward the entrance to the living room, as if expecting someone to enter. The radiator purred and the street outside was quiet.

Grandpa Ray smiled and it made Benji shiver.

"It's the reason I fell in love with her. Her optimism. Her sunny side, which was all sides. It sounds like a fairy tale now, but I met your grandmother on the side of the road. My car had broken down and I was under the hood fixing it and she pulled up in her old Buick, all alone, and she asked me if I needed any help. I told her I knew how to fix my car, and she smiled and drove off. But not far. This was all out on the Chaps-Samhattan exchange before it was called that. I figured her for a Samhattanite heading into Chaps for some shopping, and I didn't think much more on it till she pulled back up, seconds later, and said, 'You may not need help fixing the car, but everybody could use some conversation.' She parked ahead of me on the side of the road and got out and came and leaned on the side of my Chevy and just started . . . talking. And do you know what she talked about, Benji?"

"Perception?" Benji asked.

Grandpa turned to face him now. One of the eyes had gone a little uneven and Benji thought of a poorly made stuffed rabbit.

"That's right. That's exactly right," Grandpa Ray said. "Goddammit if kids don't say the smartest things. *Perception*, indeed. Your grandmother started talking about how everything's in the mind. How your entire day is shaped by how you react to the events of the day. She asked me to imagine that everything was all right, that every worry I had wasn't as much trouble as I thought it was. I told her I didn't know if I knew how to do that, and she asked me to pretend. So I pretended. And I saw things as she wanted me to see them. And she asked, 'Did you feel it?' 'Feel what?' I asked back. And she said, 'You know exactly what. You felt it. I saw it in your posture. You felt good. You felt light.' And she was right. I *had* felt light. For those two seconds I felt weightless and like the problems that so consumed me were all fixable, after all. Now, you might've got a taste of this in your time with her, but believe me when I tell you this is a *rare* trait in a person. But Meryl was like that from the start. And . . . we got to dating. We fell in love. And through it all, Meryl spoke endlessly of how to solve problems and how, two years from now, two years from any day, when you look back, whatever you thought your problems were would be problems no more. That was Meryl's Two Year Rule. Two years ago you thought it would ruin you. But it didn't. Two years ago you thought you lost it all, but you hadn't. Two years ago all of life and living was hell and here now you got a whole new version of Hell and that old Hell has been forgotten and so why wouldn't this current version be one day forgotten, too? Oh, Benji, she went *on* with this. Over time, through the years, even as we had children, as we had your mother, even after your Uncle Gary died."

Benji recalled the look in his mom's eyes when she told him about Uncle Gary.

"I know your mother told you about your uncle dying when he was a child no older than you. I also know she couldn't possibly have passed along the horror of such a thing, as she hadn't ever experienced the loss of a child herself and so couldn't know how to describe it. But let me tell you, it was a hell much wider and more barren than any I knew before. A landscape bereft of all hope and happiness. It'd be a terrible experience for anyone. But most certainly for the parents. Right?"

Benji nodded even though Grandpa Ray couldn't see him.

"Right?" he asked again.

"Right."

"Well, one would think, Benji. *One would think.* Except Meryl . . . she cried for a couple days and then reacted no worse than if we'd been too late for a play and weren't granted entrance because of it. She turned sunny on me, Benji, at a time when I knew no sun existed. Your grandmother talked of time and timing and how bad things are part of this cycle of life and how even parents have to be prepared to continue, not only for the remaining child, your mother, but for each other, Meryl and me. She smiled as she spoke, and I detected zero bullshit in her face. That woman had moved on, Benji. That woman had assimilated this horror the same way she had every other nasty event we'd lived through, as if her Two Year Rule had been condensed to two days and forever after, when Gary's name came up, Meryl smiled sympathetically my way, and she'd wink, as if to silently say, *We made a good one with Gary. We had a victory there.*"

"Where did you get your eyes?" Benji asked.

He hadn't meant to blurt it out. But the words had been rising in him for many minutes.

Grandpa Ray waited a minute before responding. And when he did, he didn't totally answer the question.

"You know where I got 'em. You just don't know how yet."

He cleared his throat and Benji nearly jumped at the sound.

"Fifty-five years this continued," Grandpa Ray said. "If we fell behind on bills, she said don't worry. When the crime went up in our neighborhood, she said don't worry. When your mother struggled with her grades, don't worry. When money was tight, things broke down, the house was falling apart, don't worry. When I worried? Don't worry. When I got sick with pneumonia? Don't worry. When the world seemed to be falling apart, what with wars and lunatic politicians, terrible horror stories from across the globe, global warming, don't worry. And, mind you, Meryl didn't fake this. Understand, Benji, she spoke from as real a place as any cynic you'll ever meet, and you're sure to meet many. And the more I came to realize she used no façade, the more I determined her optimism wasn't coming from an insecure place, and her optimism wasn't hiding some deep, dark truth. It was her true nature! And the more I learned to accept this . . . the more envious I got. Do you understand what I mean by that?"

"You wanted to be like her."

Grandpa Ray laughed.

"*Yes.* I wanted to be like your Grandma Meryl. I wanted so badly to be just like her, to react to the world the way she reacted, to say the things she said, to mean the things she meant, and to see the world the way she saw the world."

Benji looked to the carpet and when he looked back up, Grandpa Ray's big blue eyes were fixed on his own.

Benji stifled a gasp.

"We got sick about the same time," Grandpa Ray said. "You know this. I'm sure your mother and father were all abuzz with it. I got sick with my eyes. And Meryl got something worse. And even as her time was coming up, even as she lay upon her deathbed (just a floor above where you sit right now, Benji), she spoke of our accomplishments, our victories, the goodness in our lives. She was optimistic, even then." He waited a beat, then: "It drove me mad, Benji. Do you know what I mean by that?"

Benji couldn't speak. Those eyes. Unblinking.

"And do you know what fifty-five years of envy can do to a person?" Grandpa Ray asked. "I'm telling you this because if I don't tell *somebody* I might lose my mind entirely. And you? Nobody will believe you when you say Grandpa took Grandma's eyes and jammed them up into his face."

"I gotta go to the bathroom," Benji said.

Grandpa Ray smiled.

"No you don't," he said. "You need to stay seated. Right there. And you need to listen to what I have to say. Because, what good would her eyes do for me if I got them after she died? What good would dead eyes do me? Do you get it, Benji? I needed to see the world through Meryl's eyes. I needed to see the colors she saw. I needed to see how war and pestilence and famine and murder looked to *her*, not to some long dead objects on a hospital tray."

Benji was crying. No way to stop it.

"She'd already purchased for me a set of glass eyes," Grandpa Ray said, "because of what was happening with me. Because she was exactly the kind of person to tell a man who was about to lose both eyes that he need not worry, two more were on the way. But once those glass eyes arrived, I knew exactly what needed to be done." He paused, to stare, it seemed, at Benji. "She was awake when I took hers. There was no smile then, Benji. She didn't tell me not to worry *then*, Benji. She cried out as I tore 'em from her face and she died as I jammed the glass replacements in the new holes in her head."

The front door opened and Benji jumped at the sound.

Mom and Dad were back from the movie.

Benji got down from the couch quick and ran to the living room entrance, just as his parents got there.

"Benji," Dad said. "Christ! You look like you just ran a marathon."

"Did Grandpa Ray wear you out?" Mom asked.

She looked over Benji's head to Grandpa Ray on the old easy chair.

The old man sat still as a statue, the sleep mask squarely over his eyes.

"Hi, Dad," she said.

"How was the movie?" Grandpa Ray asked.

"It was whatever," Dad said.

"I liked it," Mom said. "You hungry, Dad?"

"Yes. Benji and I did nothing but talk. This kid, I tell you, he says the craziest things. Wish I could tell stories like he does."

"Mom . . ." Benji said.

Mom smiled down at him.

"Let's make some lunch together," she said.

Dad was already in the kitchen, opening the refrigerator. Mom joined him. And Benji looked back to Grandpa Ray in the chair. From the shadows pooled at the old man's right arm came the old man's right hand, and in that hand, both blue eyes, both aimed, it seemed, directly at Benji.

"You two want sandwiches?" Dad called from the kitchen.

Grandma's blue eyes. Preserved. In the old man's right hand.

Not only aimed Benji's way, but a little lower than Benji's eyes. As if Grandpa Ray were staring somehow at his mouth.

"*Mom!*" Benji called, his voice trembling. He ran to be with his parents, leaving the old, blind man in the shadows of the old, dying living room.

"Easy," Dad said, as Benji crashed up against his legs near the kitchen table.

And from the living room, Grandpa Ray's voice, speaking just loud enough for those in the kitchen to hear, said, "There's no greater gift than a sunny disposition. And for those who it was not given, it's taken."

"Jeez, Dad," Mom called over her shoulder from the kitchen counter. "You sound like Mom."

THE DONNER PARTY

DALE BAILEY

Dale Bailey is the author of nine books, including *This Island Earth: 8 Features from the Drive-In*, *In the Night Wood*, and *The End of the End of Everything: Stories* and *The Subterranean Season*. His short fiction has been adapted for television and often appears in best-of-the-year anthologies. He has won the Shirley Jackson Award and the International Horror Guild Award and has been a finalist for the World Fantasy, Nebula, Locus, and Bram Stoker Awards. He lives in North Carolina, where he teaches in the MFA in Creative Writing program at Lenoir-Rhyne University.

LADY DONNER was in ascendance the first time Mrs. Breen tasted human flesh. For more years than anyone cared to count, Lady Donner had ruled the London Season like a queen. Indeed, some said that she stood second only to Victoria herself when it came to making (or breaking) someone's place in Society—a sentiment sovereign in Mrs. Breen's mind as her footman handed her down from the carriage into the gathering London twilight, where she took Mr. Breen's arm.

"There is no reason to be apprehensive, Alice," he had told her in their last fleeting moment of privacy, during the drive to Lady Donner's home in Park Lane, and she had felt then, as she frequently did, the breadth of his age and experience when measured against her youth. Though they shared a child—two-year-old Sophie, not the heir they had been hoping for—Mr. Breen often seemed more like a father than her husband, and his paternal assurances did not dull the edge of her anxiety. To receive a dinner invitation from such a luminary as Lady Donner was surprising under any circumstances. To receive a First Feast invitation was shocking. So Mrs. Breen *was* apprehensive—apprehensive as they were admitted into the grand foyer, apprehensive as they were announced into the drawing room, apprehensive most of all as Lady Donner, stout and unhandsome in her late middle age, swept down upon them in a cloud of taffeta and perfume.

"I am pleased to make your acquaintance at last, Mrs. Breen," Lady Donner said, taking her hand. "I have heard so much of you."

"The honor is mine," Mrs. Breen said, smiling.

But Lady Donner had already turned her attention to Mr. Breen. "She is lovely, Walter," she was saying, "a rare beauty indeed. Radiant." Lady Donner squeezed Mrs. Breen's hand. "You are radiant, darling. Really."

And then—it was so elegantly done that Mrs. Breen afterward wasn't quite certain *how* it had been done—Lady Donner divested her of her husband, leaving her respite to take in the room: the low fire burning in the grate and the lights of the chandelier, flickering like diamonds, and the ladies in their bright dresses, glittering like visitants from Faery that might any moment erupt into flight. Scant years ago, in the era of genteel penury from which Mr. Breen had rescued her, Mrs. Breen had watched such ethereal creatures promenade along Rotten Row, scarcely imagining that she would someday take her place among them. Now that she had, she felt like an impostor, wary of exposure and suddenly dowdy in a dress that had looked little short of divine when her dress-maker first unveiled it.

Such were her thoughts when Lady Donner returned, drawing from the company an elderly gentleman, palsied and stooped: Mrs. Breen's escort to table, Mr. Cavendish, one of the lesser great. He had known Mr. Breen for decades, he confided as they went down to dinner, enquiring afterward about her own family.

Mrs. Breen, who had no family left, allowed—reluctantly—that her father had been a Munby.

"Munby," Mr. Cavendish said as they took their seats. "I do not know any Munbys."

"We are of no great distinction, I fear," Mrs. Breen conceded.

Mr. Cavendish seemed not to hear her. His gaze was distant. "Now, when I was a young man, there was a Munby out of—"

Coketown, she thought he was going to say, but Mr. Cavendish chuckled abruptly and came back to her. He touched her hand. "But that was very long ago, I fear, in the age of the Megalosaurus."

Then the footman arrived with the wine and Mr. Cavendish became convivial, as a man who has caught himself on the verge of indecorum and stepped back from the precipice. He shared a self-deprecating anecdote of his youth—something about a revolver and a racehorse—and spoke warmly of his grandson at Oxford, which led to a brief exchange regarding Sophie (skirting the difficult issue of an heir). Then his voice was subsumed into the general colloquy at the table, sonorous as the wash of a distant sea. Mrs. Breen contributed little to this conversation and would later remember less of it.

What she would recall, fresh at every remove, was the food—not because she was a gourmand or a glutton, but because each new dish, served up by the footman at her shoulder, was a reminder that she had at last achieved the apotheosis to which she had so long aspired. And no dish more reminded her of this new status than the neat cutlets of ensouled flesh, reserved alone in all the year for the First Feast and Second Day dinner that celebrated the divinely ordained social order.

It was delicious.

"Do try it with your butter," Mr. Cavendish recommended, and Mrs. Breen cut a dainty portion, dipped it into the ramekin of melted butter beside her plate, and slipped it into her mouth. It was nothing like she had expected. It seemed to evanesce on her tongue, the butter a mere grace note to a stronger, slightly sweet taste, moist and rich. Pork was the closest she could come to it, but as a comparison it was utterly inadequate. She immediately wanted more of it—more than the modest portion on her plate, and she knew it would be improper to eat all of that. She wasn't some common scullery maid, devouring her dinner like a half-starved animal. At the mere thought of such a base creature, Mrs. Breen shuddered and felt a renewed sense of her own place in the world.

She took a sip of wine.

"How do you like the stripling, dear?" Lady Donner asked from the head of the table.

Mrs. Breen looked up, uncertain how to reply. One wanted to be properly deferential, but it would be unseemly to fawn. "Most excellent, my lady," she ventured, to nods all around the table, so that was all right. She hesitated, uncertain whether to say more—really, the etiquette books were entirely inadequate—only to be saved from having to make the decision by a much bewhiskered gentleman, Mr. Miller, who said, "The young lady is quite right. Your cook has outdone herself. Wherever did you find such a choice cut?"

Mrs. Breen allowed herself another bite.

"The credit is all Lord Donner's," Lady Donner said. "He located this remote farm in Derbyshire where they do the most remarkable thing. They tether the little creatures inside these tiny crates, where they feed them up from birth."

"Muscles atrophy," Lord Donner said. "Keeps the meat tender."

"It's the newest thing," Lady Donner said. "How he found the place, I'll never know."

"Well," Lord Donner began—but Mrs. Breen had by then lost track of the conversation as she deliberated over whether she should risk one more bite.

The footman saved her. "Quite done, then, madam?"

"Yes," she said.

The footman took the plate away. By the time he'd returned to scrape the cloth, Mrs. Breen was inwardly lamenting the fact that hers was not the right to every year partake of such a succulent repast. Yet she was much consoled by thoughts of the Season to come. With the doors of Society flung open to them, Sophie, like her mother, might marry up and someday preside over a First Feast herself.

The whole world lay before her like a banquet. What was there now that the Breens could not accomplish?

Nonetheless, a dark mood seized Mrs. Breen as their carriage rattled home. Mr. Cavendish's abortive statement hung in her mind, all the worse for being unspoken.

Coketown.

Her grandfather had made his fortune in the mills of Coketown. Through charm and money (primarily the latter), Abel Munby had sought admission into the empyrean inhabited by the First Families; he'd been doomed to a sort of purgatorial half-life instead—not unknown in the most rarified circles, but not entirely welcome within them, either. If he'd had a daughter, a destitute baronet might have been persuaded to take her, confirming the family's rise and boding well for still greater future elevation. He'd had a son instead, a wastrel and a drunk who'd squandered most of his father's fortune, leaving his own daughter—the future Mrs. Breen—marooned at the periphery of the *haut monde*, subsisting on a small living and receiving an occasional dinner invitation when a hostess of some lesser degree needed to fill out a table.

Mr. Breen had plucked her from obscurity at such a table, though she had no dowry and but the echo of a name. Men had done more for beauty and the promise of an heir, she supposed. But beauty fades, and no heir had been forthcoming, only Sophie—poor, dear Sophie, whom her father had quickly consigned to the keeping of her nanny.

"You stare out that window as if you read some ill omen in the mist," Mr. Breen said. "Does something trouble your thoughts?"

Mrs. Breen looked up. She forced a smile. "No, dear," she replied. "I am weary, nothing more."

Fireworks burst in the night sky—Mrs. Breen was not blind to the irony that the lower orders should thus celebrate their own abject place—and the fog bloomed with color. Mr. Breen studied her with an appraising eye. Some further response was required.

Mrs. Breen sighed. "Do you never think of it?"

"Think of what?"

She hesitated, uncertain. Sophie? Coketown? Both? At last, she said, "I wonder if they reproach me for my effrontery."

"Your effrontery?"

"In daring to take a place at their table."

"You were charming, dear."

"Charm is insufficient, Walter. I have the sweat and grime of Coketown upon my hands."

"Your grandfather had the sweat and grime of Coketown upon his hands. You are unbesmirched, my dear."

"Yet some would argue that my rank is insufficient to partake of ensouled flesh."

"You share my rank now," Mr. Breen said.

But what of the stripling she had feasted upon that night, she wondered, its flesh still piquant upon her tongue? What would it have said of rank, tethered in its box and fattened for the tables of its betters? But this was heresy to say or think (though there were radical reformers who said it more and more frequently), and so Mrs. Breen turned her mind away. Tonight, in sacred ritual, she had consumed human flesh and brought her grandfather's ambitions—and her own—to fruition. It was as Mr. Browning had said. All was right with the world. God was in his Heaven.

And then the window shattered, blowing glass into her face and eyes.

Mrs. Breen screamed and flung herself back into her husband's arms. With a screech of tortured wood, the carriage lurched beneath her and in the moment before it slammed back to the cobbles upright, she thought it would overturn. One of the horses shrieked in mindless animal terror—she had never heard such a harrowing sound—and then the carriage shuddered to a stop at last. She had a confused impression of torches in the fog and she heard the sound of men fighting. Then Mr. Breen was brushing the glass from her face and she could see clearly and she knew that she had escaped without injury.

"What happened?" she gasped.

"A stone," Mr. Breen said. "Some brigand hurled a stone through the window."

The door flew back and the coachman looked in. "Are you all right, sir?"

"We're fine," Mrs. Breen said.

And then, before her husband could speak, the coachman said, "We have one of them, sir."

"And the others?"

"Fled into the fog."

"Very well, then," said Mr. Breen. "Let's have a look at him, shall we?"

He eased past Mrs. Breen and stepped down from the carriage, holding his walking stick. Mrs. Breen moved to follow but he closed the door at his back. She looked through the shattered window. The two footmen held the brigand on his knees between them—though he hardly looked like a brigand. He looked like a boy—a dark-haired boy of perhaps twenty (not much younger than Mrs. Breen herself), clean-limbed and clean-shaven.

"Well, then," Mr. Breen said. "Have you no shame, attacking a gentleman in the street?"

"Have *you*, sir?" the boy replied. "Have you any shame?"

The coachman cuffed him for his trouble.

"I suppose you wanted money," Mr. Breen said.

"I have no interest in your money, sir. It is befouled with gore."

Once again, the coachman moved to strike him. Mr. Breen stayed the blow. "What is it that you hoped to accomplish, then?"

"Have you tasted human flesh tonight, sir?"

"And what business is it—"

"Yes," Mrs. Breen said. "We have partaken of ensouled flesh."

"We'll have blood for blood, then," the boy said. "As is our right."

This time, Mr. Breen did not intervene when the coachman lifted his hand.

The boy spat blood into the street.

"You have no rights," Mr. Breen said. "I'll see you hang for this."

"No," Mrs. Breen said.

"No?" Mr. Breen looked up at her in surprise.

"No," Mrs. Breen said, moved at first to pity—and then, thinking of her grandfather, she hardened herself. "Hanging is too dignified a fate for such a base creature," she said. "Let him die in the street."

Mr. Breen eyed her mildly. "The lady's will be done," he said, letting his stick clatter to the cobblestones.

Turning, he climbed past her into the carriage and sat down in the gloom. Fireworks exploded high overhead, showering down through the fog and painting his face in streaks of red and white that left him hollow-eyed and gaunt. He was thirty years Mrs. Breen's senior, but he had never looked so old to her before.

She turned back to the window.

She had ordered this thing. She would see it done.

And so Mrs. Breen watched as the coachman picked up his master's stick and tested its weight. The brigand tried to wrench free, and for a moment Mrs. Breen thought—hoped?—he would escape. But the two footmen flung him once again to his knees. Another rocket burst overhead. The coachman grunted as he brought down the walking stick, drew back, and brought it down again. The brigand's blood was black in the reeking yellow fog. Mrs. Breen looked on as the third blow fell and then the next, and then it became too terrible and she turned her face away and only listened as her servants beat the boy to death there in the cobbled street.

"The savages shall be battering down our doors soon enough, I suppose," Lady Donner said when Mrs. Breen called to thank her for a place at her First Feast table.

"What a distressing prospect," Mrs. Eddy said, and Mrs. Graves nodded in assent—the both of them matron to families of great honor and antiquity, if not quite the premier order. But who was Mrs. Breen to scorn such eminence—she who not five years earlier had subsisted on the crumbs of her father's squandered legacy, struggling (and more often than not failing) to meet her dressmaker's monthly reckoning?

Nor were the Breens of any greater rank than the other two women in Lady Donner's drawing room that afternoon. Though he boasted an old and storied lineage, Mr. Breen's was not quite a First Family and had no annual right to mark the beginning of the Season with a Feast of ensouled flesh. Indeed, prior to his marriage to poor Alice Munby, he himself had but twice been a First Feast guest.

Mrs. Breen had not, of course, herself introduced the subject of the incident in the street, but Mr. Breen had shared the story at his club, and word of Mrs. Breen's courage and resolve had found its way to Lady Donner's ear, as all news did in the end.

"Were you very frightened, dear?" Mrs. Graves inquired.

Mrs. Breen was silent for a moment, uncertain how to answer. It would be unseemly to boast. "I had been fortified with Lady Donner's generosity," she said at last. "The divine order must be preserved."

"Yes, indeed," Mrs. Eddy said. "Above all things."

"Yet it is not mere violence in the street that troubles me," Mrs. Graves said. "There are the horrid pamphlets one hears spoken of. My husband has lately mentioned the sensation occasioned by Mr. Bright's *Anthropophagic Crisis*."

"And one hears rumors that the House of Commons will soon take up the issue," Mrs. Eddy added.

"The Americans are at fault, with their talk of unalienable rights," Mrs. Graves said.

"The American experiment will fail," Lady Donner said. "The Negro problem will undo them, Lord Donner assures me. This too shall pass."

And that put an end to the subject.

Mrs. Eddy soon afterward departed, and Mrs. Graves after that.

Mrs. Breen, fearing that she had overstayed her welcome, stood and thanked her hostess.

"You must come again soon," Lady Donner said, and Mrs. Breen avowed that she would.

The season was by then in full swing, and the Breens were much in demand. The quality of the guests in Mrs. Breen's drawing room improved, and at houses where she had formerly been accustomed to leave her card and pass on, the doors were now open to her. She spent her evenings at the opera and the theater and the orchestra. She accepted invitations to the most exclusive balls. She twice attended dinners hosted by First Families—the Pikes and the Reeds, both close associates of Lady Donner.

But the high point of the Season was certainly Mrs. Breen's growing friendship with Lady Donner herself. The *doyenne* seemed to have taken on Mrs. Breen's elevation as her special project. There was little she did not know about the First Families and their lesser compeers, and less (indeed nothing) that she was not willing to use to her own—and to Mrs. Breen's—benefit. Though the older woman was quick to anger, Mrs. Breen never felt the lash of her displeasure. And she doted upon Sophie. She chanced to meet the child one Wednesday afternoon when Mrs. Breen, feeling, in her mercurial way, particularly fond of her daughter, had allowed Sophie to peek into the drawing room.

Lady Donner was announced.

The governess—a plain, bookish young woman named Ada Pool—was ushering Sophie, with a final kiss from her mother, out of the room when the *grande dame* swept in.

"Sophie is just leaving," Mrs. Breen said, inwardly agitated lest Sophie misbehave. "This is Lady Donner, Sophie," she said. "Can you say good afternoon?"

Sophie smiled. She held a finger to her mouth. She looked at her small feet in their pretty shoes. Then, just as Mrs. Breen began to despair, she said, with an endearing childish lisp, "Good afternoon, Mrs. Donner."

"Lady Donner," Mrs. Breen said.

"Mrs. Lady Donner," Sophie said.

Lady Donner laughed. "I am so pleased to meet you, Sophie."

Mrs. Breen said, "Give Mama one more kiss, dear, and then you must go with Miss Pool."

"She is lovely, darling," Lady Donner said. "Do let her stay."

Thus it was decided that Sophie might linger. Though she could, by Mrs. Breen's lights, be a difficult child (which is to say a child of ordinary disposition), Sophie that day allowed herself to be cosseted and admired without objection. She simpered and smiled and was altogether charming.

Thereafter, whenever Lady Donner called, she brought along some bauble for the child—a kaleidoscope or a tiny chest of drawers for her dollhouse and once an intricately embroidered ribbon of deep blue mulberry silk that matched perfectly the child's sapphire eyes. Lady Donner tied up Sophie's hair with it herself, running her fingers sensuously through the child's lustrous blonde curls and recalling with nostalgia the infancy of her own daughter, now grown.

When she at last perfected the elaborate bow, Lady Donner led Sophie to a gilded mirror. She looked on fondly as Sophie admired herself.

"She partakes of her mother's beauty," Lady Donner remarked, and Mrs. Breen, who reckoned herself merely striking (Mr. Breen would have disagreed), basked in the older woman's praise. Afterward—and to Sophie's distress—the ribbon was surrendered into Mrs. Breen's possession and preserved as a sacred relic of her friend's affections, to be used upon only the most special of occasions.

In the days that followed, Lady Donner and Mrs. Breen became inseparable. As their intimacy deepened, Mrs. Breen more and more neglected her old friends. She was seldom at home when they called, and she did not often return their visits. Her correspondence with them, which had once been copious, fell into decline. There was simply too much to do. Life was a fabulous procession of garden parties and luncheons and promenades in the Park.

Then it was August. Parliament adjourned. The Season came to an end.

She and Mr. Breen retired to their country estate in Suffolk, where Mr. Breen would spend the autumn shooting and fox hunting. As the days grew shorter, the winter seemed, paradoxically, to grow longer, their return to town more remote. Mrs. Breen corresponded faithfully with Mrs. Eddy (kind and full of gentle whimsy), Mrs. Graves (quite grave), and Lady Donner (cheery and full of inconsequential news). She awaited their letters eagerly. She rode in the mornings and attended the occasional country ball, and twice a week, like clockwork, she entertained her husband in her chamber.

But despite all of her efforts in this regard, no heir kindled in her womb.

Mrs. Breen had that winter, for the first time, a dream that would recur periodically for years to come. In the dream, she was climbing an endless ladder. It disappeared into silky darkness at her feet. Above her, it rose toward an inconceivably distant circle of light. The faraway sounds of tinkling silver and conversation drifted dimly down to her ears. And though she had been climbing for days, years, a lifetime—though her limbs were leaden with exhaustion—she could imagine no ambition more worthy of her talents than continuing the ascent. She realized too late that the ladder's topmost rungs and rails had been coated with thick, unforgiving grease, and even as she emerged into the light, her hands, numb with fatigue, gave way at last, and she found herself sliding helplessly into the abyss below.

The Breens began the Season that followed with the highest of hopes.

They were borne out. Lady Donner renewed her friendship with Mrs. Breen. They were seen making the rounds at the Royal Academy's Exhibition together, pausing before each painting to adjudge its merits. Neither of them had any aptitude for the visual arts, or indeed any interest in them, but being seen at the Exhibition was important. Lady Donner attended to assert her supremacy over the London scene, Mrs. Breen to bask in Lady Donner's reflected glow. After that, the first dinner invitations came in earnest. Mr. Breen once again took up at his club; Mrs. Breen resumed her luncheons, her charity bazaars, her afternoon calls and musical soireés. Both of them looked forward to the great events of the summer—the Derby and the Ascot in June, the Regatta in July.

But, foremost, they anticipated the high holiday and official commencement of the London Season: First Day and its attendant Feast, which fell every year on the last Saturday in May. Mr. Breen hoped to dine with one of the First Families; Mrs. Breen expected to.

She was disappointed.

When the messenger from Lady Donner arrived, she presumed that she would open the velvety envelope to discover her invitation to the First

Feast. Instead it was an invitation to the Second Day dinner. Another woman might have felt gratified at this evidence of Lady Donner's continued esteem. Mrs. Breen, on the other hand, felt that she had been cut by her closest friend, and in an excess of passion dashed off an indignant reply tendering her regret that Mr. and Mrs. Breen would be unable to attend due to a prior obligation. Then she paced the room in turmoil while she awaited her husband's return from the club.

Mrs. Breen did not know what she had anticipated from him, but she had not expected him to be furious. His face grew pale. He stalked the room like a caged tiger. "Have you any idea what you have done?"

"I have declined an invitation, nothing more."

"An invitation? You have declined infinitely more than that, I am afraid. You have declined everything we most value—place and person, the divine order of the ranks and their degrees." He stopped at the sideboard for a whisky and drank it back in a long swallow. "To be asked to partake of ensouled flesh, my dear, even on Second Day—there is no honor greater for people of our station."

"Our station? Lady Donner and I are friends, Walter."

"You may be friends. But you are not equals, and you would do well to remember that." He poured another drink. "Or would have done, I should say. It is too late now."

"Too late?"

"Lady Donner does not bear insult lightly."

"But she has insulted me."

"Has she, then? I daresay she will not see it that way." Mr. Breen put his glass upon the sideboard. He walked across the room and gently took her shoulders. "You must write to her, Alice," he said. "It is too late to hope that we might attend the dinner. But perhaps she will forgive you. You must beg her to do so."

"I cannot," Mrs. Breen said, with the defiance of one too proud to acknowledge an indefensible error.

"You must. As your husband, I require it of you."

"Yet I will not."

And then, though she had never had anything from him but a kind of distracted paternal kindness, Mr. Breen raised his hand. For a moment, she thought he was going to strike her. He turned away instead.

"Goddamn you," he said, and she recoiled from the sting of the curse, humiliated.

"You shall have no heir of me," she said, imperious and cold.

"I have had none yet," he said. His heels rang like gunshots as he crossed the drawing room and let himself out.

Alone, Mrs. Breen fought back tears.

What had she done? she wondered. What damage had she wrought?

She would find out soon enough.

It had become her custom to visit Mrs. Eddy in her Grosvenor Square home on Mondays. But the following afternoon when Mrs. Breen sent up her card, her footman returned to inform her as she leaned out her carriage window that "the lady was not at home." Vexed, she was withdrawing into her carriage when another equipage rattled to the curb in front of her own. A footman leaped down with a card for Mrs. Eddy. Mrs. Breen did not need to see his livery. She recognized the carriage, had indeed ridden in it herself. She watched as the servant conducted his transaction with the butler. When he returned to hand down his mistress—Mrs. Eddy was apparently at home for some people—Mrs. Breen pushed open her door.

"Madam—" her own footman said at this unprecedented behavior.

"Let me out!"

The footman reached up to assist her. Mrs. Breen ignored him.

"Lady Donner," she cried as she stumbled to the pavement. "Lady Donner, please wait."

Lady Donner turned to look at her.

"It is so delightful to see you," Mrs. Breen effused. "I—"

She broke off. Lady Donner's face was impassive. It might have been carved of marble. "Do I know you?" she said.

"But—" Mrs. Breen started. Again she broke off. But what? What could she say?

Lady Donner held her gaze for a moment longer. Then, with the ponderous dignity of an iceberg, she disappeared into the house. The door snicked closed behind her with the finality of a coffin slamming shut.

"Madam, let me assist you into your carriage," the footman said at her elbow. There was kindness in his voice. Somehow that was the most mortifying thing of all, that she should be pitied by such a creature.

"I shall walk for a while," she said.

"Madam, please—"

"I said I shall walk."

She put her back to him and strode down the sidewalk as fast as her skirts would permit. Her face stung with shame, more even than it had burned with the humiliation of her husband's curse. She felt the injustice of her place in the world as she had never felt it before—felt how small she was, how little she mattered in the eyes of such people, that they should toy with her as she might have toyed with one of Sophie's dolls and disposed of it when it ceased to amuse her.

The blind, heat-struck roar of the city soon enveloped her. The throng pressed close, a phantasmagoria of subhuman faces, cruel and strange, distorted as the faces in dreams, their pores overlarge, their yellow flesh stippled with perspiration. Buildings leaned over her at impossible angles. The air was dense with the creak of passing omnibuses and the cries of cabbies and costermongers and, most of all, the whinny and stench of horses, and the heaping piles of excrement they left steaming in the street.

She thought she might faint.

Her carriage pulled up to the curb beside her. Her footman dropped to the pavement before it stopped moving.

"Madam, please. You must get into the carriage," he said, and when he flung open the carriage door, she allowed him to hand her up into the crepuscular interior. Before he'd even closed the latch the carriage was moving, shouldering its way back into the London traffic. She closed her eyes and let the rocking vehicle lull her into a torpor.

She would not later remember anything of the journey or her arrival at home. When she awoke in her own bed some hours afterward, she wondered if the entire episode had not been a terrible dream. And then she saw her maid, Lily, sitting by the bed, and she saw the frightened expression on the girl's face, and she knew that it had actually happened.

"We have sent for the physician, madam," Lily said.

"I do not need a physician," she said. "I am beyond a physician's help."

"Please, madam, you must not—"

"Where is my husband?"

"I will fetch him."

Lily went to the door and spoke briefly to someone on the other side. A moment later, Mr. Breen entered the room. His face was pale, his manner formal.

"How are you, dearest?" he asked.

"I have ruined us," she said.

She did not see how they could go on.

Yet go on they did.

Word was quietly circulated that Mrs. Breen had fallen ill and thus a thin veil of propriety was drawn across her discourtesy and its consequence. But no one called to wish her a quick recovery. Even Mrs. Breen's former friends—those pale, drab moths fluttering helplessly around the bright beacon of Society—did not come. Having abandoned them in the moment of her elevation, Mrs. Breen found herself abandoned in turn.

Her illness necessitated the Breens' withdrawal to the country well before the Season ended. There, Mr. Breen remained cold and distant. Once, he had warmed to her small enthusiasms, chuckling indulgently when the dressmaker left and she spilled out her purchases for his inspection. Now, while he continued to spoil her in every visible way, he did so from a cool remove. She no longer displayed her fripperies for his approval. He no longer asked to see them.

Nor did he any longer make his twice-weekly visit to her chamber. Mrs. Breen had aforetime performed her conjugal obligations dutifully, with a kind of remote efficiency that precluded real enthusiasm. She had married without a full understanding of her responsibilities in this regard, and, once enlightened, viewed those offices with the same mild aversion she felt for all the basic functions of her body. Such were the consequences of the first sin in Eden, these unpleasant portents of mortality, with their mephitic smells and unseemly postures. Yet absent her husband's hymeneal attentions, she found herself growing increasingly restive. Her dream of the ladder recurred with increasing frequency.

The summer had given way to fall when Sophie became, by chance and by betrayal, Mrs. Breen's primary solace.

If Mr. Breen took no interest in his daughter, his wife's sentiments were more capricious. Though she usually left Sophie in the capable hands of the governess, she was occasionally moved to an excess of affection, coddling the child and showering her with kisses. It was such a whim that sent her climbing the back stairs to the third-floor playroom late one afternoon. She found Sophie and Miss Pool at the dollhouse. Mrs. Breen would have joined them had a book upon the table not distracted her.

On any other day she might have passed it by unexamined. But she had recently found refuge in her subscription to Mudie's, reading volume by volume the novels delivered to her by post—Oliphant and Ainsworth, Foster, Collins. And so curiosity more than anything else impelled her to pick the book up. When she did, a folded tract—closely printed on grainy, yellow pulp—slipped from between the pages.

"Wait—" Miss Pool said, rising to her feet—but it was too late. Mrs. Breen had already knelt to retrieve the pamphlet. She unfolded it as she stood. ***A Great Horror Reviled,*** read the title, printed in Gothic Blackletter across the top. The illustration below showed an elaborate table setting. Where the plate should have been there lay a baby, split stem to sternum by a deep incision, the flesh pinned back to reveal a tangle of viscera. Mrs. Breen didn't have to read any more to know what the tract was about, but she couldn't help scanning the first page anyway, taking in the gruesome illustrations and the phrases set apart in bold type. ***Too long have the First Families battened upon the flesh of the poor!*** one read, and another, ***Blood must flow in the gutters that it may no longer flow in the kitchens of men!***—which reminded Mrs. Breen of the boy who had hurled the stone through their carriage window. The

Anthropophagic Crisis, Mrs. Graves had called it. Strife in the House of Commons, carnage in the streets.

Miss Pool waited by the dollhouse, Sophie at her side.

"Please, madam," Miss Pool said, "it is not what you think."

"Is it not? Whatever could it be, then?"

"I—I found it in the hands of the coachman this morning and confiscated it. I had intended to bring it to your attention."

Mrs. Breen thought of the coachman testing the weight of her husband's walking stick, the brigand's blood black in the jaundiced fog.

"What errand led you to the stables?"

"Sophie and I had gone to look at the horses."

"Is this true, Sophie?" Mrs. Breen asked.

Sophie was still for a moment. Then she burst into tears.

"Sophie, did you go to the stables this morning? You must be honest."

"No, Mama," Sophie said through sobs.

"I thought not." Mrs. Breen folded the tract. "You dissemble with facility, Miss Pool. Please pack your possessions. You will be leaving us at first light."

"But where will I go?" the governess asked. And when Mrs. Breen did not respond: "Madam, please—"

"You may appeal to Mr. Breen, if you wish. I daresay it will do you no good."

Nor did it. Dawn was still gray in the east when Mrs. Breen came out of the house to find a footman loading the governess's trunk into the carriage. Finished, he opened the door to hand her in. She paused with one foot on the step and turned back to look at Mrs. Breen. The previous night she had wept. Now she was defiant. "Your time is passing, Mrs. Breen," she said, "you and all your kind. History will sweep you all away."

Mrs. Breen made no reply. She only stood there and watched as the footman closed the door at the governess's back. The coachman snapped his whip and the carriage began to move. But long after it had disappeared into the morning fog, the woman's words lingered. Mrs. Breen was not blind to their irony.

Lady Donner had renounced her.

She had no kind—no rank and no degree, nor any place to call her own.

A housemaid was pressed into temporary service as governess, but the young woman was hardly suited to provide for Sophie's education.

"What shall we do?" Mr. Breen inquired.

"Until we acquire a proper replacement," Mrs. Breen said, "I shall take the child in hand myself."

It was October by then. If Mrs. Breen had anticipated the previous Season, she dreaded the one to come. Last winter, the days had crept by. This winter, they hurtled past, and as the next Season drew inexorably closer, she found herself increasingly apprehensive. Mr. Breen had not spoken of the summer. Would they return to London? And if so, what then?

Mrs. Breen tried (largely without success) not to ruminate over these questions. She focused on her daughter instead. She had vowed to educate the child, but aside from a few lessons in etiquette and an abortive attempt at French, her endeavor was intermittent and half-hearted—letters one day, ciphering the next. She had no aptitude for teaching. What she did have, she discovered, was a gift for play. When a rocking horse appeared on Christmas morning, Mrs. Breen was inspired to make a truth of Ada Pool's lie and escort Sophie to the stables herself. They fed carrots to Spitzer, Mr. Breen's much-prized white gelding, and Sophie shrieked with laughter at the touch of his thick, bristling lips.

"What shall we name your rocking horse?" Mrs. Breen asked as they walked back to the house, and the little girl said, "Spitzer," as Mrs. Breen had known she would. In the weeks that followed, they fed Spitzer imaginary carrots every morning, and took their invisible tea from Sophie's tiny porcelain tea set every afternoon. Between times there were dolls and a jack-in-the-box and clever little clockwork automata that one could set into motion with delicate wooden levers and miniature silver keys.

They played jacks and draughts and one late February day spilled out across a playroom table a jigsaw puzzle of bewildering complexity.

"Mama, why did Miss Pool leave me?" Sophie asked as they separated out the edge pieces.

"She had to go away."

"But where?"

"Home, I suppose," Mrs. Breen said. Pursing her lips, she tested two pieces for a fit. She did not wish to speak of Miss Pool.

"I thought she lived with us."

"Just for a while, dear."

"Will she ever come to visit us, Mama?"

"I should think not."

"Why not?"

"She was very bad, Sophie."

"But what did she do?"

Mrs. Breen hesitated, uncertain how to explain it to the child. Finally, she said, "There are people of great importance in the world, Sophie, and there are people of no importance at all. Your governess confused the two."

Sophie pondered this in silence. "Which kind of people are we?" she said at last.

Mrs. Breen did not answer. She thought of Abel Munby and she thought of Lady Donner. Most of all she thought of that endless ladder with its greased rungs and rails and high above a radiant circle from which dim voices fell.

"Mama?" Sophie said.

And just then—just in time—a pair of interlocking pieces came to hand. "Look," Mrs. Breen said brightly, "a match."

Sophie, thus diverted, giggled in delight. "You're funny, Mama," she said.

"Am I, then?" Mrs. Breen said, and she kissed her daughter on the forehead and the matter of Ada Pool was forgotten.

Another week slipped by. They worked at the puzzle in quiet moments, and gradually an image began to take shape: a field of larkspur beneath an azure sky. Mrs. Breen thought it lovely, and at night, alone with her thoughts, she tried to project herself into the scene. Yet she slept restlessly. She dreamed of the boy the coachman had killed in the street. In the dream, he clung to her skirts as she ascended that endless ladder, thirteen stone of dead weight dragging her down into the darkness below. When she looked over her shoulder at him, he had her grandfather's face. At last, in an excess of fatigue, she ventured one evening with her husband to broach the subject that had lain unspoken between them for so many months. "Let us stay in the country for the summer," she entreated Mr. Breen. "The heat is so oppressive in town."

"Would you have us stay here for the rest of our lives?" he asked. And when she did not reply: "We will return to London. We may yet be redeemed."

Mrs. Breen did not see how they could be.

Nonetheless, preparations for the move soon commenced in earnest. The servants bustled around packing boxes. The house was in constant disarray. And the impossible puzzle proved possible after all. The night before they were to commence the journey, they finished it at last. Mrs. Breen contrived to let Sophie fit the final piece, a single splash of sapphire, blue as any ribbon, or an eye.

They arrived in London at the end of April. Mrs. Breen did not make an appearance at the Royal Academy's Exhibition the next week, preferring instead the privacy of their home on Eaton Place. The Season—no, her life—stretched away before her, illimitable as the Saharan wasteland, and as empty of oasis. She did not ride on Rotten Row. She made no calls, and received none. A new governess, Miss Bell, was hired and Mrs. Breen did not so often have the consolation of her daughter. In the mornings, she slept late; in the evenings, she retreated to her chamber early. And in the afternoons, while Sophie was at her lessons, she wept.

She could see no future. She wanted to die.

The messenger arrived two weeks before First Feast, on Sunday afternoon. Mrs. Breen was in the parlor with Sophie, looking at a picture book, when the footman handed her the envelope. At the sight of the crest stamped into the wax seal, she felt rise up the ghost of her humiliation in Grosvenor Square. Worse yet, she felt the faintest wisp of hope—and that she could not afford. She would expect nothing, she told herself. Most of all, she would not hope.

"Please take Sophie away, Miss Bell," she said to the governess, and when Sophie protested, Mrs. Breen said, "Mama is busy now, darling." Her tone brooked no opposition. Miss Bell whisked the child out of the room, leaving Mrs. Breen to unseal the envelope with trembling fingers. She read the note inside in disbelief, then read it again.

"Is the messenger still here?" she asked the footman.

"Yes, madam."

At her desk, Mrs. Breen wrote a hasty reply, sealed the envelope, and handed it to the footman. "Please have him return this to Lady Donner. And please inform Mr. Breen that I wish to see him."

"Of course," the footman said.

Alone, Mrs. Breen read—and reread—the note yet again. She felt much as she had felt that afternoon in Grosvenor Square: as though reality had shifted in some fundamental and unexpected way, as though everything she had known and believed had to be calibrated anew.

Mr. Breen had been right.

Lady Donner had with a stroke of her pen restored them.

Mr. Breen also had to read the missive twice:

Lord and Lady Donner request the pleasure of the company of Mr. and Mrs. Breen at First Feast on Saturday, May 29th, 18—, 7:30 P.M. RSVP

Below that, in beautiful script, Lady Donner had inscribed a personal note:

Please join us, Alice. We so missed your company last spring. And do bring Sophie.

Mr. Breen slipped the note into the envelope and placed it upon Mrs. Breen's desk.

"Have you replied?"

"By Lady Donner's messenger."

"I trust you have acted with more wisdom this year."

She turned her face away from him. "Of course."

"Very well, then. You shall require a new dress, I suppose."

"Sophie as well."

"Can it be done in two weeks?"

"I do not know. Perhaps with sufficient inducement."

"I shall see that the dressmaker calls in the morning. Is there anything else?"

"The milliner, I should think," she said. "And the tailor for yourself."

Mr. Breen nodded.

The next morning, the dressmaker arrived as promised. Two dresses! he exclaimed, pronouncing the schedule impossible. His emolument was increased. Perhaps it could be done, he conceded, but it would be very difficult. When presented with still further inducement, he acceded that with Herculean effort he would certainly be able to complete the task. It would require additional seamstresses, of course—

Further terms were agreed to.

The dressmaker made his measurements, clucking in satisfaction. The milliner called, the tailor and the haberdasher. It was all impossible, of course. Such a thing could not be done. Yet each was finally persuaded to view the matter in a different light, and each afterward departed in secret satisfaction, congratulating himself on having negotiated such a generous fee.

The days whirled by. Consultations over fabrics and colors followed. Additional measurements and fittings were required. Mrs. Breen rejoiced in the attention of the couturiers. Her spirits lifted and her beauty, much attenuated by despair, returned almost overnight. Mr. Breen, who had little interest in bespoke clothing and less patience with it, endured the attentions of his tailor. Sophie shook her petticoats in fury and stood upon the dressmaker's stool, protesting that she did not *want* to lift her arms or turn around or (most of all) *hold still.* Miss Bell was reprimanded and told to take a sterner line with the child.

Despite all this, Mrs. Breen was occasionally stricken with anxiety. What if the dresses weren't ready or proved in some way unsatisfactory?

All will be well, Mr. Breen assured her.

She envied his cool certainty.

The clothes arrived the Friday morning prior to the feast: a simple white dress with sapphire accents for Sophie; a striking gown of midnight blue, lightly bustled, for Mrs. Breen.

Secretly pleased, Mrs. Breen modeled it for her husband—though not without trepidation. Perhaps it was insufficiently modest for such a sober occasion.

All will be well, Mr. Breen assured her.

And then it was Saturday.

Mrs. Breen woke to a late breakfast and afterward bathed and dressed at her leisure. Her maid pinned up her hair in an elaborate coiffure and helped her into her corset. It was late in the afternoon when she at last donned her gown, and later still—they were on the verge of departing—when Miss Bell presented Sophie for her approval.

They stood in the foyer of the great house, Mr. and Mrs. Breen, and Miss Bell, and the child herself—the latter looking, Mr. Breen said with unaccustomed tenderness, as lovely as a star fallen to the Earth. Sophie giggled with delight at this fancy. Yet there was some missing touch to perfect the child's appearance, Mrs. Breen thought, studying Sophie's child's white habiliments with their sapphire accents.

"Shall we go, then?" Mr. Breen said.

"Not quite yet," Mrs. Breen said.

"My dear—"

Mrs. Breen ignored him. She studied the child's blonde ringlets. A moment came to her: Lady Donner tying up Sophie's hair with a deep blue ribbon of embroidered mulberry silk. With excuses to her husband, who made a show of removing his watch from its pocket and checking the time, Mrs. Breen returned to her chamber. She opened her carven wooden box of keepsakes. She found the ribbon folded carefully away among the other treasures she had been unable to look at in the era of her exile: a program from her first opera and a single dried rose from her wedding bouquet, which she had once reckoned the happiest day of her life—before Lady Breen's First Feast invitation (also present) and the taste of human flesh that it had occasioned. She smoothed the luxuriant silk between her fingers, recalling Lady Donner's words while the child had admired herself in the gilt mirror.

She partakes of her mother's beauty.

Mrs. Breen blinked back tears—it would not do to cry—and hastened downstairs, where she tied the ribbon into Sophie's hair. Mr. Breen paced impatiently as she perfected the bow.

"There," Mrs. Breen said, with a final adjustment. "Don't you look lovely?"

Sophie smiled, dimpling her checks, and took her mother's hand.

"Shall we?" Mr. Breen said, ushering them out the door to the street, where the coachman awaited.

They arrived promptly at seven thirty.

Sophie spilled out of the carriage the moment the footman opened the door.

"Wait, Sophie," Mrs. Breen said. "Slowly. Comport yourself as a lady." She knelt to rub an imaginary speck from the child's forehead and once again adjusted the bow. "There you go. Perfect. You are the very picture of beauty. Can you promise to be very good for Mama?"

Sophie giggled. "Promise," she said.

Mr. Breen smiled and caressed the child's cheek, and then, to Mrs. Breen's growing anxiety—what if something should go wrong?—Mr. Breen rang the bell. He reached down and squeezed her hand, and then the butler was admitting them into the great foyer, and soon afterward, before she had time to fully compose herself, announcing them into the drawing room.

Lady Donner turned to meet them, smiling, and it was as if the incident in Grosvenor Square had never happened. She took Mrs. Breen's hand. "I am glad you were able to come," she said. "I have so missed you." And then, kneeling, so that she could look Sophie in the eye: "Do you remember me, Sophie?"

Sophie, intimidated by the blazing drawing room and the crowd of strangers and this smiling apparition before her, promptly inserted a knuckle between her teeth. She remembered nothing, of course. Lady Donner laughed. She ran her finger lightly over the ribbon and conjured up a sweet, which Sophie was persuaded after some negotiation to take. Then—"We shall talk again soon, darling," Lady Donner promised—a housemaid ushered the child off to join the other children at the children's feast. Lady Donner escorted the Breens deeper into the room and made introductions.

It was an exalted company. In short order, Mrs. Breen found herself shaking hands with a florid, toad-like gentleman who turned out to be Lord Stanton, the Bishop of London, and a slim, dapper one whom Lady Donner introduced as the Right Honorable Mr. Daniel Williams, an MP from Oxford. Alone unwived among the men was the radical novelist Charles Foster, whom Mrs. Breen found especially fascinating, having whiled away many an hour over his triple-deckers during her time in exile. The sole remaining guest was the aged Mrs. Murphy, a palsied widow in half-mourning. Mrs. Breen never did work out her precise rank, though she must have been among the lesser great since she and Mr. Breen were the penultimate guests to proceed down to dinner. Mrs. Breen followed, arm in arm with Mr. Foster, whose notoriety had earned him the invitation and whose common origin had determined his place in the procession. Mrs. Breen wished that her companion were of greater rank—that she, too, had not been consigned to the lowest position. Her distress was exacerbated by Mr. Foster's brazen irreverence. "Fear not, Mrs. Breen," he remarked in a whisper as they descended, "a time draws near when the first shall be last, and the last shall be first."

Mr. Foster's reputation as a provocateur, it turned out, was well deserved. His method was the slaughter of sacred cows; his mode was outrage. By the end of the first course (white soup, boiled salmon, and dressed cucumber), he had broached the Woman question. "Take female apparel," he said. "Entirely impractical except as an instrument of oppression. It enforces distaff reliance upon the male of the species. What can she do for herself in that garb?" he asked, waving a hand vaguely in the direction of an affronted Mrs. Breen.

By the end of the second course (roast fowls garnished with watercresses, boiled leg of lamb, and sea kale), he had launched into the Darwinian controversy. "We are all savage as apes at the core," he was saying when the footman appeared at his elbow with the entrée. "Ah. What have we here? The *pièce de résistance*?"

He eyed the modest portion on Mrs. Breen's plate and served himself somewhat more generously. When the servant had moved on down the table, he shot Mrs. Breen a conspiratorial glance, picked up his menu card, and read off the entrée *sotto voce*: Lightly Braised Fillet of Stripling, garnished with Carrots and Mashed Turnips. "Have you had stripling before, Mrs. Breen?"

She had, she averred, taking in the intoxicating aroma of the dish. Two years ago, she continued, she had been fortunate enough to partake of ensouled flesh at this very table. "And you, Mr. Foster?"

"I have not."

"It is a rare honor."

"I think I prefer my honors well done, Mrs. Breen."

Mrs. Breen pursed her lips in disapproval. She did not reply.

Undeterred, Mr. Foster said, "Have you an opinion on the Anthropophagic Crisis?"

"I do not think it a woman's place to opine on political matters, Mr. Foster."

"You would not, I imagine."

"I can assure you the Anti-Anthropophagy Bill will never become law, Mr. Foster," Mr. Williams said. "It is stalled in the Commons, and should it by chance be passed, the Peers will reject it. The eating of ensouled flesh is a tradition too long entrenched in this country."

"Do you number yourself among the reformers, Mr. Williams?"

"I should think not."

Mr. Foster helped himself to a bite of the stripling. It was indeed rare. A small trickle of blood ran into his whiskers. He dabbed at it absent-mindedly. The man was repulsive, Mrs. Breen thought, chewing delicately. The stripling tasted like manna from Heaven, ambrosia, though perhaps a little less tender—and somewhat more strongly flavored—than her last meal of ensouled flesh.

"It *is* good," Mr. Foster said. "Tastes a bit like pork. What do ship-wrecked sailors call it? Long pig?"

Lady Stanton gasped. "Such a vulgar term," she said. "Common sailors have no right."

"Even starving ones?"

"Are rightfully executed for their depravity," Lord Donner pointed out.

"I hardly think the Anthropophagic Crisis is proper conversation for this table, Mr. Foster," said Mr. Breen.

"I can think of no table at which it is more appropriate." Another heaping bite. "It is a pretty word, anthropophagy. Let us call it what it is: cannibalism."

"It is a sacred ritual," Mrs. Murphy said.

"And cannibalism is such an ugly word, Mr. Foster," Lord Donner said.

"For an ugly practice," Mr. Foster said.

Lady Donner offered him a wicked smile. She prided herself on having an interesting table. "And yet I notice that you do not hesitate to partake."

"Curiosity provides the food the novelist feeds upon, Lady Donner. Even when the food is of an unsavory nature. Though this"—Mr. Foster held up his laden fork—"this is quite savory, I must admit. My compliments to your cook."

"I shall be sure to relay them," Lady Donner said.

"Yet, however savory it might be," he continued, "we are eating a creature with a soul bestowed upon it by our common Creator. We acknowledge it with our very name for the flesh we partake of at this table."

"Dinner?" Mrs. Williams said lightly, to a ripple of amusement.

Mr. Foster dipped his head and lifted his glass in silent toast. "I was thinking rather of ensouled flesh."

Mrs. Breen looked up from her plate. "I should think First Feast would be meaningless absent ensouled flesh, Mr. Foster," she said. "It would be a trivial occasion if we were eating boiled ham."

The bishop laughed. "These are souls of a very low order."

"He that has pity upon the poor lends unto the Lord," Mr. Foster said.

"The Lord also commands us to eat of his body, yes? There is a scripture for every occasion, Mr. Foster. The Catholics believe in transubstantiation, as you know." Lord Stanton helped himself to a morsel of stripling. "Ours is an anthropophagic faith."

"My understanding is that the Church of England reads the verse metaphorically."

"Call me High Church, then," Lord Stanton said, stifling a belch. There was general laughter at this sally, a sense that the bishop had scored a point.

Mr. Foster was unperturbed. "Are you suggesting that our Savior enjoins us to eat our fellow men?"

"I would hardly call them our fellow men," Lady Stanton said.

"They are human, are they not?" Mr. Foster objected.

"Given us, like the beasts of the field," Lord Donner remarked, "for our use and stewardship. Surely an ardent evolutionist such as yourself must understand the relative ranks of all beings. The poor will always be with us, Mr. Foster. As Lord Stanton has said, they are of a lower order."

"Though flesh of a somewhat higher order may be especially pleasing to the palate," Lady Donner said.

Mr. Williams said, "This must be flesh of a very high order indeed, then."

"It is of the highest, Mr. Williams. Let me assure you on that score." Lady Donner smiled down the table at Mrs. Breen. "You have partaken of ensouled flesh at our table before, Mrs. Breen. I trust tonight's meal is to your taste."

"It is very good indeed, my lady," Mrs. Breen said, looking down at her plate with regret. She would have to stop now. She had already eaten too much.

"And how would you compare it with your previous repast?"

Mrs. Breen put down her fork. "Somewhat more piquant, I think."

"Gamy might be a better word," Mr. Williams put in.

"As it should be," Lady Donner said, looking squarely at Mrs. Breen. "It was taken wild."

Mrs. Breen was quiet on the way home.

The hatbox sat on the shadowy bench beside her, intermittently visible in the fog-muted light of the passing streetlamps. Outside, a downpour churned the cobbled streets into torrents of feculent muck, but the First Day revels continued along the riverfront, fireworks blooming like iridescent flowers in the overcast sky. Mrs. Breen stared at the window, watching the rain sew intersecting threads upon the glass and thinking of her last such journey, the shattered window, the blood upon the cobbles. She wondered idly what such a debased creature's flesh would have tasted like, and leaned into her husband's comfortable bulk, his heat.

After the meal, the men had lingered at the table over port. In the drawing room, Lady Donner had been solicitous of Mrs. Breen's comfort. "You must stay for a moment after the other guests have departed," she'd said, settling her on a sofa and solemnly adjuring her to call within the week. "And you must join us in our carriage to the Ascot next month," she said, squeezing Mrs. Breen's hand. "I insist."

There had been no need to open the hatbox she'd handed Mrs. Breen as the butler showed them out. It had been uncommonly heavy.

Mrs. Breen sighed, recalling her husband's confidence in their restoration.

"This was your doing," she said at last.

"Yes."

"How?"

"Letters," he said. "A delicate negotiation, though one somewhat mitigated, I think, by Lady Donner's fondness for you."

"And you did not see fit to tell me."

"I feared that you might object."

Mrs. Breen wondered if she would have. She did not think so. She felt her place in the world more keenly now than she had felt it even in her era of privation, when she had striven in vain to fulfill her grandfather's aspirations.

The carriage rocked and swayed over an uneven patch of cobblestones. Something rolled and thumped inside the hatbox, and she feared for a moment that it would overturn, spilling forth its contents. But of course there was no danger of that. It had been painstakingly secured with a sapphire blue ribbon of mulberry silk. Mrs. Breen could not help reaching out to caress the rich fabric between her thumb and forefinger.

She sighed in contentment. They would be home soon.

"I do wish that you had told me," she said. "You would have put my mind much at ease."

"I am sorry, darling," Mr. Breen said.

Mrs. Breen smiled at him as the dim light of another streetlamp jolted by, and then, as darkness swept over her, she took an unheard-of liberty and let her hand fall upon his thigh. Tonight, she vowed, she would give him the heir he longed for.

WHITE NOISE IN A WHITE ROOM

STEVE DUFFY

Steve Duffy lives and works in North Wales; his most recent collection of stories, *The Faces At Your Shoulder*, was published by Sarob Press in 2023, and he's currently at work on the next. A winner of the International Horror Guild's short story award and the Shirley Jackson Award for Best Novelette, he's written for publications in the US and the UK. "White Noise in a White Room" was inspired by stories told by veterans of various wars, some from 1970s Ireland, some from 1950s Cyprus, and some from the postwar ruins of Germany.

THE SCHOOLHOUSE stood apart from the rest of the village, at the top of a small rise on the road to Crossmaglen. Originally, it had been enclosed by a low wall with railings; now, steel shuttering ten feet high blocked it from the view of passersby. Those few people who gained admittance through the solid steel gates found themselves in the old playground, still marked for five-a-side and handball but now a parking space for army vehicles. Ahead of them was the schoolhouse, its high windows shuttered against the daylight, and against whatever else Armagh might launch at it.

Inside the building, the window glass was painted over in regulation drab green. The former headmaster's room was lit by fluorescent strips; their light reflected wanly from the institutional brown gloss on the walls before it lost itself on the dusty parquet floor. Filing cabinets stood behind the large desk which confronted the guest directly on entering. The tableau reminded the visitor of courts-martial he had attended in his past life.

In the whole of the room there were only two splashes of vividness: the egg-and-bacon MCC tie of the man who sat before the desk in a cheap stacking chair, and the carmine-red folder placed squarely in the centre of the desktop.

From outside in the corridor came the sound of footsteps. The visitor rose as the door opened. "Captain—I'm sorry, Major now, I see. Congratulations."

"Hello, sir—very glad you could come. Much appreciated." The two men shook hands. "I hope the crossing was uneventful?"

"The ferry, you mean? Or the soft crossing at Dogans Bridge? Both entirely straightforward, I'm glad to say."

"That's a relief. Tell me, did you like Staniforth? He's my driver—one of the few people I can tolerate being driven by. Now then, let's see." The major settled himself in the chair behind the desk. "Have they given you a cup of tea and a biscuit? Ah, they have, good. Smoke?" He pushed a tinfoil ashtray towards his visitor.

"No, thanks all the same." The visitor looked around the room. "So this is your operation now?"

"Since my promotion in '74, yes, sir. And how about you? Enjoying retirement and so forth? Do you miss your old place up in the Welsh wilds?"

"Since Merlyn Rees mothballed us? Not really. I still do the odd bit of civvy work at the barracks in Ashford, you know, visiting lecturer for the new intake. This"—he patted the canvas holdall at the side of his chair—"has been at the back of the wardrobe for quite a few years now."

"It's very much their loss." The major paused. "I'd heard you hadn't been well?"

"Nothing to write home about," the visitor said levelly. "People make a lot of these things. Unnecessarily, I think. One arrives at a certain equilibrium."

"I mean, obviously, I wouldn't have involved you if the situation hadn't been . . ." The major shook his head. "Unusual."

"Whatever help I can give," the visitor said. "Perhaps if you let me have a look?" He gestured towards the red file on the desk. "I take it this is Chummy?"

"Yes, sir." The major pushed the file across to his visitor. He took from his pocket a packet of cigarettes, and placed them in the same central spot on the desk that the file had previously occupied, as if it was somehow important in the scheme of things. "You'll notice there isn't a name."

"Yes, so I see." The visitor folded the cover of the file back, began to read.

"That's not just because he isn't talking. Though he isn't, you know. We've taken his prints, gone through his belongings, even asked Special Branch to turn over his digs. Absolutely nothing. The name he was renting under is not a name that appears in any register of births."

"Puts us at something of a social disadvantage," remarked the visitor. His tone was easy, yet the major took it as an invitation to silence. Accordingly, he waited the fifteen minutes or so it took his visitor to read all the way through the file. When he closed it and replaced it on the desk, the officer stubbed out his JPS in the exact centre of the ashtray and took up more or less where he had left off.

"As things stand, sir, that file represents the only bit of paperwork on Chummy in the system. And I mean in any system: he's not on the electoral register; he hasn't got a jacket with the local police; he doesn't own a home, pays cash on the nail for a rented room; and most pertinently of all, he turns up nowhere in regular intel. When he came on the army's radar, he was pushed all the way up the line to us immediately. He didn't have time to accumulate anything in the way of bumf."

"I see. Well, on the one hand it's a little hard to see how one might proceed with the case. But on the other, I suppose the circumstances grant you a certain latitude, don't they?"

"Well, there is that, sir." The major grinned ruefully. "It's a relief to know there won't be any knocks on the door from the civil rights brigade, or the local padre wanting to give him Holy Communion."

The visitor was studying him narrowly, in a way that some people might have found disconcerting. "But that's your only relief in the matter, really. I mean, reading through the file, this is a terrible thing that he did."

The major grimaced, raised his hands vaguely, folded them back on his desk. "It is. Thank God we made our move before the civilian authorities got wind of it, that's all. Our men were in and out of there in an evening: we got our man, brought him back across the border, and the Gardai knew nothing about it till the morning after, when somebody stumbled on the cave.

"By then the legend was already in place, to the effect that what was found in there were the bodies of suspected informers, people who'd been kidnapped, subjected to kangaroo courts, then been the victims of summary Republican justice. Naturally, the Provos denied it, and naturally, people will believe whatever they're predisposed to believe. Already, events have moved on. Except here, at the schoolhouse."

He sighed. "Basically, we're complicit in the covering up of half a dozen deaths, and we haven't even got the one thing that would make that remotely acceptable in the bigger scheme of events."

"You haven't got the intel."

"Exactly, sir."

The visitor regarded him as closely and as nonjudgmentally as he had examined the red folder. "Very well. Let's take this business in the file about how he came into your hands."

"Yes, sir: well, that was curious from the very beginning. We had a tip-off about him from one of our best and most trusted sources inside the Provisional IRA. Nighttime flits across the border to a site on a beach in County Louth, vague talk of a cave in the cliffs, people disappearing. All very suggestive. But what was most interesting was the commentary on all of this, so to speak, from our deep source. So far as we could make out, the Provos were washing their hands of him. He wasn't just being cut loose, he was being offered to us quite deliberately, as if they wanted rid of him."

The visitor nodded. "Normally, of course, when the Provisionals want rid of somebody . . ."

"He ends up face down in a ditch, quite. So the fact that this hadn't happened—that they were willing in fact to betray him to the enemy—was the first indication that all wasn't what it seemed.

"Our first thought was that this was a plant: that he was being handed over to us stuffed to the gills with phoney intel, which he'd deliver up to us with a becoming show of reluctance. We were entirely prepared for that. We felt ourselves perfectly able to sift through the nonsense and get to the facts of the matter; we prided ourselves on it, you might say. But then we took him—ambush at the scene of the crime, into the back of a van with a bag over his head, spirited seamlessly out of the world in the course of a night's work—and we found . . ." He tailed off.

"You found him uncommunicative," the visitor suggested.

"For which we were signally unprepared."

"The level of his uncommunicativeness—is that even a word?"

"The level and the *nature* of it. Unlike anything I'd ever, we'd ever, encountered. There wasn't anybody who'd come across anything quite like it. Which was why, eventually, I came to think of you. As my mentor, you might say."

"Charmed." The two men shared a weary smile.

"I always remember something you said, on that very first course I attended. That there was a crack in everybody's armour, that all you had to do was turn him around and around till you caught sight of it. Good advice, I thought. It's certainly worked up till now."

"Regarding Chummy, then. I take it all the usual procedures were followed?"

"Well, I don't need to tell you, do I, sir? The squad who picked him up followed RA1 to the letter, working straight from the trade textbook. By the time he was handed over to us he ought to have been ready for processing. So we started right in on the five techniques." He counted them off on his fingers.

"Hooding: more or less continuous, and he seems fine with it. White noise: ditto. Sleep deprivation: the bugger scarcely seems to sleep at all as it is. Postural: again, we could have him doing ballet poses on one leg and it wouldn't faze him. Dietary: he's been on bread and drain since he came in. He eats what we give him with no complaint, and it has no effect."

"So you moved to the specialized procedures."

The major nodded. "Yes. I'll be honest, we don't operate under much scrutiny here. Water treatment, jump leads, you name it. After a spell with us, Castlereagh probably feels like the Europa Hotel. We have been patient and creative in our techniques. You'd have been proud of us." The visitor raised an eyebrow. "And the sum total of our efforts so far? He hasn't even opened his mouth to confirm the name he was using when he was snatched. Nothing."

"I see," said the visitor. "So that's the reason you brought me over, is it?"

"Yes and no. It's for my own peace of mind as much as anything, by this time. You see what he's done. Terrible things. Terrible. Like nothing we've ever seen, even over here."

"Like nothing I've ever seen anywhere."

"Quite, sir. And that's saying a lot, given your experience."

"And we believe them, do we? Even the rumours, these stories from the informers?"

"Where they're checkable, they have indeed checked out, sir. As the evidence in the cave confirms."

The visitor grimaced. "And of course, whatever happens, you can't just produce him now, can you?"

"Of course not." The major took another cigarette from the packet, tapped it nervously on the desk. "No, we bypassed the chance of a judicial outcome when we vanished him. He'll never face trial. We thought it would be worth it if he was high up in the Provisional structure, in terms of the intel we might glean. And now, we're stuck with him."

"And he's no good to anyone."

"Up to a point. Though it would be good to know. Necessary, in fact, to know that it was him. That all of it was down to him and him alone. I mean, it's gone beyond intel gathering now. But without a confession nobody's the wiser."

The major lit his cigarette, and the visitor noticed a slight tremor in the hand that applied the lighter. "I keep coming back to the Provos. To the reason they effectively handed him over to us. I've come to the conclusion they were like us: they were afraid of him. Because we are afraid of him, very much so."

The words hung in the stuffy air between them. The visitor said nothing, but continued to watch the major as he drew on his cigarette. After a while, the major said: "Not a thing to be particularly proud of, is it?"

"Pride shouldn't really come into it," said the visitor instantly. "It's always important for an inquisitor to be completely honest with himself when assessing his reactions in the interrogation process. There is no shame in honesty."

"I know, sir," the major said. "Still: there it is. Simply by being there—by sitting in a crate and not lifting a finger—he's beating us. And I feel . . . I feel it's important that he not beat us. After what he's done."

The visitor considered this for a minute. Then he said: "You'd like me to have a go at him."

"Yes, sir. Yes, I would. I realise this is totally irregular, that you're retired, a civilian. I could end up on a hell of a fizzer if anybody found out about it. But this is the schoolhouse: nobody will ever find out what goes on in here. Nobody cares to know."

The visitor considered this. "If the Provos have disowned him, and more to the point, if he was never really working for them, then anything he gives you will hardly be relevant in the military sense."

"Doesn't matter, sir. At this stage, it really doesn't matter. I just want to hear from his own lips who he is and what he did—why, too, if you can possibly get that out of him—and then I just want to be rid of him." The visitor looked up sharply. "One way or the other," the major added.

The visitor nodded. "Over and above all this, you realise that there's a reason I was invited to retire? You know that a medical tribunal reviewed my work and decided I was to be cut loose? I don't expect the details ever came out, but you know that I had no choice in the matter? That had I not retired, I would have been removed? On psychiatric grounds?"

The major was already shaking his head. "Quite aware of that, sir. I still regard you as the best. There is literally nobody else I would trust in the matter. Nobody whatsoever. My show; my rules."

The visitor allowed himself a smile. "You're too kind, major. After such a ringing endorsement, I only hope I don't let you down. Very well, then. I shall see what I can do. This need never be mentioned outside this room?"

"No, sir, absolutely not."

"I shall want to see him alone, I think. No guards present. What's his current status?"

"At the moment, lights out, shackles, hooded. To be honest, that's as much to do with our own delicate sensibilities as anything. Nobody wants to be in there with him. I've spent hours in there, we all have, and it's a profoundly disturbing experience. He was fed at 0400 hours, and it's now"—he consulted his watch—"nearly midday. I think we might forgo lunch."

The visitor rose from his chair, stretched, and cracked his knuckles. The noise seemed very loud in the stillness of the schoolroom. "Righto," he said, and bent to pick up his holdall. "Take me to Chummy, then."

The major breathed deeply for a second or two, then rose in his turn.

The two men walked along the ill-lit corridor to a door at the farther end, which was stencilled in white paint with the words ABSOLUTE SILENCE. Inside the large bare assembly hall stood what looked like a rectangular shipping container, made of steel and painted military grey. In the middle of the container's long side there was a padlocked door, next to which Staniforth and a corporal were sitting on two more of the plastic stacking chairs. The visitor assumed they had belonged in the schoolroom, back in the day. Hanging from the back of the corporal's chair was a Sterling Mk.4 submachine gun.

They scrambled to attention as the major approached, but he waved them back down. "Stand easy, you two," he said quietly. "Our guest is going to have a word with Chummy. I want you to listen very carefully, and if you hear anything untoward, anything, I want you in there right away, firearms at the ready, understand? Do not wait to be invited."

"What's the disposition of the seating?" asked the visitor.

"He'll be on the left as you enter, sir," the guard said, "and your seat will be on the right."

"Bear that in mind if you do feel the need to join us," the visitor said. "And if I do give the signal, don't stand on ceremony. Well." He smiled at each man in turn. "Are we ready, then?"

The two men looked at the major, who nodded. The guard turned a key in the padlock and stood aside from the door. The visitor nodded his thanks and went in. The men heard a click and a buzz as the fluorescent light came on inside the container, saw flat light spilling from the doorway for a moment before the door was quietly and firmly closed.

"Are you ready to come out, sir?"

Staniforth's voice reached him as if from a long way away. Standing there in the gloom, his ears had been filled with the sound of waves on pebbles, or it might have been one of his own tape recordings of white noise. At high volume it could break a man; played softly, it had often helped him fall asleep.

"Yes; yes, I'll be with you now." When he turned towards the mouth of the cave, Staniforth was silhouetted there, with the grey shingle beach and the waves behind him.

"We've got plenty of time, sir. The ferry doesn't sail till eight."

"Righto." He picked his way around the saltwater pools and clumps of seaweed. Staniforth watched him solicitously.

"It's been cleaned up, of course, sir," he said. "Off bounds as far as the authorities can make it, though to be honest, sir, I don't think anybody wants to come here anyway."

"No, I should think not," said the visitor. He emerged into the drab afternoon, the susurrus of the waves still loud in his head. "Have you by any chance got a smoke, sergeant?"

"Certainly, sir." Staniforth produced a packet of Bensons, held his lighter for the visitor.

"I don't, normally," he said, turning the cigarette this way and that as if unsure how to hold it. "Still."

"Absolutely, sir," Staniforth said. "Mind if I join you, sir?"

"Please." The two men smoked in silence for a minute or two. Then the visitor asked, "Were you a member of the patrol that first entered the cave, sergeant?"

"I was, sir," Staniforth said. A spasm of disgust pulled at his face. "A nasty business, sir. Fucking horrible, actually, beg your pardon."

"I completely agree." The visitor was carefully not looking in Staniforth's direction. "I think I saw in the case file that one of the men is still on psychiatric leave."

"That's right, sir," Staniforth agreed. "Young Belkin." He paused, as if wondering how much he could, or should, say. "I did say to the lieutenant, sir, at the time. I mean, he's only on his first tour. The lieutenant, too," he added, scrupulously.

"Oh, it's no respecter of experience or of rank," the visitor said. "I've been through a mandatory evaluation myself, you know. Quite a thorough one, for all the good it did me." He flicked his cigarette butt onto the wet sand. "How long have you been out here, sergeant? In Erin's green valleys?"

"Four years this coming January, sir," he said. "I tell you, though, in all that time, I've never seen anything like what we found in there."

"I imagine not," said the visitor.

"Sir?" There was an earnest, hesitant quality in Staniforth's voice that made the other man turn and look at him. "Sir, me and the lads were just saying before—well, we wanted to thank you."

"Thank me? For what?"

"For what you did back there. For taking it out of the major's hands, sir."

"I see." The visitor threw his cigarette into the thin wash of the tide. "Well, I dare say you've all been ordered not to talk about that, no?"

"'Course, sir. And you needn't have any worries on that score, sir, not at all. But between ourselves?" He paused, and again some strong emotion seemed to cramp the muscles in his face. "I don't think there was any other way around it, is all."

"It was hardly textbook." The visitor was watching Staniforth's face narrowly. "It wasn't a thing I have ever done before, not in all my years in the service. Looked at in that light, it was not only a failure, it was inexcusable. It was, in fact, the very sort of thing I was warned might happen. Why I was instructed to retire, several years ago. Why I ought not to have come back. You don't just . . ." He trailed off.

"But what was the alternative, sir?" Staniforth offered him another cigarette; with a slight hesitation he accepted. "What were we going to do with the bastard?"

"Not that." He gripped the hand that offered him the flame. "Never that."

"You say that, sir, but what, then? The Provos didn't want him. The rozzers might think they want him, but they don't, not really, and we couldn't give him up if they did. Nobody wanted him, and we were stuck with him. And we couldn't get rid of him. And now, you've managed to get the job done at a stroke. Good show, sir."

He released the sergeant's hand. "But of course we'll never learn the truth now, will we?"

"Suppose that doesn't matter, sir?"

"But the truth is supposed to matter. That's supposed to be our job, to uncover it. Magna est veritas et praevalebit."

"That's a value judgement, sir. They're above my pay grade, those."

The older man drew deeply on his cigarette, exhaled the smoke as if it disgusted him. "I see," he said. "Very fair point." After a pause he went on:

"Let me tell you a story, Staniforth. A war story, the ones we old soldiers bore you young fellers half to death with. Or I should say a postwar story.

"At the very beginning of my time in the service, I was part of the British Army's team in Nuremberg, for the trials of the Nazi war criminals. I saw them all, all those monsters you know from the newsreels and the history books. I saw Göring and Ribbentrop and Dönitz and Hess. I saw Ley hanging in his cell; I saw Göring sprawled out on his bunk after swallowing his cyanide pill. I saw Streicher the Jew-baiter, the editor of *Der Stürmer*, the man who paved the road to the gas chambers, groaning in the latrines with a colossal dose of diarrhoea.

"These were all men who to a greater or lesser degree had committed unspeakable evil. And I looked at them in the dock, shabby downcast prisoners with buttons missing from their clothes and stubble on their chins, and I asked myself, 'Well then: is this the face of evil?' And you had to keep reminding yourself of what they'd done, because in the dock they looked . . . normal. Unexceptional. It's rather hard to believe in monsters when they ask for darning wool to mend their holey socks, or beg you for pile ointment or whatever. It was in a very real sense the beginning of my education.

"Now Nuremberg was in the American zone of occupation, but the trials were obviously a quadripartite arrangement. There were the Americans, the French, the British, and there were the Russians. Each nation had its own people at the court, and just as we represented the British Army, there were military teams from the other three allied countries. I got to know some of them pretty well: I socialized with several of the French junior officers, played chess with one of the Russians, their military liaison chap, when I had an evening spare. Anyway, there was one other man on the Soviet team I found quite striking: a reserved man, I didn't think he spoke any English, though I could never be sure how much of it he understood. I noticed that he didn't always use the headphones for translation in court, for instance.

"I became slightly obsessed by this man. For all sorts of reasons, my curiosity was engaged: by his manner, which was imperturbable; by his complete self-possession. Do you understand what I mean? He was, you'd say, an enigma. Over the weeks and months, I became preoccupied with him—I think I almost came to idolize him, in a way, even though I hardly knew the first thing about him.

"There was a feeling abroad at that time, you see, that the Soviets were the bravest of the brave. We all had a pretty good idea of the scale of the battles on the Eastern Front, the sacrifices they'd made, and, well, I looked at this chap and I seemed to see all the immense resolve of the Russian national character. The inner strength, the nobility, the determination to carry on no matter what. Silly, I know, but you must remember I was a young man in extraordinary times, and young men are prone to that sort of sentimental thinking.

"Well, it so happened that one evening in the January of 1946, this officer came into the watch room when I was playing chess with my Russian colleague. He sat down and watched our game, and when it came to an end—I'd won, which didn't happen nearly as often as I'd have liked—I offered him the next round, out of politeness.

"He seemed not in the least surprised. He nodded, and sat at the table, and I switched to black, and . . . well, I won't burden you with the details, but he ground me down over the course of one of the longest hours you could imagine. He picked me off remorselessly, piece by piece. In the end there was nothing for it but to resign, which I did, and he smiled, just slightly, shook my hand, and left the room. A firm handshake, correct, not overlong. I've often thought about it since.

"That was the end of the chess for the evening, but my curiosity about the other man was stoked even higher than it had been. I pressed my Russian colleague for details, just between the two of us. He looked at me for a long time, then suggested we go outside for a breath of air. Here, it was understood, we would not be overheard.

"It was snowing outside, and all the ruins—Nuremberg was smashed all to pieces still in that winter, great black heaps of rubble and charred timbers and the shells of buildings open to the sky—all the ruins were blanketed in white. All sounds were deadened; not a person moved on the streets.

"The Russian buried his chin deep in his fur collar, so that the steam of his breath hardly escaped, and this is what he said, just barely loud enough for me to hear:

" 'There is a monastery, not far from Moscow, near Lenin's dacha at his Gorki estate. It is a prison now, called Sukhanovka. Of all the prisons, it is the most feared. When a prisoner in one of our other facilities is threatened with Sukhanovka, he will confess on the spot, confess to anything, sign any declaration of guilt that is placed before him. Yezhov of the NKVD established it, Yezhov who was feared by all. Within a year he himself had been swallowed up by it. This is its power. Everything, everybody, it devours alike.

" 'You are taken there in a truck, by yourself. No other prisoners travel with you, and the guards are under instruction never to respond if you try to talk to them. This is how you arrive. How then do you leave? You do not leave. Nothing comes out of there: there are sixty-eight cells, cells of the monks, now cells of the prisoners, and nothing comes out of them. Nothing and no one. Not even a sound. Prisoners simply vanish; sometimes they scream, because they must, but their screams are instantly silenced. After a while they go insane and then they disappear, and in the space they leave behind there is only a terrible stillness.

" 'Your opponent at chess this evening: he was at Sukhanovka from the beginning. He was the most feared of its operatives. Stalin chose him personally to come here to Nuremberg, because he is certain that sooner or later our allies will come to their senses, these ridiculous trials will come to an end, and these prisoners, these fascists, they too will vanish. And this duty will be entrusted to my comrade, the man with whom you played your game of chess.'

"And there it was. He would say no more about it, not that evening, not ever again. And I think ever since that night, when I have looked at myself in the mirror at the end of a day's work, I have asked myself: who is it that you see? Whom do you most resemble today? The nondescript monsters of Nuremberg, or the quiet man of Sukhanovka? And as I stare at that reflection I wonder if what we see in the white room mightn't also be a mirror, of sorts. In a room filled with mirrors, I wonder what we'd really see? Might not anybody go mad in such a place as that, sergeant?"

Staniforth listened in silence, his face scrunched up a little with the strain of comprehension. For a while he said nothing, then, as if contradicting the visitor: "That one in the schoolhouse, though? We didn't drive him bonkers, sir. Quite the opposite, I'd say. And if you hadn't done what you did, sir, I honestly think he might have finished us all off in the end.

"I saw it with my own two eyes, sir. Men would go in with him, trained men, tough men, the toughest, and they'd come out no use for anything. Ruined, some of 'em. Finished. It wasn't natural. I can't find an explanation for that, sir. *Are* there just monsters, is that it? Like your Nazis, or that Russian bastard, or like Chummy? Do they come along once in a blue moon, sir? Real, honest-to-goodness monsters?" The sergeant's face was creased up in incomprehension and disgust.

"Am I the judge?" The other spoke so softly that it was hard to hear him above the noise of the waves sifting through the shingle.

"More of a judge than me, at any rate. More than any of us. That's why you were called in, wasn't it, sir?"

"No." Instantly. "I don't have any magical ability to discern the truth. I'm not St. George fighting the dragons. I can't see what others don't. I was called in because . . . well, because of my historical track record in getting results from interrogations. A record, let me remind you, that has been called into question in the severest possible terms. Results, sergeant: not dead ends."

"Perhaps a dead end was the best thing for everybody, sir."

"Maybe. But you'll never know now, will you?"

"Don't care about that sir." The sergeant was dogmatic. "The whys and wherefores—I honestly don't give a toss."

"Don't you? It seems to be the only thing that matters to me. Why he came to do it, why such a thing came to be. That seems to me to be a necessary question, a question worth asking."

The sergeant considered this for a while. "But . . ." he began, then seemed to lose his way. After a moment or two he resumed: "What it is, sir, I'm happy with it all being a mystery. Not happy. Satisfied; whatever. Resigned to it. Like I said, it's above my pay grade." He seemed very anxious to convince the visitor. "You're better off leaving some things be, sir, if you ask me. If you look into the void for too long . . . well, you know how that one goes, sir, better than me, probably. There's such a thing as asking too many questions."

"Life asks us questions," said the other man. "That's what life does. I don't know, Staniforth. Perhaps where we go wrong is assuming that these questions always have an answer."

"Well, that's what I was saying, sir."

"Is it?" There was genuine surprise in his voice. "Is it really? Then perhaps we're just talking at cross purposes." The thought seemed to pain him.

The sergeant shook his head. "I think we're on the same hymn sheet really, sir. You know what I reckon? Sometimes, the hardest thing to do is to see what's right in front of you."

The other seemed hardly to hear him, staring out at the grey that met the grey at the indefinite cold horizon. "Anyhow," he said eventually, "I suppose we'd better be on our way."

The sergeant started to say something; then his face folded in on itself and he kept his mouth closed. In the end he simply nodded and saluted. The two men walked away from the cave mouth and towards the rotting wooden steps that led up to the parked car at the top of the bluffs.

The lounge of the passenger ferry hosted a small group of determined drinkers: to call them "revellers" might be to overstate the case. The man with the canvas holdall sat on the opposite side of the room from them, writing in a notebook, with a cup of instant coffee untouched on the table in front of him. The liquid was sloshing gently in the moderate swell of the passage, and after a while he began to find this motion actively unpleasant. He got up and moved the coffee to the next table, then resumed his place.

The book was a school notebook. It might have come from a pile of such books in the schoolhouse on the Crossmaglen road. For the last hour he had been filling it with homework of a very particular kind, writing in his neat, tightly compacted script, barely pausing to search for the words. The current page began:

"In that cave I thought of the dakhmas of the Zoroastrians, the towers of silence. The temples of excarnation, where the bodies of the dead are pecked apart by birds so that demons might not rush into the corpses and pollute them.

"All around the edges of silence there lies madness. Just as matter begins to warp at the edge of a black hole, sanity begins to warp in the borderland of silence. In that cell I was morbidly conscious of the tinnitus that has plagued me in my advancing years, the sound of the blood rushing through my arteries that my doctor has warned me bodes no good. I heard the hum of electricity in the fluorescent tube, which might for all I know be the sound of the cloud of electrons flowing from filament to filament, ionizing the mercury vapour and coaxing light from it. I thought I might go mad. Perhaps if I had stayed in that room I might have heard the magnetic field of the earth, or the tectonic plates shifting a millimetre somewhere infinitely far beneath us. I might have heard the voice of God, or even worse, His critical and everlasting silence."

He picked up his pen and without bothering to reread what he had written, he went on:

"If I thought any of this made sense to anybody but the subject, it wouldn't be quite so bad. Of course, he knew. Chummy knew. It was the source of his strength, or at least the outward manifestation of it. It is why he remained invulnerable while the rest of us faltered, one by one. He was comfortable with it, if you like. He had accepted it.

"When the shot came I was so relieved to hear it. I thought the hammer might have fallen as if on fresh air, the primer might have exploded into a vacuum, the propellant might have puffed noiselessly from the barrel, the bullet struck its target and never made a single sound. I wondered whether that terrible vortex might have swallowed the shot entire, leaving no sign of its existence. It does not seem impossible to me that such a thing might happen, out beyond the event horizon. The Dionysiac architects, it is said, knew the secret of constructing chambers in which people could not hear their own screams."

For a while he considered what he'd written, then added another sentence: "Those places in which God is silent, while we babble." He closed the book, and then opened it again. Below the rest of the text he scribbled: "Burn this once you've read it."

Out on deck, the gangways were slick and treacherous. A fog had fallen on the Irish Sea since they had left Dun Laoghaire, and the ferry's speed had been reduced on the approach to Holyhead. The man made his way to a place that was not overlooked by a lighted window, and stood at the rusted rail. He withdrew from his holdall a compact service revolver, hefted it as if to assess its weight. He held it out over the rail, high above the waves, let it dangle from his finger by the trigger guard, and hesitated a long moment before dropping it back into the bag. The ferry pushed on through the night, the sound of the engines baffled by the fog. After a while lights, red and white with an eerie halation, signalled the approach to South Stack and the terminal beyond, and he went back indoors.

On disembarking, the land seemed uncertain under his feet, as if it might suddenly begin to tilt and pitch like the deck of the ferry. Flashing a pasteboard card the size of a library ticket, the man slipped past the customs officials. Leaving the terminal building by a side door, he crossed the car park to his vehicle, a two-tone brown estate car drained of colour beneath the sickly sodium lights. Absent-mindedly he removed the parking ticket from under the windscreen wiper, tore it to pieces, and got in.

The fog stayed with him through the drive across the flat scraped plains of Anglesey, and the crossing of the Menai Strait, the waters invisible beneath the dark iron bulk of Telford's bridge. On the A55, headed for England and home, he found himself, almost unconsciously, taking the A5 exit then turning off past Bethesda. This was quarry country, bare rough rock crowding on either side of the narrow road, sharp friable layers of slate tipped precariously as if caught in the act of sliding down.

One more turn onto a minor road that nosed between the Snowdonia foothills, and then on to a track hewed between vertical cliff faces that fell away after a mile or two to a dark unknowable space filled with fog. Barring the way was a high chain-link fence with a padlocked gate, and he left the engine idling while he searched in his holdall for a key ring. A sign on the fence read STRICTLY NO ADMITTANCE: MINISTRY OF DEFENCE—CONTAMINATED SITE. It was true that chemical weapons had once been stored here; lethal deposits still leached up through the stony soil in wet weather, of which there was plenty hereabouts. But he knew there were residues more toxic, and of newer vintage, locked away behind the fence.

Outside the car the night air smelled rusty, tainted. The man selected a key that sprung open the padlock, and leaned on the gate till it shuddered open. Back in the Saab, he disengaged the handbrake and let the car roll forwards into the forbidden space.

Parking up by a portacabin, he took the schoolbook from his holdall and positioned it deliberately on the dashboard, where it would be seen. He fetched an emergency fuel can from the back compartment of the car, glancing above him at the ramparts of notched rock, bitten out of the mountains generations ago by mechanical digger and explosive charge. At the side of the portacabin was a generator: he fed it a gallon of petrol and yanked the ripcord until it chugged into life. Flat white security floods lit up the freezing mist. In the wall of fractured slate ahead stood a double metal doorway. Stencilled on it was the word DANGER. The warning was swallowed up in the cliff face as the man undid the padlocks and slid the door open.

Moss had grown on the glass of the caged bulbs at the tunnel mouth, giving the light a soft greenish cast. At the farthest limit of the light, before the darkness swallowed everything, stood a large grey metal container, the twin of the one in the Irish schoolhouse. The man closed the sliding doors behind him and walked over to it.

His fingers trembled a little as he searched among his keys. Once he'd opened the lock on the door, he took from the holdall an inspection lamp. It didn't work at first, then as he shook the loose contact to life, shadows leaped and lunged around the tunnel walls. After a moment's hesitation, he stepped into the container.

Inside there were two plain chairs, one bolted to the floor, one free-standing. In the corners of the ceilings there were a couple of small cast-metal tannoy speakers. Nothing else; no independent source of light. Only white-painted walls, discoloured here and there with old stains. The man surveyed the scene, then closed the door behind him. He placed the lamp on the floor behind the bolted chair before seating himself, holdall across his knees.

The weak lamplight cast a grotesquely large shadow of the chair and its occupant on the farther wall. It was as if some great shapeshifting figure sat across from him, too massive for the claustrophobic space inside the container. What face might this shadow figure have, thought the man; what lies behind the shadow? Is there only one face behind all the shadows in the world?

The sound of his breath seemed very prominent in the enclosed space: white noise in a white room. He strove to breathe more shallowly, to disengage himself from events inside the container, to vanish, as far as was possible, from the process underway. With infinite care, he reached into the holdall and brought out the snub-nose Smith & Wesson .38 he'd toyed with on the deck of the ferry. He broke the revolver, removed the three expended casings, closed it again and spun the cylinder. With a hand that no longer shook he cocked the hammer.

SINGING MY SISTER DOWN

MARGO LANAGAN

Margo Lanagan has published two dark fantasy novels (*Tender Morsels* and *Sea Hearts*) and eight short story collections, and has collaborated with Scott Westerfeld and Deborah Biancotti on the *New York Times*–bestselling *Zeroes* trilogy.

Her work has won four World Fantasy Awards, nine Aurealis Awards, and five Ditmars. It has been listed for the Locus, Nebula, Hugo, Bram Stoker, Theodore Sturgeon, Shirley Jackson, James Tiptree Jr., International Horror Guild, British Fantasy, British Science Fiction Association, and Seiun awards, and has been translated into nineteen languages. Margo lives in Sydney.

We all went down to the tar-pit, with mats to spread our weight. Ikky was standing on the bank, her hands in a metal twin-loop behind her. She'd stopped sulking; now she looked, more, stare-y and puzzled.

Chief Barnarndra pointed to the pit. "Out you go then, girl. You must walk on out there to the middle and stand. When you picked a spot, your people can join you."

So Ik stepped out, very ordinary. She walked out. I thought—hoped, even—she might walk right across and into the thorns the other side; at the same time, I knew she wouldn't do that.

She walked the way you walk on the tar, except without the arms balancing. She nearly fell from a stumble once, but Mumma hulloo'd to her, and she straightened and walked upright out to the very middle, where she slowed and stopped.

Mumma didn't look to the chief, but all us kids and the rest did. "Right, then," he said.

Mumma stepped out as if she'd just herself that moment happened to decide to. We went after her—only us, Ik's family, which was like us being punished, too, everyone watching us walk out to that girl who was our shame.

In the winter you come to the pit to warm your feet in the tar. You stand long enough to sink as far as your ankles—the littler you are, the longer you can stand. You soak the heat in for as long as the tar doesn't close over your feet and grip, and it's as good as warmed boots wrapping your feet. But in summer, like this day, you keep away from the tar, because it makes the air hotter and you mind about the stink.

But today we had to go out, and everyone had to see us go.

Ikky was tall, but she was thin and light from all the worry and prison; she was going to take a long time about sinking. We got our mats down, all the food parcels and ice-baskets and instruments and such spread out evenly on the broad planks Dash and Felly had carried out.

"You start, Dash," said Mumma, and Dash got up and put his drumette to his hip and began with "Fork-Tail Trio," and it did feel a bit like a party. It stirred Ikky awake from her hung-headed shame; she lifted up and even laughed, and I saw her hips move in the last chorus, side to side.

Then Mumma got out one of the ice-baskets, which was already black on the bottom from meltwater.

Ikky gasped. "Ha! What! Crab! Where'd that come from?"

"Never you mind, sweet-thing." Mumma lifted some meat to Ikky's mouth, and rubbed some of the crush-ice into her hair.

"Oh, Mumma!" Ik said with her mouth full.

"May as well have the best of this world while you're here," said Mumma. She stood there and fed Ikky like a baby, like a pet guinea-bird.

"I thought Auntie Mai would come," said Ik.

"Auntie Mai, she's useless," said Dash. "She's sitting at home with her handkerchief."

"I wouldn't've cared, her crying," said Ik. "I would've thought she'd say goodbye to me."

"Her heart's too hurt," said Mumma. "You frightened her. And she's such a straight lady—she sees shame where some of us just see people. Here, inside the big claw, that's the sweetest meat."

"Ooh, *yes*! Is anyone else feasting with me?"

"No, darlin', this is your day only. Well, okay, I'll give some to this little sad-eyes here, huh? Felly never had crab but the once. Is it yum? Ooh, it's yum! Look at him!"

Next she called me to do my flute—the flashiest, hardest music I knew. And Ik listened; Ik who usually screamed at me to stop pushing spikes into her brain, she watched my fingers on the flute-holes and my sweating face and my straining, bowing body and, for the first time, I didn't feel like just the nuisance-brother. I played well, out of the surprise of her not minding. I couldn't've played better. I heard everyone else being surprised, too, at the end of those tunes that they must've known, too well from all my practising.

I sat down, very hungry. Mumma passed me the water-cup and a damp-roll.

"I'm stuck now," said Ik, and it was true—the tar had her by the feet, closed in a gleaming line like that pair of zipper-slippers I saw once in the shoemaster's vitrine.

"Oh yeah, well and truly stuck," said Mumma. "But then, you knew when you picked up that axe-handle you were sticking yourself."

"I did know."

"No coming unstuck from this one. You could've let that handle lie."

That was some serious teasing.

"No, I couldn't, Mumma, and *you* know."

"I do, baby chicken. I always knew you'd be too angry, once the wedding-glitter rubbed off your skin. It was a good party, though, wasn't it?" And they laughed at each other, Mumma having to steady Ikky or her ankles would've snapped over. And when their laughter started going strange Mumma said, "Well, *this* party's going to be almost as good, 'cause it's got children. And look what else!" And she reached for the next ice-basket.

And so the whole long day went, in treats and songs, in ice and stink and joke-stories and gossip and party-pieces. On the banks, people came and went, and the chief sat in his chair and was fanned and fed, and the family of Ikky's husband sat around the chief, being served, too, all in purple-cloth with flashing edging, very prideful.

She went down so slowly.

"Isn't it hot?" Felly asked her.

"It's like a big warm hug up my legs," said Ik. "Come here and give me a hug, little stick-arms, and let me check. Oof, yes, it's just like that, only lower down."

"You're coming down to me," said Fel, pleased.

"Yeah, soon I'll be able to bite your ankles like you bite mine."

Around midafternoon, Ikky couldn't move her arms anymore and had a panic, just quiet, not so the bank-people would've noticed.

"What'm I going to do, Mumma?" she said. "When it comes up over my face? When it closes my nose?"

"Don't you worry. You won't be awake for that." And Mumma cooled her hands in the ice, dried them on her dress, and rubbed them over Ik's shoulders, down Ik's arms to where the tar had locked her wrists.

"You'd better not give me any teas, or herbs, or anything," said Ik. "They'll get you, too, if you help me. They'll come out to make sure."

Mumma put her hands over Felly's ears. "Tristem gave me a gun," she whispered.

Ikky's eyes went wide. "But you can't! Everyone'll hear!"

"It's got a thing on it, quietens it. I can slip it in a tar-wrinkle, get you in the head when your head is part sunk, fold back the wrinkle, tell 'em your heart stopped, the tar pressed it stopped."

Felly shook his head free. Ikky was looking at Mumma, quietening. There was only the sound of Dash tearing bread with his teeth, and the breeze whistling in the thorn-galls away over on the shore. I was watching Mumma and Ikky closely—I'd wondered about that last part, too. But now this girl up to her waist in the pit didn't even look like our Ikky. Her face was changing like a cloud, or like a masque-lizard's colours; you don't see them move but they *become* something else, then something else again.

"No," she said, still looking at Mumma. "You won't do that. You won't have to." Her face had a smile on it that touched off one on Mumma's, too, so that they were both quiet, smiling at something in each other that I couldn't see.

And then their eyes ran over and they were crying *and* smiling, and then Mumma was kneeling on the wood, her arms around Ikky, and Ikky was ugly against her shoulder, crying in a way that we couldn't interrupt them.

That was when I realised how many people were watching, when they set up a big, spooky oolooling and stamping on the banks, to see Mumma grieve.

"Fo!" I said to Dash, to stop the hair creeping around on my head from that noise. "There never was such a crowd when Chep's daddy went down."

"Ah, but he was old and crazy," said Dash through a mouthful of bread, "and only killed other olds and crazies."

"Are those fish-people? And look at the yellow-cloths—they're from up among the caves, all that way!"

"Well, it's nearly Langasday, too," said Dash. "Lots of people on the move, just happening by."

"Maybe. Is that an honour, or a greater shame?"

Dash shrugged. "This whole thing is upended. Who would have a party in the tar, and with family going down?"

"It's what Mumma wanted."

"Better than having her and Ik be like this *all day*." Dash's hand slipped into the nearest ice-basket and brought out a crumb of gilded macaroon. He ate it as if he had a perfect right.

Everything went slippery in my mind, after that. We were being watched so hard! Even though it was quiet out here, the pothering wind brought crowd-mumble and scraps of music and smoke our way, so often that we couldn't be private and ourselves. Besides, there was Ikky with the sun on her face, but the rest of her from the rib-peaks down gloved in tar, never to see sun again. Time seemed to just have *gone*, in big clumps, or all the day was happening at once or something, I was wondering so hard about what was to come, I was watching so hard the differences from our normal days. I wished I had more time to think, before she went right down; my mind was going breathless, trying to get all its thinking done.

But evening came and Ik was a head and shoulders, singing along with us in the lamplight, all the old songs—"A Flower for You," "Hen and Chicken Bay," "Walking the Tracks with Beejum Singh," "Dollarberries." She sang all Felly's little-kid songs that normally she'd sneer at; she got Dash to teach her his new one, "The Careless Wanderer," with the tricky chorus. She made us work on that one like she was trying to stop us noticing the monster bonfires around the shore, the other singing, of fishing songs and forest songs, the stomp and clatter of dancing in the gathering darkness. But they were there, however well we sang, and no other singing in our lives had had all this going on behind it.

When the tar began to tip Ik's chin up, Mumma sent me for the wreath. "Mai will have brought it, over by the chief's chair."

I got up and started across the tar, and it was as if I cast magic ahead of me, silence-making magic, for as I walked—and it was good to be walking, not sitting—musics petered out, and laughter stopped, and dancers stood still, and there were eyes at me, all along the dark banks, strange eyes and familiar both.

The wreath showed up in the crowd ahead, a big, pale ring trailing spirals of whisper-vine, the beautifullest thing. I climbed up the low bank there, and the ground felt hard and cold after a day on the squishy tar. My ankles shivered as I took the wreath from Mai. It was heavy; it was fat with heavenly scents.

"You'll have to carry those," I said to Mai, as someone handed her the other garlands. "You should come out, anyway. Ik wants you there."

She shook her head. "She's cloven my heart in two with that axe of hers."

"What, so you'll chop hers as well, this last hour?"

We glared at each other in the bonfire light, all loaded down with the fine, pale flowers.

"I never heard this boy speak with a voice before, Mai," said someone behind her.

"He's very sure," said someone else. "This is Ikky's Last Things we're talking about, Mai. If she wants you to be one of them . . ."

"She shouldn't have shamed us, then," Mai said, but weakly.

"You going to look back on this and think yourself a po-face," said the first someone.

"But it's like—" Mai sagged and clicked her tongue. "She should have *cared* what she did to this family," she said with her last fight. "It's more than just herself."

"Take the flowers, Mai. Don't make the boy do this twice over. Time is short."

"Yeah, *everybody's* time is short," said the first someone.

Mai stood, pulling her mouth to one side.

I turned and propped the top of the wreath on my forehead, so that I was like a little boy-bride, trailing a head of flowers down my back to the ground. I set off over the tar, leaving the magic silence in the crowd. There was only the rub and squeak of flower stalks in my ears; in my eyes, instead of the flourishes of bonfires, there were only the lamps in a ring around Mumma, Felly, Dash, and Ikky's head. Mumma was kneeling bonty-up on the wood, talking to Ikky; in the time it had taken me to get the wreath, Ikky's head had been locked still.

"Oh, the baby," Mai whimpered behind me. "The little darling."

Bit late for darling-ing now, I almost said. I felt cross and frightened and too grown-up for Mai's silliness.

"Here, Ik, we'll make you beautiful now," said Mumma, laying the wreath around Ik's head. "We'll come out here to these flowers when you're gone, and know you're here."

"They'll die pretty quick—I've seen it." Ik's voice was getting squashed, coming out through closed jaws. "The heat wilts 'em."

"They'll always look beautiful to you," said Mumma. "You'll carry down this beautiful wreath, and your family singing."

I trailed the vines out from the wreath like flares from the edge of the sun.

"Is that Mai?" said Ik. Mai looked up, startled, from laying the garlands between the vines. "Show me the extras, Mai."

Mai held up a garland. "Aren't they good? Trumpets from Low Swamp, Auntie Patti's whisper-vine, and star-weed to bind. You never thought ordinary old stars could look so good, I'll bet."

"I never did."

It was all set out right, now. It went in the order: head, half-ring of lamps behind (so as not to glare in her eyes), wreath, half-ring of garlands behind, leaving space in front of her for us.

"Okay, we're going to sing you down now," said Mumma. "Everybody get in and say a proper goodbye." And she knelt inside the wreath a moment herself, murmured something in Ikky's ear, and kissed her on the forehead.

We kids all went one by one. Felly got clingy and made Ikky cry; Dash dashed in and planted a quick kiss while she was still upset and would hardly have noticed him; Mumma gave me a cloth and I crouched down and wiped Ik's eyes and nose—and then could not speak to her bare, blinking face.

"You're getting good at that flute," she said.

But this isn't about me, Ik. This is *not at all* about me.

"Will you come out here some time, and play over me, when no one else's around?"

I nodded. Then I had to say some words, of some kind, I knew. I wouldn't get away without speaking. "If you want."

"I want, okay? Now give me a kiss."

I gave her a kid's kiss, on the mouth. Last time I kissed her, it was carefully on the cheek as she was leaving for her wedding. Some of her glitter had come off on my lips. Now I patted her hair and backed away over the wreath.

Mai came in last. "Fairy doll," I heard her say sobbingly. "Only-one."

And Ik. "It's all right, Auntie. It'll be over so soon, you'll see. And I want to hear your voice nice and strong in the singing."

We readied ourselves, Felly in Mumma's lap, then Dash, then me next to Mai. I tried to stay attentive to Mumma, so Mai wouldn't mess me up with her weeping. It was quiet except for the distant flubber and snap of the bonfires.

We started up, all the ordinary evening songs for putting babies to sleep, for farewelling, for soothing broke-hearted people—all the ones everyone knew so well that they'd long ago made rude versions and joke-songs of them. We sang them plain, following Mumma's lead; we sang them straight, into Ikky's glistening eyes, as the tar climbed her chin. We stood tall, so as to see her, and she us, as her face became the sunken centre of that giant flower, the wreath. Dash's little drum held us together and kept us singing, as Ik's eyes rolled and she struggled for breath against the pressing tar, as the chief and the husband's family came and stood across from us, shifting from foot to foot, with torches raised to watch her sink away.

Mai began to crumble and falter beside me as the tar closed in on Ik's face, a slow, sticky, rolling oval. I sang good and strong—I didn't want to hear any last whimper, any stopped breath. I took Mai's arm and tried to hold her together that way, but she only swayed worse, and wept louder. I listened for Mumma under the noise, pressed my eyes shut and made my voice follow hers. By the time I'd steadied myself that way, Ik's eyes were closing.

Through our singing, I thought I heard her cry for Mumma; I tried not to, yet my ears went on hearing. *This will happen only the once—you can't do it over again if ever you feel like remembering.* And Mumma went to her, and I could not tell whether Ik was crying and babbling, or whether it was a trick of our voices, or whether the people on the banks of the tar had started up again. I watched Mumma, because Mumma knew what to do; she knew to lie there on the matting, and dip her cloth in the last water with the little fading fish-scales of ice in it, and squeeze the cloth out and cool the shrinking face in the hole.

And the voice of Ik must have been ours or others' voices, because the hole Mumma was dampening with her cloth was, by her hand movements, only the size of a brassboy now. And by a certain shake of her shoulders I could tell: Mumma knew it was all right to be weeping now, now that Ik was surely gone, was just a nose or just a mouth with the breath crushed out of it, just an eye seeing nothing. And very suddenly it was too much—the flowers nodding in the lamplight, our own sister hanging in tar, going slowly, slowly down like Vanderberg's truck that time, like Jappity's cabin with the old man still inside it, or any old villain or scofflaw of around these parts, and I had a big sicking-up of tears, and they tell me I made an awful noise that frightened everybody right up to the chief, and that the husband's parents thought I was a very ill-brought-up boy for upsetting them instead of allowing them to serenely and superiorly watch justice be done for their lost son.

I don't remember a lot about that part. I came back to myself walking dully across the tar between Mai and Mumma, hand-in-hand, carrying nothing, when I had come out here laden, when we had all had to help. *We must have eaten everything,* I thought. *But what about the mats and pans and planks?* Then I hear a screeking clanking behind me, which was Dash hoisting up too heavy a load of pots.

And Mumma was talking, wearily, as if she'd been going on a long time, and soothingly, which was like a beautiful guide-rope out of my sickness, which my brain was following hand over hand. *It's what they do to people, what they have to do, and all you can do about it is watch out who you go loving, right? Make sure it's not someone who'll rouse that killing-anger in you, if you've got that rage, if you're like our Ik—*

Then the bank came up high in front of us, topped with grass that was white in Mumma's lamp's light. Beyond it were all the eyes, and attached to the eyes the bodies, flat and black against bonfire or starry sky. They shuffled aside for us.

I knew we had to leave Ik behind, and I didn't make a fuss, not now. I had done my fussing, all at once; I had blown myself to bits out on the tar, and now several monstrous things, several gaping mouths of truth, were rattling pieces of me around their teeth. I would be all right, if Mai stayed quiet, if Mumma kept murmuring, if both their hands held me as we passed through this forest of people, these flitting firefly eyes.

They got me up the bank, Mumma and Auntie; I paused and they stumped up and then lifted me, and I walked up the impossible slope like a demon, horizontal for a moment and then stiffly over the top—

—and into my Mumma, whose arms were ready. She couldn't've carried me out on the tar. We'd both have sunk, with me grown so big now.

But here on the hard ground she took me up, too big as I was for it. And, too big as I was, I held myself onto her, crossing my feet around her back, my arms behind her neck. And she carried me like Jappity's wife used to carry Jappity's idiot son, and I felt just like that boy, as if the thoughts that were all right for everyone else weren't coming now, and never would come, to me. As if all I could do was watch, but not ever know anything, not ever understand. I pushed my face into Mumma's warm neck; I sealed my eyes shut against her skin; I let her strong warm arms carry me away in the dark.

BACK SEAT

BRACKEN MacLEOD

Bracken MacLeod is the Bram Stoker, Splatterpunk, and Shirley Jackson Award–nominated author of the novels *Mountain Home*, *Come to Dust*, *Stranded*, and *Closing Costs*. He's also published two collections of short fiction, *13 Views of the Suicide Woods* and *White Knight and Other Pawns*. Before devoting himself to full-time writing, he worked as a civil and criminal litigator, a university philosophy instructor, and a martial arts teacher. He lives in the Boston area with his wife and son, where he is at work on his next novel.

The cold made her feet hurt. She was wearing the same sneakers she'd had since before the beginning of the school year, even though her feet had grown and her toes were pushing up against the ends. They were thin canvas and the flat soles were slippery on the black ice coating the road, but they were what she had. To combat the cold, she doubled up on socks even though that made the shoes feel even smaller and crunched up her toes more. Layering her socks worked at first, but the cold still crept in like needles slowly being pushed through the canvas and into the layers of cotton underneath.

There was snow on the ground on the side of the road, but it wasn't deep, not like the year before. She didn't have to slog through it like then. This was that dry, powdery kind that you couldn't make a snowman or even a ball out of—it just sifted through your fingers like weightless sand when you tried to shape it. It was the kind of snow that fell when it was so cold the condensation from her dad's breath froze tiny icicles in his mustache and beard. When that happened, she used to laugh and try to pick the little pieces of ice out of his facial hair. He'd smile and bat her hands away, telling her to keep her paws off his beard diamonds. But the novelty of it wore off after the second week of record low temperatures, and neither of them acknowledged the tiny icicles anymore. They were headed into the second *month* of frigid temps now. That's what they said on the radio. Record lows, not felt in New England in a century. At nine years old, a century was a mythical length of time. Like "once upon a time" and "happily ever after." One hundred years only existed in stories. Though plenty of things in New England were much older, she'd never met a *person* who'd lived a hundred years. She knew she wouldn't be around in a century to tell anyone how numb her toes were. Cold wasn't supposed to last like that.

They walked along the side of the road toward the next house. She didn't want to leave tracks, but the ice on the road was too slippery to walk on. She'd fallen a couple of times when they first got out of the car and her dad told her it was okay for them to walk in the snow on the shoulder. That was tricky because it was dark and there were no street lights out here to illuminate something in the shallow snow that might trip them. Just a faint, unsettling glow from the reflection of the moon behind the clouds. Hidden roots or not, if anyone came driving along, neither of them wanted to be *in* the road.

The snow crunched softly beneath her feet. Her dad's footfalls were louder, though he did his best to stay quiet—he couldn't help his size. He walked in front of her and she tried to step in his footsteps. Though the snow wasn't deep, it still got in over the tops of her shoes and froze her ankles along with her stinging toes. Walking in his tracks kept that from happening as much, though it still did.

She made a game of it, pretending she was a ghost stalking him, walking in his tracks so when he looked behind him, he couldn't see where she'd been. She'd stand in his footsteps and he'd see right through her and shiver at the thought that something was following him. What could it be? The spirit of a tragically lost girl he once knew? She thought it might be fun to be a ghost. Then, she could sneak into some of these houses—pass right through the doors and walls—and sleep in an empty room all by herself. Instead of in a car.

The shelters in the city wouldn't take them. A single man with a child was bad enough, but they definitely wouldn't take in a single man with a *girl.* Men and women were kept apart for safety reasons, they said. Her dad argued that she was his daughter, and they said it was policy. She couldn't stay in the men's area and he couldn't go in the women's. We're sorry, they told them. So, they had to sleep in the car. Her dad turned on the engine every couple of hours to run the heater. The sound of it turning over woke her up every time, but she pretended to sleep through the noise. She knew he wanted her to get good sleep so she could be alert in school. But then every few nights, they had to go for "The Walk."

She moved quietly behind him, pretending to be a spirit until they reached a driveway and he turned to remind her with a raised finger to be extra quiet. She didn't need reminding. She knew.

Stepping around her dad, she glanced at the mailbox, as if it mattered whose address this was. Most people bought those brass-colored metal numbers to stick on the side of their mailboxes, but this one had been carefully hand-painted. It was hard to read in the dark, but up close she could see. The person who'd done it hadn't painted the street name, just the numbers five and seven. That was enough. She remembered they were on Summer Street. That had made her smile at first. It was nothing like summer out that night, but it was nice to think about warm weather. She was ready for some.

Her father leaned down and whispered in her ear. She wanted to pull back her stocking cap to hear him better, but her ears were as cold as her feet. They hurt in the biting wind, so she leaned closer and turned her head, but left the hat in place.

"You know the drill. Don't forget the cup holders."

She nodded. She never forgot, though when she came back without anything in hand, he worried that she wasn't looking hard enough. She tried to find what he wanted everywhere she could think of. Sometimes, she even checked under the floor mats in the footwells.

She crept up the driveway. It was clear of snow, though there was some salt spread out. She tried not to crunch when she stepped, but couldn't help it. She was small and the noise was slight. Still, it sounded loud to her. At this time of night, every house on the street was dark; everyone was asleep. She knew how tiny little sounds outside of the car made her wake up all night long. She tried to move as silently as a ghost.

She hesitated beside the car and looked back at her dad. He'd melted into the shadows of the trees beside the driveway. The shadow he'd become nodded at her, and she turned back to the passenger door and pulled up on the handle, gritting her teeth, waiting for the electronic chirp that would tell her to let go and run for the shadows. The door clicked faintly and popped out an inch. No alarm. She lifted and pulled hard and it swung open. And *that's* why they were in the town they were, instead of Manchester or Concord. No one out here locked their doors.

She jumped inside and pulled the door shut to extinguish the dome light overhead. It was still cold with the door closed, but the breeze couldn't get in anymore. She wished she had the keys so she could start the engine and let it idle for a little bit and heat up—take some of the chill out of her feet and hands. That was as sure a way of getting caught as leaving the dome light on or just standing out on the front step and ringing the doorbell. No. She had to wait. The drive back to Manchester would be warm. She'd snuggle up under her blanket and get some sleep when they were through. And tomorrow was Saturday. No school. She could sleep in. Though she never did.

She opened the center console, knowing she probably wouldn't find any quarters in the coin slots, but still hopeful for something. No one out here locked their doors, but they didn't need meter money either. Free street parking in small towns meant no one kept quarters in their cars. The best she ever seemed to find was what someone got handed back in change from the drive-thru window along with their Whopper and Coke. That ended up in the cup holders most often, as her dad reminded her. But she checked everywhere. Her mouth watered at the thought of a hamburger. She loved Whoppers so much! They were better than a Big Mac or those dry, square burgers from the other place with the girl on the sign.

She gasped when she saw the roll of quarters wrapped in one of those paper bank sleeves in the console. Ten dollars! Whoever drove this car must go into a city a lot. Maybe even Boston if he needed that much change. She'd never found a whole roll of change before and her heart started to beat fast with excitement. Dad would be so happy. Maybe he'd even let them quit early tonight. They could be out for hours on any other night before she found as much. She tried to imagine what his face would look like when she showed him. How the crinkles at the corners of his eyes would deepen and that one eyebrow would arch up the way it did. She loved that eyebrow. It only went up when he really smiled. It was how she could tell when he was faking.

Still, there was more looking to do before she could go back to him with her treasure.

She stuffed the coin roll in her pocket, closed the console, and started feeling around in the cup holders. Nothing. As if she hadn't found enough. She popped open the jockey box and felt around inside. Once, she'd found a checkbook and had taken it back to her dad. He'd gotten excited at first, and then his face fell and he told her they couldn't keep it. He didn't say why, he just said he couldn't write bad checks. She didn't know what made them bad. If they were filled out they were good, right? Still, he'd thrown the checkbook in the garbage and told her to focus on cash and anything they might be able to pawn.

Once, she found a toy. Nothing big. Just a tiny fashion doll of a blue-skinned girl with bright pink hair. It had little removable bracelets and a belt that she was careful not to lose, and the blue girl was beautiful even though she had little fangs. She knew it was a Monster High figure, though she didn't know the character's name. She'd hidden that find from her dad. She didn't want him to accuse her of having bad toys and throw that in the garbage too. When he found it in their car a week later, he'd asked where she got such a thing and she lied to him and said that her friend at school, Holly, had given it to her. She was ashamed to lie to him, but it wasn't a bad toy; it was a good toy and she wanted to keep it. The kid she took it from had a big house and her parents drove a big SUV and she didn't even care enough about the figure not to leave it on floor in the back seat like an empty wrapper. She loved that monster girl better than that other kid had.

There was a book in the jockey box. Who kept books in a place like that, she wondered. It was some grown-up book with a pair of bare feet on the cover. She thought for a minute about taking that too and giving it to her dad. She didn't know whether he liked books, but maybe it was like the figure. Something he could love better than whoever had left it in a car. Sometimes, they went to the library and she sat and read while he looked at his email on the public computers. He never checked anything out. He never had time to read, he said. This book though, stuffed in with the car papers like it wasn't anything important, could be his and he could read it and not worry about it being due or late fees or anything. He could take all year to finish it if he wanted. And he could love it like she loved her blue girl.

It was probably a bad book. Like a bad check. He'd throw it away and then no one would have it. She put the paperback novel with its one-word title back and closed the jockey box.

Her dad would be getting impatient soon. He didn't like her to take too long. She had to hurry. She checked the floors under the mats and stuffed her fingers deep in the cracks in the seats, but she knew the quarter roll was all she was going to find. It was enough. Still, she turned to crawl into the back seat and look for other treasures.

The boy sitting there stared at her from the shadows.

A shout she couldn't control escaped her lips. She clapped her hands to her mouth. She lurched away from the boy, hitting her back against the gear shift and then the dashboard. Another cry escaped her lips at the sudden insult of the little knobs that jutted out of the dash jabbing into her back between her shoulder blades. If she'd been in the driver's seat, she would've honked the horn and they'd be caught. She arched her back and her foot slipped. She fell face-first into the passenger seat, dragging her cheek down the cold leather. The quarter roll in her jacket pocket pulled heavily, like a weight, but didn't fall out.

She whimpered at the pain of her neck craning back against the upright seatback as she pushed up. The side of her right leg hurt where it scraped against the plastic of the center divider. She wanted to cry and call out for her dad, but she had to keep herself together. At least until they got back to their own car. She sniffled and gritted her teeth and got up on her knees.

Peeking over the back of the seat in the dark, it looked like a doll. Pale and still and small. And for a single second, an unwelcome thought about how much she'd love to have a baby doll intruded in her mind. But this wasn't a toy. It was a boy. He sat in his car seat, the harness over his shoulders holding him upright, head tilted to the side on a thin neck. His skin wasn't like a piece of plastic painted to look like a real kid; it was pale in the moonlight and looked unreal. His eyes were open, but they were dull and unfocused. Not like sharp plastic eyes that looked alert and had bright irises. His eyes weren't any of those things.

He had on mittens and a snowsuit with little built-in booties. She didn't want to know what his tiny fingers and toes looked like. She didn't want to know anything. Tears blurred her eyes as she struggled not to scream. But . . . the boy. The tears in her eyes made him waver in the dark, and it looked like he might be wriggling against the straps of the car seat, trying to get free, trying to reach for her and close his tiny little fingers around her throat and squeeze. Once, she'd seen a part of an old movie about dead people coming back to life and they were a horrible blue color that made her laugh because it was so fake-looking and how could anyone be scared by a blue person? And then they bit people and the crazy extra-red blood squirted out and she got scared. Even though that was fake-looking too—like a living cartoon—it was terrifying. Because it was blood and nobody lost that much blood and stayed alive.

In the diffuse moonlight, this boy was blue like that. The thought of him biting her and crazy bright blood spurting out of her body onto his round baby face made her breath hitch and she pushed away from the seatback.

The boy didn't move. He didn't look up or cry or even breathe. He sat there in the dark and looked somewhere, a million miles away—maybe in a whole different world. Looking at her from the ghost world.

She pulled off one of her gloves and leaned forward to touch his cheek with the tip of a shaking finger. She didn't know why she wanted to touch him, but she did. The boy terrified her, but she *needed* to touch him. Needed to know he was real and not a ghost. It felt like he needed her to touch him.

He was so cold.

The car moved, and she heard laughter and loud talking. She tumbled into the back seat as the car took a corner too fast and she heard a woman say, "Take it easy, Louis." The driver replied, "I'm fine. It's fine," and he gassed the engine. The baby in the seat next to her sat there, his head dropping with heavy sleepiness until his eyes closed and he slumped down. The grown-ups in the front seat kept talking and it sounded like when her own dad and mom had wine and their words got mushy. She could smell wine and bad breath like when her own mom would kiss her goodnight. They turned another corner and the car stopped too fast and the woman snapped at the man and he repeated, "It's fine. I'm fine." She said, "Go open the door and I'll carry the baby in," and he replied, "Let him sleep for a minute." He pawed at her chest through her coat and she shoved at his hands and said, "Your hands are cold," but he insisted and started kissing her neck and she moaned and let him put his hands back inside her coat. They kissed and then got out of the car, laughing, and she heard the woman say, "I should get the baby," and he said, "He'll be fine for ten minutes." "Ooh, I get *ten* minutes, huh?" She fumbled at the man's pants and he unlocked the door to the house and they nearly fell inside. They kept laughing and then the door slammed. And the baby woke up and began to sniffle and then started to cry. She tried to comfort him, saying, "Shh" and "It's okay; they'll be out in a minute." But they didn't come out. Not in a minute, or in ten, or in an hour. They stayed inside and she knew they fell asleep like Mom and Dad used to sometimes after too much wine and she saw the baby's breath in the car and he started to cry harder and harder and she got more worried and tried to get out of the car, but she couldn't move. She was frozen. It was cold. So cold. And the baby cried more, until it started to lose its voice and then his head began to bob again like he was tired and he sobbed and looked at her with glassy, accusing eyes she didn't want looking at her. She wanted to look away and be anywhere but in this car, but she couldn't get out. The baby boy looked at her and his lips were turning blue and then his head bobbed down and he stopped crying.

Everything was quiet for a long time while she watched the little puffs of breath from his mouth grow smaller and less frequent, until they stopped altogether.

Then she blinked and was back in the front seat reaching out to touch the blue boy's cold cheek. She drew her arm back like her hand had been burned and fell against the dash again. She started to cry harder, unable to control the hitching sobs that were building in her chest and her throat. She let them out and it was wrong because they could get caught but there was nothing she could do to stop it. She was only nine, after all. So, she cried.

The door to the car swung open and the dome light lit up the night and she screamed and stiffened, waiting to hear the angry shouts of the owners of the car, demanding to know in that way angry grown-ups did *what the fuck* she was doing. Instead, the dark blur in the door was her dad, and she lurched toward him, wrapping her arms around his neck.

"Daddy, daddy! There's a boy back there! He's in the back seat and he's blue and—"

He shushed her a little too sharply. Angrily. She repeated herself, trying hard to keep her voice down. "There's a boy in the back seat. A baby."

He shushed her again, softer, and held her tightly, pulling her out of the car and turning away. "It can't be," he said. "I'm sure it's just a doll."

All she could manage was "no" and "no" and "no" again. She said it and he replied with "Shh, it'll be all right," and "Calm down," as if she could. Not after what the blue boy had shown her.

Her dad looked at the house at the end of the driveway. Her crying was noisy and they had to be quiet . . . like ghosts. *Ghosts don't cry,* she told herself and tried to stop sobbing. But they do cry. They were sad and lonely. That's why they were ghosts on Earth instead of souls up in Heaven.

But being a ghost meant being dead.

Like the boy in the back seat of the car.

He's dead.

He froze *to death, because his parents left him in the back of the car and they went inside and fell asleep.* She'd seen them do it. The blue boy had shown her. He showed her the things she didn't want to see. The man's hands on the woman's chest and her hands in his pants, each other touching their private places, and then laughing and going inside while their baby froze to death in the back of a car. Now he was a ghost and he was sad, and he gave her a little piece of his death and now she was a ghost too, like him. Except not a dead one. He killed her inside. It felt like she'd never be happy again.

She tried to calm down, but her heartbeat and her breathing were beyond her control. Instead, she put a hand over her mouth, so at least she wasn't sobbing out loud. Snot slipped out of her nose and she felt ashamed for being a baby, but she couldn't help it. She wiped it away with the back of her glove and sniffed hard. The sound was loud and she gritted her teeth when her dad flinched at the noise of it in his ear.

Her dad whispered, "Are you sure?" She nodded. He set her down on her feet and dragged his hand down his mustache and beard the way he did, smoothing it down. It was the way he moved when he was feeling troubled. Even when he said he wasn't, if he did that, she knew he was. And that worried her. If the grown-ups were afraid, what hope was there for a kid?

"You go stand over there in the trees, okay? Go wait for me over there where it's dark and I'll be right over."

"Don't leave, Daddy."

"I'm not leaving. But I gotta have a look, okay?"

She drew in a long wet sniffle and pleaded quietly with him. "I'll be good, I promise. I won't shout or cry or anything, I swear. Just don't go. Don't touch him!" Her heart thundered in her little body. She didn't want him to get in the car with the blue baby. She didn't want him to be frozen with the sadness like she had been. If he did then they'd both be ghosts and nothing would ever be right again. She had been so wrong. The blue boy gave her what she'd wished for and it felt so bad.

It's a dream. I'm in the car and I'm dreaming we're out for The Walk. We're sleeping and the boy is blue because I found that stupid blue girl toy in the back seat of a car and I'm having a nightmare about her and that movie and none of this is real, it's all a nightmare. I have to wake up!

A chill breeze rustled through the trees and it hurt her face and made her eyes tear up more and convinced her she wasn't asleep and dreaming. The wet lines the tears had traced down her cheeks stung and she wiped at them with the glove she hadn't wiped her nose with. "Can we just go? Look, I found money." She reached in her pocket and pulled out the roll of quarters. She held it out to her dad, trying to press it into his hand. "I'll stop crying and be good if we go. I promise."

Her dad got that look, the one when he was worried. She knew it because his eyebrows came together and his eyes looked bigger somehow and his lips got so thin and tight they disappeared in the hair on his face. He looked like that a lot, so she knew it very well. He looked like that now. She knew *all* his looks.

"You *are* good, honey. You're the best. And I'm not leaving. I just want you to go stand over there and wait for me so I can have a look."

"I'll stay with you. Right up next to you. I can be brave." She wasn't sure if that last part was a lie, but she wanted it to be true, so she meant it even if she couldn't actually do it. *That* wasn't a lie, was it?

"Oh, honey. You don't need to look again, okay? Let me be brave for both of us." He put his hands on her shoulders and gently turned her toward the tree line at the edge of the property. "Go wait for me over there. Don't move. Just wait and be brave over there. I'll be right over."

"Promise you won't touch him." It wasn't a question. "Don't touch him. Promise."

He blinked. "I promise," he said, and nudged her away. She did as he told her and walked toward the darkness in the trees, wanting instead to hold on to her father and hold him back. She hadn't wanted to touch the blue boy. But then, she had. Something moved her arm like she was in a dream and what she wanted to do and what she actually did were two separate things. Before she realized what was happening, she'd reached out, and there was no way what she *wanted* was going to stop what happened next. Just like now that her dad had sent her away, and all she wanted was to make him come with her instead, leave the car and the boy in it alone. What if he made her dad do it even if *he* didn't want to? She wanted to plead with him to just leave. She could show him the roll of quarters again and say "Breakfast is on me," the way grownups did on TV, and he would smile and kiss her forehead and they could go out for an eggamuffin and stare into each other's eyes because it was the weekend and she didn't have to go to school and they could go window-shopping at the mall the way they liked to do and look at all the things they'd buy if they had the money to buy anything and she'd promise to get him a big leather chair he could put in his own room of the big house they owned in her dream and she would sit in his lap while he read her books all her own and not borrowed from the library or anywhere else and fall asleep and he'd carry her to her room where she'd lie in a warm bed with cozy Monster High sheets and on a shelf nearby would be a whole collection of beautiful dolls that would be her friends because she would buy all of them so they'd never be lonely or sad ever again. Except for the blue one. She didn't want the blue one anymore.

Except, that was only a dream.

Her feet crunched in the snow in the dark of the trees. She turned and waited. It was cold, standing still. Her breath billowed out in front of her face and hung there for a half second before blowing away.

She watched her dad open the rear passenger door and he gasped and said, "No," loud enough for her to hear, even though he'd never made a sound before on any of the nights they went walking on the road. She looked at the house. No lights went on. No one emerged with a shotgun or phone in hand already dialing 9-1-1. There was nothing. Like the night had swallowed everything up, leaving them all alone.

Don't touch him. Don't touch him. Don'ttouchhim!

He leaned into the car. She watched his broad back convulse once. Twice. Was he crying? She'd never seen her dad actually cry. He'd look like he might feel bad for a second and then he swallowed it up. She knew he swallowed it up for her. That's why she tried to be brave, so he wouldn't have to eat so much sadness.

Her dad backed out of the car and closed the door. He turned and walked toward the house. She said, "Daddy." He held up a finger to shush her and climbed the front steps. The door was unlocked. He walked inside.

The girl wanted to run after him. This was the worst thing to do. They'd be caught. And if they were caught, people would take her away from him, because it was mommies that raised girls, not daddies. She knew they'd send her to live with someone else and then she'd be a real ghost—sad *and* alone all the time. She stayed put. Her feet were numb and felt frozen to the ground, and she was too afraid to follow him into the house. She tried to picture the people inside blue like the little boy. As if they were all dead and this was the end of the world like that movie and she and her dad were the only non-blue people left alive. They weren't though. She knew they were pink and warm and asleep.

After a few short minutes her dad walked out of the house. To her it had felt like forever, the way time feels to a child. Long and uncrossable, like an ocean. Or a hundred years. He came walking out, wiping at his eyes, and joined her in the dark. "Time to go," he said. She wanted to ask why he had to go inside. What he'd seen. But she didn't say anything. Instead, she grabbed his hand and they walked up the driveway to the road.

In the distance, she heard a siren wind up.

They turned back the way they'd come, in the direction of their car. The weight in her pocket made her remember and she pulled her hand away and dug out the roll of quarters and held it out to him. "Here, Daddy." She wanted to see him smile. Ten dollars was a lot. It would make him smile.

A tear rolled down his cheek. He didn't bother to wipe it away. He said, "That's yours. Maybe you want to buy a new toy. A new monster doll."

"No. It's for breakfast."

He shook his head. "Uh-uh. That's yours sweetie. We'll go find something you can buy with it this afternoon." He paused. The siren was getting louder and she wanted to run. But he stood there. He crouched and more tears dripped down his face. "I'm so sorry, baby. I'll never make you do that again."

"It's okay. I understand."

"No. It isn't."

"How will we eat if I don't go look in the cars?"

He shook his head. "I don't know. We'll find a way. But you don't ever have to do that again. Not ever."

Her dad picked her up like he did when she was six and carried her the rest of the way back to the car, walking slowly so he wouldn't fall on the ice. She held on to the roll of quarters.

When they got over the hill and were on their way down the other side, she saw the flashing blue and red lights appear behind them. The sirens were loud now and lots of lights were coming on in the houses along the road. People were looking out their windows.

They reached the car and he tried to put her down so they could get in, but she didn't want to let go of him. With her chest pressed to his, she felt her dad's heartbeat. She held him tighter and never ever wanted down. But she had to get down to get in the car. "Can I sit in the front?" she asked. He nodded.

"We'll both sleep in the front tonight," he said.

"Did you touch him?"

He shook his head.

"Are we going to be okay?"

He nodded. "We're going to be fine, hon. Everything'll be okay." She let go and climbed in ahead of him, dragging her blanket out of the back seat up front with her. He climbed in behind her, started the engine, and turned the heater on full. Cold air blasted out, but soon it'd be warm.

For a while, anyway.

ENGLAND AND NOWHERE

TIM NICKELS

More a reader than a writer, **Tim Nickels** continues to work as an undertaker in Dorset, England.

THERE WAS SOMETHING about the couple downstairs.

No, really.

I thought they'd both been boys. Felt that stab as the blond one lay back, hands behind head; ginger-smudged armpits, smooth chest.

Huddled on that little finger of headland over the beach, they had taken out mugs of tea, sugared—one might say—with their own private chuckles. Footballs skimmed the sand below them; terriers shook their sea salt on groaning masters. All unnoticed, unheeded. They lived in each other's movie: one could imagine a cinema sun shafting to touch where their lips might have met.

He had taken his empty mug and crossed the sand track into the flat below me. She sat up, slipped her slight breasts into a bikini top, awkward arms trying to fasten it. I heard him pee—the house gave its echoes easily—and then he was out again with a kite. It was one of those big new ones you have to control with a pair of handlebars.

He'd made it to the beach when I came back onto the balcony with the binoculars. She was down there too by now—blond and boyish—very carefully laying out the kite strings for him. The balcony had no rail to lean on, and I pressed elbows into ribs to stop my hands shaking.

He was older than you might think. Strong, veiny forearms: all dark curls and Mediterranean eyes. But his face was just taking on that hardness that creeps up when you're in the thirties.

The kite was flying by the time I'd come out again with another drink. She was standing by him but was careful to keep out of his way. She put something silver to her face. A movie camera. A Super 8. She was laughing. The kite was lifting him off the sand, dragging him through rock pools and the dam works of five-year-olds and their dads.

An old man, shrunken and absurd in a purple Speedo—his splayed legs revealed scrotum as shiny as his shaven head—was trying to adjust his hearing aid when the boy careered into him. The man looked up blankly then continued to work his dial.

The boy kept moving.

But I remember he glanced back once or twice.

She carefully wound the kite strings when he'd finished, each string wiped free of sand with a hanky. He did some arm and shoulder exercises, jerked his head left and right, laughed and whispered in her ear when she'd finished winding. They both bent down and hunched about the beach making monkey noises, wiggling their arses and grooming each other for nits.

Then they scrambled back up the path still giggling. When the girl reached the top, she stopped and filmed me.

Pulling the cocktail stick from my martini, I sucked off the olive and gave her a grin.

And later—in their big glass porch—she started taking more footage. The porch's roof formed my balcony floor. Both flats fronted the cul-de-sac sand track with its carpet of fir cones; the track that ended at the big white house around the point with the peacocks that you see on the postcards.

Well, you don't see the peacocks on the postcards, but you *do* hear their lost cries in the night like weirded-out mermaids.

I knew about their filming session because I saw her through the window when I came back from the hotel bar in the sunset and long shadows. The camera was a little thing—a cheaper Chinese model maybe or one of those the Russians made for their aborted Games. What the hell did I know. She swivelled it on a tripod as if it were the prism of a lighthouse.

As he lolled and posed on the daybed, I noticed a pretty drastic scar running up his thigh. But we've all got a few of them, whether inside or out.

And I certainly envied him his urchin curls as they fell against the pillow.

The boy went out at midnight and came back around two. I was on the balcony wide awake. Don't ask: my throat was sore and the night was clear and I'd done enough sleeping in my life. Done enough waking up and wishing I hadn't.

I looked down as he searched for a key in the luminous summer shadows. He knocked his trainers off on the door rim as he entered. They must have been pretty sandy.

A light snapped on and the girl slipped out and across the path with the tripod.

Five minutes later a great light lit up the beach—only to quickly fail and plunge the night into deeper darkness.

The sea was just beginning to take the shells.

In the breakfast sunshine I sat on a rock, popped some seaweed, and watched the limpets and cockles on the sand. In ten minutes the shell shape would disappear underneath the tide and I would only have a memory.

The artist had a punning sense of humour: I remember the shells had been placed in the shape of an ear.

I was about to cross the track to fix the first drink of the day when a woman glided by in a wheelchair. A collie dog followed closely, a chunk of driftwood in its mouth. The woman's lap held a bottle of milk and a copy of *The Western Morning News*. Those wheels were impressive: big gnarly things that you'd find on a truck. She paused in her progress and peered out across the beach; stared at the ear of shells as the tide stole them away. But the dog soon became restless, and they both continued their journey around the point.

Curious, I quietly changed course and followed, padding ten yards behind. When I turned the corner, the woman had disappeared.

Into the air.

As if she'd been a magician.

I took a walk and thought about the kids.

Their apartment was brightly coloured inside its beach-blasted glass: blue walls, a wide-screen blue canvas with further, deeper shades of blue. Found object sculptures. Rush mats. Tablets of surf wax, a couple of longboards. Yes, surf wax melted with candles into little shrines. Maybe I'd even heard some Stevie Nicks slipping up from below.

But they didn't quite fit.

Did they own or rent? I could certainly imagine her leafing through the catalogues, carefully sourcing the flat's decor—while *he* might have made do with whatever the last board bum had left behind. I fancied the boy was on first-name terms with every hostel owner from here to Bali—yet I don't suppose she'd even toyed with a backpack that wasn't made of some sort of designer nothing-fluff.

Yes: scared or disdainful of water, she was too much in the shallows.

And was he too much out of his depth?

I took the path out to The Mine.

Well, we called it The Mine when we holidayed there as kids—but I'm pretty sure now it was just a glorified quarry. I can remember the gargoyled slates on the cliff top; the way they terrified my toddler sunsets.

I walked home through the lanes, enjoying the foxgloves and hart's-tongue and talking to the cows. I was working out the timing for my latest medication when I came out onto the crossroads and stopped.

It must have been twenty-five years since I'd last seen or even thought about those crossroads. The signpost was quite distinctive: the post and letters and mileages to the villages were painted in a poppy red. One of those lanes still led you down to the big barn; and back in the days of transportation the barn had ejected its livestock in favour of convicts bound for the New World. Lying there in the hay in a place of suspended animation. Neither here nor there. England and nowhere. A limbo land. *Boys in the sweating darkness; the hard walls, the pale flesh shafted by sunlight that swayed through the cow parsley; the light freckling their skin, every mole and scratch thrown up into a shining relief with nothing but themselves to feed on . . .*

I knew how they felt. I popped some pills and loped home in strange good humour, my erection fading.

Brother and sister?

That was my feeling as I thought of her taking cartridge after cartridge of Super 8. As they laughed together quietly, they might seem to share an age of time; a relaxation with self and selves not gained through romance, however passionate.

But my boy-man was dark and she was blond. He was a frayed-out beach urchin born for the surf and some hazardous sex, while the girl had nervously clutched a pair of spiky-heeled Russell & Bromleys as she tiptoed across the beachhead stream that morning.

For all her buzz-cut practicality, water certainly didn't appear to be her natural element.

I passed from countryside shadows through the scrubby fields to the coast.

I'd never seen so many butterflies; they clustered in the rough corners where the ploughs couldn't reach. Some of the previous season's swealing had revealed a path I hadn't noticed before: the blackened undergrowth held no scent. I plunged on down, the ground uneven. Wasps rose angrily from their gorse bushes.

The gorse gave way to camellias, their flowers long gone. Beyond *them*, an overgrown tennis court and cypress trees; a tired-looking pavilion with a parked-up Italian sports car.

I was in the grounds of the white house.

Assuming the unhurried innocent gait of the misplaced hiker, I attempted to wander casually through the tussocks, the sharp grasses spearing my thin knees. The house itself seemed in good order, one of those vaguely Arts & Craftsy jobs the Edwardians did so well. But the grounds were a forgotten jungle, as if the owner lived more inside his head than out of it.

His head?

Something glittered beside a rancid ornamental pool, a longtime stranger to frog spawn. A brooch made up of three circles. I picked it up and brushed off the dried salt. Everything was covered with it here. Three faces. Mad children?

No.

The faces of monkeys.

There was something going on in the water when I reached the beach.

A couple of boys on surf canoes had been caught on a rip and slammed into the rocks. Blood and broken bones. The helicopter from Culdrose stood by offshore, but the lifeguards managed to get them up to the ambulance unaided.

Children played with the smashed fibre-glassed fragments, throwing them at each other as if they were splintered Frisbees.

"Someone's going to get injured," I heard a mother's voice say.

Although I couldn't see it, I smelt a bonfire.

They were eating toast on the porch when I came up from the beach. On the opposite side to the daybed were a table and two chairs. Thing is, they weren't eating at the table, they were eating in the bed. That's not strange, is it? And yet—peeping in sideways as I hosed my sandy feet off—it was as if I was a second groom at the wedding.

Uncomfortable.

Have you ever seen red and green together? Really bright red and really bright green? Do you understand? There was a buzz, a vibrant sudden disharmony, a wrongness that clashed against their previous brother-and-sister act.

I caught his Mediterranean eye: but he waved in that quick English way. The mouth swiftly wrinkled up then straightened as he turned back to study her.

Easy to say—in that blissed-out, seems-so-long-ago Cornish summer—that they were high on each other. That in the already sea-thick ionised air, their oxygen was a little too abundant.

They went out hand-in-hand that evening, skipping down the track to the village. The village: a post office selling shrimping nets and a tired hotel with a bar and a quiz night on Wednesdays. I lay looking up at the stars, pretty done in from my hike. I thought of the light-damaged windbreaks in the post office window, impressed by my ability to still be in awe at the wonder of it all.

Bright red, bright green:

I'd noticed that the boy—the thirty-ish-year-old—kept a knackered green Renault 5 in a corner of the public car park, while my afternoon adventure had confirmed *her* little red Alfa Romeo slept under the cypress shadows along the cul-de-sac road. She wandered along there quite often, humming a funny little tune and spinning her fluffy rabbit key ring. The road was narrow. Parking was impossible unless you were In the Know. And she must have been pretty well In the Know with the white house people. They were always using their Land Rover to drag some poor tourist's vehicle back to the main road. The house was the last stop before the coastal path, and its wide drive must have been tempting for the fair-weather hikers to dump their cars in.

The boy returned first. He had someone with him; not the girl, someone taller with frizzy hair who rattled. Another boy. Yes. I thought so. The newcomer had a bit of a stagger going on and was giving my neighbour—and bloody me, by now—a loud talking tour through the bars of Thailand. He was a bit odd-looking though. Sort of scrunched-up. With an eye patch.

No really. Like Bowie had once.

I don't think the boy—my boy, ouch, the boy downstairs—actually spoke at all. They hung around outside for maybe twenty minutes while Thailand exhaled great plumes of hashish smoke. He said he wanted to put his tongue into somebody's ear.

They took the path down to the beach and were gone. The surf was ebbing, distant, faraway. Another sound: sheep in the darkness? Surely not.

I shone my little Maglite down onto the track and realised the One-Eyed Pirate would rattle no more.

Bitch had dropped his Tic Tacs.

My boy was back with the girl in an hour. He was calm. She was gasping, breathless and intent on her camera as they scrambled up from the beach. They went inside, and the old house awoke and sent up conversational vibrations. They talked till dawn then walked slowly to the beach in a warm, white, misty drizzle.

They each carried a long fantastical object, green and blue. And as they planted them in the sand and walked away, I realised they were peacock feathers: the amber eyes swayed and winked at me through my shaking binoculars.

I swim through the forests: thick brown kelp like tripe, green clouds, anemones, darting fish smudges. I feel like the angel I wanted to be as a boy. I think about the Etruscan blues of Cala Domestica. The whiter whites of Fire Island. The sun shafts perfectly through the ten-foot-tall water. My eyes open, balls freezing and recessing in the cold Channel current as if I were wingless in deep space. I surface: foam-skirted rocks, the cliffs hazing away . . .

My towel lay waiting. A book and a sandwich. The pills. A can of Diet Coke with a squirt of something extra.

Shadows spun across the rocks: they were up there, the neighbours, peering down at me from an overhang. I think she smiled before they began the slide down the narrow sheep path.

Perhaps I really had heard sheep.

I hauled myself onto the rock, found my trunks, wrapped myself in the sun-warmed towel, aware of my scrawny dying little body. I'd found the little cove just last year: *my* cove, I thought, in the selfish way a child's mind slips into that of the man.

They were dressed for hiking. Expensive boots (I figured) and matching too. She carried the pack: a proper, mush-like-shit-for-the-Pole rucksack. I'd been wrong.

"We were going to pass by," he said. Soft accent—somewhere northern. "And then saw you."

"And we thought we'd come down." Hers was sharper. London or trying to be. Texting vocalised. "You're above us, aren't you."

They both had grey eyes.

You live for yourselves, right? I couldn't shake the thought. I suppose I'd written their life stories while they'd barely noticed me.

She said: "You probably think we just live for ourselves."

I nearly dropped off the rock.

"Well, we do," he said.

"Kind of," they chorused together, smiling, perfect.

Fantastic.

I wondered again whether she swam, my glance shifting from the water to my small picnic, the child-me wondering if they were hungry, the me-me pondering if they had eaten of anything but each other.

"Dan." He gave the little wave. "By the way."

My hand was still salt-clammy so I didn't offer it.

"Yes, we love swimming," she said. "Don't we, Da—" The pause was so brief as to be almost undetectable, half an eye blink at most. "Dan," she finished quickly, simply.

As she slipped to one knee and peered at the sunlit submarine sand, I realised she could have been no more than fifteen or sixteen. But she drove a car. It's hard with girls, isn't it.

"She swims like a fish." Dan was already turning away, first foot back on the track.

So there you are. She swam like a fish.

They stopped halfway up the path, and she turned—the blond girl without a name—and took another little film.

Living for themselves.

Had they realised that I hadn't spoken?

I rinsed my trunks out in the basin, fascinated by my body in the long, stained mirror. The sun haloed my shoulder hairs like I was an angel already. I never realised I had so many ribs.

An outdoor tap spluttered below the window. My bathroom was at the rear of the flat, and I peered down into the kids' little backyard, shading my eyes. Their expedition hadn't lasted long. Dan was naked and washing out a wetsuit.

He turned the tap off. "Say again?"

Her head popped out of the French windows, clamped to a mobile: "She says she might need to move it."

"Is that all? Why are you telling me? What's it got to do with me?"

He turned the tap back on.

Her voice rose half-heard, half-imagined through the tap water as it spoke into the phone: "Yeah. Don't worry. Yeah. Catch you later."

She was amazing, a real gymnast. She could spin the chair on one wheel, a postage-stamp turn using the impetus to throw the rubber bone fifty metres. The dog was good too, catching the toy in midair, teasing the abyss beyond the cliff edge—but always falling safely back into the long coarse sea grass.

The woman was in her fifties. She wore a dark roll-neck sweater that was a little out of place on a summer evening. She had a rug over her lap too—and by the way it fell I reckoned she had no legs at all.

Yes. Quite a magician.

Too late, she caught my eye. Christ. But she smiled. A really big grin and a wave before throwing the bone again. I smiled and raised my glass—nearly fell off the balcony—and nodded my head in that meaningless, pants-down way that you'd probably do too.

Suddenly—or so it seemed—Dan and the girl were there. First they just leant against the outside glass of the porch. Then they ventured onto the grass—unflinching, uncaring—as the collie raced around them barking deliriously. The old girl—sorry, the same-age-as-*me* girl—was roaring with laughter, tarting it up big time for the movie camera, pulling the roll-neck over her nose and doing wheelies.

She was having such a party with herself that she didn't immediately notice when the dog trotted up to the boy with the bone to throw. The woman quickly wheeled up and took the slobbery toy from Dan's fingers.

I could hear her, even in a hissy whisper. "Come on, Beth," she said, and the dog followed her down the track home to the big white house.

I slipped in for a leisurely refill. When I came out Dan was alone on their headland finger. The sea would soon be snapping at the rocks below.

He had her fluffy bunny car keys and he threw them at the sunset.

There was a firework party that night.

A couple of families had got together and made a camp above the high-water mark. The display was pretty good; I think one of the dads did it for a living—he had a red boiler suit and everything. The applause echoed over as the rockets shimmered and spat.

In the gaps between the explosions, I could hear sharp laughter from the track below. And I mean sharp: derisive, brittle, ungiving.

Presently, I saw the girl walking quickly down to the beach. There were a couple of guys in Bermudas with her, young and wiry. They both wore graffitied plaster casts on their forearms: the canoe dudes had come back to party. They were talking loudly, booming about the latest beach riot over in Rock. I could hear them even above the biggest bangers.

Cracked posh voices privately honed for leadership. England and somewhere. Tongues of glory.

The porch door crashed, and Dan was out and running to the promontory, standing amidst the fireworks; heedless of the warning voices, the air full of shooting stars.

He came to my flat three hours later.

I heard bare feet creaking up the stairs as I lay out in my usual stellar-mesmeric position on the balcony. I never lock the front door—what the hell have I got that no one else has?—so I counted and calculated when the door was most likely to open and then peeped inside.

Yeah, it was Dan all right. Naked again, fearless and flushed. He stood in the light of the twenty-watt economy bulb, the leg scar reaching from thigh to lower stomach. His fingernails were filthy. He stalked from room to room nursing his semi-engorged penis; trying to make sense of the artwork I'd rented with the flat. I could tell he sat on the bed for quite some time: the springs have a way about them. He was in the bathroom for a while as well—I could hear him going through the pill bottles.

Another footfall from the stairs. Lighter. The girl, chest heaving, dressed in a man's fleece that nearly covered the Bermudas. Dan came out of the bathroom, and I thought they were about to kiss. But he just shook his head as she pulled the top off and gave it to him to wrap around his waist. For a moment, Dan seemed to look right at me, then he turned and they both hurried off down the stairs together.

I held the three monkeys up in my shivery fingers, turning them so they caught little pieces of moonlight.

Black-headed gulls were fighting over a ragworm breakfast, the tide sliding in an hour behind yesterday as I bent down closer to see: they told me the drugs would make my corneas swell and pop. Someone had planted hart's-tongue in the ribbed sand. Two bunches: long fleshy leaves, lightly corrugated and redolent of moist hedgerows. As unexpected here as . . . *as a second groom at a wedding*, I thought, peering in through their window as I came back; observing a scattering of hart's leaves on the daybed.

I smiled at the woman and the woman smiled back.

"Did you hear the fireworks last night? Bloody summer." She was still smiling, looking up at me as I traversed the track. The sun caught her cropped grey hair as if it were pewter. Might have been blond once. "Did I see you up at the crossroads the other day?"

God. Maybe she had.

"You know the story?"

I said nothing of course.

"All to do with the old convicts. It's a corpse way as well. And rather notorious for road accidents."

I must have raised an eyebrow.

"Oh, I mean nobody's ever died or anything." She spun the chair. "Well, well. Hear no evil, see no evil."

And speak no evil, I thought, wondering what all this was about.

She grunted good-naturedly—a gruff sort of saint—and wheeled herself home for more spells.

Sea caves: the pounding mirror of echoes and the smell; organic, salty, slippery. The uncertain discovery in the darkness: jammed pallid buoys and polystyrene. The vacated egg sacs of sharks. I squatted in the coolness, picked up the blanched quill of a cuttlefish and rubbed it against my loosening teeth.

The caves lay on the other side of the beach. They were far below the high tide mark and submerged themselves twice a day. I admired the cleansing action of the sea most especially here. The grains rubbing and changing themselves. Changing and shrinking and wearing themselves down to nothing.

I waddled out towards the sunshine, crouching to save what was left of my head from the cave roof. A little clump of sea anemones caught my eye. They were no fools, hidden in a hollow to avoid the crushing surf of autumn. One of them had closed while trying to gorge on something that looked joyously like a methamphetamine capsule. Unable to resist, I gently released it from its captor and nibbled the end.

Salty. Minty.

Did I have any sense of moment? Of sudden crisis after the torpor of an anticipation unrecognised?

I took a stroll along the beach track that night. Actually, more like four the following morning. I carried a vermouth-free martini with me: laugh if you like, but I was still determined to burn down in style.

The track led around the head of the shore and curved naturally into the drive of the big house with its forgotten garden and cypresses. I say cypresses, but I'm not quite sure now: they just looked elegantly tall and French. Mid-point on the bend was an orange street light: it was slightly unexpected, but I guess the council had been nabbed for public liability a few too many times.

I counted: one, two . . . *three* bats chasing insects around the streetlamp's glow; caught briefly, tiny, black. I threw an olive at the lamp but it sailed over—a pickled green beetle—uninterrupted.

Three bats. Three monkeys. Three people. The boy, the girl, the woman. And me.

The white house had a light on.

It was in the left-hand corner, to landward. No sea view at all, I reckoned, as I filtered gin through my teeth and counted bats out there on the beach road. And the very moment I looked back—extraordinarily—the light went out. Moments later, another replaced it facing the sea. Then two lights together in the midriff of the building.

Darkness.

I was turning for home when headlamps shot out over the beach, catching a cat running up the big rusty sewerage pipe from the sea. A peacock's call rose into the night. A diesel engine rattled; gears shifted.

I slipped into the bushes by the street lamp, lost the last of my drink as I tripped over a discarded barbecue. It was silly: the road was perfectly public. And yet—

The Land Rover was making reasonable progress, given its load. The bats sliced the air over my head as the groaning red sports car—wheel-locked, hand-braked—lurched behind on its tow rope.

I struggled out and stalked the two vehicles as they rounded the bend—but I wasn't fast enough. They were way ahead of me and I had the exaggerated caution of a drunk. Something was happening—or rather what was happening was ceasing to happen: it sounded as if the Land Rover had stopped. I tried to make my ears curl around the corner: the little convoy had obviously reached the kids' porch; a car door opened . . . quickly shut . . . one person maybe . . . muffled speech perhaps . . . porch door, opened, shut . . . gear change . . . vehicles moving off again—

I turned to look back at the lamp-post. A couple of moths fluttered too close to one another and a bat took them with a single snap.

I must have stayed awake till six, lying out on the balcony in my underpants. I seemed to have run out of olives but otherwise I was doing okay. It was early July, so it never really got completely dark. The Atlantic swells were coming in good and the pre-breakfast surfers would be down and waxing before seven. The A30 at Bodmin would be like a car park.

There was a noise from the flat below. A floorboard creak, the clack of plastic on plastic. A toilet seat. Up or down? Then the sound of somebody peeing, long and loud, in the hour before dawn.

And as the morning entered in earnest, a bonfire burst out from somewhere inland.

But by then I might have been dreaming.

I'd somehow rolled up in a towel and my mouth tasted like someone else's. I crawled in through the balcony door, found some juice and the last bottle of vodka; scrambled for the binoculars and was out again.

The surf: low tide, three foot and clean, flags keeping the real hangtenners and the weekend bodyboarders apart. Was Dan down there? It was hard to tell in the mass of foam and heads and flailing leashes.

I focussed out beyond the crowds towards the point. There was a small group sitting astride their long boards, doing the cosmic thing. It seemed like Dan's speed—but they were too far away. It could have been a group of seals for all I could tell.

The sun shot across the ocean, seemingly intent on setting the waves alight.

Bright, bright as a bonfire.

A bonfire.

She was dancing when I got to the red crossroads.

Do you remember Jordan waltzing around the bonfire in Jarman's *Jubilee*? That unreal Super 8 slow motion, the flames licking in the sunlight, trying to defeat it. The girl even had a maxi dress hitched into her knickers in a semblance of a tutu. She arched and flitted through the smoke while the Fire & Rescue held off with their big hoses, fearful that they might blow her over.

"Daft maid," murmured a fireman. "Too late for the bastard in the Alfa though."

And I could see through the nearly brighter-than-day blaze that a solitary charcoal figure slumped itself in the driver's seat.

I ran.

I ran almost all the way back to the beach. My lungs were full of hot crawling crabs as I collapsed on a bench and vomited.

The lifeguards were carrying something up across the sand. Dozens of semi-naked people followed as if processing a saint's effigy through a South American village.

The body was distinctively dressed in a purple Speedo. Across the short distance, I could imagine a pale dead hand clutching a hearing aid.

"How long have you got?"

The woman was suddenly there on silent wheels, her dog resting its head on my knee. She had her morning paper, her pint of milk.

I wiped my mouth, fingered my throat. Or what the surgeons had left of it.

"You have something of mine." She looked at me long and hard. "And if you hand it back I'll give you something in return."

She spoke for maybe fifteen minutes.

And when she'd finished, I reached into my pocket and gave her the brooch. She took it and called the dog and left without another word, the pine cones cracking beneath her wheels.

I must have sat there for quite some time. Staring children were shooed away.

I suppose I made quite a sight.

The girl was looking down at me.

Christ. How long had I been there?

Her camera was raised for a final sequence. I would quietly learn later—there was only ever a passing reference to the matter in court—that it was never even loaded, the Super 8 cartridges just demonstration dummies.

So their unreality was truly unreal.

You probably think we just live for ourselves . . .

She seemed dressed for a journey, her dancing skirt now pulled down, Tic Tac's eye patch wrapped like a bracelet around her wrist. The bare arms were just beginning to turn pinkish; this blond Ariel, this . . . *creature . . .*

I knew I wouldn't forget her then: my mind's easily lost other things in its life; pretty much sapped itself of interest in anything but *Jeremy Kyle* and the morning makeovers here at the hospice. Dangling between life and death; England and nowhere.

And I do remember one thing in particular as she lowered the camera from her face that final time.

She had her father's eyes.

ENDLESS SUMMER

STEWART O'NAN

For Paul Cody

Stewart O'Nan was born and raised and lives in Pittsburgh. He's the author of twenty books, including *Snow Angels*, *The Speed Queen*, *A Prayer for the Dying*, and *The Night Country*. With Stephen King, he cowrote *Faithful*, about the 2004 Red Sox, and the short story "A Face in the Crowd."

THEY SAW ME at the lake, when I had the cast on, the one I made in the basement. They saw me messing with the trailer hitch. They came over.

"Hey," they said, "need a hand with that?"

Guys and girls both, the young ones. That's who went there.

They had long earrings like chandeliers. They had long blonde hair parted in the middle, their bright combs poking out of their cutoffs. They had muscle shirts and puka beads, they had shaved legs and baby oil for the sun.

"How'd you do that?" they said.

"How do you sail with one hand?" they said.

"Let me help you," they said.

When there were two of them, I let them fix it so the taillights worked, then I thanked them and left.

They were all leaving; that's why they were in the parking lot. I could leave and come back and they'd be gone.

"How much can a Bug tow?" they said. "Nothing heavy, I bet."

They saw me from across the lot, putting away their blankets, their wet towels around their waists. Suits still wet and smelling of the lake. They walked out into the shallows and stood there sipping beers. The garbage was full of cans, every one of them worth a nickel. I almost wanted to stop and fill a bag.

"Thanks," I said. "It's hard with this on."

"No problem," they said.

"No sweat."

"My dad has one like this," they said.

They had wallets, licenses, credit cards. They had keys I had to throw in the river. Rolling papers, little stone bowls. They had bubble gum. They had Life Savers.

"How does it go together?" they asked.

"How did it come apart?"

They knelt down in front of me to see what they were doing. They had freckles from coming to the lake; they had sunburnt shoulders, and their hair was lighter than in the winter. The ends, and around the top. They smelled like lotion, they smelled hot. They wore flip-flops so you could see their toes, the hard skin of their heels.

They liked my car. They asked how old it was, if I might sell it, how much I'd ask.

"How do you shift with that?" they asked.

They lifted the two ends of the connectors. They didn't see the other set electrical-taped under the tongue. They didn't know they couldn't put it together, that it was impossible. They tried to do it the regular way, like you would.

"Here's your trouble," they said.

They turned to say it, to show it was two male ends.

The parking lot was empty, everyone down at the beach. Kites in the sky. Hot dogs on the free barbecues the county put in. Charcoal smoke.

They smiled as they turned, like I didn't know. Like I was an idiot or something, so dumb I'd busted my arm. Pathetic. A little weak thing.

The lot was empty, kites in the sky.

I had the cast over my head and brought it down hard.

"Oh," they said, the bigger ones.

Or "Uh."

Nothing really interesting.

They fell across the hitch, and the first thing I did was grab them by the hair and pull them up. I could use the hand. It looked like I couldn't but I could all along.

So stupid.

I grabbed them by the hair and the back of the waistband and spun them into the car. Because I already had the door open. They saw me like that first, with the door open. Helpless. They came over to see what they could do.

Most the same age. The older ones I let go. They were young, with good skin. I liked them best that way. Blonde, tall. The boys had muscles. They were everywhere that summer, like a song on the radio you can't get away from. You start to sing it anyway.

They came from the city, or just outside of it. They lived with their parents, or with friends over the G. C. Murphy's, or they were at school for summer semester. They had IDs for work, they had chips for free drinks. They had bottle caps in their pockets. Heineken and Löwenbräu, Bud and Bud Light.

Love, love will keep us together. . .

They lay back in the seat when I folded it down and put a towel over them. They were breathing, they were making breathing sounds.

The lot was full, windshields all glinting in the sun. You could hear the little sound of the lake.

"Oh God," they said.

"Please," they said.

They had freckles on their chests. They had bright white tan lines. They had the red marks their suits made around their waists. Their hair was still wet from the lake, and smelled like it. They had sand there.

They got up to see what was happening and I hit them with the cast again, backhand. Bam, straight-out. I didn't even have to look.

"Oh," they said again. "Uh."

The highway was empty, the fields, the barns. All of it hot. A mile away from the lake, you couldn't tell it was there. Just hills.

They didn't see the dust in the mirror, didn't hear the rocks clunking in the wheel wells.

"What year is it?" they asked.

I laughed then. Me, pathetic. Weak.

"An accident," I said. "Nothing major."

"I really appreciate it," I said, and already I wanted to hit them and never stop. Right there in the lot. But I waited.

They smelled like pot, like wine, like the cheap beer from the concession stand. Old Milwaukee. Sometimes I didn't even kiss them after.

They stayed that way until I got them down to the rec room. They woke up when I opened the vinegar under their noses. I already had them tied up, their ankles to their wrists and then their necks. You could raise and lower them over the beam to make them shut up.

I didn't really need the mask; it was more for them.

"Please," they said. "Oh my God please."

They were all lying there in the sun with the waves coming in. That summer, it seemed it was always a beautiful day. The outlook for the weekend was good. They heard it in the morning, waking up to the clock-radio, drinking coffee, thinking of taking Friday off. Hard to find a parking spot. They circled the lot, signaled to stake their claim.

They drove little pickup trucks and Camaros with pinstriping. They drove their mother's old Volare with the peeling woodgrain decal. Their keychain had the name of their insurance company on it. Their keychain had a picture of their niece.

Think of me, babe, whenever . . .

They prayed. They closed their eyes and they prayed.

They had a favorite sweater around their necks, in case it got cold later. They had a dab of mustard above their upper lip. They had a bump where the cast hit them. They had a tattoo of a moon, its eye winking just below where their tan stopped. They had gold chains that broke if you pulled on them too hard, and blue eye shadow you couldn't rub off.

"What happened to you?" they asked, like it was funny.

"You do that sailing?"

They screamed when they saw the knife.

They said, "Oh my God."

They said, "No."

The lot. The lake. A beautiful day, highs in the mid eighties.

Some sweet-talking girl comes along . . .

They screamed.

"Be quiet," I said.

The windows were boarded over, with cinder blocks piled against them, but they didn't know that.

I lifted them up. Now I was doing all the talking.

"Shhh," I said.

"Please," I said, and they looked like all of them by then. They looked like they knew how it felt to be me, and for a second even I was sorry for them. For a second we were together there, me and them. We knew.

How I wanted to be honest then. You don't know.

I reached over and touched their hair, the two of us quiet in the still air of the basement.

"It's all right," I said. "I'm not going to hurt you."

MY MOTHER'S GHOSTS

PRIYA SHARMA

Priya Sharma's work has won multiple British Fantasy Awards and Shirley Jackson Awards. *Pomegranates*, her latest novella, is nominated for a British Fantasy Award, a Shirley Jackson Award, and a World Fantasy Award. More information can be found at priyasharmafiction.wordpress.com.

The dark and stormy night is welcome after the long, hot summer that's scorched the grass and put me in a stupor. I'm in a perpetual sweat. I lie awake through airless nights in my bedroom.

The violence of the dark and stormy night breaks the tension and brings a kind of peace.

I am my mother's ghost and she is mine.

She follows me around the house. Right now she's outside the toilet. I know this because her sigh penetrates everything, even my sleep. It verbalises her emotional exhaustion. She doesn't need words now that she has her powerful sigh. It creates a vacuum that sucks out all my feelings.

"Are you okay in there?" Her voice is low and slow. I pretend not to hear her.

"Charlotte?" There's a tentative knock.

"Go away."

"Charlotte, are they talking about us?"

She means in the village. I went out today for supplies, carting them back in my rucksack. Mum imagines the village as it was years ago, when her and Dad bought this house. There was a butcher's, greengrocer's, post office, and tearooms. A crucible for gossip.

I've tried to explain to Mum that I cut through the trees to the main road and walk the half mile to the supermarket. It's a great barn of a building in which to be anonymous.

Mum can't take it in. She's stuck in the past. I'm stuck in *her* past.

"Nobody's talking about us."

I wash my hands. When I open the door she's right outside, as if her nose was pressed against the wooden panelling.

People used to tell me that I'm a younger version of Mum. I wouldn't know. I've no idea what either of us looks like.

Wash day is a chore. Mum has the demeanour of a beaten dog.

"I don't want to."

Her hair is lank and greasy, clumping in patches to reveal the thick flakes on her scalp. She used to spend hours in front of the mirror, doing her hair and makeup. We live in the country but Mum dressed like something from a film.

I bully Mum into the bath, pouring water over her head with a plastic measuring jug before she tries to climb out.

"The water's cold."

"It's the hottest I can get it." I push her back down.

Her crying makes me scrub harder. I stop when I realise that I'm raising red welts on her back.

"What will become of us? Who'll look after us?"

As if I've not been here my whole life doing exactly that. I must be strong so that she can be weak.

"Where's Jack."

Now I want to scrub until I draw blood. To hold her head under the water, like she did to Arthur. He must have been terrified. At least Jack survived.

I sluice Mum down and wrap her in a towel instead. Action brings memory. I'm on this very spot, but time recedes to when the tiles were clean and whole, not cracked and mouldy. I'd wrap Arthur in a fluffy towel, warmed on the radiator. The one in my hands now is stiff and scratchy. I hope it takes her skin off.

Wherever Jack is now, at least he's out of it all.

"Come on, old man. It's your turn."

I unbutton his shirt and unzip his trousers.

"Get off me. You're young enough to be my daughter."

"Dad, please."

"Help! Get off me!"

I unbuckle the belts strapping him into his wheelchair so that I can undress him.

"Somebody help me!"

An unmistakeable smell rises from him. His pants are stained. He used to be able to tell me when he needed to go. I get him to stand but he grapples with me before I can get his y-fronts down. There's still so much strength in those bony hands.

"Mum, calm him down, will you?"

She hovers, getting in the way without offering help. The heat's made her even more sluggish than normal. She moves so slowly that I want to shake her.

"Charlie." She takes his hand.

"Eva." The use of his last mistress's name used to make me furious.

The intricacies of the brain are alarming in their dysfunctions. Dad can see faces, his brain can process the image, but he can't remember whose face it is. I can see faces but can't process the image. The outcome's the same. Neither of us knows who we're looking at.

Dad grasps Mum's forearms to steady himself. At least she calms him, if only for a little while. He puts his head close to hers.

"Penelope." He's correct this time. He kisses her cheek.

I gag as I wipe his smeared buttocks. You'd think I'd be used to it by now.

I sit in the armchair I've put beside the landing window, overlooking the drive. It's a nice spot. I get the last of the light. There's a stained-glass panel down the centre of the window, put in by a previous lord of the manor. It's of Demeter, arms laden with corn sheaves. I like the patches of colour it sheds on the floor and walls.

Bats flit through the warm twilight, feeding on the fly. Birds serenade the arrival of the night. I should feel settled but something gnaws. I want to shrug myself off and become something else.

I freeze. A flashlight's moving through the trees, a swinging line that lands on the defunct fountain in front of the house. Cars used to circle it, stopping to drop off partygoers. The drive itself is wrecked, potholed and cracked by vicious winters, allowing new growth through it. The only access is from the main road and the gates have rusted shut.

The beam of light climbs up the front of the house. I duck out of sight. I wish I had a gun. I peep from behind the curtain, watching his progress. Everything about the figure marks it as male. It's confirmed when he stumbles and swears. A burglar would be stealthier.

Then he does the unthinkable. He comes up to the front door. The knocker lands on the wood with a series of heavy thuds.

A light goes on below. It must be Mum. I thought she was in bed. Running hurts my bare feet. They slap clumsily on the floor. Too late. She draws back the bolts as I reach the bottom step.

"Jack?" Mum says, then she collapses.

The man's as tall as me but broader. He drops the torch and sweeps Mum up. He manages her easily.

"Where shall I take her?"

"Up there."

He carries her up the stairs.

"That door." Mum's bedroom.

He's used the moment to take charge, kicking the door open with his foot and laying her on the bed. He smells of cigarette smoke. Wonderful in this house of decaying flesh.

Mum tips her head from side to side, her eyelids fluttering. "Jack?" She puts out a hand.

"It's okay, Mum." He hesitates over the word *Mum*. "You need to get some sleep."

"Will you be here when I wake up?"

"I promise."

She smiles, or something that passes for a smile.

I can see expressions and distinctive features but it's the face itself that's elusive. When I was younger and went out more, I used haircuts or clothes to recognise a person. Uniforms made negotiating school a nightmare, making me wary and shy. People thought I was stupid as I stared at them, trying to work out who they were.

Jack was young when he was taken into care. Too young to have a stance, a walk, or a gesture that would help me now. There was nothing on his face to mark him out. There are no vestiges of the boy I knew.

What I see now are sturdy legs, and sleeves rolled up to reveal knotted arms. Hair brushing his collar.

I close the door behind me so that Mum can't hear.

"Who are you?"

"It's me, Charlotte. Don't you recognise me? I'm Jack. I've come home."

The past is a hungry animal. It devours me, piecemeal.

Dad's a poor sleeper. Maybe it's because of his illness, or his guilty conscience. He's started wandering the corridors, which is punishing. I fret he'll fall and break something. When I'm too tired to supervise him, I tie him down and plug my ears against the shouts.

Tonight I let him roam. He shuffles along, stopping to pick at the wallpaper. I don't want to fall asleep with a stranger in the house. The man went straight up to Jack's room without prompting. I should've made him leave right then.

"Penelope, what have you done with the children?"

"They're in bed." There's no point trying to correct him. "You shouldn't have left like that, Dad."

Talking about it all now he's lost his mind isn't fair, but it makes me feel better to tell him what I couldn't when I was younger. I was scared of Dad. He was a stranger in our midst, who could destroy us all with a few words.

Now he stops and turns around. The way he looks at me makes my stomach lurch, but his clarity is short-lived.

"Where's Eva?"

"You phoned from the airport." Dad knew Mum never answered the phone. It brought on a panic attack. "You told me to tell Mum you were leaving with Eva. You said, 'Promise you'll look after them, Charlotte. They'll never cope without you. They need you.'"

"Jack, Jack, Jack." Raps on the wall as he walks along.

"Before you hung up you said, 'You can love someone too much.' What did you mean?"

Love hurts. That's what he meant. I resolved not to love anymore as I put the receiver back in its cradle.

Dad gets away from me. He raps at the first door he comes to. It opens and our uninvited guest is in the doorway, rubbing his face.

"Jack, Jack, Jack," Dad says.

My favourite time of day is before anyone else is awake. The house is pleasant this way. The quarry tiles in the kitchen are cool underfoot. Everything is quiet.

I make a pot of tea and take a cup to Mum. Her legs stick out from under the sheet, skin flaking all over the bed and carpet. I arrange the pillows behind her as she sits up. As I lean over her, I smell something sour in her morning breath.

Drawing the curtains shows the room up. One wall is lined with framed images from her photoshoots. Her dressing table is thick with dust. The perfumes are stale. The potions separating in their glass jars. The prongs of her hairbrush are clogged with dirty hair.

"Mum, is it really Jack?"

She looks past me. I hate that. It's like she's seen someone behind. I seize her chin and turn her head in my direction. There's a delay before her gaze follows.

"Yes."

"How can you be sure?"

"I'm sure."

She's suddenly forbidding and formidable. Then, after she's stared me down, comes great gusts of self-indulgent sobs. A confusing contrast.

Yes, there she is. The mother I grew up with.

There's nothing for it. I slip a kitchen knife into my pocket and go up to where would-be Jack is sleeping.

I used to clean Jack's room when I had time. He was fascinated by animal bones. Birds. Small mammals. Each specimen was labelled in his childish hand with its Latin name, where and when he found it.

Mum wrinkled up her nose at his collection. *You little psychopath.* It was one of the few things she found funny.

Except it wasn't so funny when Jack punched Arthur until he sobbed. Mum put Jack out in the rain as punishment. He stood, face against the window, watching Mum pretending to read by the fire. Neither of them would give in. Dad broke the deadlock when he came home.

For God's sake, Penelope, do you want him to get pneumonia?

Dad picked him up and carried him in, Jack's smile triumphant over Dad's shoulder.

Is this Jack?

I stand in the door. The sheet's pushed down to the man's waist. Light brown hair covers his upper chest. Everything about him is lean and long. He's an undernourished wolf.

"Get up."

I open the curtains and sun floods the bed.

"How did you get that?"

There's a long scar along his left collarbone. He touches it, as if he's forgotten it, then laughs.

"You'd be shocked by my life, Sis."

There's a hardness to him that makes me think, *Yes, you might be Jack after all.*

I reach out and run my forefinger along the irregular, thick line. His lips part, just a fraction.

"You could be as beautiful as Mum was, if you took care of yourself."

Mum was a model. People joked that Dad, who inherited a fortune from a German uncle, chose her from a magazine.

The man flings back the sheet and I look away.

Life's suddenly uncertain. The only thing I can rely on is routine. So-called Jack offers to help. I let him.

He shaves Dad and then feeds him breakfast, coaxing him with spoon after spoon, long after I've lost patience. He wipes the porridge from Dad's chin with a gentleness that I can't second-guess. Would real Jack be so kind?

Mum sits in the chair opposite and stares. She eats like the food's choking her.

"What next?" Jack asks.

"Wheel him out onto the patio for a dose of morning sun while I pick some food."

If this weather doesn't break soon everything I've planted will die. I take a colander out to the rose bed, now filled with peas. They're starting to wither, the leaves yellowing, like the grass. The sun is bleaching the colour from the world. I peel a pod at intervals to taste the tender greenness nestling within.

When I look up, Jack's knelt beside Dad's chair. He talks to Dad, but he's watching me. Then he comes over.

"You've done a good job here." He helps me pick.

"It's not picturesque, but I like it."

"I'm not talking about the garden."

I know what he meant but he can go to hell if he thinks his opinion matters. He responds to my silence with, "This used to be full of flowers."

"Yes, Mum and Dad were all about the spectacle."

Before Dad's dalliances and Mum went off her rocker, there were guests who stayed for weekends. Staff were brought in for parties that went on all night. Where are those free-loading champagne-guzzlers now?

The girls at school used to call me *New Money* and snigger. They mocked my parents for buying the old hall and playing at being the landed gentry. Their mothers looked away, embarrassed, when they saw me pushing Arthur in his pram. They'd mutter to each other or give me a patronising smile. *They're so happy, Down's children, aren't they?*

No, they're just children, like yours. They cry. They laugh.

I wanted to tear their faces off.

The memories still smart. I want Jack, if he is Jack, to leave it all alone, but he doesn't. I'm not sure what bothers me more—the subject or that it's proof that he *is* Jack. And that maybe that I don't want him to be.

"Dad called us a bunch of headcases."

"Well, he's one too now, isn't he?"

"When did he come home?"

"A few years after Mum was released. Eva didn't want a man with dementia."

Sad, really. I think Dad really loved her. Or at least more than he loved us.

"So the old goat dragged his carcass back here."

"Mum was glad to see him." I was too.

The colander's full now. I have to ask him.

"What do you remember about that day?"

If this is Jack, he'll know exactly what I'm talking about.

"You and Mum were fighting. I'd never seen you so angry. Mum started with her normal stuff."

You're not safe out there. All you have is us. No one will love you like we do. People laugh at you. They'll hurt you.

"But you wouldn't have it, Charlotte. You wanted to go out. Mum was crying, saying you were going to leave us because of Arthur, just like Dad did. Where were you going that was so important?"

"I went for a walk. I just wanted to be alone for a while." My mouth contorts. I should be crying now. My heart should be in tatters but there's a place beyond tears, pleasure, or love. It's the sanctuary of the ultimate safety and despair. "Dad didn't leave because of Arthur. He left for Eva."

We tell ourselves the most outrageous lies.

"Arthur was screaming. He wouldn't stop. You were the only person who could comfort him, but you didn't because you were furious at Mum."

There's no reproach in his voice. There should be. I could've picked Arthur up. Soothed him. I went for a walk instead, and Mum drowned him in the bath.

Well, I would ask. It serves me right.

Mum's come outside. She stands, clutching one handle of Dad's wheelchair. Her gaze is unfocused. She sways. She'd stand there forever if I let her. Dad's chatting to himself and plucking at the fabric of his trousers.

We go in for lunch. Jack pushes Dad, flanked by Mum, her step hesitant and faltering. I bring up the rear. Here we are, me and my fucked-up family.

"Help me bring the chickens in."

It's dusk. Jack and I head out to the part of the garden overlooked by the drawing room. The chickens scratch around out here by day, coming and going through the long doors. They've decimated the lawn.

Jack throws his head back, bellowing with laughter.

"Bloody hell. *We* weren't allowed in there."

We herd the chickens in. The green room used to be a calm space. The green silk moire wallpaper shimmered in the sun, making the room a lagoon. Mum loved it. Maybe that's why I let the chickens defile it. One wall was soaked after a pipe broke and now verdant mould blooms on the peeling paper. All I care about are fresh eggs.

I like the chickens, too. They recognise me. I like the warmth of their breasts through their feathers and their throaty clucks as I stroke them. My affections are pragmatic. I'm not above killing and skinning one.

Jack can't stop laughing as they roost on bookshelves and in open drawers.

"Just wait until you have to shovel out the shit and feathers."

We're both laughing now, fit to bring tears to my eyes. I can't remember when I last laughed with someone. I'm overcome with the urge to reach out and embrace him.

Jack reaches below a chicken and pulls out an egg.

"This is cause for a celebration. Do you have any whisky, Sis?"

The library was Dad's favourite room, just as the green drawing room was Mum's. I associate it with the smell of cigars and men's laughter from those weekend-long parties.

The books in here were bought with the house. Rows of encyclopaedias, reference manuals, the classics in leather binding, art books, and atlases. I daren't remove the ones on the far bookshelves in case they're holding the wall up.

Jack sloshes whisky into heavy crystal tumblers after rinsing them out. It's never occurred to me to try some. It was Dad's drink. I take a sniff, then a slug. It's antiseptic and scalding. Jack sits back, cradling the glass in his hands. It's gone unsaid that I've accepted he's Jack.

"I wanted to stay here with you when they arrested Mum."

"That's funny. You never seemed to need me when you were little."

He never seemed to need anyone. Our mother doesn't feature in this parenting equation.

"Not true. I always wanted you, but you were too busy with Arthur when he came along."

"Arthur needed me more. And I was never going to get custody of you. I was only eighteen, and with my condition . . ." I sound like I'm justifying myself. "The only reason I was allowed to stay here myself was Mr Baines."

Mr Baines, Dad's solicitor. A dull, solid man who helped me with bills and tradesmen.

"Your condition." Jack waggles his forefinger at his own face. "You seem to manage okay now."

"Barely."

I've been called maladjusted, misfit, personality-disordered, and a fucking weirdo. I think Dad was the most relieved when a private neuropsychiatrist diagnosed a form of prosopagnosia. Face blindness.

At least she's not retarded.

On the contrary, your daughter's exceptionally bright.

"Why didn't Dad come home? I kept asking for him."

"He was in India with Eva, searching for enlightenment in an ashram in the middle of nowhere. Nobody could find him."

We fall silent. A fly skitters along the wall, high up, out of swatting range. My emotions are up there too, buzzing.

"This is expensive stuff. It's from Japan." Jack picks up the bottle of whisky and examines the label. "They had the best of everything, didn't they?"

"So?" I don't know why I'm so defensive.

"I didn't understand that we were loaded when I was a kid."

"What's your point?"

"I've seen a very different side of life to you." He strokes the scar on his collarbone.

"Yes, because my life's *so* easy." I spit the words at him.

"It's all relative."

"Where exactly have you been all this time, Jack? I wrote to you. Every week. You never wrote back. You refused to see me. Then you disappeared."

"I was angry."

"That's it? You were angry?"

"Yes. Angry at all of you. None of you wanted me."

You can't negotiate with pain, so I don't even try.

"So what's changed?"

"There's stuff I've done, bad things, to survive. I'm in trouble. I need to lie low."

"For God's sake . . ."

"It's okay. They won't look for me here."

The buzzing fly's incessant in its futile rage. There's a band of grey clouds in the distance, sucking the light out of the sky. They bleed dark lines into the trees below.

"Tomorrow. You go tomorrow."

He sighs, as if he expected this reaction.

"Do you remember the flour bin?"

The change of subject throws me.

"Yes."

We'd gone into the pantry to steal biscuits. The narrow space was cold and dark, lit by a single bare bulb. It was lined by shelves, stacked with boxes and cans. The flour bin was large, with a loose lid. It sat on the floor beside a drum of cooking oil.

There was a rapid thudding inside the bin and followed by silence. Then the thudding started again, followed by a high-pitched squeal. Jack and I looked at each other.

"We pulled back the lid." Jack drained his glass. "There were three rats inside."

"One was a gnawed carcass." I continue the story for him. "One was thrashing around, blood on his neck."

"And the third one was sleek and healthy," he finished pointedly.

I wonder what Jack means by reminding me of this salutary lesson in survival.

I'm the last to have a bath. I step out, dripping and shivering. The house is cooling rapidly as the storm approaches.

"Damn!"

The floor's still wet from the struggle with Dad. I slip, calling out as I go down. I try to breathe through the shock, taking an inventory of what hurts.

"Are you okay?"

Jack's right outside the door. The flimsy bolt pops off. I snatch at my towel, trying to cover myself.

"Get out."

"Sorry. I thought you were hurt."

"I'm fine. Just winded." I wince as I move. "Pass me my bathrobe."

He hands it to me, bunched up in his fist, then turns around very slowly. I tie the robe's belt, aware of my body, my unloved, untouched body beneath the thin cotton.

"Let's get you up."

He slips his arm under mine. There's a distant rumbling.

"One, two, three."

His heat seeps into me. He takes my weight easily. His T-shirt is cut away at the neck. Of all life's mysteries, sex is the one that we can experience every day if we choose. Except for me. The only mystery I'm acquainted with is death.

"I can manage."

I draw away when we reach my bedroom door. My thigh's throbbing. I landed heavily. Jack follows me in, shutting the door behind him. When I sit down on the bed, he kneels beside me and takes my leg in his hands, pushing at the bone from calf to thigh. His fingers are on my inner thigh, close to my most private place.

"Nothing's broken, but you'll have an almighty bruise tomorrow."

He sits beside me on the bed. His pregnant pause is leading up the something.

"I'm worried about you, Charlotte. You can't carry on looking after Mum and Dad on your own. You're run ragged."

"You won't talk me into letting you stay."

"Just hear me out. They need proper care. A nursing home and specialists. When was the last time Mum saw a psychiatrist? And the house, the whole thing needs rewiring and replumbing."

"We've only got enough to see us from month to month."

"Where did all the money go?"

"We've been living on it."

"Even in this state, the house is still worth something. And the land. You could sell it."

"I don't know. Mum and Dad wouldn't want that."

"Do you think they'd want you living like *this*? What do *you* want, Charlotte?"

I've never been asked that before.

"I don't know."

"Fuck." He shakes his head, like something's tearing loose in him. "I can't do this anymore. I'm not your brother. Sorry."

"I don't understand."

"We shared a squat. Jack knew this guy, said he'd give us both work. Stuff you don't want to know about. Jack used to talk about you. About what happened."

"I don't believe you."

The thunder's getting closer. I'm shaken to my foundations.

"It's the truth."

"Then where's Jack."

"We both got greedy. Our boss caught up with Jack. I only came here because I had nowhere else to go. I was only going to stay for a few days." He reaches out for my hand. I pull away. "We could go somewhere. Just the two of us."

There's a flash of light.

"Don't tell me, you were looking for somewhere to hide but now you've fallen in love with me."

"We both need a new start. We need each other."

This pulls me up short because it's the truth, whoever he is.

"How can I trust you?"

The air crackles. The distance between us is charged.

"Would I do *this* if I were Jack?"

He reaches out and cradles my face in his hands. His thumb strokes the skin beneath my ears. It's not the touch of a brother for his sister. He leans in. The involuntary sound of yearning escapes my lips.

What surprises me most is the tenderness. No, this can't be Jack.

I need to check on Dad. I put him to bed before I had my bath, buckling him to the wrought-iron bedframe for safety.

Mum's hovering outside the door. Always hovering.

"Your dad's crying. He's scared of the storm."

Not *Charles*. Not *my husband*. He's my responsibility. She abdicated long ago.

Mum peers into the darkness behind me. At the bare leg tangled in the blanket. Then her head swivels, taking in my nakedness beneath the robe. Her movements are slow and her eyes look blank, but she's assembling these pieces. I close the bedroom door.

Her mouth's downturned. The rain's hammering on the roof, pouring from the broken gutter onto the front of the house. It feels like it'll never stop.

"He's not Jack," I whisper. "He's—"

I don't know his name.

The door behind me opens with a click. He's there, bare-chested, doing up the buttons of his jeans' fly. A visceral thrill shoots through me. My face burns.

"Tell her," Mum says. There's a thunderclap.

"Tell her what?"

The lightning flash illuminates the hall's stained-glass panel. We're directly below the tempest. It's a timeless drama played out on a greater scale than ours.

"You're Jack. Tell her."

"You're crazy." He sounds uncertain.

"I know you, you little psychopath."

"No."

"I lied for you. I should've told them."

"About what?" I ask, even though I'm scared of the answer.

"You're a confused old woman."

"Tell her about Arthur."

I look from one of them to the other.

"Tell Charlotte," Mum musters all the venom she can, "or I will."

Her anger still has power. He throws up his hands. "I told you before. Arthur wouldn't stop crying. You left me and he wouldn't shut up."

"What did you do?" I sound as slow as Mum.

"He liked having a bath. I was trying to calm him down. It was an accident."

It's like he's explaining how he broke a toy. Arthur was fully dressed when I pulled him out of the water, his sodden clothes flooded my lap. Jack wasn't giving him a bath.

"You knew exactly what you were doing."

"I thought you'd walked out on us, just like Dad. I thought you weren't coming back."

I cover my mouth with my hands. The lightning feels biblical. It's true. It's all true, and the whole world has changed. Jack killed Arthur. I slept with Jack. No amount of rain will wash this away.

Jack reads me like a book.

"The rules don't apply to you and me. This doesn't have to change anything." He reaches out for me. "We can start again. Be anybody we want."

I shove him away. We're both disgusting.

"I know you. I saw your face when you found Arthur. You were relieved."

Promise you'll look after them, Charlotte. They'll never cope without you. They need you.

All I wanted to do was walk in the woods for a few hours. Mum, Jack, and Arthur were so heavy. Mum's tears filled up my lungs. I couldn't breathe.

"Don't pretend, Charlotte. You're as guilty—"

I want to shut Jack up. I slam his head against the wall as hard as I can.

"Mum, will you stay with Jack while I see to Dad?"

"Yes."

Mum and I hold vigil by Jack's bed. I've cleaned the boggy swelling on the side of his skull as best as I can. We listen to his ragged breath. His lips are dry and cracked.

"Why didn't you tell me, Mum?"

"I didn't want to ruin the rest of Jack's life. It was my fault."

"We're all to blame."

I don't feel angry at her for weeping. Not this time.

"If anyone comes, Charlotte, I'll tell them this was me."

She means what happened to Jack. Her hand hovers over my arm but she can't bring herself to touch me. It's okay. It's enough. I start to cry. Is your mother meant to be the person who breaks your heart? She looks so small and vulnerable.

If she's my mother, then I'm hers too.

Jack wakes up on the third day. His eyelids flutter, then open. The moan coming from his mouth doesn't sound human. One of his eyes is pulled up in a different direction to the other, marking his intracranial derangement.

Yes, we're a bunch of headcases.

The air in the room is cool and bright. The days have felt calm after the storm.

Jack's hand shakes as he lifts it to my cheek. His single word is mauled and elongated, but I understand it: "Mum."

THE WINK AND THE GUN

JOHN PATRICK HIGGINS

John Patrick Higgins is a writer, illustrator, and filmmaker. His short fiction has been published in the anthology *The Black Dreams*, two editions of *The BHF Book of Horror Stories*, and four editions of *Exacting Clam*. He is working on a book of short stories called *The Devil in Music*.

His debut novel, *Fine*, will be published by Sagging Meniscus Press in 2024, and the same company will be publishing his essay, *Teeth: An Oral History*. His first film, *Goat Songs*, premiered at the 2021 Belfast Film Festival. His second, *Muirgen*, will premiere at the Paracinema Cult Film Festival in 2023. He currently has two feature films languishing in development heaven. He lives in Belfast, where it rains.

I HAD TO DELIVER a birthday present to a friend, a book I'd wrapped in brown paper and secured with string rather than Sellotape. It was a book on British maritime history. We'd once had a conversation on the subject and I thought she seemed interested. Her name was Catherine and I hadn't known her very long, so I hoped I'd read the situation correctly. I slipped the package through her letterbox and listened to it crash onto the tiled hallway before going on my way.

She lived on bohemian Oakland Avenue in the east of the city. It was a street of brightly coloured doors and children's Wellingtons left on designer doormats. Fiat 500s bit into the pavements, so I walked down the middle of the road. There was nobody about.

At the end of the street was a sturdy, pebble-dashed Scout hall, the grey of dry pumice. Next to the barred windows swung a sign in a curling wrought-iron brace, artisanal in a way the street's occupants wouldn't recognise. The sign was weather-beaten into inarticulacy but retained a naive drawing of a tepee. The hall's doors were boarded up and two of the three unprotected windows were cracked and held in place with ancient orange tape. It was so odd: flat-roofed and hand-moulded, a strange projection of the past into the present—something boxy and unlovely squatting in this metropolitan street. I wondered if it was still in use.

As I reached the Newtownards Road I turned right. I was going to visit the local shopping centre and pick up some contact lenses. It was my only reason for going there, and I never enjoyed the visit, but Oakland Avenue was equidistant between my house and Connswater and, besides, it was a sunny day, and I had to pick them up at some point.

I was brought up in east Belfast, but lived elsewhere for many years. My job took me all over the world—I was a cameraman for sporting events—so it didn't much matter where I lived as long as it was near an airport. At the age of forty, I returned to the city, taking advantage of the house prices: you get a lot of brick for your buck in Northern Ireland.

I rarely left the house when at home. The city centre was completely foreign to me. I didn't know the good pubs and restaurants or if there were any. I kept my head down.

The natives of Belfast are gregarious and affectionate, though if you say that to people who haven't been here they don't believe you. They are a soulful, gentle people. Equally, they are loud, community-minded, and interested in your business, and I'm not like that. I keep myself to myself. I don't have any family left. I'm just me, not rooted but stuck in the mud—buying contact lenses, but not making eye contact.

As a child I enjoyed sport: I wasn't good at it, but I liked the rules. They were exact, impartial, and invented by stern Victorians. Rules were good. Rules were fair. My other interest was photography. It was solitary and quiet and played to my strengths: my separateness and my tireless collecting of kit. Everything reassuringly black-and-white. There was magic in birthing something new in a chemical tray in the cupboard under the stairs. So I travelled the world photographing sport and when I was at home, I stayed at home.

Connswater was one of the few places I did visit. It was an unlovely warren of discount perfumeries, pound shops, and army recruitment stands. The top tier was all fast-food outlets and toilets, the one suggesting the other in a joyless, nutrition-free exchange. The building was large and rectangular, except for a glass and metal rupture at the entrance, bulging like a swollen belly and pressed bullishly against the multistorey opposite. Pylons bristled like titans as cars beetled between their splayed legs. Everyone was on their phones, walking at a zombie's pace. There was no urgency—just grumbling, low-level menace. I hated this place, but my optician was here and I needed my lenses. I had a school reunion I didn't want to attend but probably would, and I couldn't imagine going in my specs.

Connswater was full of children, gangs of them, sharp as splinters, faces hard with purpose. They laughed and jostled and swore, but had a seriousness and self-possession that terrified me. They had the compact energy of seeds about to violently bloom. I kept my distance. Well, you have to nowadays.

I picked up a month's worth of contact lenses from the smiling optician, and I was out the door in minutes, swinging my branded plastic bag and happily free of the crowds, the dusty shells of dead shops, the persistent smell of hot fat.

I thought I would walk home along the Comber Greenway. The Greenway had been the route of the Belfast and County Down Railway for a hundred years until it was dismantled in the 1950s. It malingered, always on the cusp of becoming something for a further half century. Finally it was resurfaced and rebranded as a tranquil green corridor providing local people with a "traffic-free route for walking or cycling." It is seven miles of meandering valley, with soft verges rising on both sides. It's chiefly used by joggers, cyclists, and dog-walkers, the latter marking their territory with black bags of animal waste, hung from the branches of trees like foul Christmas decorations. Still, on a fine day, it was preferable to the exhaust fumes and graffiti of the main road. I headed past the trolley bay and crossed over to Bloomdale Street, a short terrace of houses with the usual proliferation of Union flags sagging in front. Cigarette butts formed fairy circles next to cars parked on the pavements. Down an entry, a shopping trolley looked guilty.

A woman walked towards me with a bichon frise on a short leash. She was wearing sportswear in a manner which suggested she didn't always wear sportswear. Her black hair was scraped back from her face, which was thinner than the last time I had seen it, her eyebrows fuller and darker. But there was no mistaking her. It was Tanya Millar. Tanya Millar from school. I hadn't seen her for a quarter of a century and she looked great.

"Tanya?" I said. She turned sharply, her eyes narrowing as she flicked through some mental Rolodex. Her eyes widened with her smile.

"McCullagh! For goodness' sake," she said.

"What are you doing here?" I asked.

"I've been walking my dog, what do you think? This is Beattie." The dog jumped up and sniffed my groin in a friendly manner.

"What are *you* doing here?" she asked. "I heard you moved away."

I confirmed I had moved away, but was now back. She looked at me with her large, dark eyes. She was twenty years older and her hair hadn't always been that colour, but she'd aged beautifully. I occasionally bumped into my male classmates on my short sorties to the shops, and time appeared to have made an example of them, but not her.

"How long has it been?" she said.

"Shut up!" she replied when I told her. "I can't be that old. You can't. We're too good-looking."

I laughed. I could think of nothing to say but I was pleased to have made a noise, just to join in.

"Are you going to the reunion?" she said.

It seemed more than likely.

"I might see you there. I've got to run on here, but I might see you there. Fancy that—Ol' Blue Eyes is back."

I enjoyed watching her jog off down the street, and I thought back to school: I'd always liked her, but never did anything about it. She barely spoke to me then. But, twenty years on, she remembered my name and thought I was good-looking. She specifically reminded me to attend our school reunion. It was all very exciting.

She had come through a gap in the wall leading out to the Greenway. The red paint on the wall looked like it had been touched up several times, but had never properly taken. Its lividity spread in patches and odd mineral clumps were pressed into it. It looked like the rusting hull of a landlocked trawler. The stone was bitten into and the gap seemed broken away, snapped off like a tooth, sharp as coral.

My mind was still racing from meeting Tanya Millar as I approached the wall and passed through. I felt slightly drunk. I had to admit I was lonely. I never went out as I had no one to see and nothing to do. This brief meeting had changed everything. It had opened up Belfast for me. The sky was suddenly a magnificent blue. Perhaps I could be happy in this city. It was, after all, my home. I could go to pubs, to restaurants, anywhere. I could start to live. I could learn to love Belfast.

As I climbed the dirt path on the other side of the gap, something unexpected pushed into view: a familiar object rendered unfamiliar. The light suddenly changed, the landscape pulled out of joint, as though I had stumbled into the prestige of a magic trick without seeing the setup. The canopy of trees over the Greenway was no longer there. Instead a crude, wooden ziggurat had landed like Dorothy's house in Oz, sudden and strange. It was thirty feet high and neatly constructed of slatted wooden pallets. It was a bonfire, a Twelfth bonfire. And it was April.

It shouldn't have been there, and the shock of its presence made me miss my footing. Tipping forward, my shopping spilled in front of me and my hands skidded across the pathway, skinning my palms and catching my left thumb awkwardly. The pain was sudden and sharp. I drew myself up to my knees and pushed the hand into my armpit. My thumb throbbed angrily. With my good hand, I returned the lenses to the bag and looked around to see if anyone had noticed. And that was when I saw the boys.

There were two of them, standing about five yards apart and staring at me. I was, maybe, thirty feet away, so they must have seen the whole thing. I could add embarrassment to the list of indignities. I got to my feet and dusted myself down with my good hand. The boys continued to stare. There was something odd about them, something I couldn't place. They just stood there, their faces expressionless.

I thought back to when I was their age, perhaps ten or eleven. If I had seen a flushed middle-aged man tripping over his own feet, holding an optician's carrier bag, I would have thought it hilarious. The cornerstone of all humour is a fat man falling, and there was an added transgressive edge because I was an adult and I was belittled. Schadenfreude is sweeter when dignity is punctured and, to a child, a humiliated adult is the funniest thing of all.

But these two just stood there. They didn't react in any way. I sensed no aggression, and I didn't feel they were trying to intimidate me. They just *stared*, as though I were something new that had stumbled into their world, and for which they had no taxonomic reference.

There was something else. It didn't strike me then, not as a conscious thought, but occurred to me much later. I would have cause to reflect on the encounter at some length.

They didn't *look* like other children. The other kids in the area were tough and pinched, with tight haircuts and branded clothing. Their footwear was more expensive and better cared for than my own. They understood the value of presentation. Their style was performative, tied in with their aspirations and the larger ideas they wished to express about themselves.

These two boys betrayed no such information. They were spare-looking, undernourished and hollow-eyed, and their hair was shaggy and grown out. They wore green woollen jumpers patched at the elbow and their jeans looked as if they'd known previous owners. It struck me that I hadn't seen a child wearing jeans in a very long time. Their gutties were laughably simple affairs: tiny coracles of rubber and canvas, the only decoration a Plimsoll line running the length of the shoe.

But it was their silence and stillness and the deadness of their eyes . . . Their faces were masks, revealing nothing. They didn't move, but their bodies seemed permanently on the point of doing so, coiled for action.

My left hand was still throbbing and, seeing no need to prolong our silent acquaintance, I began to move off down the Greenway. The moment I started to move the nearer boy moved too. His arm jerked at the elbow; his thumb and forefinger extended; his face creased into a heavy wink.

"Pow!"

He was giving me the wink and the gun. It was so strange and sudden that I started backwards, nearly stumbling again. I walked away, looking back several times before finally winding around a corner and losing sight of the boys. Every time I looked, he was still frozen in this strange attitude, gun pointed at me, his face still clearly contorted into a wink, long past the point I could make out individual features.

At home, I ran my thumb under the cold tap—it was stiff but not hugely painful. There was some swelling, so I wrapped it in a dishcloth and took two paracetamol. I went to unpack the carrier bag and realised one of the boxes of lenses was missing. I checked the optician's initial on the remaining box: the squiggled "L" meant the right eye lenses were gone. I could have gone back to the Greenway to look for them or I could have ordered more, but I was too excited. Tanya Millar looked amazing and I wanted to see if I could track her down on social media. I sat down in my office and switched on the computer when there was a loud rap at the door as though from a doorknocker, though I didn't have one.

Opening the front door, there was nobody there, but lying on the doormat was my packet of right eye contact lenses. The boys must have found them. They'd followed me home. They knew where I lived. I scooped up the box and looked about, but there was no sign of the boys anywhere in the street. The strangeness of our encounter shivered through me once again. Though really, what had happened?

I stared out of the living room window for a few minutes, watching the schoolchildren, their blazers at right angles to their bodies, their school bags trailing behind them like unloved pets. Joggers puffed past, the street echoing with their flat-footed slaps. The people who lived on my street were mostly old. They didn't have funky cars or *personality* front doors like the denizens of Oakland Avenue. They were neat and careworn and so were their houses. There was nothing strange in my world and there never had been until those boys had rattled me. I felt scolded by their seriousness and their silence, by the strange, sustained gesture of the wink and the gun. There was no cheek in it, no play: it felt like a warning, even a threat.

The thumb didn't get better. After a few weeks I went to the doctor who sent me to A&E. They sent me to get the thumb X-rayed and I finally spoke to a specialist who told me that it had broken and was already healing badly. They could rebreak it and pin it, but the damage looked irreversible, and the middle joint in my thumb might never work again. And so it proved. They gave me a sandwich bag of blue putty, some plastic squares, and a photocopy of some physiotherapy exercises, and that was it for my thumb. To this day it will not bend, but it doesn't hurt in the least.

About a month later, I put on my suit and tie and booked a cab for eight. It was the evening of the school reunion. I opened a bottle of wine and either sat or paced, occasionally passing the invitation on the kitchen counter.

By eight, the first bottle was finished, I had started on a second, and I realised that I was not going to go to the school reunion. Relief washed over me. I wouldn't have to humiliate myself in front of Tanya Millar and the rest of the school. I was risking disaster on a chance meeting in a local beauty spot. I had read too much into our minute-long exchange. I was being a fool. The taxi driver beeped outside at eight and my phone vibrated. I sank deep into my chair and listened to the taxi pull away, accelerating in anger.

I examined my face in the mirror over the mantelpiece and, in fact, I didn't look too bad with the wine goggles on. I still had hair. I had money. I wasn't *too* fat and the suit looked pretty good. We would have been a viable couple. I really *should* have gone to the reunion. Of course Tanya would be there. She'd more or less invited me and, anyway, a few weeks of *minor* online stalking had revealed she was divorced and almost certainly a free agent. My research had been thorough. There was some unfinished business there or, at least, some not-yet-started business. I *had* to go—I could get another cab. And I would wear my contact lenses—give Tanya the benefit of my baby blues. "Ol' Blue Eyes is back."

I opened the box of right eye contact lenses and noticed a tiny hole had been made at the top of each sachet. In each of the thirty capsules a pinprick had allowed the saline to evaporate, the lenses hardened into brittle translucent molluscs. The boys had done it. It had all the hallmarks of schoolboy cruelty: the wantonness, the pointlessness, the sloppy execution. They would never see the outcome of their destruction, but they had destroyed. It was enough. But it wasn't *quite* enough. They had missed one. A single plastic bulb was still intact, its contents still workable. I tore away at the foil, removed the lens with a forefinger and, tilting my head back, pressed it on to my eye.

I had never known pain like it. It was immediate and searing, dizzyingly focused. My eyelid clamped down, the ruined eye filling with tears in an attempt to cushion this foreign body, to lift it free of the surface and wash it away. I pushed it around the eye, howling in torment, unable to switch off the penetrating agony. The lens felt like it was breaking into shards, puncturing the soft film, scraping it, scorching it. I could smell hot copper as I clawed my face, stumbling into the kitchen to push my eye under the tap, to flush away the pain, filling the sink with pale, roseate blood. Panicked, I stabbed 999 into my phone and vomited, my eye socket an open wound. I fainted, but came to in time to stagger to the door for the ambulance.

The doctors couldn't tell me what had happened or what kind of corrosive was on the lens. I lost the eye.

Catherine came to visit me in hospital to thank me for the book. She was shocked when she saw my face. "My God," she said, "what will you do for a job?"

I laughed it off. "I only need one eye to take photographs," I said. I held my phone to my bad eye and took a picture of her. "I see no ship." She smiled, but clearly didn't get the reference. But, then, she was French, so there was no reason why she should.

I was discharged before the bandages came off, but a nurse would visit a couple of times a week to help with the dressing. I took to wearing an eyepatch when I went out. It wasn't worth it around the house.

I often went back to the Greenway. I traced the path I had taken that day. By then, it was the start of July and the bonfire was huge and densely populated with young, industrious ordinary people. Never the ones I was looking for. I saw no sign of Tanya either.

One day, there was a loud rap at the door. It sounded like someone slamming a door knocker, though I don't have one. I answered and there they were: the boys. They looked exactly the same, same clothes, everything. They stood there, expectant and silent on my doorstep. I couldn't speak. Words would not come. I simply lifted my hand to point at them, gasping, my thumb rigid, the hollow of my ruined eye closed over, and we three stood in the paralysed moment.

"Pow!" said the boy in front. They both started to laugh.

ONE OF THESE NIGHTS

LIVIA LLEWELLYN

Livia Llewellyn is a writer of dark fantasy, horror, and erotica whose fiction has appeared in over eighty anthologies and magazines, including *The Best Horror of the Year, Year's Best Weird Fiction,* and *The Mammoth Book of Best New Erotica.* Her short fiction collections *Engines of Desire: Tales of Love & Other Horrors* and *Furnace* were both nominated for the Shirley Jackson Award, and her story "One of These Nights" won the 2020 Edgar Award for Best Short Story. You can find her online at liviallewellyn.com.

NICOLE'S FATHER doesn't say a word when he drops us off at Titlow Park, and that's fine with me. Mr. Miller's car is hard and lean and long, with dents all along the side and a giant rusty grill in the front that looks like a monster's grin. His car looks like the kind that would roll down the streets at night all by itself, latching onto you with its lidless glass eyes and running you down like the neighbor's mangy dog, backing up over and over again until there was nothing left but a sticky red smear on the blacktop. His car reminds me of him.

"Time to get wet," Nicole says.

I peel myself off the sticky leather and lurch out of the car and into piercing summer sun and noise, the sounds of a hundred kids shrieking and thrashing in the park's Olympic-size pool like they're being murdered. From the other side, Nicole unfurls into the humid air, all long, tanned limbs and bikini-top ties, the tips of her black curls wet against her neck from heat and sweat and coconut oil, from secretions of adulthood that still haven't settled over me. I don't understand how she can look so much older when we're both fifteen. I'm not exactly a kid myself, but the way she's moving forward, I'll never catch up. Then again, I don't have a father like hers to get me there. I have to do everything myself.

"Can I have a dollar for the vending machine, Daddy?" Nicole asks, swaying her body back and forth as if she's still five. She lets the last word drawl and drip out of her mouth, just like I've heard her mother do when she's drunk and itching for a fight.

"Ask your little friend Julie. I already gave her all my spare change."

Nicole's fake smart-ass smile vanishes. Some other type of smile takes its place, and it's real.

"I know," she says.

Mr. Miller sneers at her, then flicks his cigarette ash out the window. "You know nothing." Soft grey flecks drift onto Nicole's face.

"You know what's going to happen, don't you."

Mr. Miller shrugs. "Do what you gotta do, daughter. You know you want to."

"Come on." I tug at Nicole's arm, then touch her tote bag, so heavy it doesn't sway. She looks at me, then stares back at him with those same pale, green-grey eyes that are in his worn, fox-sharp face. After a second, she slowly walks away. I hook my thumb in the belt loop of my shorts and lean forward slightly, my face hovering just outside the window. He can see right down my top. I give him my most earnest, respectful gaze.

"How about that dollar, Mr. Miller?"

Mr. Miller smiles at me, a wide grin that makes his lips curl up like he's pretending he isn't smelling something bad.

"Is that all you want from me, honey?" he says, plucking the cigarette out of his mouth. " 'Cause Julie asked for more than that, and I gave it to her. I can give you some, too."

I lean in closer. "Right here, Mr. Miller? You can't wait?"

"Can you?"

He drapes his hand out of the car window, and his thick fingers hang in the air, moving back and forth in front of my breasts as more ash floats from the red tip. A few flecks catch against my skin. He's waiting for me to say it, beckoning it out of me with those rough hands. A soft pop escapes my lips as they part. But nothing else comes out of me, all my thoughts have gone fuzzy red, and suddenly like thunder the car is rolling across the blacktop, so fast and loud that I jump back in fright. He's gone just like that, out on the road and leaving me behind in a shimmering sea of cars, mothers snarling and tut-tutting at me as they rush their kids past. I don't know why they're glaring at me. I don't control what he does. Most of the time.

I make my way across the lot over to the low building. Paint bubbles and peels off its concrete sides in fading aqua strips, and grime streaks the glass double doors. Above the entrance, fading brass letters read TITLOW PARK POOL, but it's clear that some of the letters have been vandalized and replaced multiple times—LOW is spelled with much shinier metal, making the TIT that much more noticeable. Like everything in Tacoma, it's seen better times. I like it this way.

Julie Westhoff hangs outside the doors, staring at her reflection in the filthy glass as she sprays something on her long pink tongue. Julie thinks she's more Nicole's friend than mine—even though I knew Nicole first, Julie quickly took her place as the favorite, and treats me as the interloper with the quiet confidence of girls who always look like her. Thin and blonde and pretty, always wearing low-cut blouses and halter tops with open spaces that travel down forever. So cool, she's not even a cheerleader, instead standing on the sidelines at pep rallies and games, making all the other girls lose their shit as she leans against the railing and slowly plays with her hair. She's the kind of girl Nicole and I used to wish we could look and act like—above it all, never letting anything get under her skin. It took us a while to realize there's a world of difference between looking that way and being that way, and we had it going on, long before she came along.

"Where's Nicole?" I ask.

"Somewhere, I don't know, she disappeared around the corner. She's pissed at me, or life. I don't know." Julie lets out a small, satisfied sigh as she inspects her face. It always makes her a little satisfied when she thinks we're miserable.

"Is this about her father? Did you two—did you and he . . ." I let my voice trail off.

Julie's eyes narrow. "What the fuck are you talking about? I don't even know him." She looks down at her hand, at the small cylinder rolling between her fingers.

"Really."

"Really." Her voice has turned steely, meaning the conversation is over.

"New poison?" I ask.

Julie points the spray at me. "Open your mouth and find out."

I know my place in the Bermuda Triangle of our relationship. I open my mouth. Julie squeezes bottle and mists my tongue. A powerful scent of mint hits my nostrils before I taste it, and a small *uck* escapes the back of my throat. Julie started smoking like a chimney when she turned twelve and got boobs, so it's pretty strong. She's probably swallowed her weight in breath freshener by now.

"I thought you didn't like mint."

"Not at first. But the taste goes better with coffee." She tosses the bottle into her tote bag and gives me a smile and a wink. "And urine. You'll see."

I laugh. "I don't drink urine, you freak."

"If you swim in that pool, you do."

"Funny."

We follow a group of parents and their kids through the doors. I can't help but frown at the familiar, nauseating smell of chlorine. We haven't even gotten to the dressing rooms yet and already it clogs my lungs, slowing my movements and weighing me down. It's the smell of my childhood, of graceless flailing, of choking, of always fighting the sensation of sinking into oblivion. Back in '68, the year I turned five, some Tacoma chick won three medals in swimming at the Olympics. By the next summer every mother in the city was dragging her daughter here for lessons, and every summer after that was spent struggling in the lanes of the competition-sized pool, swallowing great gulps of warm chemical water as we thrashed our way through the four-hour sessions like drowning cats. Every summer at least one kid drowned or got sent to the hospital, and they still kept pushing us into the bright blue water, hoping for one more girl who'd bring home the gold. Mom finally stopped taking me when I got my first period and threw a huge shit-fit about wearing a bathing suit with a big old brick of wet cotton between my legs. But I think she was tired of driving all the time, and I was never a good swimmer, anyway. Nicole was the good one. All I learned how to do was hold my breath underwater until the instructors forgot about me or left me alone. It's been a little over three years since I've been here. Nothing's changed.

Well, a few things have. We pay our entrance fees, then make our way into the women's changing room, echoing with high voices and laughter, the slap of bare feet and shower water against tile, the metallic bang of locker doors. It smells the way it always has, like perfume and soap and damp crotch, but the rooms seem smaller and dingier than I remember, and so many girls look younger. As we strip out of our clothes, I catch a girl I recognize from the seventh-grade class staring at me, then some kid on the bench beside her giving me the eye, super-young, maybe ten. I realize with a slight start that I've become the unsettling older creature the younger me always wanted to be. The kid's eyes are round and startled as she stares at our naked bodies, at our breasts and the dark hair between our legs. That's how I used to look at the older girls when I was a kid. *Those are women*, I would think to myself, *I'm going to be one of them someday.* And now I am.

"Nicole still isn't here," I say as I set the numbers spinning on the lock. "Did you see her come in?"

Julie makes a sniffing noise. "Maybe she's not coming? I don't really care."

"Did you two have a fight?"

"I'm not fighting with her. She's fighting with me. It's more of a disagreement, really. You know what she's like."

"I don't know, it doesn't sound like her. What is she disagreeing with you about?"

"My rightful place in the world."

I almost laugh out loud—that phrase is so Nicole. "And your rightful place is . . ."

"The one place she can't go."

"There are always places we can't go. Until we do."

"That's not true. You know what I mean. You've seen how she looks at him. She's just jealous of me. Because I can do what she can't."

"I thought you said you didn't know him."

"Well." Julie smiles and rolls her eyes. "Maybe."

"Maybe what?" I stare at her like I don't know what she's talking about, but she only raises her eyebrows and sniffs, gives me that old "you couldn't *possibly* understand" look, then picks up her towel. "Ready?" she asks.

"Always."

We make our way through the maze of rooms and into the blinding gold of a late afternoon sun. It looks exactly the same—the pool seems to stretch on forever, and there's movement everywhere, water and waves and limbs all vibrating and shimmering. Oscillating—a word I remember from science class last year. Past the chain-link fence surrounding the pool, the green grass of the park rolls in low waves around a small lake to thick rows of evergreens. Black cables pierce through their branches, converge around high telephone poles, dash across train tracks that line the entire coast. Beyond that, the smooth-pebbled beach and the dark blue waters of the Sound that look so warm and inviting and are only ever cold.

"Jesus Christ, this pool is big. Look at all these kids—and their parents, my god. Everyone's so fat and old." Julie's eyes are covered in glasses so dark and large, she looks like an insect. "Why are we here again?"

I shrug. "I met Nicole here—did she tell you? We used to swim here every summer. Four hours a day, five days a week, every June and July for eight years. It's like, this is what summer is to us. It's our ritual."

"Ugh. You are so suburban."

"It wasn't that bad. The lifeguards are handsome—look at him."

"I guess. He's kind of—what the fuck. How did she get here before we did?"

Julie points to the far opposite corner, to Nicole's slender body wrapped around the base of the lifeguard chair, her wet body curved against the thick steel poles, her lips moving silently. She's watching the divers at the deep end plunge in, disappearing in one spot and appearing elsewhere, breaching the surface like miniature whales. The Selkies, that's what they used to call Nicole and me.

"Come on." I lead Julie through clumps of bodies, past the shallow end where groups of parents form protective rings around their toddlers and first-graders, and then down the long side of the pool. I watch the pool depth numbers painted on the concrete beneath my feet and just underneath the surface of the water grow larger. It was somewhere past the middle that Nicole and I grew comfortable over the years. The shallows are too supervised, and the deep end is for divers, and too empty. The middle is both crowded and deep, but most of all it's deceptive. It's where you can get lost if you become unsure, or if you're overconfident and think you can easily get back to the walls. It's not for amateurs; you have to spend a long time there to learn how to make it all the way back.

"You don't have to swim, you know," I say. "It's fine to just hang out along the side." Julie's grown a bit more quiet than usual, her fake adult face wrinkling a bit with anxiety or worry, although it's hard to see it under those massive shades.

"I know. It's not that I'm against swimming, it's just"—she makes a circular motion about her face—"none of this is waterproof. I don't need to look like Alice Cooper, you know?"

"That's fine. We can just hang out by the wall and stare at the guys in Speedos. Like that one."

Julie shrugs. "I've seen bigger. I've had bigger. Is Nicole talking to herself? What a psycho."

I shield my eyes and squint. "Oh, that. Yeah, it's nothing. We used to do that all the time here. Just an old habit—going over all the rules and routines we were taught. The way you position your body before you dive, how you move your arms and legs when you do laps, even how and when you breathe. It looks easy, but it's not. It's all very coordinated, like a dance."

I can almost see Julie's eyes rolling underneath her sunglasses. "Wouldn't it be easier to just dance? At least you can drink when you dance . . ." Her voice mutters away into nothingness. For someone who's such a bitch all the time, it's almost sad how the sight of a large body of water is breaking her. I remember all the summers before, all those bullies breaking my nose as they lunged through the water with their raised fists, all the kicks to my sides, all the angry embraces. No one just lets it happen. Everyone fights, to the very end. I have high hopes for Julie. She's a fighter, too.

We reach the lifeguard's chair, and now I feel my emotions draining away, and it's the most wonderfully disorienting feeling in the world. It's like everything is underwater now, blurry and distant. Nicole and Julie speak to each other in small sonic waves: they're talking about Nicole's father, and Julie is triumphantly confessing even as Nicole admits tearful jealousy. I meander over to the chain-link fence, inspecting the tear in the links that runs up the side of one of the poles. I push the fence, and the tear widens into a body-sized slit: I pull it back, and the fence appears whole again. On the other side, a filthy black garbage bag sags into itself at the pole's base.

I turn back toward the pool. Families are pulling themselves out of the water, lumbering back into the changing rooms as their land-dry replacements make their way toward the shimmering water. It's a pattern, endless and unchanging in repetition, but I couldn't tell you what it represents, only that we're not part of it. Julie has taken her sunglasses off and placed them on top of the neat, folded pile of her and Nicole's towels, and she's sitting at the pool's edge, her long legs dangling in the water. Nicole sits next to her, leaning back slightly on one arm that crosses Julie's back. The sun is against our necks, hot and relentless as it slips further down into the day, and goosebumps run up and down my arms, cold bumps that send the fine hairs standing to attention. Nicole motions me over with a tilt of her chin, and I slip next to Julie's free side. We slowly kick our legs back and forth, watching the spectacle of arms and legs and heads rippling before us, florescent-print-clad bodies on blue foam paddleboards clumsily churning the waters. The oily scent of sunscreen drifts through the chlorine-heavy air, clogging my lungs. I stop kicking, and begin to take long, deep breaths as I stare out into the middle of the pool. There's always one place, one perfect place.

Nicole leans farther back, catching my eye. "What's the number?" she asks me.

"58. Same combination as usual."

Nicole shoves Julie against her back, sending her into the pool.

I wait for her to emerge, and she does, enraged and flailing. "You fucking bitch, I told you not to do that!" Julie tries to rub her eyes dry, but her wet hands only smear her mascara across her cheeks. With her hair all dark from the water, she really does look like Alice Cooper now. She reaches for the wall, but Nicole slips in, blocking her. I stand up, all of my muscles singing in anticipation.

"You shouldn't have fucked my father," Nicole says, grabbing Julie's slippery arms. "I told you I'd fucking kill you if you touched him." Quick as a flash, she butts Julie's head. Julie's eyes go wide, and she screams. There's the fight, the anger, along with all the majestic panic that heralds incoming doom: I knew she had it in her. I can't see it, but Julie's kicking out now, trying to push Nicole off of her by using her feet. We know that trick. We've been in these waters for over a decade.

I watch Nicole kick back and push off from the wall, shoving Julie deeper into the pool's interior. She's laughing, hard and loud, almost screaming like Julie is—it looks like what my mother calls horseplay, or roughhousing. Just two loud girls in a pool filled with a couple hundred other loud girls and boys and men and women all moving like they're having fits. Nicole keeps herding her farther into the pool, pushing her down and pulling her up, getting her good and tired. Julie's choking, she can't fight the water coming into her mouth, she doesn't know the rhythm, the routine. She doesn't know the dance. I pace down the side of the pool, never losing sight of them, then back away, take a few quick steps, and I'm in the air. My dive isn't perfect, it's been a year, but I'm powerful and methodical and determined, and I go deep, like I always do. I could always go deepest. Underneath the surface of the water, everything moves about and above me like a tapestry, dappled with blobs of liquid gold sunlight. I make my way through the floating forest of legs over to Nicole, her bright cherry ankle bracelet that I wove for her beckoning me near. I pat her right calf twice with the flat of my hand, and then I take hold of Julie's nearest leg, running my hands down until I have her foot. I pull down.

Above me, Nicole is steering us into the most crowded section in the middle. I'm kicked in the head a few times, but that's nothing, there is only the breath that I hold in my lungs, the lean curve of Julie's body rising out of my hand like a dying flower. Nicole pushes her head down one last time, holding it under the water. Julie looks like a mermaid, her hair fanning in waves like silky sea grass. She convulses, contorts, bubbles of air flowing out of her grimacing mouth. Like she's speaking to me, shouting, but no one can hear her down here, below all the muted thunder of the surface. I don't think she even sees me. None of them probably ever have. Her legs stop shaking, and I loosen my grip. Little dots of black start crinkling at the corners of my sight, and my lungs are burning, but I linger for just a second longer, watching how graceful Julie is now, all sleepy-languid and peaceful as she floats. She's finally dancing, I think as I shoot past Nicole to the surface, letting the air back into my lungs in one ragged, greedy gasp. I take my time getting back to the wall—Nicole is somewhere in the middle, still holding Julie, maybe telling her some final secret, I don't know. She'll eventually leave her there, wedged between people who don't even understand what's happened, and slip out of the pool and into the changing room, where she'll go to locker 58 and take my tote bag out and get into my clothes and leave. 707 for the combination. It's a lucky number. It hasn't failed us in almost ten years.

I make my way back to the wall and pull myself up. The neat pile of towels is still in place—I'm surprised no one took Julie's sunglasses, so I put them on, and tuck the towels under my arm. I can hear the familiar commotion behind me begin. No one's going to look at me, I'm completely forgettable. I slip through the long gap in the chicken-wire fence and pull Nicole's tote out of the garbage bag. I pull out her dress and sandals and slide them on, then slick my wet hair back from my face with Julie's sunglasses as I serenely walk onto the wide grass lawn. I don't look back. I never look back, it does no good. All across the lawn, families gather up the remains of their picnics, teams pack up volleyball nets, park volunteers shove trash into round cans. Overhead, a sun so dark gold it's almost black drips behind needle-thick trees and into the Puget Sound, and massive bands of orange and purple stain the darkening sky. Afternoon is ending, bleeding out into night. To my left, porch lights begin to flicker like fireflies, and street lamps glow. I love the sun, but when it starts to die is when I'm most alive.

Behind me, the sirens sing.

Following no particular path, I head toward the intersection next to the train tracks, where several old wood buildings hunker. Strips of red neon letters flash on and off like a stoplight: BEACH at TITLOW. Beneath the tavern sign, several cars are parked, including a car that looks like it would slide out from behind bushes in the heat of the night, engine throbbing like the heart of a mechanical minotaur as its fat tires pressed your frozen body against the filthy pavement, grinding you down into motes of blood and bone. This car would follow you to the ends of the earth, its horn crying out to the vast ocean of stars above as it pursued you until you succumbed, until you drowned in the gasoline smoke of its quaking embrace.

This car reminds me of me.

Mr. Miller rolls down the window. "So I guess it's done," he says between long pulls at his bottle of beer. "Another one bites the dust, right?" I don't say a thing. He opens the door and stands, stretching. I watch the muscles of his arms stretch and contract under his tanned skin. "She suited the both of you."

"Apparently she suited you, too."

"Hey now. Julie was a good girl."

"Uh-huh. Well. I know my rightful place in the world. Julie didn't."

"Well, maybe Nicole can patch things up with her someday. It's not right that you're her only friend."

"I don't know. She took it pretty hard. She was crying when Nicole talked to her. I mean, she was really freaking out—I mean, she acted like she was going to kill herself. Anyway, I don't think she's ever going to speak to Nicole again."

"Damn that girl. She goes through friends like toilet paper."

"Nicole wasn't that bad to her. But you know, she doesn't like competition."

"It wasn't like that. You know it wasn't like that."

"Well, tell that to her the next time it happens."

We lean against the car, watching the distant red and blue lights flash and wink like carnival rides, watching cars whoosh around the wide, clean curve of the park, watching evening slowly creep down into the vast horizon of the Olympic peninsula. The warm lights of the tavern windows grow brighter, the conversations louder inside, and a cool evening wind spider-steps up my spine and across my neck. We wait until Nicole emerges out of the dark streets, her wet curls pressed flat against her cheeks and forehead, looking as if she's emerging out of some other, faceless girl. She's wearing my clothes. Perhaps that faceless girl is me.

"It's getting late," Mr. Miller says as she walks up to the car. "Time to go home." Nicole looks amused at his sudden fatherliness.

"Since when did you get so concerned about the time? It's not even nine yet."

"Did anyone see you?" I ask.

Nicole bristles. "Did anyone see you?" she shoots back.

"What do you think?!" I shouldn't snap at her, she always acts this way after, but I can't help it. It takes a lot out of me, too. "You know we have to be prepared."

Mr. Miller sighs and pitches the empty beer bottle into a nearby trash can, then motions to the car door. "Yeah, this is why we're going home. It's past your dinner, and you're getting cranky. Come on now, get in. Back seat, both of you. I've got a case on the front seat."

I slide in after Nicole. She pulls my top off and hands it over. "It's still wet."

"That's fine. Can I give you your dress back tomorrow?"

"Whatever."

"Say, what was going on back there at the pool?" Mr. Miller asks as he heads out of the tavern lot and onto the worn two-lane road, back to our quiet corner of Tacoma, deep in the dry interior of the city, far from ponds and beaches and pools.

"What are you talking about?" Nicole says.

"All those sirens, the ambulances. Someone have an accident?"

"I don't know."

"We weren't there when it happened," I add. "Everything was fine when we left."

"You can read about it tomorrow morning," Nicole says as she reaches over to the front seat. "How about one?"

"You know we'll just steal them if you don't," I say.

Mr. Miller laughs. "Just one." Mr. Miller hands her a beer. I reach across the stiff leather seat, holding out my hand. Mr. Miller places a bottle into it, but as I draw it toward me, he grabs my wrist. His hand is so large, his skin dark against the white of mine. He lowers his head, and in the dark of the car, I feel his lips against my skin. "Someday, girl," he whispers, his rough whiskers scratching the letters out against my flesh.

He thinks his mouth is a volcano, that my blood is exploding into hot vapor, that my bones are shattering at his touch. He thinks he's going to make me a woman like he did with Julie. That little girl in the changing room knows how a woman is made. He doesn't have a clue. My heart is a cluster of wires, transmitting all the terrible longings from the dark spaces inside my body into Nicole's gelid gaze. We stare at each other, stare at her father, who stares down the black, empty road.

Do we dare? I soundlessly mouth the words to her in the rumbling space of the car.

One of these nights . . . Nicole slides a hand onto my bare thigh, lets it rest there, gentle and warm, so light I can hardly feel it at all.

LD50

LAIRD BARRON

Laird Barron spent his early years in Alaska. He is the author of several books, including *The Beautiful Thing That Awaits Us All*, *Swift to Chase*, and *The Wind Began to Howl.* His work has also appeared in many magazines and anthologies. Barron currently resides in the Rondout Valley writing stories about the evil that men do.

DESPITE THE PERVASIVENESS of instant communication, smart phones, video-capable eyeglasses, and twenty-four-hour cable media, I generally slip under the radar. While I'm not homely, I've got one of those faces you can't help but forget even though the name Jessica Mace trips off the tongue, the answer to a crossword puzzle, no doubt. In this age of daily horrors going at ten cents a bushel, what happened to me in Alaska three years ago is ancient enough news to be cataloged alongside floor plans for the pyramids.

The first thing people ask if they catch me without a turtleneck or a scarf is, Oh my god, what happened to your neck? Then I tell them to go piss up a rope, with a rasp because the blade went deep, and that is inevitably that. We aren't going to discuss it now, either.

Moving on.

I won't give you the entire picture. You can have snapshots. Order them any way you please. Make of them what you will. This is your mystery to solve.

Late one summer I was hitching through Eastern Washington.

Joseph on a camel, *there's* a whole lot of nothing for you. Chatted up a few locals and got the lay of the land. Twigged to the fact that that part of the world rivaled Alaska for incident rates of theft, murder, rape, and diabolism—amateur and professional.

A long-haul trucker who gave me a lift bragged that the meth labs were so prevalent they formed a Crystal Triangle, the Mexicans were taking over, first wave was migrants working the apple orchards, and now the cartels had their hooks in just like in Arizona and Texas. Tourist attractions included the Hanford Nuclear Reservation, Walla Walla state prison, and the J. W. Trevan Memorial Testing Facility. The first and the last concocted the poison and the middle supplied the control population. Just kidding, everybody knew big animal shelters in Seattle and Spokane provided the subjects, forever homes his foot. He offered me a twenty-spot to blow him and I bailed at the weigh station before the wheels stopped rolling.

A farmer and his grandson chided me for thumbing, it wasn't safe for a young lady, insert lecture here. The farmer was aggrieved because somebody poisoned his German shepherd and hacked off its paws. Stole the paws, left the dog. I mean, damn. That bad news was making the rounds. The waitress at the diner where I got dropped by Farmer Brown said it was a shame, the Devil Hisownself at work through the instrument of some godless sicko. *Thirty dogs since Easter,* said the fry cook as he watched me push my cheeseburger aside. *Nuh-uh, eighty or ninety,* chimed in a barfly who was sipping from a brown paper bag at nine in the A. M. *A serial killer of mutts,* said the cook, shaking his head. Pooches snatched from yards and kennels, later found stabbed, decapitated, pierced with arrows, ritually dismembered. *You know what mutilating animals leads to,* said the waitress. *People!* said the barfly and grinned. The sheriff's department was on the case, which meant there'd be three hundred dogs slaughtered before that nimrod Sheriff Danker Brunner caught a clue. Then cookie got going on a rape trial concerning a high school football team the next county over, and I tuned my brain to another frequency.

Did some loon think a dog's foot might be a lucky charm? Did he string them from his rearview? Did he mount the heads on the wall of his shack? Did he have a Fido to call his own? Those interstate hookers might want to watch themselves, being a lateral link in the food chain, except nobody cares about hookers the way they get out pitchforks and torches for the plight of mutts.

Rednecks flying Dixie colors from the antenna of their monster truck chucked a bottle at me as I waited for the next hitch at the pull in. Who says you can't go home again. Who says you ever get away.

I danced with a cowboy named Stefano Hoyle at a tavern near the freeway off-ramp. His shirt smelled of Old Spice and tobacco. He possessed an aura reminiscent of the Yukon fishermen and hunters I'd known in the Forty-Ninth State. A radioactive strangeness that drew me like a magnet, made me all tingly. Said he'd never been to Alaska, had always lived here in purgatory. Hated the cold and Eastern WA got plenty. He didn't have much more to give, measured his words as if they were pearls. I am a reader between lines kind of gal so we got along dandy.

One Cuervo led to a shitload more Cuervo, and we fucked away half the weekend back at his trailer. Basking in the afterglow, I decided to hang around and see where the ride went.

Hoyle didn't ask about the bitchin' scar in his haste to get my clothes off, although he was also pretty goddamned drunk and it was dark, so I figured for sure by the cold light of morning, et cetera, and still not a peep. Tall, dark, and handsome fixed us bacon and toast, and I finally became exasperated lounging there in a bra and Hello Kitty panties and told him the score, how I got my throat cut and how I got back my own, or maybe got back *some* of my own, at the end of that spooky fairytale in the frozen north. Real-deal fairytales are all about nasty sex, blood, and cannibalism, just like real life. I tend to babble after a righteous fuck, but I possessed the presence of mind to leave out a few details of the incident, such as me busting caps into a dyed-in-the-wool mass murderer. Girl's gotta hold something in reserve for the second date.

He shrugged and tipped his Stetson back and said how'd I like my eggs and then served them to me overdone as steel-belted tires anyway. That Stetson, incidentally, was the only thing he ever wore until five minutes before exiting the trailer to perform his cowboy routine.

Nice enough body, could have made the grade for a young nekkid Marlboro Man calendar in a pinch. It was also obvious that between chain smoking Pall Malls, chugging booze, and taking a beating from the elements, he'd be a woofer in a few more years. *Weathered* is the polite term, and it's why my policy is to snag them while they're young.

He pulled on a long-sleeve shirt and blue jeans and grabbed a rifle from where it rested against a pile of laundry. Flicked me a Gila monster glance as he limped into the yard. Real-deal cowboys, not assholes who wear ten-gallon hats and dinner plate belt buckles to the office or while sipping wine coolers, are bowlegged, and *all* of them limp. When you call to a real-deal cowboy, he turns his body, not his neck. Busted ribs, busted vertebrae, and yeah getting kicked in the face by a bucking bronco smarts. They all chew, or smoke, or both, and they drink. Every mother-loving one of them.

His trailer was an Airstream from the fifties. One door. Windows so tiny you'd have to be a rattler to shimmy through. It teetered on cinderblocks, verging that big-ass nothing I mentioned earlier. Two acres of empty chicken coops, junk cars, and a pair of corrals taken over by ant mounds. A fire ant colony, the advance guard of a South American invasion force. The barn had collapsed. Country & Western version of the projects. He'd inherited the whole shebang from his folks. Dead for ten years, Mom and Dad; a brother, or sister, in Canada soaking up that sweet, sweet socialized everything. No pets, pets were a tie-down. I looked around at the desolation when he said that, kept my mouth shut for once.

Hoyle proudly showed off his motorcycle, a Kawasaki he'd gotten on the cheap from his pal Lonnie. Did I know anything about motorbikes? Told him my late uncle was a motocross fanatic, took me riding on the Knik Flats when I was a kid, showed me how to tune a carburetor and change a spark plug, just the basics. Hoyle seemed impressed with my tomboy ingenuity. His bike had some problems, it stalled and stuttered, and he wasn't exactly a mechanic, although he tinkered with it every chance he got. His cousin died in a motorcycle crackup, rear-ended a semi at highway speed, and after divulging that info he changed the subject by not speaking again for half an hour.

Way off through the haze and the hayricks and rough hills were mountains, the ancient worn-down kind. The landscape was arrested mid-evolution; all the worst qualities of salt plain and high desert and not a tree for miles, frozen like that forever. Could have been tar pits from the look of things, mammoth tusks scattered. Even in hot weather, and Jesus it was hot that year, the dry wind had an edge. The grit between my teeth tasted of alkali and it was always there, always made me yearn to rinse my mouth. Made me wonder if it was the same phenomenon here as on the tundra, if the emptiness treated your mind like a kid deforming a slinky.

I asked where to as he climbed into his old Ford flatbed. Gods, I hated my voice. Sounded like a rusty hinge. Another detail that raised brows, but not his. Unflappable he, I bet a scorpion could scuttle over him and not get a rise. He laid the rifle on the rear window rack and cranked up his rig. Of course the radio was dialed to a station that spun the ghosts of Hank Williams, Roger Miller, and Ernest Tubb.

The roads were either cracked blacktop, dirt, or wagon trails, depending. You traveled in a cloud of dust. I lighted another cigarette and squinted through a pair of sunglasses I'd swiped at a liquor store in Vancouver.

"Last book I read was *Stallion Gate*," Hoyle drawled. A recitation. "Favorite movie is *The Food of the Gods*. You agreed to come home with me because there's something about my eyes." This was in response to a survey question I'd asked at the bar thirty-six hours prior. So it went with him. Drop in a quarter and the music would play sooner or later if you stuck in there.

"Smith's least appreciated book, that movie is terrible, and yeah. You're right on. You've got angel eyes, like Lee Van Cleef." I shifted on the bench seat because the Ka-Bar strapped to my hip was digging in. I'd ditched the .38 since I didn't qualify for a concealed carry permit and none of the cops I'd met had any kind of a sense of humor, so a pistol was too risky for my taste. The knife had already earned its keep when a sketchy dude hassled me at a campsite along the AlCan Highway. Scared him off, no slicing necessary. I didn't think Hoyle harbored ill intentions, hoped not. Time would tell. Mr. Ka-Bar gave me a little security anyhow.

"You like to shoot?" he said out of the blue.

The road reeled us farther and farther into North American badlands variety of veldt. I almost laughed, caught myself, lowered my shades, and gave him a bug-eyed glance that passed for innocence.

"What are we shooting?" I said.

"Sunday's my day of rest," he said. "So, coyotes."

"One thing leads to another."

"What?"

"It's not a country song," I said.

Hoyle parked in the middle of nowhere and we walked to a blind of grass and brush built on the lip of a gully. Perfect three-hundred-and-sixty-degree view of the great empty. Patches of cattle tried to stay in the shade of cloud dapples. Fences between them and us. Corroded barbed wire, petrified posts, rocks, tumbleweeds, lightning-struck charred bones.

He brought a jug of water and a pair of binoculars; decided against the Varmint Suit, as he called it: an olive-gray camo set of matching pants and coat; a sniper outfit webbed with netting and faux vegetation. Gave me the chills just to see it bundled there by the spare tire like some discarded rubber monster suit from a Universal sound stage, and I felt relief that he didn't climb inside, didn't strip away his humanity through the addition. The VS was hot and bulky, and he saved it for tricky hunts, the kill of kills. Today wasn't tricky; it was straightforward as she got.

We nestled onto a mat in the near darkness of the shelter and peeked through cunning slits in the blind at the bright old world. The blind was one of a dozen he'd erected across the prairie. His custom was to tour them over the course of a season, catch as catch could. Mainly, he strung wire and drove tractors for the neighborhood farmers. This was how he earned tequila and cigarette money. Picking up bitches money, is what he mumbled, or what I heard.

"I don't think I like this," I said, quiet as if we were in church.

He told me how it was, laconic, nothing wasted.

Government paid fifty bucks a pelt with a waterproof form to fill in—time, date, sex, method, latitude and longitude, a tiny-print wall of other bureaucratic bullshit. The state predator culling program guide claimed winter and spring to be superior to late summer for purposes of controlling the population. Hunters didn't give a damn. Fifty bucks was fifty bucks, and a dead coyote was one less coyote, which was good.

"Predators, schmedators. Everything's got a right to live," I said, believing it.

"They eat kittens," he said.

"Coyotes do not eat kittens. Where the hell do they find kittens?"

"Kittens. Puppies. Lambs and calves. Foals if they can get 'em. You name it. Scarf 'em bloody and bawlin' out a mama's womb. Wile E. is a merciless fucker." He smiled at me and his eyes had a bit of merciless fucker in them too. Made me a teeny bit hot.

"Kittens? Really?"

"Yep. A pack went for a baby at a picnic a few years back. A human baby."

"Ah. This is a noble enterprise. You're an exterminator. That it?"

"Sure. I guess."

"You enjoy it so much, I'm kind of surprised you don't do something about all these fire ant condos."

He cracked a smile. "Now, that's not neighborly. They're just getting a foothold this far north. Besides, I don't get paid to blow up anthills, Jess."

Normally, Hoyle used electronic decoys and artificial scents and other kinds of high-tech bait. Culling was an art, and he'd learned everything that he knew from a true master. Wouldn't say who, though. That afternoon he kept it simple with a pocket call. A piece of plastic that created a spectrum of horrendous screeches, squeals, and yowls. Distressed and dying rabbit was his specialty. A scrawny female coyote slunk from the tall grass and froze, nose lifted to get a fix on lunch. He shot her dead at two hundred yards.

We went to the carcass and he dressed it on the spot with a buck knife while the sun hammered and cooked. The slices went A, B, C. Done it before a thousand times, easy, you could tell. Blood, guts, the works went into a plastic bag, and he made his notations of record on the waterproof form. Then back to the truck and a hop, skip, and a jump to another vast quadrant of prairie and a fresh killing blind.

"Next one's yours," he said and handed over the rifle.

"No way, José," I said. "I'm not bushwhacking some hapless critter."

"Oh, yeah you will."

"Get bent," I said.

"This is sacred. You'll offend the gods."

I worked the bolt to test the action, and maybe to back him off his he-man perch a tad. An ex taught me plenty about shooting, it simply wasn't my pastime of choice. That said, the rifle, a Ruger .223, was sleek and ultra-phallic. I tasted the linseed and 3-in-One oils on it, whiffed the powder tang from the barrel. The stock fit my shoulder, snug. Deer gun, a woman's gun.

I shot two males, but made him do the skinning.

It got dark, and we knocked off for dinner at that seedy tavern of our initial fateful rendezvous. I compounded my daily quota of moral transgressions by chomping a steak and powering a couple of beers on his tab. Although, much as it pained me to acknowledge, blasting coyotes hadn't been bad.

In fact, I'd rather enjoyed it, tried to convince myself coyote murder was therapy, if not law of the jungle justice. Doing unto predators who surely did unto the weak and the wounded, and kittens. I am human, thus a justifier of irreconcilable behavior. Therapy, right.

Therapy shouldn't get the pulse pumping, no. Lining up the trotting coyote in the scope, waiting for the precise instant, then half an exhale, squeezing the trigger, and watching the animal kick over, its slyness no bulletproof shield. Goddess of death, that's me. We aren't so far removed from the primitive iterations of our species that slurped blood from the jugular. Like dirty, sleazy sex with a complete stranger, I'd probably hate myself later. Meanwhile. As long as my pet cowboy plied me with drinks and physical comfort, that eventuality could be held at bay. I could drown myself in his bad influence and not worry about the bill that was surely coming due.

The waitress, a double-dee bimbo, hung on him as floozies will do, called him Steffy and batted her fake lashes to put out a fire. I wondered if he'd fucked her, thought probably, definitely. He went to the men's room and I caught her in passing, asked how they knew each other, sizing up the competition, I told myself. Flexing the claws, that was it. She gave me a dead cow stare and said she didn't know my boyfriend, slung him drinks and that didn't mean shit from Shinola, and kept trucking. Busy woman. Bumpkins at every table and bellied to the bar, even on a Sunday night. Her whore purse would be stuffed with folding green by last call and the long walk in the dark to her Pinto at the employee end of the lot.

Hoyle returned with more beer. Sauntered back to the table with more beer, to be accurate. Bar lights limned him Travolta style. Best-looking dude in the joint that night, maybe every night. His totem animal was something savage and furtive, it watched me from beneath heavy lids.

Expansive with alcohol, I said, "It occurs to me that this dog mutilation spree could be the work of a coyote hunter. Or any kind of hunter."

"What spree?" Hoyle sipped Pabst. His lips were thin and secretive. His lips and his teeth also belonged to the animal.

"The thing. The thing. Ninety dogs, minus heads and paws. A satanic cult or a thrill kill club, according to the yokels. The sensation sweeping the nation."

"Yeah, that. I don't really like dogs very much. Haven't paid attention to the gossip. On your mind, huh?"

"*I* like dogs. A lot."

"Coyotes get no love?"

"Humans have a pact with dogs. You don't break a pact."

"Not particular to them. Not really."

"Humans or dogs?"

"Dogs. Animals. They're filthy."

"It's an unattractive quality in a man."

He smiled, slow and easy. Occurred to me that I wasn't expansive, I was drunk.

"You think I'm stupid. The way you speak to me." He didn't sound mad.

"Shallow. I think you're shallow." The double-dee bimbo with her Daisy Dukes and red pumps, the fact he'd had her every which way, provoked my mean streak.

He studied his fingernails. Took a long pull on his brew, wiped his mouth. When he looked at me I saw myself, a pale blur, Casper the Friendly Ghost's sarcastic little sister. "Did you hear they're building a telescope in Hawaii that's more powerful than anything ever invented?"

"Why, no, Steff. I did not." *Steffy* is what nearly escaped.

"Know what they're going to look at with that super-duper telescope?"

"The mother of all telescopes? Let me guess . . . the stars?"

"The beginning."

"The beginning of what?"

"Of everything."

He poured cheaper-than-Cuervo tequila all over my skin and lapped it up. No lights, no radio serenade, his breath hot in the hollow of my throat, kissed bruises on my arms, my inner thighs. After, the trailer became cold as a grave and an inkling of the consequences began to sink into my thick skull. Stars blinked through the window slot. Coyotes sang of death and vengeance on the prairie.

Hoyle rolled onto his side. His breathing steadied. I thought he'd fallen asleep when he said in a slurred voice, "It doesn't follow that a coyote hunter is going after dogs. Not a real coyote hunter, I mean." His lighter snicked and soon came a slow roll of smoke. That cigarette was almost gone before he finished his thought. "The coyotes are business. This other thing. It's pleasure."

My nakedness became quite acute.

He laid his rough hand on my belly and said, "Considering what you've seen, what you've been through. Maybe you should leave this alone."

The trailer settled. Out there, a breeze moaned and wind chimes clinked to accompany the coyote chorus. All those dead stars shone on.

"But this has been waiting for me," I said to him, him snoring.

Monday was riding-a-tractor-in-the-back-forty-of-some-hayseed's-ranch day, and Hoyle departed before sunrise. I slept in until the heat made an oven of the Airstream. Glass of warm water from the tap in hand, I explored the property, ducking under withered gray clotheslines, and forging through stunted shrubs, stumps, and earth mounds that disgorged ant convoys that streamed black in the sand. Little biting fuckers were everywhere underfoot. Tried to avoid crushing too many, but you know. That ubiquitous breeze whispered in the grass, fluted through soda bottles arranged as dingy candelabrums made of sticks, rattled the chimes and mussed my hair. The wind chimes were clumped in the petrified grasp of bushes and scrub trees, dozens of them. Metal tinged and pinged, and it was almost there for me, almost but not quite. The puzzle resisted, refused to crystallize.

I got that sense of unfriendly scrutiny, of being the object of a malevolent desire, how the coyote must feel as crosshairs zero in right before its brains are blasted out the other side, yet different, this was all around me, and I ditched the glass and beat it for the trailer, ran no different from the panicked heroine in a horror flick with a chainsaw-gunning maniac on her heels. Locked the door and had a breather, fists clenched, heart in spasms, gulping for air. No safer inside, though, I knew that.

Nothing happened, and I calmed down, tried the television, got no picture, tried the radio, a scratchy gospel station only, and for a long stretch I sat in a lawn chair, knife balanced on my knee, while dust motes swirled and sweat poured into my socks. I put the knife away and eyed the clutter. Laundry, boxes upon boxes of magazines and Christmas lights and photograph albums, yellow receipts, camping gear, miscellanea.

Better believe I took the opportunity to ransack the place. It didn't amount to anything.

There wasn't a discussion regarding how long I'd stay or what it meant. Hoyle drove into the dark heart of each dawn. I'd smoke my first cigarette while his taillights dwindled. Evenings he'd straggle in from the red haze, caked in range dirt, pockets full of hay and gravel, shower and wolf his supper, down a six pack, collapse, roll onto me to fuck me somewhere along the line. My contribution was to shovel the long-neglected barbeque pit and throw on hamburgers to chase all that beer, and to get fucked. Could have been worse duty and it got me where I wanted to go, or at least it got me closer and closer.

Other nights we hit the tavern.

Weeknights it was just us chickens in a suddenly cavernous hall. *Everybody off hunting Grendel*, I said, curious if he'd get it. With him it was impossible to tell. He was a cold one, my Steffy Hoyle, sharper than he appeared, possibly. No stray emotions. He didn't raise his voice or get overly excited, not even during sex, except I woke from a nightmare of strangulation to hollering and war whooping, the strident whine of an engine, stared out the window and he had that Kawasaki hell bent for leather, headlight drilling a hole into the perfect darkness. Dead drunk, naked but for hat and boots, he shrieked in atavistic joy as he slalomed through the minefield of stumps and gopher holes in the field, revving that bike for crazy-as-a-motherfucker jumps over fallen logs and grassy berms. Crashed it in the yard while cutting donuts. Laid the machine over and it flew fifty or sixty feet, smoked and died. Took some skin off his shins and palms, the bloody mess not quite as bad as it looked. I cleaned him up, picked gravel and bits of grass from the wounds. He didn't flinch, sat stinking of alcohol, legs akimbo, eyes wild, then dull and duller, sank into a stupor, then fell asleep, and in the morning it hadn't happened. But it did happen, and several other times, although he managed not to wreck the bike so badly that he needed medical attention. Matter of time. Man with a death wish usually gets what he wants.

Once, we cruised over to his friend Lonnie's house, a shotgun shack not far from the county landfill. Lonnie was a biker, or a biker wannabe, kept a massive Harley in a makeshift carport under a canvas tarp because he didn't have a garage. Guy was brawny and hairy, wore tinted aviator glasses indoors and out. Smelled of hair gel and musk. His fingernails were blacked from getting mashed. Tats and a death metal T-shirt. Death to Tyrants, Death to Infidels, Death to Everybody. Chained a pair of scarred and muscular pit bulls to the bumper of a truck on blocks. Grizzled brutes with jaws wide enough to crush my head. Sweet as puppies, not a mean bone in them. He didn't appear overly fond of the dogs and they were indifferent to him. Dogs were real friendly toward me, though. Slobbery kisses and paws-to-the-jaw roughhousing, and such. I played with them while the boys chatted about riding choppers and hunting and guns. Lonnie also moonlighted as a coyote culler. Birds of a feather, right?

On the ride home I asked if Lonnie fought the dogs, tried to make it sound casual. Hoyle didn't answer. He pressed on the accelerator and drifted into the oncoming lane as we rounded a bend. Needle pegged at eighty. Almost went head-to-head with a good old boy on a road grader with the blade up. Got to give it to Hoyle—he tapped the brakes and swung us past with inches to spare, and his free hand never stopped stroking my leg.

During the second week I dragged a ten-speed from under the trailer where it rusted among abandoned tire rims and sheets of tin siding. A bit of chain oil and wrench work, I got the bicycle fixed right up and I pedaled my ass into town. Hadn't ridden a bike since high school and the six-mile slog just about precipitated a coronary conclusion. Instant blisters, instant sunburn, steam rose from me in a trailing shadow. I staggered inside the mom-and-pop on Main Street and drank two quarts of lime Gatorade while Methuselah the Clerk observed my antics with gap-toothed bemusement. Goddamned Gatorade made a snowball in my gut that wanted to ricochet right back out, but I held on, held it down. I hung tough and paid the clerk, smiled sweetly as if my lobster sunburn and chattering teeth weren't nothing but a thing.

I composed myself and moseyed around town for the rest of the afternoon. Youngish female and not terribly unattractive, nobody mistook me for a pervert or a weirdo as they would've if I'd been some bearded, sunbaked dude lurching in off the prairie. People skills, I had them, and most folks were willing to shoot the shit with me as they watered lawns, or washed cars, or slumped in the shade of their porches. I wore my shades and gave everybody a different story, all of them pure baloney. Nobody knew Hoyle, although stoner skateboard kids loitering in the mom-and-pop parking lot had seen him around, and I'm confident the pancake makeup tarts at the realtor and plumbing supply offices would've gotten misty-eyed at his mention.

A wasted Vietnam vet parked in a wheelchair at the entrance to the Diamond Dee Gentleman's Club panhandling for change knew Lonnie, of course he fought his dogs, Leroy and Gunther, tons of locals did. Pit fighting was real popular. The veteran owned a collie mix with the softest, saddest brown eyes I ever did see, and he covered the dog's ears when he leaned close to confide that the hardcore crowd used house pets and strays as bait for the killer breeds. The bait thing notwithstanding, fighting dogs in gladiatorial exhibitions was innocent, really! Death was rare, usually an ear or an eye got removed at the worst, a lot of yip and yelp signifying nothing, so to speak. The other stuff going down? The dogs piled into sacrificial mounds off Route 80, or buried alive in burlap bags down to Stabinham Creek? Now, *that* was insane. Whoever was scragging dogs wholesale was a psycho sonofabitch from the darkest pit of hell, and woe unto the sap he eventually turned his knife and arrows against, because sure as horses made little green apples it would come to human butchery. See if it didn't. That assessment seemed to be the consensus, and a page-three story in the paper confirmed law enforcement, including the FBI, agreed. Whether the Feds planned to make it a priority was another matter.

Damned if I knew what I hoped to learn from this shotgun approach to detective work. Definitely I was bored out of my skull, lurking at Hoyle's trailer. Definitely recent life events had activated a recessive sleuthing gene.

I pedaled home, slowly. Redness pooled on the horizon.

In a disappointing development, Hoyle and I didn't screw for four nights running. He poured liquor down his throat and fell into a slumber that was as unto death itself. Did not even snore, did not so much as twitch. I began to wonder what was in it for me because my days in that backwater town weren't proving out in any way, shape, or form. I dreamed of old loves lost to shipwreck and mayhem, and I dreamed of dogs I'd known, all of them gone back into the dirt. Dad waved to me from a distance where he stood amid knee-high grass, a warning in his grim smile, the white skull of a cow he raised in his left hand. He'd seldom tried to tell me anything requiring words when I was a hellion child, and he didn't now. A golden darkness radiated from him and pushed me into the territory that lies just on the other side of waking. Erotic nightmares followed. These involved Hoyle, although his face was obscured by the shadow of his hat. After he'd gotten his rocks off he'd shove me from the moving truck, or leap from it himself, leave me to tumble down a cliff, be consumed in fire. Or I'd emerge unscathed and a piece of the underbrush would detach and come after me, a bear covered in leaves, bits of a shredded net, reared on its hind legs and full of Satan's own desire to fuck me or devour me, one then the other.

I'd emerge into consciousness, aroused and afraid.

With the frustration of one type of lust, the wandering kind crept into my thoughts, had me eyeing the straight shot to the distant highway, phantom engines rumbling, phantom exhaust on my lips, headlights branding an SOS into my frontal lobes. Except, Sunday came around before I got resolved and it was coyote sniping time again.

Hoyle pushed coffee at me, said he hadn't toured this particular zone in several months, then we were in the rig and moving toward a seam of light above the mountains. We didn't talk, not that there was ever much chatter, but this was two-cactuses-on-a-date quiet. The drive was longer than I expected. The road went on and on, degraded from blacktop to gravel, to dirt, to scabbed tracts of bare earth in a sea of bleached grass. Plains spread around us, larger and deeper than the sky. Spectral and wan, gradually acquiring substance like film in an acid bath. Landmarks I'd learned recently were absent or in the wrong direction.

He stopped the truck and shut it off. Reached into a duffel bag and presented me with a rabbit facsimile. Plush and brown, wired to emote vulnerability at various decibels. My task was to pace one hundred steps upwind and set the decoy in play. Once I trotted back we'd find a likely spot with a clear line of fire and settle ourselves to wait. He pecked my forehead by way of dismissal and began to scribble in his culling book. I was tempted to argue, to sneer and inform him he wasn't the bwana of me. Wasn't worth the hassle. I had a hunch I'd get on the highway east any day now, leave this shitkicker paradise in the rearview. Thus and so.

I trudged into the prairie, sullenly counting paces, each step precisely, more or less, one yard as my Dad the Marine had taught his kiddies. Made the football-field-long hike and set the robot rabbit on a log in a patch of sand and weeds. I turned and saw the truck, grill blazing with reflected sunlight, and no sign of Hoyle.

As I approached, I fully expected him to step from behind the opposite side of the cab, shaking the morning dew off his pecker, but he didn't. It became apparent he wasn't crouched in hiding and I came over and tried the doors. Locked tight, no keys in the ignition, no duffle bag with food and water. His rifle was missing from the rack. I shaded my eyes and turned a full circle, scanning for his outline against the blankness. I shouted his name, and in the middle of all this I glanced at the bed of the truck and realized the Varmint Suit wasn't there either. The spit in my mouth dried.

Oh, what goes through a woman's mind at a moment like that.

Instinct kicked in and I went from a standstill to a sprint, six maybe seven strides in a random direction, and did a Supergirl dive. Scratched, bruised, winded, I didn't feel a thing except my heart trying to climb out of my mouth. Those newsreels about trench fighting in World War I, GIs belly-down kissing the dirt as they wriggled under barbed wire? That was me navigating a shallow depression away from the track.

I wormed along until my arms failed. I rolled over and lay still, half covered in swaying grass. Clouds inched past my face. Horses, a hound, Dumbo's lopsided head. A pair of hawks drifted along crosscurrents, wheeling and wheeling. Gnats bit me and I didn't care, my being was consumed with listening for the crunch of footsteps, although I imagined if he spotted me I would hear exactly what the doomed coyote did in its last split second on earth.

A wail rose and fell somewhere to the left. A trilling *eee-ee-eeee* that made my flesh prickle, made me bite my tongue lest I cry a response.

The robot rabbit's sobs described an arc that moved closer, then farther from my hiding place. I considered crawling some more once my arms revived. Too afraid to move, I pissed myself instead, counted down the seconds until the end came brutal as a tomahawk blow to my noggin. Had time to think back on a wasted youth, a life of misdeeds. I contemplated my possibly fatal morbid fascination with things better left alone. Sure, I was furious with myself. Two weeks playing chicken with dark forces, yet never truly admitting I was in over my head. I'd known, always known, and the colossal scope of my pride and selfishness bore down to smother me as I bit hard on the flesh of my arm and tried to keep it together, tried not to whine like prey.

The sky grew dim, then dark. Lightning tore the blackness and thunder cracked a beat or two afterward. The cavewoman running the show in my brain, the primordial bitch dispensing adrenaline and endorphins, knew what I'd listened to throughout the day hadn't been any mechanical rabbit and that almost undid me, almost got the waterworks going.

I sucked it up and stood. Every muscle in me complained and for a few seconds I couldn't bring myself to actually breathe. What Dad and his hunting buddies told me back in the Alaska days was if I felt the bullet, it'd be like a heavy punch. A few seconds of that and it became apparent I wasn't going to be smote from afar.

The truck was gone, probably had been for hours. It began to rain.

Sonofabitch had my purse and knapsack with the spare clothes, the handful of knickknacks and keepsakes I brought with me when I split from AK. All that shit was in a burn barrel by then, and no, I didn't equivocate or second-guess myself, didn't say, *Jess maybe this is a misunderstanding, maybe life has made you a wee bit paranoid. Maybe there's a logical explanation.* I was indeed a wee bit paranoid. Thank the gods. And yep, there was a logical fucking explanation.

Saving grace was I'd dressed sensibly for the trip. I had my wallet, a pack of Camel No. 9s, and a lighter. I veered due east, walked until lights from a farmhouse appeared, kept going, and the clouds rolled back and stars glowed. Dawn came and I crossed a rancid stream. Dunked my head underwater, drank until I was fit to puke, and rambled on, came to a two-lane road I hadn't seen before and followed it back to the highway. Getting dark again. Cleaned up in a gas station john, then walked into a no-tell motel one block down and rented a single. Delivery pizza and two scalding showers, no booze, but that was fine. Cigarette burns in the carpet, broken box springs, and an ammonia reek was all fine too.

Comatose for eighteen hours with the TV and air conditioner humming white noise, a chair propped under the doorknob, Mr. Ka-Bar cool against my cheek. Dreamless sleep, except in those moments before I came fully online again and a misshapen shadow lunged, made a hissing, shushing sound as it trampled the grass. I stabbed it with my knife and poof. The fact I'd doubtless be haunted by that goddamned Varmint Suit until my dying day filled me with the white-hot rage men are always being warned about. Could be that's what changed my plans from flight to payback. An old high school enemy called me VH1. Vindictive Hoochie Number One, and she wasn't wrong.

Hopped a ride to the next town with a salesman going to Seattle for a conference. He politely declined to mention the gouges on my face and arms, left me at the off-ramp, and went his way. Thinking to hell with hitching, I haggled with a kid over the hatchback gathering rust in front of his house. The engine had a million miles on it and sounded iffy and the tires were screwed to hell. Nonetheless, that jalopy only had to get me down the road a state or two. Better would come along. I paid three hundred cash and put a lie on the receipt. Kid was so stoned, I doubt he even knew I was a woman, much less be able to ID me if it came to such a pass. As for where I got the dough, listen. Just because I enjoyed pilfering stores for sundries didn't mean I was destitute. *People* magazine once gave me sixty grand for an interview they pared to three and a half sentences and a muddy headshot. I socked that shit away.

I bought basic camping gear at a sporting goods store and spent four nights on the grounds of a state park, four more along a big river where it didn't feel as if anybody would notice. On the ninth day I parked in a gravel pit a half mile from Hoyle's trailer, sneaked closer for recon. He wasn't around. I proceeded with caution, stealthy as any woodland critter, and let myself in. Forty-five minutes on the property was forty more than necessary. Did what needed doing and got the hell out and drove to another motel, a nicer setup, and treated myself to an evening on a soft bed and half a bottle of red wine.

Swung back to check on him late the next afternoon. Hoyle's truck sat in the yard. I glassed the property with a pair of binoculars, gave it an hour before moving in. My ex-lover lay behind the trailer, sprawled face down, stark staring naked except for his boots. Nearby, his bike was a crumpled mess of spokes and leaking fluids. The results were certainly more spectacular than I'd hoped for while sawing through the brake lines.

I poked him with a stick, unsure whether he was dead or playing possum. Neither, as it developed. Rolled him over and he smiled at me, teeth stained with grass and dirt. His arms worked, but that was it. I didn't see any marks beyond some bumps and abrasions. Whatever was wrong with him, I bet he'd be fine with proper medical attention.

"Hi, darling," he said. "You had me worried, runnin' off like that."

I squatted and hooked under his armpits and lifted, began to shuffle backward. His legs bumped along lifelessly. Went a few steps, rested, and repeated. I dragged him into the nearer of the two corrals and propped him in a seated position, his spine braced by a post. He didn't say anything the whole time except to ask for his Stetson because the sun was powerful warm on his neck. I fetched the hat and gave it to him. An ant climbed atop the toe of my boot, another clung to my pants cuff. I bent and brushed them aside, moved my feet to discourage the rest. Hoyle stared at the looming mound, its teeming inhabitants. The breeze stirred.

"Why?" he said, as if genuinely curious.

I strode to a dead dogwood and tore free the chimes strung in its branches, flung the mess at Hoyle. He snatched it midflight, glanced at the handful of dog tags—rabies vaccinations and ID tags—and nodded. Dozens upon dozens more clinked in their constellations on bushes, posts, clotheslines, woven into the trailer vents, every-fucking-where. I let him think about it while I used a branch to cover my tracks, the grooves where I'd towed him.

"Don't you think the cops will put it together? They'll catch you, Jess."

"I hear Sheriff Brunner is a dumbass," I said.

He chuckled. "Yeah. It's true enough."

Daylight was burning and restlessness overcame me. I gave the old boy a sip from my water bottle and tried to think of the proper words, settled for a goodbye kiss, quick and dry. We didn't say anything for the longest time and eventually I turned and walked away.

I looked over my shoulder once, right as I crested a rise that led to the road. Hoyle, indistinct at that distance, reached forward and passed the Stetson over his legs, back and forth.

On the way through town to wherever, I stopped, bold as brass, at Lonnie's house. There was a bad moment where I worried Gunther and Leroy might've forgotten, had visions of getting rent limb from limb as I knelt to unleash them from the bumper of the truck. Not a chance. And when I popped the hatch, those bruisers piled into the back like they'd always belonged there.

We hit the highway eastbound, ascended into the hills and then the mountains. Kept right on going, flying. The car eventually crapped out in

Idaho. I spent a time with a reverend and his family on what had been a potato farm until the latter seventies. God works in mysterious ways, so said the right reverend. He'd lost a pair of mastiffs to old age and cancer respectively. His kids fell in love with Leroy and Gunther. I left the dogs in their care when I slipped away one night by the dark of the moon. Headed east across the fallow fields with a knife, backpack, and a pocket bible I lifted from the reverend's shelf.

I hollowed out that good book. It's where I stash my possibles.

Camped in the lee of an abandoned barn, I rolled over onto a black widow. Little bitch stabbed the living shit out of me. Sorry, so very sorry that I crushed her in my thrashing. Spent two days curled tight, guts clenched into a slimy ball. In my delirium, I chewed dirt and fantasized about being skinned alive. Laid my bottom dollar on dying out there in that lonely field.

I didn't die. Nah, I did what I always do. I got over it.

CAVITY

THERESA DeLUCCI

Theresa DeLucci is an author and journalist based out of New York City. Her short fiction has appeared in *Strange Horizons*, *Lightspeed*, *Weird Horror*, and on *Reactor*, where she also covers film, television, and the occasional videogame. She loves covering pop culture for *Den of Geek* and Wired.com's *Geek's Guide to the Galaxy* podcast. Find her hot takes on horror, HBO prestige dramas, and more at www.theresadelucci.com.

1. THE FIRST TIME you meet a murderer, you are in kindergarten. At the exact moment you are at the dentist getting a lesson about avoiding cavities, the parent volunteer at your after-school program—a woman who has been babysitting you for the past two months—brings in a plate of cookies laced with rat poison that sickens and kills three of your classmates. You will think of that near-miss again and again when you get older. Your parents never let you forget. Your good fortune is like rock candy on your tongue, sweet, but turn it over and shards scrape your soft palate. Sugar forever tastes of pleasure mingled with guilt. You vow to avoid it entirely.

Most people don't encounter their first murderer so young. Most people won't meet the Fermi estimation of the national per-person lifetime average of thirty-six murderers, either. Some will meet many more, but that's usually an occupational hazard. An unlucky minority will only ever meet one—their own. But you, a mostly unremarkable female, will meet a murderer thirty-two times, though you will know that you did far fewer times than that.

Thirty-two: one for every adult tooth.
This may count for something, later.

2. You are in fourth grade when Adam, your neighbors' little boy, gets so mad that you won't let him play on your swing set, he kicks your dog. You feel it would have been fairer if Adam had kicked *you* instead, but he already knew that it would bother you much more if he hurt someone you loved. You didn't play with him after that. When your dad finds one too many dead skunks in your yard he assumes it's coyotes and keeps your dog inside after sundown. It will be about fifteen years before you see Adam again, on the national news. If you were still his neighbor and if any reporter had asked *you* about him, you would never have said that Adam seemed like such a nice, quiet boy.

3. Some murders are old. Your sixth-grade social studies teacher served in the Second Gulf War and while some would consider that cause enough to call him a killer, others would not. But there were things his unit did to a non-combatant that semantics cannot cover. The incident was hidden on his record and he was honorably discharged, but he remembers how black the blood looked on the dusty road outside of Mosul, under a starlit sky.

4. Billy, the new boy in your seventh grade class, who doesn't just *seem* nice and quiet, but really is? This time last year he was playing with his little brother. Neither boy knew their father's gun was loaded, only that it wasn't locked up. But this is a death so common, no one seems to think it worth counting anymore. You imagine Billy's guilt must taste much more bitter than your own, like smoke and lead.

5. The driver of the SUV that sideswiped your father's car after he picked you up from soccer practice was given her first DUI summons. Her third DUI came attached to a vehicular homicide charge for killing a twenty-nine year-old mother of two.

6. Your parents would think twice before letting you take your dressage lessons from a woman who bludgeoned her own mother to death. But she was a minor when the crime was committed and the court records were sealed. She changed her name, but was that all that she changed? If you watch her very closely, you still would not be able to name what mixture of emotion clouds her eyes when she spurs her horse just a bit too hard.

7. You are right to trust your instinct that hot summer day when you are twelve and the man stocking shelves at the grocery store looks at your bare legs a little too long. This is the first time you notice a man looking at you at all. While it thrills you the tiniest bit, to think that someone has seen you, mostly you feel like you are the one doing something wrong. So, too, thought the other young girl whose bones molder in the clerk's crawlspace.

8. Do you count your fourteen-year-old best friend, Myra, for hanging herself in her bathroom?

9. Do you count her twice because Myra made you pinky-swear that you wouldn't tell anyone that she was pregnant?

10. Or do you just count Frankie Geller, the boy who raped Myra three months ago? You know what he did and that his friends watched. There was a video that you and your friends watched, along with the whole high school, maybe the whole town. But people still called Myra a liar and a slut and, yeah, Frankie goes to another school while he's awaiting trial, but he didn't have to change his name. No one outright tells you that sometimes there's one set of rules for boys and another for girls, but no one needs to after that.

You'll think of Myra when you catch a whiff of green apples, like the Jolly Ranchers she used to love. Her breath always smelled so sweet and your stomach lurches with missing the scent of Myra's lost voice for a long, long time after.

11. Walmart. It could be a nightclub, a movie theater, a place of worship, definitely a school, but for you it was walking past the young man in a long coat on a hot day entering the store as you left.

12. The most popular girl in your school, Cathy Ong, becomes even more popular, in a ghoulish way, after she texts her boyfriend while driving through a crosswalk. The little boy she hit was killed instantly and Cathy spun her cautionary tale into speaking engagements at high schools across the nation. A tiny inner voice bemoans that she'll probably get into a better college than you, but you *do* remember to keep your phone in your purse when you drive.

13. Do you count Billy twice? You and Billy are both in senior year when he decides he can't spend another day feeling like the wrong brother survived that accident. Smoke and lead, you think. Guilt was the last thing he had in his mouth. You come home from his memorial service and raid the kitchen pantry, suddenly starving. You eat an entire package of molasses cookies, barely swallowing one before going for the next, until your mouth is filled with gritty, wet sugar sludge and you nearly choke. You eat until you vomit and you can taste the sweetness again as it leaves you. It becomes addictive, that act of filling and emptying a deep, dark hole inside.

14. Your first date with your murderer is at the concert of a band he insists any intelligent person must love. You thought the band was pretentious and boring; you wonder aloud if he thinks you're dumb, then immediately apologize for offending him. You want him to like you.

15. You don't want to know what's in the smoky, meltingly tender pork belly you're eating. You give the restaurant four stars on Yelp. The bathroom could've been cleaner.

16. Because your (perfectly respectable) college campus is in a big city and sometimes you want nothing more than solitude, you take up jogging. Because you are a woman jogging alone at night, you catch the eye of a man . . . but he can't catch you. He runs behind you, oblivious you, for almost a quarter mile before you turn toward a better-lit trail and he thinks twice. The next week, he chases down another woman on the

same path. He rapes her, he beats her, he keeps her teeth, then sets fire to her hands and feet. The story is on the cover of every paper in the city and for a week there is a woman on every treadmill at your gym, every woman outrunning her own would-be killer in her mind. It's an impossible balancing act, being desirable enough but never in too easy reach.

17. You and your murderer broke up for the first time after he said you were getting fat. How could he not appreciate how much you ran, how much you didn't eat? You run more, eat less, and say you're a different, stronger, and lighter person without him. A lonely month later, he lays a honey trap of promises to do better at your doorstep. You look at him and think that this is how idiots invite vampires into their homes, but you tamp down the bad feeling in your gut and let him cross your threshold.

18. You forced a thin smile for the catcaller skulking outside your bank but the next woman would not.

19. The tandem skydiving instructor that you are strapped to on your vacation in New Zealand is self-medicating for depression. He never tells you. He never tells the man strapped to him two days later, either. The tourist only recognizes this mutual and critical distrust when their chute never opens.

20. Natalie, who works in your department, has an ex-husband everyone agrees is a creep. Everyone also agrees that even if the court had granted

her that restraining order, it wouldn't have stopped what he was determined to do to her. It's as if Natalie's murder was inevitable, ordained from on high, because she did what she was supposed to do, and it still made no difference.

21. That actress who was gracious enough to take a selfie with you when you see her walking on Fifth Avenue never got out of her car to check if the paparazzo she hit outside her home in Malibu was still breathing. She was too scared to face the man who had been stalking her for a year. But the truth wouldn't drive up the revenue of gossip blogs who questioned her motives. In death, he finally got his wish: she would never be allowed to forget him.

22. When you tasted the back of your murderer's hand for the first time, you broke up again. Sweetness always turns to rot. There's a doubt inside that you want to explain as the lack of him, so you say he was missed. You say what came before doesn't really count even as you understand that whatever happens to you from here on out, it will be your fault. Like Myra. Like Natalie and solo joggers and girls with bare legs. No one outright says that there are a thousand ways to tell a woman that she's wrong, but after this, no one needs to.

23. The train you take home from a cozy, bright Christmas upstate to see your parents has a lot of people on it. You suck on the end of a candy cane until it becomes a sharpened point that stabs the underside of your tongue. You snap the end off in your mouth and hold it there until it dissolves. Not everyone in your car makes it home. Six hours after you reached your destination, police found the body of a young black woman

rolled up in her own coat and left in an alley near the train station. Her killer was in your train's car, too. He saw your white skin and blonde hair and knew that you would bring him a lot more of the wrong kind of attention. You would both actually agree that some women are more disposable than others, but only you see that as an injustice, not an opportunity.

24. The pregnant woman you make small talk with on line at the supermarket will drown her baby within a year because she cannot tell anyone how afraid she is of the voices that are telling her to drown her baby; they'd take her baby away and everyone would know she's a terrible mother, which is the only thing worse than being crazy. It seemed perfectly sane at the time.

25. Your dentist—not the same one you went to in kindergarten—will eventually mistake his cheating boyfriend for the steak he meant to spear with a serving fork. Twenty-three times.

26. Your murderer buys you a corgi puppy without consulting you and you both know you can't refuse such an apology gift. You share custody of the puppy's demanding training schedule, which is a much more adorable, sometimes messy way to keep you dependent on your partner, like the rent for the apartment you moved into that's too high for you to afford on your own. But how can you be upset? You *like* the nicer apartment. You *did* say you've wanted a dog of your own since you moved out of your parents' house. Gimli (what else would you name a corgi?) is the size of a throw pillow. When you cuddle him, you feel how tiny his ribs are beneath all that fuzz. For the first time in years you remember your long-ago neighbor Adam and the whimper of a different dog.

You find it easier to think of others before yourself, so you leave your murderer before either one of you can get kicked.

27. Starbucks and murderers are about equally pervasive, so the odds of meeting a murderer in a Starbucks is higher than you'd guess.

28 and 29. Two different wives in your bulimia support group were strangled by two different husbands in the same weekend. You try to decide which is worse: the odds of that being highly likely or hideously random. Their two empty seats are like missing teeth in a smile and you seethe so much that you don't realize you're gnawing on your lower lip until it bleeds. The pain soothes the howling inside for a bit, so you keep devouring little pieces of yourself.

30. The final time you meet your murderer, you're in a dark corner of the garage underneath your friend's apartment building. You don't see him until he grabs you from behind because you, oblivious you, are digging your phone out of your purse to text your friend, who's letting you and Gimli crash at her place. Thanks a lot, Cathy Ong and your fucking school assemblies.

31. If intent is all that counts, then he only actually becomes your murderer the moment he squeezes the trigger. In the struggle to pin you to the back seat, his shot goes wide and grazes your left ear. He twists your clawing hands over your head and grinds his shoulder into your chest. You try to scream, but you're not sure if any sound comes out above the

ringing in your head. His neck is pressed so close, his sure pulse on your lips becomes your entire world.

There's no time to doubt what swells up in your gut on a tide of desperate fear and lifelong need. Nor is there time to wonder if it's just luck that gives you the opportunity to use a weapon that you've only ever turned against yourself: hunger.

You open your mouth again, and this time it's not to scream.

32. You don't stop biting until you're full.

You keep it all down.

In the absence of adrenaline, your jaw throbs and your left ear rings softly for weeks, rattling your sinus, your loosened upper molars. Your whole body is a stripped raw nerve.

His attempt to annihilate you succeeded in ways he did *not* intend; the defining bisection of your life and the blithe denial of Before replaced with the memory of trauma that never dissolves. Its imprint crystalizes within you down to the cellular level. No one sees you as murderer, but nor do they think, even now, that you are entirely blameless. You will meet yourself in a mirror and some days you won't know your reflection, but mostly you look exactly as you did before. That feels wrong, too, as if there should be something you could recognize in another person after such a life-altering event. You'll seek it on every new face, just the same. There are more murderers you've yet to meet, but you have a harder time ignoring your gut.

There is one big change that you keep to yourself: every time you startle, which is often now, a metallic tang leaps into the back of your throat. You had wondered if the lemony icing on your next birthday cake, the birthday you should be grateful to see, would frost over that singular flavor, but it doesn't. You have a second slice anyway, without guilt.

Your body's response to fear is the aftertaste of your survival. Your survival tastes like meat grown plump with satisfaction. You savor it. You want more.

Much more.

SOUVENIRS

SHARON GOSLING

Sharon Gosling is the author of multiple historical adventure books for children, including *The Golden Butterfly* and *The Extraordinary Voyage of Katy Willacott*. She is also the author of YA Scandi horror *FIR* and several adult novels, including *The House Beneath the Cliffs* and *The Lighthouse Bookshop*. Her short stories have been published in *The Mammoth Book of Halloween Stories* and *Close to Midnight*. Sharon lives with her husband in a tiny village in Cumbria that is best known for being the home of one of the earliest vampire legends in the UK.

The rain had been tilting at them all day. Above the motorway the wide sky was a slick bruise of cloud, dark in the middle and a sick grey-green at its distant edges. It reminded Reg of the weeks he'd spent on Kamchatka, so many moons ago, although those skies had spread wider still, and when it rained it had felt as if it were the end of the world, probably because it very nearly was.

Donna was behind the wheel, peering through the slashing wipers of the Transit at the spray sent up from the tarmac by the surrounding traffic.

"I'll drive, if you like," he told her, not for the first time.

"It's all right, Dad," she said, voice somewhere between distraction and anxiety, not looking at him. "You just relax."

Reg leaned back in his seat and studied his daughter's profile. It seemed like only yesterday that he was scooping her off pavements and teaching her to ride a bike. Now here they were, on his last journey. Not that she'd appreciate hearing him call it that.

"It's not the end of your adventures," she'd said, as they'd pulled the door shut on the house that had kept him still for the past twenty years. "It's just the start of a new one, that's all."

He turned his head toward the wet window and went back to Kamchatka. Wild green pastures full of vivid bursts of meadow flowers that stretched towards the climbing crags of snow-capped mountains, bears roaming the forests, beluga sinuous in the waters. He hadn't been prepared for East Russia to be so beautiful, and all told, he'd ended up staying six weeks. Six weeks at the end of the world. He could have stayed longer. Perhaps he should have, but there was always a reason to move on.

A face floated to him, dark hair beneath a white headscarf, khaki shirt, sturdy boots, firm thighs, a figure lying back amid that lush pasture grass. He searched the years for a name and came up with Elise. He'd met her in Osaka, Reg remembered now, an American nurse with dark eyes and a beautiful smile, perfect white teeth. It had been a while since he'd had a companion and she'd declared herself open to adventure, but as usual it had turned out that Reg's understanding of the word exceeded that of others.

He'd travelled on alone, at twenty-five the years stretching ahead of him like an endless road, the ones behind having already woven through a dozen countries. He'd boarded a cargo ship in Petropavlovsk and lumbered across the Bering Sea towards Alaska with winter closing in. Cold enough to freeze the proverbials off a mythical metal ape, but there wasn't a single day he hadn't gone up on deck. *Now though,* he thought, *now I quake at the slightest drop in temperature, a weak old man perpetually wrapped in a blanket.* Reg shifted in his seat, dispelling the bitterness. There was no sense in it, after all. Life was what it was and his had been a good one, no doubt about that.

He'd enjoyed that first time in Alaska, even in ice. The hugeness of it, the clear white cold, the secrets it must hold. He'd worked his way along the fishing routes, heading for Canada, restless and uncontained. Somewhere in the midst of it he'd met Natasha. The clarity of the name after all these years surprised him, but then he supposed their dalliance had lasted longer than others. Two years they had travelled together, crisscrossing the barest expanses of Canada and then down beneath the big skies of the American Midwest, traversing both Dakotas and on. They'd both been heading for Colorado until her eye had been caught by a cowboy somewhere just south of Broken Bow, Nebraska, and that had been the end of that. He'd found himself alone again, pausing to walk the central vertebrae of the Rockies before spending the next ten years moving ever farther south until he eventually dropped off the end of the continent.

After Natasha there had been many other faces, attached to less memorable names: beautiful, all of them, in their own ways, he was sure. Reg spent a few minutes trying to recall each, but faltered after the first two or three and wasn't convinced that he'd remembered even those correctly. Some had barely lasted a night a handful of decades ago, so it was inevitable that the strength of his memories would wane, he supposed. Besides, it had never been about the company but about the journey. So much to see, so many places to visit. Why else would he have spent so long moving on, always moving on?

Reg glanced at Donna, wondering what she'd make of her father's early exploits. Not that he felt guilty, exactly. That had been a different life, long before she'd been even the merest twinkle in her mother's eye—long before, in fact, he'd had any notion that Agnes even existed. Donna had been a late addition to a late marriage, neither advent something he'd anticipated but had found himself welcoming nonetheless, a journey into a different type of country.

"I think I could do with a cup of tea," Donna announced now, as through the wet afternoon gloom shone a sign that indicated civilisation in the form of Harrogate. "Perhaps a bite to eat, too. What does the clock say? It must be past time for lunch, anyway."

They were barely an hour from Doncaster, but Reg wasn't going to argue. Anything to postpone the inevitable. He hadn't been in this neck of the woods for years, but Donna had insisted that the best thing he could do now was move closer to her and Michael. "It's time you came home, Dad," is how she'd actually termed it, although she'd only grown up in Doncaster because her mother had been born there. Reg hadn't had the heart to point out that it wasn't home for him, aware that such a statement would probably hurt his daughter's feelings. He didn't want to rock the boat. Reg didn't want to cause a bother at all—he would have been quite happy to fade away in his own small house, the one he'd bought in the Borders after Agnes had shuffled off. Donna had put that move down to grief, perhaps unwilling to acknowledge that her father was merely attempting some small return to a pattern of life that had predated her appearance and that she only knew through half-told stories that must have seemed more like legend than history. The house had been miles up a dirt track in a forest so dense that he could be cut off for weeks over winter if the snows were bad. It reminded Reg of those weeks in Colorado and then New Mexico and, much later still, the Andes. If Britain had been that kind of country, it was where the bears would have been, and that suited Reg just fine. But of course, the reason he'd bought the place became the reason he was forced to leave it. What was manageable when one was knocking sixty became lethal when fast approaching eighty.

Donna pulled off the motorway. Reg expected her to head for the service station but instead she made for Harrogate itself.

"I've read about a great place a little further on," she told him. "I've been meaning to visit it for ages. A salvage warehouse with a café and all sorts of interesting independent stalls. It sounds like just your sort of place, Dad. Let's go there."

Reg said nothing, but nodded. Behind them his accumulated possessions of years, many of them brought back from his overseas trips, sat in boxes along with the last of his furniture. Donna had nagged and nagged him to "minimise" on the basis that his room in the residential home would be too small for the majority of it. What he had saved had been by way of argument, cajoling and outright stubbornness, and was still deemed to be too much. Why she thought a warehouse housing bric-a-brac of the sort he would habitually gladly take home would be a good place to stop he had no idea.

The rain eased as they approached the town, a shaft of sunlight illuminating the Yorkshire sandstone of its oldest buildings. They did not head for the centre, but instead pulled down what seemed like a residential street.

"It's hidden behind here somewhere," Donna said, leaning over the steering wheel as the van crawled forward over speed humps. "There, look."

A break in the houses heralded a narrow road that ran between two large rusty open gates. Donna turned in and through them. Beyond, the road widened into a yard with parking space at the near end, closed off at the other by a substantial old barn. The arched entrance, which would once have featured solid wooden doors, had been replaced by glass panels, through which Reg could see laden pitches stretching back into the dimly lit interior. A sign proclaimed that the café was somewhere to the rear.

"Come on," Donna said, killing the engine and unbuckling her belt. "Let's get inside before the rain starts again." She opened her door and hopped from the driver's seat, rounding the bonnet to help him as he clambered out of the passenger side. His hip protested as his feet hit the pocked tarmac and Reg cursed, just a little, under his breath.

"I'm sorry, Dad," Donna said, one arm under his, as if to hold him up. "We should have stopped sooner."

He extricated himself from her grip, trying not to show his annoyance at his own frailty. There was a time when he'd been the strongest man she knew.

They headed for the bathrooms first, situated just inside those big glass doors. As he left the men's, Reg looked out into the grim grey daylight and saw Donna back out beside the Transit. She was talking to a large man in weathered black overalls, gesticulating as she explained something. Reg blinked, slowly, assimilating this new information. His daughter's decision to bring him here suddenly made a lot more sense.

They saw him coming. Donna took a hurried step back, as if she'd been caught in a compromising position, which Reg supposed she had been, in a way. The man greeted Reg's approach with an encouraging smile.

"Dad," said Donna. "This is Adrian, he owns this place."

Reg nodded at this new acquaintance. "I gather I've been the victim of a ruse, Adrian. I'll have a word with my daughter alone, please, if I may."

Adrian smiled again. "Of course. I'll let you two come and find me in a bit. No rush."

Reg watched him walk across the wet tarmac.

"Dad—" Donna began.

"Poor show, love," Reg said, mildly. "Poor show."

Donna sighed, half in sadness, half in exasperation. "Dad, you can't keep everything. You just can't. Your room at Wisteria Lodge—"

"Wisteria Lodge," Reg repeated, bitterly. "Why don't they just call it what it is? The Death Wagon."

"Don't," Donna said. "I'm doing the best I can, Dad. There was no way you could carry on living on your own up there at the house. Look at you, you can barely walk ten paces. You know Mike and I would have you at ours if we could, but we can't, there's barely room for the two of us as it is. Wisteria Lodge is the best option close by, and we've got you the biggest room there that we could. Try to understand, why can't you?"

"Understanding," Reg said, "is not the problem. Acceptance, my dear, is the issue."

They stood facing each other, and he realised, perhaps for the first time, that his daughter stood head and shoulders over him. The thought imbued Reg with a sense of hopelessness he'd hitherto held at bay.

"Adrian will take everything you don't want," she said.

"Fine. Get him out here. Let's get this show on the road. Can't keep Wisteria Lodge waiting."

"Dad," Donna said, softly, but he turned away.

When Adrian returned, he had a couple of younger men with him, also dressed in black overalls. As they rolled up the back of the Transit, Reg said, "You can take it all."

There was a pause.

"Dad, that's not necessary. You don't have to get rid of everything. You just have to be a bit more selective."

Reg, who thought he'd already been pretty damn selective back at the house, shook his head. "There's only one thing I want to keep. Burn the rest, for all I care."

He watched as the men went about their work, lifting down tables, chairs, curiosities from far and wide, pieces of art, even an old wooden globe set on its own legs.

"Don't you want to keep the globe?" Donna asked, probably because she remembered it from her childhood. "There's room for that, at least, I'm sure."

"You have it, if you want it," Reg told her, trying and failing not to let his voice slide into sullenness.

The single remaining object of his desire had been jammed unceremoniously between the carved oak legs of a large armchair. One of Adrian's lads pulled it out, coughing slightly as a faint plume of dust flickered from the chair's upholstery.

"There," Reg said. "That's it. Give it here, would you, son?"

"Oh, Dad," Donna said. "You can't be serious."

Reg held the old rucksack up before him. He'd bought it from one of the American army boys he'd met in the Philippines when his first such companion had finally given out. He'd lost count of the years they'd passed through together since, this old pack and him. The straps were frayed and in places worn through entirely. There were patches of oil on the base where he'd set it down to crawl beneath that waste-of-money truck he'd rented in Namibia. A black pillow of duct tape signalled the spot where a good old-fashioned cutpurse had tried to slash through its base that time in Mozambique. There were the holes the families of mice had nibbled in it over the twenty-five years it had stood on the metal utility shelves in their garage in Doncaster, not fifty miles from this very spot.

"It's falling apart, Dad," Donna tried, again. "It's full of dust and god knows what else. That can't be the thing you want to take with you, not to your beautiful new room."

"This is what I want," Reg told her, stolidly, "so you'll have to make a decision. Let me take it or leave me here with it and the rest of Adrian's relics, because I'm not leaving without it."

They didn't stop for lunch in the end. Reg wandered around inside the barn while Adrian and his boys finished unloading the truck into the intermittent rain. Donna hovered nearby, apparently too uncomfortable to accompany him indoors. Reg didn't feel the need to set her at ease. He was the one being asked to give everything up, after all.

He kept hold of the bag, just in case. When he put it over his shoulder, Reg found that it fit there just the same as it always had. It struck him that he should have taken better care of it in those years after he'd abandoned his travels. It seemed now that it had always been the best home he'd never had.

Back on the motorway, he kept it between his feet, a familiar weight he'd all but forgotten.

"What's so important about it?" Donna asked. "I can understand it went a lot of places with you, but surely all your photographs—they must be better memory keepers than that disgusting old thing."

Reg looked out of the window at the looming bulk of Doncaster. He tried to remember the last strange city he'd arrived in and couldn't. He knew the pack would have been with him, though, its bulk settled firmly against his back.

"It was there," he said. "It was always there."

Wisteria Lodge was a large Victorian building of red brick, standing in an adequate amount of greenery that had reached the end of its season. A gravel driveway led up to the large arched front porch. It might once have been impressive, but its wide steps had been augmented by a ramp with a handrail on one side and a wheelchair lift on the other, both of which had been installed with practicality in mind rather than any sense of aesthetics.

"Mr Sanderson!" squeaked the nurse who came out to greet them, in that tone caring types reserve for the very old or the very young. "I'm Nancy. How lovely to meet you. Your daughter's told us all about you—we're all excited to hear your stories about travelling. I hear you've been all over the world, not just once but many times! Can I call you Reg? I can, can't I? Oh, good."

Reg regarded her, close-lipped. Nancy was short and dumpy and looked as if wiping elderly arses was about as much exercise as she ever got. Not unattractive, though, at a push, especially if one only looked at her face.

"We've had a long journey," Donna confided, as an apology for her father's silence. "It's been rather fraught."

The nurse maintained her bright mask, still smiling as she ushered them inside. "Of course. We'll get you settled, then you'll feel much better. We've got the boxes you brought down earlier, Donna, with your father's clothes and whatnot, they're all unpacked and waiting for Reg in his room. It's this way . . ."

She led them down a corridor carpeted in a thick, loud pile that might have been considered stylish for a week or so sometime in the late seventies. It smelled of old boiled food that had been liberally sprayed with air freshener. There were more handrails, this time on both walls. Reg felt the passageway closing in, threatening to squash him between its patchy papered walls. His hand tightened on the strap of his pack, wondering if together they could make a bolt for it—one final trip for two empty old sacks.

"There, you see," Nancy gushed, as she pushed open the door to number twenty-three, the siding into which the long train of Reg's life had now been shunted once and for all. "It's a lovely room, this one—looks right out over the rose garden. They're not in bloom now, obviously, but in summer it's beautiful. You'll like that."

Donna let him go ahead of her. Reg walked in and looked around. It was bright and airy, but there wasn't much to take in. Single bed, chest of drawers, wardrobe, bookcase, and a small desk, which was bare apart from a tray bearing a kettle, a couple of mugs, and a bowl of PG Tips sachets alongside mini long-life milk cartons.

"It might feel a bit sparse at the moment," Nancy agreed, to Reg's silent assessment, "but we'll get more of your own things around you and it'll feel like home in no time, mark my words."

Reg looked at Donna, whose cheeks coloured a little. Then he swung the pack from his back and dumped it on the bed. Flakes of dust hit the pristine white coverlet.

"I'd like to be alone now, please," he said. "If that's not too much to ask."

He felt rather than saw the two women exchange glances.

"Supper is at six, Reg," said Nancy. "I'll pop back and get you then. It'll be a good chance for you to meet the other residents."

"I'll leave you to it then, Dad," said Donna. "Mike and I will come in and see you tomorrow. All right?"

Reg didn't answer either of them. They made a quiet exit and he could hear them murmuring to each other beyond the blank white of the fire door that closed him off from the rest of the world. He hobbled to the window to look out over the garden. It was barely five o'clock but the light was already beginning to disintegrate. The faded roses, dead but with their heads still waving aimlessly on their stalks, seemed to him to be a particularly malicious joke. He turned away and pulled the curtains, returning to the bed.

"Just you and me now, kid," he muttered, perching beside his old pack. "Just like the old days."

Reg unzipped one of the small outside pockets, the one where he knew his trusty old Leatherman was waiting. It had saved his life many times, this piece of kit—literally as well as metaphorically. He pulled open the blade, which had stiffened during its long period of disuse. Then he turned the pack over and went to work on the duct tape. He took his time, worrying at the edges, pulling a little here, peeling a little there. He didn't want to just rip it off. That might cause more damage. The pack was plenty threadbare in places already.

Reg worked carefully, the time slipping away as the light faded still further. He left Wisteria Lodge and Doncaster far behind, passing down the narrow lanes of time and memory as he worked. He'd just about freed enough of the tape to reach what was stored beneath it when there was a knock at the door.

"Reg? It's Nancy again," said the familiar voice. "It's five to six. Are you ready for something to eat? Your daughter said you hadn't stopped for lunch, so you must be starving."

Reg didn't answer. He was too busy coaxing out the string. It made him smile to see it after all these years. He'd just succeeded in freeing it completely when Nancy opened the door, knocking softly, as if doing so precluded the need for guilt at the intrusion.

"Reg, is everything all right? Are you—"

She stopped in the doorway. The light from the hall behind her spilled into number twenty-three.

Reg slipped from the bed, still holding the string as he looked around for somewhere to hang it. He settled on the mirror of the dressing table, which had round wooden handles on either side so that it could be adjusted. He shuffled across the floor and hooked the old string over one of these knobs. The long line of yellowing molars clacked gently against the wood and one another as they settled themselves. As he looked at them Reg was satisfied to realise that more names were coming back to him. A little aide-mémoire, that's all he needed, and he was right back amid the brightest of his days. He'd give them each a good clean later, he decided, treat himself to a real trip down memory lane.

Reg turned towards the nurse. She was still standing at the door. The expression on her face was uncertain. As he watched, she looked at the pack on the bed, then back towards his little souvenirs, then at the open knife still in his hand.

"You're right," Reg said, offering a pleasant smile. "It does feel better. Now—time for dinner, is it?"

Nancy backed away as he moved towards her, the uncertainty taking on a thin edge of fear. Reg moved past her with a lighter step than he'd managed in years, the smile still on his face. Beneath his feet, the turgid carpet seemed somehow less offensive, the smell receding to the periphery of his awareness. He could hear the hubbub of voices somewhere ahead of him. Behind him, Nancy's feet began to move, albeit with a somewhat hesitant step.

Perhaps, he thought, life at Wisteria Lodge had the potential to be more fun than he'd anticipated. After all, life was what you made it, wasn't it?

WHERE ARE YOU GOING, WHERE HAVE YOU BEEN?

JOYCE CAROL OATES

for Bob Dylan

Joyce Carol Oates is the author most recently of the novel *Breathe* and the collection *Zero-Sum: Stories*. She is a recipient of the Bram Stoker Award, the National Book Award, the PEN America Lifetime Achievement award, the Bram Stoker Life Achievement Award, the President's Medal of Honor, and the Jerusalem Prize.

HER NAME was Connie. She was fifteen and she had a quick, nervous giggling habit of craning her neck to glance into mirrors or checking other people's faces to make sure her own was all right. Her mother, who noticed everything and knew everything and who hadn't much reason any longer to look at her own face, always scolded Connie about it. "Stop gawking at yourself. Who are you? You think you're so pretty?" she would say. Connie would raise her eyebrows at these familiar old complaints and look right through her mother, into a shadowy vision of herself as she was right at that moment: she knew she was pretty and that was everything. Her mother had been pretty once too, if you could believe those old snapshots in the album, but now her looks were gone and that was why she was always after Connie.

"Why don't you keep your room clean like your sister? How've you got your hair fixed—what the hell stinks? Hair spray? You don't see your sister using that junk."

Her sister June was twenty-four and still lived at home. She was a secretary in the high school Connie attended, and if that wasn't bad enough—

with her in the same building—she was so plain and chunky and steady that Connie had to hear her praised all the time by her mother and her mother's sisters. June did this, June did that, she saved money and helped clean the house and cooked and Connie couldn't do a thing, her mind was all filled with trashy daydreams. Their father was away at work most of the time and when he came home he wanted supper and he read the newspaper at supper and after supper he went to bed. He didn't bother talking much to them, but around his bent head Connie's mother kept picking at her until Connie wished her mother was dead and she herself was dead and it was all over. "She makes me want to throw up sometimes," she complained to her friends. She had a high, breathless, amused voice that made everything she said sound a little forced, whether it was sincere or not.

There was one good thing: June went places with girl friends of hers, girls who were just as plain and steady as she, and so when Connie wanted to do that her mother had no objections. The father of Connie's best girl friend drove the girls the three miles to town and left them at a shopping plaza so they could walk through the stores or go to a movie, and when he came to pick them up again at eleven he never bothered to ask what they had done.

They must have been familiar sights, walking around the shopping plaza in their shorts and flat ballerina slippers that always scuffed the sidewalk, with charm bracelets jingling on their thin wrists; they would lean together to whisper and laugh secretly if someone passed who amused or interested them. Connie had long dark blond hair that drew anyone's eye to it, and she wore part of it pulled up on her head and puffed out and the rest of it she let fall down her back. She wore a pullover jersey blouse that looked one way when she was at home and another way when she was away from home. Everything about her had two sides to it, one for home and one for anywhere that was not home: her walk, which could be childlike and bobbing, or languid enough to make anyone think she was hearing music in her head; her mouth, which was pale and smirking most of the time, but bright and pink on these evenings out; her laugh, which was cynical and drawling at home—"Ha, ha, very funny"—but high-pitched and nervous anywhere else, like the jingling of the charms on her bracelet.

Sometimes they did go shopping or to a movie, but sometimes they went across the highway, ducking fast across the busy road, to a drive-in restaurant where older kids hung out. The restaurant was shaped like a big bottle, though squatter than a real bottle, and on its cap was a revolving figure of a grinning boy holding a hamburger aloft. One night in midsummer they ran across, breathless with daring, and right away someone leaned out a car window and invited them over, but it was just a boy from high school they didn't like. It made them feel good to be able to ignore him. They went up through the maze of parked and cruising cars to the bright-lit, fly-infested restaurant, their faces pleased and expectant as if they were entering a sacred building that loomed up out of the night to give them what haven and blessing they yearned for. They sat at the counter and crossed their legs at the ankles, their thin shoulders rigid with excitement, and listened to the music that made everything so good: the music was always in the background, like music at a church service; it was something to depend upon.

A boy named Eddie came in to talk with them. He sat backwards on his stool, turning himself jerkily around in semicircles and then stopping and turning back again, and after a while he asked Connie if she would like something to eat. She said she would and so she tapped her friend's arm on her way out—her friend pulled her face up into a brave, droll look—and Connie said she would meet her at eleven, across the way. "I just hate to leave her like that," Connie said earnestly, but the boy said that she wouldn't be alone for long. So they went out to his car, and on the way Connie couldn't help but let her eyes wander over the windshields and faces all around her, her face gleaming with a joy that had nothing to do with Eddie or even this place; it might have been the music. She drew her shoulders up and sucked in her breath with the pure pleasure of being alive, and just at that moment she happened to glance at a face just a few feet from hers. It was a boy with shaggy black hair, in a convertible jalopy painted gold. He stared at her and then his lips widened into a grin. Connie slit her eyes at him and turned away, but she couldn't help glancing back and there he was, still watching her. He wagged a finger and laughed and said, "Gonna get you, baby," and Connie turned away again without Eddie noticing anything.

She spent three hours with him, at the restaurant where they ate hamburgers and drank Cokes in wax cups that were always sweating, and then down an alley a mile or so away, and when he left her off at five to eleven only the movie house was still open at the plaza. Her girl friend was there, talking with a boy. When Connie came up, the two girls smiled at each other and Connie said, "How was the movie?" and the girl said, "You should know." They rode off with the girl's father, sleepy and pleased, and Connie couldn't help but look back at the darkened shopping plaza with its big empty parking lot and its signs that were faded and ghostly now, and over at the drive-in restaurant where cars were still circling tirelessly. She couldn't hear the music at this distance.

Next morning June asked her how the movie was and Connie said, "So-so."

She and that girl and occasionally another girl went out several times a week, and the rest of the time Connie spent around the house—it was summer vacation—getting in her mother's way and thinking, dreaming about the boys she met. But all the boys fell back and dissolved into a single face that was not even a face but an idea, a feeling, mixed up with the urgent insistent pounding of the music and the humid night air of July. Connie's mother kept dragging her back to the daylight by finding things for her to do or saying suddenly, "What's this about the Pettinger girl?"

And Connie would say nervously, "Oh, her. That dope." She always drew thick clear lines between herself and such girls, and her mother was simple and kind enough to believe it. Her mother was so simple, Connie thought, that it was maybe cruel to fool her so much. Her mother went scuffling around the house in old bedroom slippers and complained over the telephone to one sister about the other, then the other called up and the two of them complained about the third one. If June's name was mentioned her mother's tone was approving, and if Connie's name was mentioned it was disapproving. This did not really mean she disliked Connie, and actually Connie thought that her mother preferred her to

June just because she was prettier, but the two of them kept up a pretense of exasperation, a sense that they were tugging and struggling over something of little value to either of them. Sometimes, over coffee, they were almost friends, but something would come up—some vexation that was like a fly buzzing suddenly around their heads—and their faces went hard with contempt.

One Sunday Connie got up at eleven—none of them bothered with church—and washed her hair so that it could dry all day long in the sun. Her parents and sister were going to a barbecue at an aunt's house and Connie said no, she wasn't interested, rolling her eyes to let her mother know just what she thought of it. "Stay home alone then," her mother said sharply. Connie sat out back in a lawn chair and watched them drive away, her father quiet and bald, hunched around so that he could back the car out, her mother with a look that was still angry and not at all softened through the windshield, and in the back seat poor old June, all dressed up as if she didn't know what a barbecue was, with all the running yelling kids and the flies. Connie sat with her eyes closed in the sun, dreaming and dazed with the warmth about her as if this were a kind of love, the caresses of love, and her mind slipped over onto thoughts of the boy she had been with the night before and how nice he had been, how sweet it always was, not the way someone like June would suppose but sweet, gentle, the way it was in movies and promised in songs; and when she opened her eyes she hardly knew where she was, the back yard ran off into weeds and a fence-like line of trees and behind it the sky was perfectly blue and still. The asbestos ranch house that was now three years old startled her—it looked small. She shook her head as if to get awake.

It was too hot. She went inside the house and turned on the radio to drown out the quiet. She sat on the edge of her bed, barefoot, and listened for an hour and a half to a program called XYZ Sunday Jamboree, record after record of hard, fast, shrieking songs she sang along with, interspersed by exclamations from "Bobby King": "An' look here, you girls at Napoleon's—Son and Charley want you to pay real close attention to this song coming up!"

And Connie paid close attention herself, bathed in a glow of slow-pulsed joy that seemed to rise mysteriously out of the music itself and lay languidly about the airless little room, breathed in and breathed out with each gentle rise and fall of her chest.

After a while she heard a car coming up the drive. She sat up at once, startled, because it couldn't be her father so soon. The gravel kept crunching all the way in from the road—the driveway was long—and Connie ran to the window. It was a car she didn't know. It was an open jalopy, painted a bright gold that caught the sunlight opaquely. Her heart began to pound and her fingers snatched at her hair, checking it, and she whispered, "Christ. Christ," wondering how bad she looked. The car came to a stop at the side door and the horn sounded four short taps, as if this were a signal Connie knew.

She went into the kitchen and approached the door slowly, then hung out the screen door, her bare toes curling down off the step. There were two boys in the car and now she recognized the driver: he had shaggy, shabby black hair that looked crazy as a wig and he was grinning at her.

"I ain't late, am I?" he said.

"Who the hell do you think you are?" Connie said.

"Toldja I'd be out, didn't I?"

"I don't even know who you are."

She spoke sullenly, careful to show no interest or pleasure, and he spoke in a fast, bright monotone. Connie looked past him to the other boy, taking her time. He had fair brown hair, with a lock that fell onto his forehead. His sideburns gave him a fierce, embarrassed look, but so far he hadn't even bothered to glance at her. Both boys wore sunglasses. The driver's glasses were metallic and mirrored everything in miniature.

"You wanta come for a ride?" he said.

Connie smirked and let her hair fall loose over one shoulder.

"Don'tcha like my car? New paint job," he said. "Hey."

"What?"

"You're cute."

She pretended to fidget, chasing flies away from the door.

"Don'tcha believe me, or what?" he said.

"Look, I don't even know who you are," Connie said in disgust.

"Hey, Ellie's got a radio, see. Mine broke down." He lifted his friend's arm and showed her the little transistor radio the boy was holding, and now Connie began to hear the music. It was the same program that was playing inside the house.

"Bobby King?" she said.

"I listen to him all the time. I think he's great."

"He's kind of great," Connie said reluctantly.

"Listen, that guy's great. He knows where the action is."

Connie blushed a little, because the glasses made it impossible for her to see just what this boy was looking at. She couldn't decide if she liked him or if he was just a jerk, and so she dawdled in the doorway and wouldn't come down or go back inside. She said, "What's all that stuff painted on your car?"

"Can'tcha read it?" He opened the door very carefully, as if he were afraid it might fall off. He slid out just as carefully, planting his feet firmly on the ground, the tiny metallic world in his glasses slowing down like gelatine hardening, and in the midst of it Connie's bright green blouse. "This here is my name, to begin with," he said. ARNOLD FRIEND was written in tarlike black letters on the side, with a drawing of a round, grinning face that reminded Connie of a pumpkin, except it wore sunglasses. "I wanta introduce myself, I'm Arnold Friend and that's my real name and I'm gonna be your friend, honey, and inside the car's Ellie Oscar, he's kinda shy." Ellie brought his transistor radio up to his shoulder and balanced it there. "Now, these numbers are a secret code, honey," Arnold Friend explained. He read off the numbers 33, 19, 17 and raised his eyebrows at her to see what she thought of that, but she didn't think much of it. The left rear fender had been smashed and around it was written, on the gleaming gold background: DONE BY CRAZY WOMAN DRIVER. Connie had to laugh at that. Arnold Friend was pleased at her laughter and looked up at her. "Around the other side's a lot more —you wanta come and see them?"

"No."

"Why not?"

"Why should I?"

"Don'tcha wanta see what's on the car? Don'tcha wanta go for a ride?"

"I don't know."

"Why not?"

"I got things to do."

"Like what?"

"Things."

He laughed as if she had said something funny. He slapped his thighs. He was standing in a strange way, leaning back against the car as if he were balancing himself. He wasn't tall, only an inch or so taller than she would be if she came down to him. Connie liked the way he was dressed, which was the way all of them dressed: tight faded jeans stuffed into black, scuffed boots, a belt that pulled his waist in and showed how lean he was, and a white pull-over shirt that was a little soiled and showed the hard small muscles of his arms and shoulders. He looked as if he probably did hard work, lifting and carrying things. Even his neck looked muscular. And his face was a familiar face, somehow: the jaw and chin and cheeks slightly darkened because he hadn't shaved for a day or two, and the nose long and hawklike, sniffing as if she were a treat he was going to gobble up and it was all a joke.

"Connie, you ain't telling the truth. This is your day set aside for a ride with me and you know it," he said, still laughing. The way he straightened and recovered from his fit of laughing showed that it had been all fake.

"How do you know what my name is?" she said suspiciously.

"It's Connie."

"Maybe and maybe not."

"I know my Connie," he said, wagging his finger. Now she remembered him even better, back at the restaurant, and her cheeks warmed at the thought of how she had sucked in her breath just at the moment she passed him—how she must have looked to him. And he had remembered her. "Ellie and I come out here especially for you," he said. "Ellie can sit in back. How about it?"

"Where?"

"Where what?"

"Where're we going?"

He looked at her. He took off the sunglasses and she saw how pale the skin around his eyes was, like holes that were not in shadow but instead in light. His eyes were like chips of broken glass that catch the light in an amiable way. He smiled. It was as if the idea of going for a ride somewhere, to someplace, was a new idea to him.

"Just for a ride, Connie sweetheart."

"I never said my name was Connie," she said.

"But I know what it is. I know your name and all about you, lots of things," Arnold Friend said. He had not moved yet but stood still leaning back against the side of his jalopy. "I took a special interest in you, such a pretty girl, and found out all about you—like I know your parents and sister are gone somewheres and I know where and how long they're going to be gone, and I know who you were with last night, and your best girl friend's name is Betty. Right?"

He spoke in a simple lilting voice, exactly as if he were reciting the words to a song. His smile assured her that everything was fine. In the car Ellie turned up the volume on his radio and did not bother to look around at them.

"Ellie can sit in the back seat," Arnold Friend said. He indicated his friend with a casual jerk of his chin, as if Ellie did not count and she should not bother with him.

"How'd you find out all that stuff?" Connie said.

"Listen: Betty Schultz and Tony Fitch and Jimmy Pettinger and Nancy Pettinger," he said in a chant. "Raymond Stanley and Bob Hutter—"

"Do you know all those kids?"

"I know everybody."

"Look, you're kidding. You're not from around here."

"Sure."

"But—how come we never saw you before?"

"Sure you saw me before," he said. He looked down at his boots, as if he were a little offended. "You just don't remember."

"I guess I'd remember you," Connie said.

"Yeah?" He looked up at this, beaming. He was pleased. He began to mark time with the music from Ellie's radio, tapping his fists lightly together. Connie looked away from his smile to the car, which was painted so bright it almost hurt her eyes to look at it. She looked at that name, ARNOLD FRIEND. And up at the front fender was an expression that was familiar—MAN THE FLYING SAUCERS. It was an expression kids had used the year before but didn't use this year. She looked at it for a while as if the words meant something to her that she did not yet know.

"What're you thinking about? Huh?" Arnold Friend demanded. "Not worried about your hair blowing around in the car, are you?"

"No."

"Think I maybe can't drive good?"

"How do I know?"

"You're a hard girl to handle. How come?" he said. "Don't you know I'm your friend? Didn't you see me put my sign in the air when you walked by?"

"What sign?"

"My sign." And he drew an X in the air, leaning out toward her. They were maybe ten feet apart. After his hand fell back to his side the X was still in the air, almost visible. Connie let the screen door close and stood perfectly still inside it, listening to the music from her radio and the boy's blend together. She stared at Arnold Friend. He stood there so stiffly relaxed, pretending to be relaxed, with one hand idly on the door handle as if he were keeping himself up that way and had no intention of ever moving again. She recognized most things about him, the tight jeans that showed his thighs and buttocks and the greasy leather boots and the tight shirt, and even that slippery friendly smile of his, that sleepy dreamy smile that all the boys used to get across ideas they didn't want to put into words. She recognized all this and also the singsong way he talked, slightly mocking, kidding, but serious and a little melancholy, and she recognized the way he tapped one fist against the other in homage to the perpetual music behind him. But all these things did not come together.

She said suddenly, "Hey, how old are you?"

His smiled faded. She could see then that he wasn't a kid, he was much older—thirty, maybe more. At this knowledge her heart began to pound faster.

"That's a crazy thing to ask. Can'tcha see I'm your own age?"

"Like hell you are."

"Or maybe a couple years older. I'm eighteen."

"Eighteen?" she said doubtfully.

He grinned to reassure her and lines appeared at the corners of his mouth. His teeth were big and white. He grinned so broadly his eyes became slits and she saw how thick the lashes were, thick and black as if painted with a black tarlike material. Then, abruptly, he seemed to become embarrassed and looked over his shoulder at Ellie. "Him, he's crazy," he said. "Ain't he a riot? He's a nut, a real character." Ellie was still listening to the music. His sunglasses told nothing about what he was thinking. He wore a bright orange shirt unbuttoned halfway to show his chest, which was a pale, bluish chest and not muscular like Arnold Friend's. His shirt collar was turned up all around and the very tips of the collar pointed out past his chin as if they were protecting him. He was pressing the transistor radio up against his ear and sat there in a kind of daze, right in the sun.

"He's kinda strange," Connie said.

"Hey, she says you're kinda strange! Kinda strange!" Arnold Friend cried. He pounded on the car to get Ellie's attention. Ellie turned for the first time and Connie saw with shock that he wasn't a kid either—he had a fair, hairless face, cheeks reddened slightly as if the veins grew too close to the surface of his skin, the face of a forty-year-old baby. Connie felt a wave of dizziness rise in her at this sight and she stared at him as if waiting for something to change the shock of the moment, make it all right again. Ellie's lips kept shaping words, mumbling along with the words blasting in his ear.

"Maybe you two better go away," Connie said faintly.

"What? How come?" Arnold Friend cried. "We come out here to take you for a ride. It's Sunday." He had the voice of the man on the radio now. It was the same voice, Connie thought. "Don'tcha know it's Sunday all day? And honey, no matter who you were with last night, today you're with Arnold Friend and don't you forget it! Maybe you better step out here," he said, and this last was in a different voice. It was a little flatter, as if the heat was finally getting to him.

"No. I got things to do."

"Hey."

"You two better leave."

"We ain't leaving until you come with us."

"Like hell I am—"

"Connie, don't fool around with me. I mean—I mean, don't fool around," he said, shaking his head. He laughed incredulously. He placed his sunglasses on top of his head, carefully, as if he were indeed wearing a wig, and brought the stems down behind his ears. Connie stared at him, another wave of dizziness and fear rising in her so that for a moment he wasn't even in focus but was just a blur standing there against his gold car, and she had the idea that he had driven up the driveway all right but had come from nowhere before that and belonged nowhere and that everything about him and even about the music that was so familiar to her was only half real.

"If my father comes and sees you—"

"He ain't coming. He's at a barbecue."

"How do you know that?"

"Aunt Tillie's. Right now they're uh—they're drinking. Sitting around," he said vaguely, squinting as if he were staring all the way to town and over to Aunt Tillie's back yard. Then the vision seemed to get clear and he nodded energetically. "Yeah. Sitting around. There's your sister in a blue dress, huh? And high heels, the poor sad bitch—nothing like you, sweetheart! And your mother's helping some fat woman with the corn, they're cleaning the corn—husking the corn—"

"What fat woman?" Connie cried.

"How do I know what fat woman, I don't know every goddamn fat woman in the world!" Arnold Friend laughed.

"Oh, that's Mrs. Hornsby. . . . Who invited her?" Connie said. She felt a little lightheaded. Her breath was coming quickly.

"She's too fat. I don't like them fat. I like them the way you are, honey," he said, smiling sleepily at her. They stared at each other for a while through the screen door. He said softly, "Now, what you're going to do is this: you're going to come out that door. You're going to sit up front with me and Ellie's going to sit in the back, the hell with Ellie, right? This isn't Ellie's date. You're my date. I'm your lover, honey."

"What? You're crazy—"

"Yes, I'm your lover. You don't know what that is but you will," he said. "I know that too. I know all about you. But look: it's real nice and you couldn't ask for nobody better than me, or more polite. I always keep my word. I'll tell you how it is, I'm always nice at first, the first time. I'll hold you so tight you won't think you have to try to get away or pretend anything because you'll know you can't. And I'll come inside you where it's all secret and you'll give in to me and you'll love me."

"Shut up! You're crazy!" Connie said. She backed away from the door. She put her hands up against her ears as if she'd heard something terrible, something not meant for her. "People don't talk like that, you're crazy," she muttered. Her heart was almost too big now for her chest and its pumping made sweat break out all over her. She looked out to see Arnold Friend pause and then take a step toward the porch, lurching. He almost fell. But, like a clever drunken man, he managed to catch his balance. He wobbled in his high boots and grabbed hold of one of the porch posts.

"Honey?" he said. "You still listening?"

"Get the hell out of here!"

"Be nice, honey. Listen."

"I'm going to call the police—"

He wobbled again and out of the side of his mouth came a fast spat curse, an aside not meant for her to hear. But even this "Christ!" sounded forced. Then he began to smile again. She watched this smile come, awkward as if he were smiling from inside a mask. His whole face was a mask, she thought wildly, tanned down to his throat but then running out as if he had plastered make-up on his face but had forgotten about his throat.

"Honey—? Listen, here's how it is. I always tell the truth and I promise you this: I ain't coming in that house after you."

"You better not! I'm going to call the police if you—if you don't—"

"Honey," he said, talking right through her voice, "honey, I'm not coming in there but you are coming out here. You know why?"

She was panting. The kitchen looked like a place she had never seen before, some room she had run inside but that wasn't good enough, wasn't going to help her. The kitchen window had never had a curtain, after three years, and there were dishes in the sink for her to do—probably—and if you ran your hand across the table you'd probably feel something sticky there.

"You listening, honey? Hey?"

"—going to call the police—"

"Soon as you touch the phone I don't need to keep my promise and can come inside. You won't want that."

She rushed forward and tried to lock the door. Her fingers were shaking. "But why lock it," Arnold Friend said gently, talking right into her face. "It's just a screen door. It's just nothing." One of his boots was at a strange angle, as if his foot wasn't in it. It pointed out to the left, bent at the ankle. "I mean, anybody can break through a screen door and glass and wood and iron or anything else if he needs to, anybody at all, and specially Arnold Friend. If the place got lit up with a fire, honey, you'd come runnin' out into my arms, right into my arms an' safe at home—like you knew I was your lover and'd stopped fooling around. I don't mind a nice shy girl but I don't like no fooling around." Part of those words were spoken with a slight rhythmic lilt, and Connie somehow recognized them—the echo of a song from last year, about a girl rushing into her boy friend's arms and coming home again—

Connie stood barefoot on the linoleum floor, staring at him. "What do you want?" she whispered.

"I want you," he said.

"What?"

"Seen you that night and thought, that's the one, yes sir. I never needed to look anymore."

"But my father's coming back. He's coming to get me. I had to wash my hair first—" She spoke in a dry, rapid voice, hardly raising it for him to hear.

"No, your daddy is not coming and yes, you had to wash your hair and you washed it for me. It's nice and shining and all for me. I thank you sweetheart," he said with a mock bow, but again he almost lost his balance. He had to bend and adjust his boots. Evidently his feet did not go all the way down; the boots must have been stuffed with something so that he would seem taller. Connie stared out at him and behind him at Ellie in the car, who seemed to be looking off toward Connie's right, into nothing. This Ellie said, pulling the words out of the air one after another as if he were just discovering them, "You want me to pull out the phone?"

"Shut your mouth and keep it shut," Arnold Friend said, his face red from bending over or maybe from embarrassment because Connie had seen his boots. "This ain't none of your business."

"What—what are you doing? What do you want?" Connie said. "If I call the police they'll get you, they'll arrest you—"

"Promise was not to come in unless you touch that phone, and I'll keep that promise," he said. He resumed his erect position and tried to force his shoulders back. He sounded like a hero in a movie, declaring something important. But he spoke too loudly and it was as if he were speaking to someone behind Connie. "I ain't made plans for coming in that house where I don't belong but just for you to come out to me, the way you should. Don't you know who I am?"

"You're crazy," she whispered. She backed away from the door but did not want to go into another part of the house, as if this would give him permission to come through the door. "What do you . . . you're crazy, you. . . ."

"Huh? What're you saying, honey?"

Her eyes darted everywhere in the kitchen. She could not remember what it was, this room.

"This is how it is, honey: you come out and we'll drive away, have a nice ride. But if you don't come out we're gonna wait till your people come home and then they're all going to get it."

"You want that telephone pulled out?" Ellie said. He held the radio away from his ear and grimaced, as if without the radio the air was too much for him.

"I toldja shut up, Ellie," Arnold Friend said, "you're deaf, get a hearing aid, right? Fix yourself up. This little girl's no trouble and's gonna be nice to me, so Ellie keep to yourself, this ain't your date right? Don't hem in on me, don't hog, don't crush, don't bird dog, don't trail me," he said in a rapid, meaningless voice, as if he were running through all the expressions he'd learned but was no longer sure which of them was in style, then rushing on to new ones, making them up with his eyes closed. "Don't crawl under my fence, don't squeeze in my chipmunk hole, don't sniff my glue, suck my popsicle, keep your own greasy fingers on yourself!" He shaded his eyes and peered in at Connie, who was backed against the kitchen table. "Don't mind him, honey, he's just a creep. He's a dope. Right? I'm the boy for you, and like I said, you come out here nice like a lady and give me your hand, and nobody else gets hurt, I mean, your nice old bald-headed daddy and your mummy and your sister in her high heels. Because listen: why bring them in this?"

"Leave me alone," Connie whispered.

"Hey, you know that old woman down the road, the one with the chickens and stuff—you know her?"

"She's dead!"

"Dead? What? You know her?" Arnold Friend said.

"She's dead—"

"Don't you like her?"

"She's dead—she's—she isn't here any more—"

"But don't you like her, I mean, you got something against her? Some grudge or something?" Then his voice dipped as if he were conscious of a rudeness. He touched the sunglasses perched up on top of his head as if to make sure they were still there. "Now, you be a good girl."

"What are you going to do?"

"Just two things, or maybe three," Arnold Friend said. "But I promise it won't last long and you'll like me the way you get to like people you're close to. You will. It's all over for you here, so come on out. You don't want your people in any trouble, do you?"

She turned and bumped against a chair or something, hurting her leg, but she ran into the back room and picked up the telephone. Something roared in her ear, a tiny roaring, and she was so sick with fear that she could do nothing but listen to it—the telephone was clammy and very heavy and her fingers groped down to the dial but were too weak to touch it. She began to scream into the phone, into the roaring. She cried out, she cried for her mother, she felt her breath start jerking back and forth in her lungs as if it were something Arnold Friend was stabbing her with again and again with no tenderness. A noisy sorrowful wailing rose all about her and she was locked inside it the way she was locked inside this house.

After a while she could hear again. She was sitting on the floor with her wet back against the wall.

Arnold Friend was saying from the door, "That's a good girl. Put the phone back."

She kicked the phone away from her.

"No, honey. Pick it up. Put it back right."

She picked it up and put it back. The dial tone stopped.

"That's a good girl. Now, you come outside."

She was hollow with what had been fear but what was now just an emptiness. All that screaming had blasted it out of her. She sat, one leg cramped under her, and deep inside her brain was something like a pinpoint of light that kept going and would not let her relax. She thought, I'm not going to see my mother again. She thought, I'm not going to sleep in my bed again. Her bright green blouse was all wet.

Arnold Friend said, in a gentle-loud voice that was like a stage voice, "The place where you came from ain't there any more, and where you had in mind to go is cancelled out. This place you are now—inside your daddy's house—is nothing but a cardboard box I can knock down any time. You know that and always did know it. You hear me?"

She thought, I have got to think. I have got to know what to do.

"We'll go out to a nice field, out in the country here where it smells so nice and it's sunny," Arnold Friend said. "I'll have my arms tight around you so you won't need to try to get away and I'll show you what love is like, what it does. The hell with this house! It looks solid all right," he said. He ran a fingernail down the screen and the noise did not make Connie shiver, as it would have the day before. "Now, put your hand on your heart, honey. Feel that? That feels solid too but we know better. Be nice to me, be sweet like you can because what else is there for a girl like you but to be sweet and pretty and give in?—and get away before her people come back?"

She felt her pounding heart. Her hand seemed to enclose it. She thought for the first time in her life that it was nothing that was hers, that belonged to her, but just a pounding, living thing inside this body that wasn't really hers either.

"You don't want them to get hurt," Arnold Friend went on. "Now, get up, honey. Get up all by yourself."

She stood.

"Now, turn this way. That's right. Come over here to me—Ellie, put that away, didn't I tell you? You dope. You miserable creepy dope," Arnold Friend said. His words were not angry but only part of an incantation. The incantation was kindly. "Now come out through the kitchen to me, honey, and let's see a smile, try it, you're a brave, sweet little girl and now they're eating corn and hot dogs cooked to bursting over an outdoor fire, and they don't know one thing about you and never did and honey, you're better than them because not a one of them would have done this for you."

Connie felt the linoleum under her feet; it was cool. She brushed her hair back out of her eyes. Arnold Friend let go of the post tentatively and opened his arms for her, his elbows pointing in toward each other and his wrists limp, to show that this was an embarrassed embrace and a little mocking, he didn't want to make her self-conscious.

She put out her hand against the screen. She watched herself push the door slowly open as if she were back safe somewhere in the other doorway, watching this body and this head of long hair moving out into the sunlight where Arnold Friend waited.

"My sweet little blue-eyed girl," he said in a half-sung sigh that had nothing to do with her brown eyes but was taken up just the same by the vast sunlit reaches of the land behind him and on all sides of him—so much land that Connie had never seen before and did not recognize except to know that she was going to it.

THE WRONG SHARK

RAY CLULEY

Ray Cluley's work has been published in various magazines and anthologies and been reprinted several times, appearing in such places as Ellen Datlow's *Best Horror of the Year* series, Steve Berman's *The Year's Best Gay Speculative Fiction*, and Benoît Domis's *Ténèbres* series. He has won the British Fantasy Award for Best Short Story ("Shark! Shark!") and has since been nominated for Best Novella (*Water For Drowning*) and Best Collection (*Probably Monsters*). His second collection, *All That's Lost*, is available now from Black Shuck Books. He lives in Wales with his partner and two troublesome but adorable cats.

When Darnell Jackson was a boy, a film crew came to the island where he lived and made a movie. The island was Martha's Vineyard, and the movie they made was *Jaws*.

Forty years later, feeling like a tourist, Darnell came back to the Vineyard. He came back on the Woods Hole ferry like he was summer people, only it wasn't yet summer, it was early May, and there was a bite in the air that had him holding his coat closed at the throat as he stood on deck for the approach. They passed the West Chop lighthouse. It wasn't on, but he felt its warning.

Stay away. Stay away.

It was cold, but as he remembered it the weather was much the same back when filming started all those years ago, actors and extras doing their best to pretend it was summer-hot. The aim had been to get most of the shoot done before the real tourists arrived and turned six thousand people into sixty thousand. For Darnell, though, this time? He had come straight from his father's funeral, renting a car with little thought to where he was going until he was already most of the way there. Still wearing his black suit, his black shirt, his good shoes. Appropriate, in its own way, as something of Darnell had died here long ago. He'd mourned it his whole life.

He headed for his rental as the ferry began the docking process. He tried to ignore the appetite that had been building throughout his long journey. He didn't want to spend much time in Oak Bluffs. There'd be no lobster roll from the Lookout, no Big Dipper ice cream. No nostalgic visit to Inkwell Beach, either, as much as he'd loved the place as a child. His mother used to take him, before *Jaws*, because of how much he'd liked to swim, but his father had hated the place and the racist roots of its name. He thought going there was volunteering for segregation.

There *were* more people of color on the island these days, Darnell noticed that right away. Better off than he'd ever been—shit, they were downright *affluent*—but that was okay. That was probably good. The Black Hamptons, some people called it. His father would have found a way to be angry about that, and he would have found a way to blame white people, but that was okay, too. That was his right. The island had been home to the same families for centuries, and progress was always ever slow. You had to keep swimming against the current until the current changed, that was all, and as his therapist was fond of saying, it was swimming against a current that made you stronger.

He was swimming against the current in coming back. That's how it felt, anyway, after years of moving deeper and deeper inland. As if things would get better depending on how far they removed themselves from the ocean. But jobs were scarce everywhere—or his father was bad at keeping one for long—and Darnell quickly discovered that the fears he'd started harboring on the island were carried with him, regardless of where they went. They were like memories that way, which are the wake you make in moving forward.

And all that moving didn't mean shit because the sharks would always follow.

Sharks have a kind of sixth sense, thanks to a remarkable electroreceptive system. The black spots on a shark's skin around the eyes and mouth and snout are the ampullae of Lorenzini, which allow the shark to sense the electromagnetic fields and movements of other animals. It means they are especially good at locating and homing in on prey.

On his way to Edgartown, Darnell stopped to walk the State Beach and look at the American Legion Memorial Bridge. Or "*Jaws* Bridge," as it was better known. State Beach was where the Kintner kid was killed, where the camera so famously zoomed in on Brody while everything else seemed to zoom out behind. On State Beach you could run upon the same rocks as Brody on his way past the bridge to the pond—Sengekontacket Pond—where his own kid was playing, sent to the estuary because Brody had thought it safer than the open sea. It had been so cold for that scene. People on the beach and in the water were freezing their asses off in shorts and tees, swimsuits, bikinis, all of them dressed like it was already the Fourth of July, all of them with jackets hidden in their beach gear for the time waiting between takes. The sun had rarely been out, and the water held its chill because the Gulf Stream didn't shift until late May, early June, and unless you were in the Polar Bear Club, you wouldn't want to swim State Beach until then *at least*, but people went in the water anyway. You had to, if you wanted to be in the movie, and *everyone* wanted to be in the movie. Like everybody else, Darnell would loiter wherever there was filming, hoping for an opportunity to get involved. For many people that tactic paid off.

It never worked for him, though.

Darnell walked beside the rocks he could have run upon and watched the sea. He watched waves sweep up the beach, each one the result of some distant force, pushed and pulled to their inevitable destination. Building to violent force in some cases, smashing against whatever tried to stop them, often to their own mutual destruction. Not these ones, though. Not today. They merely hushed their way up the beach to dissolve and disappear back the way they'd come. Darnell wondered if it was a sign that he should do the same.

The sea withdrew, and the sea came again. Did it remember what it once lifted, carried, deposited on distant shores? Did it remember what it consumed or regret any of them it drowned? He didn't think so. The tides were as cold and careless as time.

At the bridge, he remembered how he used to watch older kids jump from it, splashing into the water below. Judging by the warning sign on the rail it seemed they still did, probably even more so now it was *Jaws* Bridge. He imagined children joking about sharks before they jumped.

Jump the shark. Wasn't that something people said these days? About taking things too far? Darnell wasn't sure. And how far was too far, anyway? Hit back harder, that's what his father used to say. Pay it back with interest. Darnell had rarely agreed with him but now that he was gone, he felt adrift. Not that his father had ever been any kind of anchor. More often than not he was that current Darnell swam against. He didn't feel stronger for it, though.

He waited for a gap in the traffic and crossed the street to look at the pond where Brody's kid and his friends had been knocked from their dinghy. One of them—the Rebello boy—was nearly eaten. What was his name? Darnell had sort of known him once. He used his phone to Google. *Chris*. That was it. There'd been a time Darnell was envious of him, only to learn in later years that he'd been so scared of that fin coming at him over and over that filming needed to be cut short. Even knowing it was all fake, he'd been terrified. Darnell wondered if the experience still came to him at night the same way his own experience haunted him, or if he'd managed to reduce it to an amusing anecdote, something to dine out on. He Googled again, curious to see what the kid—what the *man*—was doing now.

He was dead.

Darnell looked again at the pond, remembering the kid's face as the camera came at him in the water and wondering, shit, did the shark get you after all, man? Because your thirties are far too young for a heart attack, aren't they? He scrolled down a few more links on his phone but found something disturbing about the younger Brody brother and put the phone away without reading more.

People were like oceans, he thought. Pushed and pulled by similar tidal forces. Prey to all the vicious things that swam within them.

He looked at the ocean and thought of all that lived there, sleek and secret beneath the waves. He thought, predictably, of sharks. Of bulls and blacktips, makos and hammerheads. Of tigers and threshers. He'd become something of a shark expert over the years, "a black Richard Dreyfuss" as he'd explained it to a partner once, when he still trusted enough to confide such things. Learning all he could about sharks was the therapy he'd prescribed himself long before he ever had a professional session.

Hammerheads have 360-degree vision. Great whites can grow ten inches each year. A shark's heart is an S with two chambers. These were some of the things he still remembered. He found comfort in the natural facts of them, albeit a cold one. Better to remember details like that than how a shark's skin felt against your own, or how sharp their teeth could be.

How hard laughter could bite.

There was a churning in his stomach he'd hoped was a lingering effect of his ferry-crossing, but now his breathing came quicker and shallower and he knew that what was happening had little to do with the ferry and more to do with where it had brought him.

"Okay," he said. "Okay." He knew what he had to do.

He looked and saw the sea. It was the same gray as the sky. He saw a boat. He saw gulls. He saw a distant buoy.

Okay.

The breeze. It carried the ocean with it as a thin mist that settled on his skin. He clutched the satiny lining of his pockets tight in his fists and held the coat open like twin sails to feel the cold.

Okay.

He turned an ear to the breeze and listened. Heard the gulls calling back and forth. Heard the clanking halyards of nearby boats. Heard his own slowing inhalations which brought to him a fishy odor and the ocean's brine. The latter was so strong, he could taste salt on his lips.

"Okay."

All those hours of therapy—all those dollars—and the best thing he'd learned was the 5-4-3-2-1 technique. The rest of it was all trite, soundbite wisdom. Like "face your fears," that was a classic. Face your fears so as to better overcome them. But then that was what Quint did and look what happened to him. Days scared in the water waiting for sharks to eat him and the rest of his life hunting them in an effort to defeat that fear, only to have it come back monstrous and chomp him down whole. The shark was an instrument of karma, that was how Darnell saw it, because as far as he was concerned, *Jaws* was Quint's movie. He'd watched it over and over—facing his fear—and the more he saw it the more he was convinced. Quint was the lead. Quint was the one with history and past trauma to overcome. That he fails just makes the film honest.

Fear never went away. Quint knew that, and so did Darnell. It accreted like coral. It built like a wave. Shit, there were people who *still* wouldn't go in the water thanks to *Jaws*, that's how strong fear could be.

Darnell turned away from the pond and headed back to the car. The breeze, as if to encourage him, strengthened into wind to push him on his way.

The color of a shark's skin helps it hunt. The blues and greys of the ocean, combined with a pale underbelly like the sky, help render it near invisible when seen from above or below. Many are named for their colors, such as great whites, brown sharks, and blacks.

Spielberg had a thing about color, but not the way Darnell's father said. As far as Darnell could tell—and he'd followed the director's career over the years—the man was not a racist. He *was* particular about color, though. Like how he didn't want the color red in *Jaws* so that when the blood came it would really pop. If Darnell had realized, he wouldn't have worn his lucky tee—the *red* one—every time he showed up for a part. He wouldn't have worn his favorite—red—baseball cap. He supposed they could have given him a different shirt if they'd really wanted him. He could have taken off his hat.

Down-island, walking through Edgartown, he remembered that cars had been moved out of shot if they were red. He remembered the red had been replaced with orange in the bunting they'd put up all along Main Street for the Fourth of July celebrations. He remembered the atmosphere, the excitement and expectation that came with the novelty of a movie crew on Main. Now, that same street was quiet. Much of it had changed, too, and yet at the same time it had not. Not really. The differences were mostly surface details. As if another film set had been erected in the time he was away, the buildings given new identities with false facades. He had a sense of floating between worlds, between past and present and something else. He recognized many of the clapboard and redwood buildings, the old whaling captains' houses, but some of the businesses were new. He remembered the hardware store that had briefly become a music store so Quint could buy piano wire for fishing line. The scene had been cut. The store was a restaurant now.

At the junction of Water Street and Main he saw where Brody had picked up his supplies for the "beach closed" signs. Afterward he had driven the wrong way down a one-way street because it was only Martha's Vineyard that had the one-way system, not Amity, and back then, when Darnell was a boy, the topsy-turvy use of his hometown had amused him. Amazed him, even. It had shown him how rules he thought were fixed in place could be broken. Showed him how the world he thought he knew could change, or at least seem to.

"If he's not racist, how come you ain't got no part in his damn movie?"

His father's voice, able to cross time to find Darnell wherever—whenever—he might be.

"Everybody else is in it, why ain't you?"

Almost all of the other kids got parts, that was true. Some of them even got two; the Edgartown kids in the marching band were the same as the Boy Scout group swimming in the sea (even though the parade and the swim were meant to be happening at exactly the same time) because who was going to notice the same kid twice? Darnell was patient, though. He'd hang around the cast and crew, collecting autographs, making sure he was seen and hoping he'd be remembered. But . . .

"Shit, there ain't no one black in that movie. No one."

That wasn't true. Darnell had checked. There were people of color in the Woods Hole ferry scene, *and* on State Beach, right before that pasty-pale mayor started hogging the camera.

Not Darnell, though. Every time his father asked he had to shake his head no, not today, hating to see his father disappointed yet again, not just by him but by the world they lived in, and he'd move quickly to show him the new signatures in his autograph book, though his father never cared for it.

"Looks blank to me," he'd once said. "Look at all them pages. They're so damn *white*."

The largest of the predatory sharks is the great white, or Carcharodon carcharias. *It relies on its heavy-hitting power, sometimes leaping out of the water to attack.*

The tiger shark, or Galeocerdo cuvier, *is a stealthier animal. It hunts mostly at night, drifting slowly before suddenly striking.*

It was a tiger shark they'd used for the scene on the docks. Thirteen feet long, or thereabouts, tied up by its tail and hooked through the mouth so it hung with its jaws gaping open. It wasn't local. Best they'd managed to catch off the Vineyard was a load of threshers and blues that lacked the striking visual impact required for a summer blockbuster. With time running out, they'd sourced the tiger shark from Florida and FedExed it in a crate of ice. Darnell hadn't known that at the time, though. He'd assumed Spielberg had said, "I need a shark," and someone had hooked the tiger right out of Vineyard waters. The idea had terrified him. Knowing there were sharks like that near Inkwell Beach? Shit, no wonder his father never went swimming.

While the hunt wore on in real life to find the right kind of shark, everyone else was filming the other hunt, the first of the chaotic dock scenes. All those different crews hurrying and jostling each other and getting in each other's way. All of that, plus the film crew, too; it made for a lot to watch. The film crew was easy to spot because by then most of them were wearing those screen-printed T-shirts Darnell had liked so much, an open-mouthed shark coming at you over JAWS, and the boat crews were easy to spot because they were locals, all of them stepping around each other and bumping left and right and swamping each other's boats in their eagerness to get out there and catch a monster. Anyone and everyone who had a boat was in that scene, and getting paid twice for it, too: once as an extra, and once for the hire of their boat. Darnell's father wasn't into boats, so he missed out on that, but he could bullshit with the best of them and managed to land himself a background part. He still complained, though. "Doubt you'll even see me," he'd said, but Darnell had gone along to watch anyway, sitting in the cab of his father's truck with the engine running for the heater.

It was May and it was cold, raining enough that there were long pauses between takes and a lot of hanging around. "Hurry up and wait" was a joke Darnell had heard plenty of times without really understanding it, and with so many people to organize for this scene, and rain as well, there was even more waiting than usual. But then suddenly the docks would come alive with a cry of "Action!" and sure enough there'd be lots of it as men overloaded their boats and bumped each other and even fell into the sea in their haste. Then they'd cut and there'd be shouting through a bullhorn, "Rick! Rick! Get over here!" and there'd be pointing and taking new positions and nodding and a lot of standing around to wait all over again. Some of the men drank from flasks they'd brought along to keep the cold at bay—and Darnell had no doubt his father was one of those—but with the rain and the cold and no coats or waterproofs, because it was meant to be July, all that waiting and waiting and waiting became too much for some of them.

Darnell's father had been one of those, as well.

"Look at this shit!"

Darnell had been staring at a truck opposite, one of the rentals the film people used. He'd been trying to figure out what they'd done to the AVIS logo to make it read JAWS, eventually seeing how lines of tape had been used to make a J, while another line from the V to the I made a W. It was clever, Darnell thought. Like the clapperboard he'd seen with its white stripes altered to a double row of teeth: snap! He smiled, thinking of that. Then the door beside him was wrenched open, startling him, and his father was shaking a flimsy fishing rod in his face.

"Look at this shit! Like this'd catch a shark. Shit, this wouldn't catch *nothin'*."

He threw it aside to reach in for his jacket.

"Catch a *cold*, though, you bet I can do *that*."

He pulled his way out of the wet sweater he'd been allowed, put his jacket on, and yanked the sweater back down over it best he could before slamming the door closed again to stomp his way back to where everyone else was hurrying up to wait.

Safe in the truck, Darnell had laughed at how suddenly fat his father looked with the jacket under his sweater, stopping only when the new cold in the truck had him looking around for his own.

Standing on the dock years later, he let his coat flap open in the wind, welcoming the cold —

an awareness of discomfort is proof of a desire to live

— and looking around at the boats and buildings. He was surprised at how little had been done to mark the *Jaws* legacy on the island, especially here. He'd half-expected a fiberglass replica of the shark to be dangling on the docks, a background prop for tourists' selfies. In the absence of such a thing, he was able to better remember the real one.

"Looks like a lynching," Darnell's father had said when they first saw it, hanging there. "It's the wrong way up, but that's what it looks like. And look at them. Bunch of happy white folk."

That had been some time after the first dock scene and by that point Darnell's father had no desire to be in the film no more. He'd agreed to let Darnell keep trying, though. Maybe as a kindness, maybe to prove a point. Either way, that was how they found themselves at the docks again, approaching the dead shark hanging in the crowd. A hook through its mouth kept it open, its rows of teeth on gruesome display. It had been stabbed and cut, and something like a crossbow bolt or harpoon protruded from its side.

They could smell it long before they were close.

The meat of a shark is different from that of other fish. It decays quickly because it's all just simple proteins and no bones, only cartilaginous tissue. For the eight-hundred-pound tiger they'd strung up, that decaying process had begun in Florida, was slowed a little by ice, then hurried along again quick just as soon as it was out of its crate. When they hung it upside down, gravity went to work on its insides until the guts kept piling up in the fish's throat. Darnell had been both delighted and repulsed to see them bulging out of the animal's mouth, ready to drop and slop on the docks. As he watched, someone stepped close to push them back in, push them back up.

"Yuck," said Darnell.

"It's just a fish. You wanna be in the film, you gotta get closer."

Darnell had felt his father's hand on his back, guiding him forward with a final, not gentle, push. He'd felt a similar thing at his grave, once the service was over. Something steering him away from where his father lay buried and pushing him toward Amity. Back toward the Vineyard.

Close up, the shark had *reeked.* It was dead, and doing what dead things do, which was rot. There could be no bringing it down between takes to store on ice because the more they handled it, the more it would fall apart, and so it stayed there, hanging in the sun. Unless you had to get close for a shot, you made sure you stayed upwind of it.

Many of the locals had complained about the hanging shark and its stench—for all those keen on the film and all it provided, there were plenty who resented the disruption of their normal lives—but whoever was running the docks back then was getting more money from the *Jaws* people than all of those complaining put together, so the shark hung there, rotting, stinking, spilling its guts and blood, while everyone waited and filmed and waited again.

Darnell had waited with them, making himself part of the crowd around the shark. He'd even had to step out of the way once so Richard Dreyfuss could measure the span of the open mouth, *and* he'd been there in the background as Dreyfuss explained to Brody it was the wrong shark, but he'd never yet spotted himself watching the scene back. They'd run that scene quite a few times, though, and much of the time he'd found himself distracted by the shark. He'd looked into that mouth, his hands over his own and over his nose, and he had been revolted. He had looked into those eyes, those dead, dark eyes—

lifeless eyes, black eyes

—and he had not liked what he saw there. Had not liked, either, what he couldn't help imagining: the whole shark descending from its unraveling rope to swallow him whole.

More than once his nightmares had put him in that shark's place. He'd be packed in ice and FedExed straight to the docks where he'd grasp and pull the sudden noose at his neck, gasping his last breaths while people in screen-printed tees and hoods like teeth gathered 'round to watch. Someone would yank his legs and he'd wake with a clapperboard snap, freezing cold and sucking for air.

That was one of the better dreams.

Darnell heard some children laugh and the sound pulled the present into sharper focus while the past dropped away, like in that famous dolly zoom. Only there were no children on the docks, there was only him, leaning into the wind coming in off the sea and staring at where a shark used to be. The ghost of young laughter lingered, clinging to him like the smell from something dead and rotten.

As well as extraordinary electroreceptors and excellent eyesight, sharks have a great sense of smell. A great white can detect a drop of blood in an area the size of an Olympic pool.

Far from Martha's Vineyard, two years after they'd moved away, Darnell's mother convinced him to try swimming in the local pool. Not to face his fears, as any of his therapists might have put it, but because her little boy had once loved to swim, and she was keen to bring that joy back to him.

He'd been anxious, but they took some time for him to control his breathing and to quietly note his surroundings, and eventually she was able to lead him to the pool edge and into the shallows, and never mind who might be watching, you're doing real good, and with her help it had worked out all right at first. The water was cool and then comfortable, and the chlorine smell was nothing like ice or the briny scent of sharkskin, and the room was so big it echoed, throwing back the cries of other children and the occasional whistle blow of a lifeguard keeping them safe. And the light! It was so bright, and the water was clear, and there were no sharks, not a single one.

Still, he stayed close, facing his mother, holding her hands until she eased him away to tread water on his own and told him that's it, that's *good*, see? You're doing it, you're doing it. And he was. He turned and saw adults swimming lengths of the pool and he saw children splashing each other, the youngest of them wearing inflatable bands around their arms to keep them afloat, and as he watched he saw . . .

He saw a shark.

He saw a dark shape in water that suddenly breached, lifting one of the children shrieking into the air, shrieking with laughter, and he panic-splashed himself around again to face his mother, but he couldn't turn quick enough, remained frustratingly in the same place, his left hand slapping the water one way and his right hand the other, both too fast, too choppy, splashing like he was swatting at flies and that splashing would draw more sharks, he knew that, but he couldn't stop. He saw the shadow of one coming for him along the bottom of the pool and another bumped him from behind and now he couldn't breathe, he was drowning in the air while his legs kicked and his arms slapped and splashed and the water was so suddenly cold, *freezing* cold, gripping him around the chest, and the reason he couldn't breathe was because all the breath he'd had was coming out in a scream. A shark fastened its teeth on his arm and pulled and his scream became so shrill that something of the sound broke and he could only expel air and suck in sobs as his mother's fierce grip pulled him close and she waded to the edge of the pool with her son in her arms.

It was the first time his fears had taken hallucinatory shape in the waking world, surfacing from his nightmares to frighten him into a state that had him shaking so violently that his mother, holding him tight, trembled with him.

Darnell woke from that remembered terror, shivering. He was on the floor of his hotel room. He'd consumed the contents of his minibar and fallen asleep fetal by the open door of the refrigerator. He remembered listening to it hum until the sound dragged him into sleep, the cold seeping deliberately into his bones.

An awareness of discomfort is proof of a desire to live.

He groaned with the ache of straightening, sitting up and putting a hand to his head. It throbbed like a boat's motor. A taste for alcohol was one of the things Darnell had inherited from his father and he'd liberated the tiny bottles from the minibar in an effort to drown the laughter that had followed him back from the docks, hoping to sleep so deep the dreams wouldn't find him.

Only the powerless are at the mercy of their trauma.

He snatched up the bottles and threw them into the wastebin under the dresser, wincing with each knock of the metal and clink of glass. Was there anyone more powerless than a child? How can a man overcome trauma born at such an early, powerless age?

You can't. That's what Darnell had learned. Instead, you drag it behind like a trawler drags its net or a shark its barrels.

It was late but still light outside, so he splashed his face, ran his wet hands over the buzz of his hair, and left the hotel.

As a child, Darnell had lived in Oak Bluffs, but coming back he'd decided to stay down-island in Edgartown. Edgartown was where most of the film crew had stayed all those years ago because it was only fifteen minutes away from Cow Bay, the area so perfect for *Jaws*, and just as Edgartown had been conveniently located for their needs, so it was for Darnell's, too. He didn't want to be driving all around the island any more than could be helped, even as small as it was. He'd do what he had to do and be gone.

He drove slowly, though. The cocktail of different drinks from the minibar was still foul in his mouth and swimming in his bloodstream. He leaned over the steering wheel to look left and right at the large, handsome houses as he passed.

A child was playing in the front yard of one of them, throwing a baseball straight-up high and watching, watching, ready to catch it with that flat, rifle-shot smack in his mitt when it came down. He was white, wearing the full baseball kit to go with his mitt. The Red Sox colors, not the purple of the Vineyard Sharks. The cap reminded Darnell of his old favourite, forever lost now.

"I know where they keep the *real* shark."

A boy exactly like the one across the street had said that once. Darnell had thought he was talking to him but when he'd turned to ask "Where?" he saw the boy was addressing his own group of friends, all of them talking about the shark hanging on the docks as they waited between takes. Darnell recognized a couple of them from school. The kid in the baseball shirt was Brad. Bradley Ladson. He was the one claiming to know where they kept the real shark. One of the others had at that moment reached forward to pull at the arrow sticking out the shark's side and then the lot of them were ushered away by an angry adult, Darnell included, even though he hadn't done nothing.

"My brother says he carved his name into it but he's full of shit," said one of the boys Darnell didn't know and the others laughed and agreed, just so they could say "full of shit" themselves.

"It's way bigger than that one," said Brad, and pointed back at the hanging tiger. Someone was measuring its mouth again, but no one was filming. They measured the distance between the mouth and one of the actors.

Can't be no shark bigger than that one, Darnell thought.

"What did you say?"

It had taken him a moment to realize that this time someone *was* talking to him, and only then because someone pulled him around by the shoulder. Not aggressively, but not exactly gently, either.

"You said something," Brad said. "What did you say?"

"He said it wasn't bigger than that one."

Had he spoken out loud?

"I bet you haven't even seen it," Brad said. "I think only people in the movie get to see it."

Darnell could feel something stirring in the air between them, something that even as a child he recognized as the vibrating thrum of violence waiting. Darnell wondered if he was going to have to fight and hoped the choice wouldn't need making. His mother had always told him to walk away from fights, especially with someone white. His father's advice, had he ever given any, would have been the opposite—he was a man of action—and of the two parents there was one he was more afraid of disappointing.

He looked for his father in the crowd around him.

"*Nobody* gets to see the shark," he said absently. "It's locked away and secret."

Someone took his hat.

Darnell turned quickly and saw Brad wearing it. He snatched it back, too quick for Brad to dodge.

"Hey, I was just trying it on."

Then he called Darnell a bad word.

The others tried to laugh as if it had been "jerk" or "butt-wipe" but it was much worse than that and all of them knew it. They didn't fully understand *how*, but they knew it was a bad word, awful, maybe a dangerous word, and their laughter reflected some of that confusion in trying to be something it wasn't. Darnell even saw a flush of shame pass over Brad's face, but it was only brief.

Without thinking—which frightened him a little then, and a lot in later years—Darnell took up a boxing stance, fists as tight as the sudden silence they made. One of the actors, the police chief, Roy, had shown him how. He used to be a boxer, and sometimes he liked to play with the kids between takes, throwing slow jabs or sweeping his whole arm for them to duck under while encouraging quicker, hard punches back from them, BAM!, into one of his open palms, WHAM! He called it the old one-two, WHAM-BAM! Once, he'd called Darnell "Tiny Tate" while shaking out his palms and pretending Darnell had hit him too hard.

So Darnell put his fists up and though he didn't know if he had it right, he must've had it close because he saw Brad back down. Not physically—Brad still had one arm up himself, a fist cocked back—but something went out of his eyes. Darnell relaxed his own stance and straightened up a bit, the moment fading, and Brad threw a pretend slap at him with such exaggerated slowness and with such a comic-book sound effect that there could be no mistaking it was just a joke. "Ka-POW!" Darnell stepped back from it though, and one of the other boys pretended to be struck instead, spinning in slow motion with his hands at his jaw, eyes mock wide and mouth growling in feigned pain as he ricocheted from a bystander like a sluggish pinball. It led the others back into a more comfortable laughter.

Brad said, "Hey, remember when that lady hit him?" and he mimed a slap again—and again, and again—making a whip-crack noise with each one. There was no need to ask what lady, or hit who, because they'd all watched it. Take after take after take, a grieving mother had slapped the police chief, over and over. For real.

"His face was all pink!"

"She slapped him so hard his glasses came off!"

"I bet they use that in the film."

Darnell said, "If you get attacked by a shark you should punch it on the nose and it will leave you alone."

Everybody looked at him.

"What?"

"They're very sensitive."

Everybody laughed again, but it was okay. They weren't laughing at him. They were laughing at the idea of punching a shark. And just like that, the rest of the violent tension they'd been wading through receded.

"Come on," said Brad. "I wanna show you something." He pushed his way through the crowd who were still hurrying to wait for the next "Action!" and his friends followed him down the dock. Darnell watched them go, feeling their fleeting acceptance slip away like a slow wave when you're standing barefoot in the surf, sand sinking beneath your feet.

Brad turned, running backwards for a moment to throw a question back at Darnell.

"You coming?"

He didn't wait for an answer. Just turned back to continue running.

Stunned for a moment by the invite, then giddy with inclusion, Darnell ran to catch up, grinning.

The thresher shark has a very long tail fin that measures half the length of its whole body. It uses this to lure prey, tricking it close only to swat it away and attacking once it's stunned or otherwise disabled.

They gathered in one of the boathouses of Norton and Easterbrook dock, standing a short distance away from a large freezer. The docks had a walk-in refrigeration unit but whether for purposes of secrecy or perhaps permission, the film crew was using a large freezer like you'd find in a regular store—only bigger—to keep some of their potential props fresh. That's what Brad said. A generator chugging nearby kept it running. A flap of cardboard torn from a box was stuck on the freezer with a piece of raggedy tape and the outline of an open-mouthed shark had been markered on the card as if to devour the sign's instruction: KEEP CLOSED.

"What's in it?" someone asked.

"What do you think?"

"The real shark?"

"The *real* shark is fake," said Brad. "It's all mechanical and fake and nowhere near here. But they caught lots of real ones like that massive son-of-a-bitch out there."

This time there was no laughter at the swearing, no joking elbows to the ribs. They were too curious, too much in awe of what might be in the freezer. They were too afraid.

They shuffled one another forward as a group, leaning to look rather than get too close. The freezer lid wasn't see-through, though, wasn't frosted glass or nothing like that. It was flat, and metal. There was a clasp with a bolt to keep it closed.

"Get it open," Brad said. "You'll see. My dad told me."

Someone pulled the bolt and flipped the clasp open and started to lift the lid and then other hands were helping. The freezer released a cold cloud that enveloped them as they bowed slightly to look inside.

Their gasped sounds of amazement and disgust drew Darnell closer, and he pushed his way among them like they'd been friends forever.

"Look at them all!"

A pungent smell came at him out of the frosty mist, but it was nowhere near as bad as the stink from what was hanging outside. Nor were the sharks he could see anywhere near as big. But there were so many!

"There's more underneath!" someone said.

"Look at that one!"

"There are *loads* of them!"

The freezer was *full* of sharks, all of them twice the size of Darnell, easy. Head to tail and tail to head, rows of them stacked on more rows of the same, none of them suitable for some reason or another but kept anyway, all blue and grey with pale bellies. They had fins like half kites, and tails too on the blue ones; the others had tails so long to be nearly ridiculous, coiled or folded like something wilted. Their torpedo bodies glistened, frozen forever wet, and slit with gills like tallies counting recent kills. Darnell reached in to touch one. He ran his palm over the skin. It was smoother than he expected. He rubbed the other way and found it rough, like sandpaper. Eyes black as night stared docile through cataracts of ice. Their mouths were open sickles of teeth.

"Even the chief couldn't punch this many on the nose."

Brad said it quietly, like it was only meant for Darnell, and the new intimacy of it was startling but welcome. Darnell glanced at him, smiling wide, then turned his attention back to the sharks. Imagine swimming into this many! He shuddered, imagining them alive and writhing around him, thrashing to bite, and for a moment he thought his imagination had flexed, like it was a muscle that could tense or spasm, because he felt something clamp around his legs and he cried out, thinking "Shark!" as he was lifted like a caught kill, breaching. He soared high as Brad stood from a crouch behind him, his arms wrapped around Darnell's calves, his shins. Darnell flailed his arms as the others laughed and he was carried, panicking for balance he'd never achieve as he twisted in Brad's grip. His hat was knocked flying and then he was coming down, dropping, deposited backward into the ice chest. Those gathered around it backed away fast, their laughing faces disappearing quick as his head struck the side of the freezer and the lid came down to plunge him into darkness.

The dark was so absolute that he thought he'd passed out, but he could feel the cold and he could hear the laughter that felt the same and he could smell the—

fish, it's fish, just fish, lots of fish

—but he couldn't move. He lay in a dark so deep it filled his mind like seawater rushing into a capsized boat and he felt himself sinking. He couldn't move and he couldn't speak but he could *feel*, and what he could feel was all the sharks beneath him and beside him, the sharks all around him in the cold pitch dark. Their hard bodies, tight with frozen muscle. The press of fins in his ribs, the scythe-blade sweep of a long tail against his neck. Prickling his skin were teeth, everywhere teeth, all of them seeming to bite as he tried to fight the fear that held him frozen amongst the sharks, so many sharks he was drowning in them, breathing the stink of them—he could breathe, he was still breathing, oh God, oh God—but he couldn't do it properly, was doing it too quick, in/out, in/out, giving him nothing, like he might not be breathing at all, and waves of shock carried him so that his chest rose and fell like a fast tide and all the sharks swum out from him, out from within, and with each attempted breath they wanted back in, *they wanted back in*, and he couldn't . . . he couldn't . . .

The paralysis was dragged out of him, pulled like sand and stones by a receding sea, and taking its place before the sharks could fill him was a titanic burst of panic that made him mighty; he thrashed and turned and kicked, beating at a lid that wouldn't open, and as he shoved and shook in his fit of fear the teeth around him opened his skin and cut a low noise out of him, stuttered grunts connecting for a keening growl rising in volume until he was *screaming*, screaming like the sound itself might free him as he tried to beat his way out of a cold darkness filled with sharks that wanted to drown him and eat the flesh that shivered from his bones.

A group of sharks is called a shiver.

Darnell thought of that now as he watched the boy across the road throwing his baseball, catching his baseball. He had the air conditioner running, keeping the temperature in the confines of the car purposefully low.

A shiver of sharks.

A shark's skin was smooth in one direction, but if you rubbed it the wrong way you got that sandpaper roughness he'd felt as a child because a shark's skin is made up of placoid scales that point back to the tail, tiny teeth-like formations called dermal denticles that help reduce friction as the shark swims.

Even its skin was all teeth.

The chill in the car had raised the hairs on Darnell's arms. He rubbed them, one way and then the other. What was skin, anyway? The cells on the surface were dead already, shedding to replace themselves until no one was the same person they once were, not on the outside.

Some sharks shed and replace so many teeth that they get through fifty thousand in a lifetime.

Darnell watched the boy play. He wondered if he had many friends and thought, *of course he does.* A white boy in Edgartown would have lots of friends. This whole place was once Amity, friendship by definition. A place where you could give a beach a racist name and watch it stick throughout the years. Where people like Darnell were only welcomed as friends if they had money to spend, and even then not for long, thank you. Hurry up, we're waiting for you to leave.

The sky was sharkskin gray with held rain, and though he had the windows closed, the smell of the sea came to Darnell thick and tangy. It tasted like something spoiled. Like childhood.

He looked at the boy and then the house behind him. White clapboard facade, large windows, a white fence that might as well have been fucking picket, all of it ghostly in the fading light. He'd only known the upper floor of a shared house, growing up, and when they moved across to the mainland they downsized again while his father looked for work. It didn't help that Darnell's sessions with doctors had cost them, as had his medication, and they could never afford either for long. His father would rage about the film people and white people and everyone else he blamed for Darnell's terrors, including Darnell himself once he'd blamed all the rest. "You gotta be strong, boy. You gotta hit back and hit back harder. Show them they're messing with the wrong—"

With the wrong N-word.

Darnell's father had been so angry, all of the time, right up until he was too old to hold it anymore and it killed him, that's what Darnell thought. It ate him up from the inside.

If you cut a shark open and throw it back to sea, it will rip itself to pieces and devour itself.

A lot of the time, therapy had felt just like that. A self-feeding frenzy of anxieties and emotions once you've opened the box you locked them in.

Darnell had come out of the dark of that freezer like he was surfacing from deep water, cold and gasping for breath. He didn't remember the lid opening, or the sudden light, just that eventually he realized he was being carried. He didn't remember being lifted out from that icy shiver of sharks, but he remembered being carried, knees to his chest. Like he'd fallen asleep in his father's truck.

When a reporter managed to sneak a peek at the mechanical monstrosity to be used in the film's finale, a security guard was fired. There was no such punishment for anyone after what had happened to Darnell. A prank gone too far, an accident, that was all, and where was Darnell's father anyway when it happened? Of course, Darnell's father had raged, threatening violence, and his mother had threatened legal recourse they couldn't afford, and eventually they did receive a little keep-quiet money as compensation, but it didn't last long. It certainly didn't cover all of the help Darnell would need.

He was given a screen-printed tee.

By the end of September, almost all signs that the film had ever been made were gone. Quint's boat was still around, and the barge they'd used to film from, out on the water, but apart from that and a few newer cars on the roads, a few newer boats, the island went back to how it had always been, and life carried on as it always had.

Except for Darnell. Thanks to Brad.

"Hey, Dad."

The kid across the street threw his ball to the man stepping out from the house who caught it effortlessly, as if he was always going to pluck a ball from the air right there.

"Hey, Roger Clemens. Better get your butt inside. Getting dark."

The resemblance between father and son was striking. Not that Darnell had needed to see Brad again to confirm he had the right place; looking at his son was like looking back through time. Like looking at the same kid twice. They were ghosts of each other, in different ways.

Brad put his hands on his hips to watch his younger self pitch a ball to the sky and the gesture spread his jacket open. Darnell saw the uniform beneath and was not surprised because—

bull sharks were the most dangerous of sharks, the most aggressive

—because of course Brad was a cop. *Of course* he was.

But shit, it didn't change nothing.

"How about we catch a few together tomorrow, you and me?"

The ball came back down; a star falling to the kid's mitt.

"'K."

He threw the ball back up to the dark.

"Maybe we could go down to the cages?"

The boy kept his eyes to the sky, mitt snug to his chest until he knew where to put it, and said, "'K."

Darnell found he had as much hate for their easy relationship as he did for what was done to him all those years ago. The relationship he'd had with his father had never been the warmest, but after the sharks it was never anything, though the man forever directed the course of Darnell's life. And though he understood how the world worked, how it belonged to the great white man—he'd endured countless discriminations his whole life, just as his father had—it was to this particular one that his hatred held fast. And there he stood, with no idea of what Darnell had lost because of him. He just waded through life, kicking up sand from the seabed and paying no attention to the mess he left behind.

As he passed his son, Brad swiped the Red Sox cap from his head—

"Hey!"

—and tossed it back, saying, "Inside, kiddo, before your mom gets home."

I should have punched you, Darnell thought. *Right on the nose.*

A police cruiser pulled up at the sidewalk and someone inside called a greeting to the kid in the yard as Brad opened the door and dropped into the car. The kid waved and there was a blerp of siren in reply. A quick flash of the lights as they went, like bioluminescence in the wet air.

Darnell had managed to put a lot of what happened behind him, but it was always there. Coming back had not helped. You had to keep moving forward to live. All he'd done was chum the waters and now something worse than his terrors had surfaced, dorsal-sleek and sharp with teeth. It fought to come out, bulging its way from his mouth until he grew tired of pushing it back in, pushing it back down.

He wasn't here for revenge. He was an instrument of karma, that was all. A wave some forty years building, ready to smash up against the shore.

The boy continued to play, even as a light rain began to fall. Darnell turned on the wipers so he could keep watching the boy throw and catch his ball. Up it went, and down it came. Inevitable.

The male great white matures at around nine, ten years of age. They have teeth as early as embryos and eat their siblings in the womb. From the outset, before they are even born, they are as dangerous as their parents.

Darnell looked into the rearview and saw, behind him, sitting upright in the back seat, his father. A chill, colder than the air con, settled over him and he closed his eyes. He felt the sharks pressing their icy bodies close, fighting to bite, to strip skin from flesh and flesh from cold, white bones.

When he opened his eyes and looked again his father was gone.

Grief was how you drowned. Better to be a shark.

He knew what he had to do.

Most shark attacks occurred in shallow water. Exactly where you thought yourself safe. Like in your front yard.

This time when he looked in the mirror all he saw was himself. His eyes were full. Lifeless eyes, black eyes. The descending dark filled his car and the cold shadows enveloped him, slipping over him like sharkskin he could wear as armor.

He who makes a beast of himself loses the pain of being a man.

The windshield wipers slowed—

thump-thump . . .

thump-thump . . .

—as a cloudy rime of ice crackled across the glass, and a quiet voice from somewhere behind him said, "Action."

Darnell stepped out into the wet, the frosty drop in temperature following him from the car. The door shut behind him with the finality of a freezer's lid.

Alerted by the noise, the boy paused in his play and looked at Darnell.

"I like your hat," Darnell said as he approached.

He smiled.

He showed the boy his teeth.

21 BROOKLANDS: NEXT TO OLD WESTERN, OPPOSITE THE BURNT OUT RED LION

CAROLE JOHNSTONE

Scottish writer **Carole Johnstone**'s award-winning short fiction has been published around the world and reprinted in many annual Best Of anthologies in the UK and US. Her debut novel, *Mirrorland*, a gothic suspense set in Edinburgh, was published in 2021. Translation rights have been sold to fourteen countries and it has been optioned for television. Her second novel, *The Blackhouse*, an unusual murder mystery set in the Outer Hebrides, was published in 2022.

She lives in the Scottish Highlands with her husband, within a stone's throw of the seventeenth-century Glencoe Massacre. More information on the author can be found at carolejohnstone.com.

We're rarely all in the house together. Not even to sleep. Whenever we are it's by accident; none of us mean to be. Families aren't supposed to like each other, are they? I don't see how they can. They save the worst of themselves for themselves because everyone needs a break from pretending. I wrote that in an essay last year and Mr. Ingles gave it a B-plus before making me stay behind after class to ask if I was alright. I said yes, why wouldn't I be?

I only came back at all to pick up some stuff before going back to Julie's: underwear, some food, more smokes, because she's been getting a bit pissy about stuff like that lately, and I like staying over at her bit. It's as shit as mine, as all the houses around here are—wooden two-bedroom bungalows that started out as holiday chalets for rich people—but it's just her and her mum. And as far as families go, they've more energy for pretending. And they've got cable.

Mum caught me stealing the food because I rooted about in the fridge for ages—there wasn't much in there worth stealing—and I forgot about the beep it makes when you've left the door open too long. She didn't get up, she never gets up, but her thin scream forced me into the front room. She made me sit down and wait for Dad. I could've just left, I guess, it's not like she's ever going to be able to stop me, but I knew I'd pay for it later if I did.

Me and Mum don't speak. We must have done once, I suppose. On days when I'm pretending that she's not pretending, I blame her drowning lungs. I sat on the sofa, she sat in her armchair opposite Dad's, and some five o'clock quiz show buzzed and clapped between us. She watched me for a bit, but I didn't look at her because I don't do that anymore either. It's not just that she's all sucked in and wrinkled like a deflating balloon now, it's more than that. I'm scared to look. When she does speak to me at all, even in those two- or three-word breaths that rattle in their beginning and end, I can hear the bile in her. She hates me and I don't know why.

The back door bangs, creaks open—squeals open—and then bangs harder again as it shuts. We never use the front door; I don't even know if it works. The back door you could hear working from three or four streets away. I think it's Dad, but it isn't, and I'm nearly disappointed. A stay of execution isn't much better. Sometimes it's worse.

It's Wendy, which is almost as bad. "Hey, Mum. Where's Dad?"

A dry and rustling shrug as familiar as bad breathing.

Wendy tuts. "Pub then, shit. Shit!"

Silence apart from the clapping, and then, "Thought you was . . . stayin . . . with Mick to—"

"Well I fucking was, but his shitheap got a flat on the Sands and we need a spare." Wendy comes into the front room, stands in the middle of it. "Think Dad's got a spare?"

Mum swallows hard. It's a dry, noisy click. "Might have." Mum doesn't like Wendy much more than me I don't think, but it's enough to speak to her. It's enough to say *might have* when we all know that even if he does Wendy won't be getting it.

The door bangs open, bangs shut. Mick's heavy footsteps fill the quiet and then his bulk fills the doorway. He winks, he grins, scratches at the big black tattoo on his shoulder. "Evening ladies. Where's the man of the house then?"

Wendy tosses him a look. Her hands stay on her hips. "Pub."

He comes in and sits on the arm of the sofa farthest from me. Grins. "Haven't seen you here in a bit, gel. What's up?"

I'm grateful that someone is finally looking at me, but not enough to answer.

"She's waitin . . . for her dad."

"Oh yeah?" Another wink, another grin. "What you done then, gel?"

"She'll have been stealing," Wendy says. "That what you've been doing?" She stays in the middle of the front room, shaking her ugly hair like a prize stallion, not even looking down on me because that would mean looking. Wendy calls herself a hairdresser, but all she does is put rollers in cauliflower heads in the back room of Bobby's Bingo. Mick's a drug dealer but everyone pretends he's a fisherman.

"I was just getting food out the fucking fridge," I mutter.

"Stealing it more like," Wendy says.

Can you steal food out of the fridge in the house you live in? It doesn't matter that I was doing exactly that, not really.

Mick gets up. "Jimmy's not goin to give us a tyre, Wends. C'mon, I'll pick one up tomorrow."

"And how are we going to get back to yours, eh? If you think I'm walkin back through this estate in the middle of the fucking night, you're thicker than you look. I keep tellin you to sell that shitheap for scrap and buy something that'll actually go. It's not like you don't have the money, Mick."

"The Baron is not a fucking shitheap. And it wasn't a fucking flat. You leave anythin on the Broadway more than five minutes these days and it's nicked, fucked, or slashed dependin on the weather." He laughs like this is the funniest thing he's ever said.

I believe him though. It probably wasn't a flat. It isn't the middle of the night either; it's five p.m. But the Baron is a shitheap. Occasionally Wendy has to be right about something.

The back door bangs, screams open, bangs again. We all hold our breath, Mick included—in that we have about as much choice as Mum does.

Dad takes a long time getting to the front room; I hear him swear at the kitchen table when he walks into it. "Ah, what the fuck is all this? What the fuck you all doin here?"

Like I said, we're rarely all in the house together, and whenever we are none of us mean to be. None of us want to be.

"Mick got a flat on the Sands, Dad. You got a spare that—"

"It wasn't a fuckin flat, Wendy, Christ! You know what the Broadway's like, Jimmy. Some bastard—"

Dad staggers through the door, past Wendy and into his beat-up armchair. I can smell him: lager, sweat, chilli, and the cold. When I get brave enough to look up, I'm relieved that his red-faced, thin-lipped rage is only for Mick.

"Fuck off, Michael Whitney. If someone did for you or your fuckin beat-up Beamer, lit up red as the fuckin sky at night, then it's for good fuckin reason." He closes one eye, but its neighbour stays half open. "Fuck off out my house."

Dad's like all the olds around here: he doesn't care that he lives in England's povviest town; he revels in it. Mr Ingles calls it the Indices of Multiple Deprivation. He showed us a spreadsheet once with entries for income, employment, health, disability, crime, and living standards. Of nearly thirty-three thousand neighbourhoods, we were in his words, literally streets ahead. Dad doesn't see it that way. When they tried to bulldoze the chalets before I was born, he went to court with all the other residents and won. I think it's the only thing he's proud of. I can't ever remember a time when any of the shops on the Broadway were anything more than shuttered, graffitied spaces with names I can't read, or when a new burnt-out anything made me stop and look, or a winter where our wooden houses didn't flood; our walls are patterned with varying tidemarks and

Mum knows the year of every one of them. Dad's still proud of it all. He calls it self-reliance. But he needs a lot of drink to say so.

"Dad, we need a spare."

He hauls himself out of his armchair. "Well, you ain't gettin one. Fuck off, the lot of you." He looks at me then, his still awake eye getting wider. "What's she done?"

I hear the louder hiss of Mum's oxygen cylinder when she turns it up; I can imagine the rise of the bobbing red ball inside its gauge. "She was . . . stealing food . . . for the . . . Martins."

"I wasn't!" My hands are angry fists until Dad starts coming toward me; I have to let them go so that I can try to get away. "I wasn't. Dad, I wasn't!"

His shadow makes me cringe and I stop trying to get up. He's too drunk to hit me right, but he still gets that soft spot just below my temple and my teeth rattle together, trapping my tongue. I make a stupid sound, like a dog that's been kicked in the ribs, and then I put my hands up in time to protect myself from the next punch. Dad's lost interest anyway; he backs up, staggering again on his way back to his armchair.

I cough, spit and it comes out red.

"Ugh," Wendy says, still not really looking.

When no one else says anything at all, I get up and run out the front room, around the narrow bend of hall and then into the bathroom. I lean over the sink and spit red again before rinsing out my mouth. I'm examining my tongue in the mirror, trying to find the bite that I've made, when Mick comes in. He looks at my reflection and winks. Grins.

"Seems a shame to waste the opportunity."

I elbow him in the chest when he tries to touch me; when his cold hands grab at my waist, when his fingers pinch at my skin.

"C'mon, Suse, don't be a bitch about it."

His hands slide up inside my T-shirt. I bite down on my swollen tongue again. Our faces look ugly in the mirror, so I stop looking. I try to push him off, try to reach the door, but he follows too fast, never letting go of my shirt, pushing me back against the tiles. His breath is hot, the bristles of his stubble spiky, his tongue hard, erect.

"You taste good."

I taste of blood.

He yanks down my jeans without undoing them and then my knickers, kicking my feet apart, making me grab hold of him for balance. He thrusts one finger inside me, then two.

"God, you're always so ready." He says it like the idea revolts him, but he's still smiling. Still grinning. "You like that, don't you, bitch?"

I don't want to, but I do. I don't want to like the words he uses and the way he always uses them, but I do. Maybe it's because I've watched him for years from my bedroom window, washing down cars in the street, his shirt tucked into his back pocket, his tattoo black against the white of his skin. It's more than that, I know. It's because he's with my sister.

The tiles are cold, cold against my shoulder blades. He never uses a condom, and I never ask him to. I try not to cry out; I try not to wonder where everyone else thinks he's gone. I try not to listen to the filth that he hisses into my ear.

He never waits for me to come. Maybe he doesn't want me to. If it's a consideration at all. And maybe I'd like myself a little more if I didn't. But I do. Almost every time.

Mr Ingles sometimes lends me books on the sly. He says I'm the only one in any of his classes that could make it out of this town. They're not the books the school makes us read. They're just as old, just as hard to read, but the difference is I want to. He gave me one I don't think he meant to once, because it was pretty dirty. I still liked it though. Instead of coming, or worse, *cumming*, they called it spending. It's a far better word for it. As if every one of my ugly and violent orgasms has cost me something.

This time it doesn't cost me anything at all. Or Mick. Because the lights go out.

He lets me go straightaway, swearing when he pulls out of me, still swearing when he zips up his jeans. I try to do the same but I'm shivering in the sudden cold, sweat drying to an itch.

"C'mon, Suse! You decent?"

I don't answer him. I can already hear Wendy shouting his name.

"C'mon to fuck, Suse. Right, I'm goin first, alright?" He pushes me back against the tiles. "Wait a few minutes, alright? Alright?"

"Alright."

I hear him swear a bit more as he feels his way towards the door; hear the lock pop, the door creak open, letting in no new light at all, and then close again behind him. I stand shivering in the dark, the tiles still cold against my back, but while they're still there I know where I am. I start counting in my head but soon give up. I can hear them all still in the front room, swearing, shouting. No one is shouting for me.

I don't like the dark. I've never liked the dark. Wendy loves it, maybe because it was her right-hand man when we were kids. But even when she was torturing me she never really got it. It's not what's hiding in the dark that scares me. It's just the dark. It makes everything small. It's heavy and thick and it's all you can see, all you can breathe. It makes a bathroom feel like a coffin.

I run out into the hall too quick and bounce off the corner of the front room wall, banging my head, my left shoulder. It hurts, but not enough to make me stop. The hall feels as small as the bathroom. Smaller. I grope my way along the wall, following the sounds of my furious family. When I stave my finger against the hinge of the front room door, I hiss, bringing it up to my sore mouth, and then I stumble in, nearly crying with relief.

Wendy is still standing in the middle of the room. She's holding up a fake Zippo that blows left and right in hidden draughts, pulling ugly at her face. Dad's swearing so much I don't need to see him to know that he's still in his beat-up armchair.

"Think the lights are out on the whole street," Mick says, and I hear the squeak of his arm against the window. "Which ones still got folk in 'em, Jimmy?"

Dad belches and swears some more. Not many, is the answer. The Old Lion pub across from us was torched nearly three years ago because of all the drug dealing. Dad hates junkies and flash gits like Mick, but he hated losing his local more. Now he has to go to The Mermaid, which is nearly on the front. More than half of the houses on our street are boarded shut with graffitied steel; half again are as burnt-out as the Lion; of the remaining three, only one is anywhere near to us. I don't know what happened to most of our neighbours—where they went before or after their houses were destroyed. They just go. People do that all the time. They just up and go.

"Fat Bob's is two houses left," I say.

Another squeak. "Can't fuckin see. Might be out too."

"Christ, Mick," Wendy snaps. "Why d'you have to get a fucking flat? I hate this place!" The last part comes out as a screech, which only stops when we all hear the nasty creak of Dad's armchair.

"Well fuck off then, gel. Fuck right off. No one here'll be stoppin you."

Wendy doesn't move, but she looks over at me. I wonder what she sees. To me, she looks like a tall-booted mannequin glowing orange. I'm probably just a shadow.

"Think I can see lights out on Breckfield," Mick says. "Nothin closer."

We've never had pavements or street lights on Brooklands, but we're luckier than most. The council stopped repairing a lot of the roads a few years back and they're either narrow dirt tracks or potholed and cracked tarmac. Some of the chalets out on the Flats don't even have mains sewage.

Mick chuckles, his voice getting closer. "You pay the electric, Jimmy?"

"We're on a fuckin meter, wise guy," Dad says, and if I was Wendy I'd have shut my lighter, because his voice is turning back into the one that wants to hit someone.

No one says anything for a bit. I think about trying to phone Julie even though the signal's always crap, but then remember I've no credit. We don't have a landline either; kids kept chucking tied trainers over the wires, and when that got dull, they just knocked the poles down. Dad said he'd rather spend the line rental down the pub.

When no one says anything for even longer, it gets a little spookier. I'm dead aware of the dark of the hall pushing at my back, so I creep into the front room a bit more, even if that means I don't have anything to hold onto anymore. I can hear Wendy and Dad and Mick breathing; I can hear Mum trying to. The hiss of her oxygen cylinder is the loudest of all.

I jump when Mick says: "You got any candles, Jeanie?" So does Dad, I think, because I hear a thud in his corner and then a curse.

"No . . . candles."

"Right, well, we can't just sit in the fuckin dark. What about makin a fire? You still got that old barbecue out back, Jimmy?"

I don't want Mick to go out back. Don't want that at all. I start feeling my way closer to his voice, but it's harder to follow than I thought it would be.

"You ain't makin no fire in my fuckin house, Mick."

"Right, so what, we do just all sit in the fuckin dark then? You know no bastard's goin to jump in their van and nip down here to fix whatever the fuck's gone wrong, right?"

"We could . . . go . . . to bed."

"It's dinner-fucking-time!" Mick bellows, and I'm surprised to remember that he's right. It doesn't feel like dinnertime. The dark is so absolute it might as well be the middle of the night.

I'm still shuffling towards Mick's voice—it's easier now he's shouting—when Wendy sparks up her lighter again, so close to my face that I can feel its heat enough to shriek.

"What are you doing?" She's looking at me now, but even though she's the only thing I can see, I don't look back.

"Trying to sit down."

She waves the fake Zippo high enough to expose the angry shadow of Mick near to the far end of the sofa. I grope for the closer edge of it and sit down. I hear rather than feel Mick doing the same; we're too far away.

"This is the third fuckin world right here," he mutters, but maybe not loud enough for Dad to hear him.

If this was one of those crap TV movies Mum watches on Channel Five every afternoon, we'd be minutes away from huddling close around Wendy's fake Zippo; Mum and Dad sharing forgotten memories from our childhoods; Mick proposing to Wendy or professing undying love for me like in Mr Ingles's books; all of us realising one way or another that we love each other really. I'm not holding my breath, and Mum couldn't even if she wanted to.

It's just so quiet, that's what I don't like the most. Worse than even the dark. Maybe. Usually the lights and those quiz shows hide the outside enough I forget it's there. The real outside, I mean. I forget we're nearly on our own now.

The worst day was the one when I realised Old Western had gone. He'd lived next door to us all my life. Even Dad liked him. On the last Friday of every month he'd bring Mum daisies and Wendy and me sweeties and Dad a bottle of white rum that they'd both drink out back or in the front room depending on the weather. He used to own the whelk and jellied eel shop on the promenade, and when he lost that he sold them door-to-door instead. Dad said he got good rates from the shore boats and he was a stand-up fella because he always passed them on. Unlike Mick, Old Western really had been a fisherman once.

His house didn't get torched. A few days after he'd gone, some men in a white van came and put in the steel shutters and doors instead. A few days after that a letter came through the back door addressed to me. I stuffed it in my bag and waited to get to school to read it. I went into the toilets at morning break. There was nothing inside the envelope except a crumpled-up bit of paper. In printed black letters:

19 BROOKLANDS: NEXT TO CHAPPELS,
OPPOSITE THE BURNT OUT RED LION

And then underneath that, in Old Western's scribble: *Carefull of the Dark Susie x*

After I'd read it, I flushed the note down the toilet because I was still angry that he'd gone. Or probably that he could. It got stuck; I could still see the black print even when the toilet started filling up to the top, spilling dirty water onto the tiles.

A few days after that the graffiti started. Everyone knew Old Western, so his was a popular spot. Dad went out on a Sunday and spent two hours cleaning a big red-painted PEEDO off Old Western's porch, because he said it was the only one that wasn't true.

When Wendy suddenly shrieks, I nearly shriek myself. I nearly stand up; I nearly lunge towards Mick.

"What the fuck, Wends?" Mick growls.

"Mick?"

I can hear her moving and moving quick. I feel the cool whisper of her body as it passes near to me; hear the gassy burst of her fake Zippo. I still flinch from the light and her lunging face.

"What is your problem, Suse? What—"

"Jesus H. Christ," Dad mutters, and I can tell by his voice he's been sleeping.

"You think it's fucking funny, Suse?" Wendy's face throws even uglier shadows. "You think it's funny to creep up behind me in the dark, trying to scare the shit out of me?"

Like she used to, I think. But I can tell from her face that she knows it wasn't me. I haven't moved since I sat down.

She looks back over both shoulders, but doesn't move the flame from my face. "If it wasn't Mick it was you!"

I wonder why she thought it was Mick before she thought it was me, and then I see her free hand and forearm clamped hard across her breasts. We both hear movement in the corner where Mum sits at the same time. Wendy spins around, shooting out her lighter arm towards it.

"There's . . . someone . . . here."

None of us move. I can hear Mum's breathing getting faster, wheezier. I can hear the loud hiss of her oxygen because no one else is making any kind of noise at all now.

"There's someone here . . . someone here someone—"

Her oxygen cuts out like she's shut off the valve. That only ever happens when the district nurse needs to change an empty cylinder for a new one. The weird silence frightens me even then—now it stands up the hairs on the back of my neck and scalp in bunches.

Mum doesn't try to say anything else, which is worse. I stare at Wendy's drunk flame, and then I try to stare past it towards Mum's dark corner. I think I hear something—a muffled something—and even though I keep trying to work out what it is, I want Dad or Mick or Wendy to start shouting and swearing so I can give it up.

Finally, it stops. That muffled nothing becomes complete nothing. I can't hear anything at all.

"Jean?" Dad. The creak of his beat-up armchair. "Jeanie?"

I screw my eyes shut black. Open them. Black.

Wendy shrieks again when something thuds without echo on the carpet. I watch her flame drop down to the floor, exposing her scuffed leather boots. Exposing the thrown armchair cushion less than two feet away from them. She doesn't move; the fake Zippo doesn't move. The cushion was a Christmas present to Mum. I made it in home ec three years ago. Wendy's light shakes over the little stone cottage next to a silver rope of river.

And then I can't see either anymore. Only dark. Wendy shrieks again and her fake Zippo flies in a feeble arc: up and then down. It goes out.

I hear a little thud, a whimper. The creak of Dad's beat-up armchair again, his curse—but it's pitched high and alien—and then Mick's better one and the feel of moving air, maybe his fist. Another thud. I'm still on the sofa, but I've started trying to climb up towards the back of it, my sore fingers gripping at its spine.

Someone taps hard on the shoulder that I banged into the wall. It sends shocks down my arm and into my fingers. I let go my right hand and my body spins round. I stare up into the dark. All I see is the dark.

I get up. My thighs are shaking. When I step away from the sofa, I immediately forget where I am. Where the door is. A hand drops onto my good shoulder. It's heavy. I feel the weight of someone behind me, though they don't make any kind of sound at all. They walk me forwards a few feet. Another hand drops onto my bad shoulder. Both start pressing down hard and I drop to my knees before I get that I'm supposed to. I hear another too close sound—a whimper—and then realise that it's me. The hands disappear.

I'm breathing so hard that it takes a while for me to realise that I'm not the only one doing it. I reach out—flail out—and hit Wendy's leather jacket on my left; Mick's bare arm on my right. I can smell Dad dead ahead: lager, sweat, chilli, and the cold. And something else—something he's never smelled of before.

I whimper. Wendy whimpers. Mick and Dad make no sound at all. I don't need light to see us kneeling on the front room floor, facing one another inside a tight square. I can feel the heavy air behind us move, pressing us closer. I can feel it pacing restlessly around us. Black inside black. Heavier, closer, quicker. As though our collective fear of what he is, of what this is, is feeding him like MiracleGro.

Minutes pass like this. None of us move; none of us speak. The owner of the hands paces faster, even though I can't see him, can't hear him.

Finally Dad clears his throat. "You got the wrong house."

Silence.

I hear him shift his knees; I smell his sour breath. "I own this shithole outright, fellas, so if you're them come lookin for back rent, you got the wrong fuckin house."

There's a sudden scuffle where Dad is. I hear him start to curse and then his voice doesn't so much stop as run out. It gurgles. Wendy screams; I hear the slap of skin against skin and only realise it's her palm against her mouth when her scream muffles, chokes. There's a new smell. It's like the pork sides Dad sometimes brings back from The Mermaid. Another thud—a big one. I only realise that my hand is covering my mouth too when I try to breathe and can't.

I need to get up. My knickers are twisted inside my jeans, cutting into my groin hard enough to give my left leg pins and needles. "Mick?" I whisper, looking right. "Wendy?" Left.

They don't answer. I know they're there: I can hear them, feel them, but they're too afraid to answer me, even if they know that it doesn't matter; even if they know that the someone in here with us knows exactly where we are. Where he put us.

I feel a whisper of cool air at the back of my neck, moving left to right. Towards Mick.

"Fuck this." Mick gets up—I feel it in a fast whoosh of coppery air to my right and then faster still in front of me. I start trying to get up too, but my dead left leg drops me onto all fours. Wendy starts screaming for Mick to take her too, but I know he won't. She pushes against me as she struggles to get back onto her feet—the someone kicks her hard enough that she falls forwards into me instead, sending us both sprawling onto the carpet. It's wet. It smells.

Mick makes it as far as the kitchen, maybe even the back door. His scream is far away, but I can hear the dismay in it before the horror gets louder. And then nothing. More silence.

Wendy is sobbing when the someone comes back. We still can't hear him, can't see him. And now we can't even feel him. But he's still here. He's here.

Would this be when Wendy and I hug and clutch at each other like we never did when we were kids? Is this when we realise that there are worse things than each other? I grab for her when she gets up; I scream for her because my leg still won't work and she's my big sister whether she wants to be or not. I remember the books Mr Ingles gave me; I remember him telling me that family is the worst and best of everything—that it's why we exist at all.

Wendy screeches and falls back against me again, scrabbling for a hold of my sweaty cold skin. I shoot out my good arm and it slides through the hot slick wet of her chest. I don't scream. I don't take my hand away. Instead, I half kneel, my heels digging into my numb bum, my free hand drawing into a fist. I feel Wendy die: she runs over my good hand in hot hiccups. I hear her die in frothy breaths that are still trying to scream.

After, I don't try to get up because there's no point. I can't smell pork sides anymore. Just blood. I know the someone is still in here with me. Prowling around the front room. And I don't much care. We're despicable, is that it? Is that why? If it is, then it's a worse reason than no reason at all. It's worse than jacked-up kids knocking down telegraph poles; worse than the olds setting fire to everything they hate; worse than drunks beating up their useless wives and children, or jealousy spent through ugly sex, or councils making fancy spreadsheets and calling dirtshit poor something no one else can pronounce. Worse than the good ones jumping ship and leaving the rest of us behind. Worse than teachers pretending that there's something else, something better. *Somewhere* better.

Eventually, I lean back, wiping Wendy's blood on my jeans. My hands are still shaking, but it's not because I'm scared. Not anymore. Even I can see that despicable people can only breed despicable people. It's no reason at all.

I reach out my palms so I can stand, and my fingers brush against metal. Wendy's fake Zippo. I pick it up. It feels very cold. I thumb the wheel once, twice; the second time it sparks but doesn't take. I stand up slowly. Swallow. The third turn bursts into bright light. I hold it up and away from me. Dad and Wendy are sprawled on the carpet: Dad on his back, his neck a red smile; Wendy on her side, still letting out hiccups of blood. Her skin is pulled back in one big flap, and I think there's the white of her ribs inside it. I can see the shadowed, open-mouthed gape of Mum in her armchair. There's no blood on her at all.

I turn the light towards the front room door and the someone scuttles across it on all fours. I balk before I remember that I can't feed him any more of my fear. I step around Wendy, being careful not to stand on her outstretched fingers. I finally hear a sound, but it's not one I like. My imagination thinks it's a chuckle, even though it doesn't sound like one.

I creep towards the door, mainly because I'm being allowed to. Is it because I'm not as despicable? Maybe the someone doesn't know about Mick or all the stealing. I hold the lighter high and out, and it makes me feel safer even if it only exposes me and more shadows; even if it only makes the dark around it darker. It feels like a torch, a priest's cross. I feel for the door's edge with shaking fingers. I step into the hall.

I smell the petrol before I feel it splash against my skin. I've flung the lighter away from me and into the kitchen before I start screaming. It lands on its side on the lino, flame hissing bigger, exposing Mick's curled up body against the kitchen unit under the sink, pulling his face about. His cut-out eye dangling against his cheek.

I forget that I shouldn't be screaming. I forget that I'm not scared anymore. And then the petrol hits my face like it's been thrown from a bucket and I gag instead of scream, trying to turn my body away. More petrol hits my shoulders, my back. Another throw soaks my jeans, sucking them in against my shaking legs. The stink is bad—the stink is terrible—but the threat of it is worse.

I don't try to run back into the front room because I don't want to die with my dead family, and I don't run down the hall towards the bedrooms because I don't want to die anywhere else. I don't run towards the front porch because the door is always locked and I don't know where the keys are. My only escape route is through the kitchen and the back door, but the still lit fake Zippo is there, spitting and hissing, barring my way. And I know—I *know*—that the someone is there too.

I cough, try not to choke. Try not to cry. I edge my way into the kitchen, my soggy feet squeaking on the lino. The fake Zippo is lying right in the centre of the room and it's not a big room. I pretend that it's my only enemy because it might as well be.

A couple of feet in and my hip bangs hard against the kitchen table, making me shriek. I grab for its edges with my sore fingers, never taking my eyes off that hissing flame. Even though I just want to run—to take my chances and run for the kitchen door and the back door a few feet past it—I don't. I'm too terrified of what it'll feel like to go up like a bonfire. I know it'll hurt a lot worse than having my oxygen cut off or my throat slashed into a smile.

I try not to look at Mick either as I keep on edging towards the door, and that's easier to do, even though the fake Zippo keeps catching the dangle of his eyeball, making me think that it's still moving.

The kitchen door is very light—I don't even think it's proper wood—when I hit it with my shoulder, it starts swinging shut. I grab for it with a nearly silent scream, yanking it back too hard, banging it off the table. I make my hands into fists and stop its backswing with my foot. The fake Zippo is now far enough away that I can move out towards the space that the open kitchen door has left. The back door is less than two feet away.

The someone stands up. Like he's been crouching on all fours inside the kitchen doorway, waiting for me to think that he's gone. I still can't see him, but I can hear him in a slow whoosh of air rising up from the lino. And I can feel him. He doesn't breathe, he doesn't sweat. But he's there. Inches away.

Two hands punch against my chest, staggering me back into the kitchen. Towards Mick. Towards the fake Zippo.

"No, please. Nopleasenopleaseplease."

He stops pushing long enough for me to run as far away from him and the fake Zippo as I can without giving up any more ground. I smack hard into the kitchen table again, doubling myself over it, whacking my chin against its top, my teeth cracking together, singing high inside my head. I spit what tastes like more blood, and then turn around.

The light from the fake Zippo has gone. I don't know if it's because it's really gone or because he's standing between me and it. I try to listen for its hiss, but all I can hear is my own breathing and the blood rushing through my ears.

And then I hear a muted thump, maybe a kick. A groan. I bite down on my swollen tongue again. The groan is Mick. Mick isn't dead.

Another kick. Another louder groan. *Mick isn't dead.*

I imagine eyes looking at me in the dark. My heart kind of stops, and then starts banging too hard and too fast, making me feel sick again. Another kick. And I suddenly understand that I'm being offered a choice. Mick and me. Or just me. In Mr Ingles' books, the main character always knows what to do. In the end, no matter how scared they're pretending not to be, they know what the right thing to do is. I don't. And not just because the petrol and the fear and my heart are making me feel sick and a bit dizzy. Not just because if one of them was still going to be alive, I'd want it to be Mick.

If the someone is a vigilante like the olds down the Mermaid and Bobby's Bingo, he wants me to leave Mick behind. But if he's the Devil like in *Paradise Lost*, and God is waiting to see what I'll do, then I'm supposed to try and save Mick too. And if he's just a man like Dad said—a man come to get money or his kicks—then I'm fucked whatever I do. Even if my mind has made him into a thing so far removed from any kind of man that it hardly matters.

A finger—I think a finger—traces the left tendon of my neck, down to my collarbone where it digs in. I hear the raspy turn of the fake Zippo's wheel. I see its brief spark inches from my face. And as far as I care, it takes away my choice.

I turn and run. I run into and then around the kitchen's flapping door, my wet feet skidding on the lino as I grab for the doorframe. My sore fingers scream. The wood feels cold against my skin. I scrabble for the handle even as I hear Mick's groans getting louder, more awake. For a few seconds I think that it's all a lie—that the door is locked; that I never had any kind of choice at all—and then the back door gives in its usual bang and cold briny air rushes in, pushing me backwards.

Not for long. I lunge through the new space, ignoring the door's stupidly loud creak. I'm already down the steps, around the house and into the street when I hear the bigger bang as it shuts again. Mick screams high and long, but I pretend it's the wind. It could be—the wind off the Sands is as sharp as a bitch's tongue, Dad says.

I stop running when I reach what I think is the middle of the street. I stand shivering instead. There are no lights anywhere in Brooklands. I look right, where I know the black skeleton of the Red Lion is, but I don't go towards it. I look in the direction of Fat Bob's chalet, but I don't want to go there either. If I squint, I can see the lights that Mick saw out on Breckfield, but that's far too far away. I look back at the dark of my house.

I should be running, I know that. But I can't. This is my home, and it's surprisingly hard to leave it. I don't know what it was all for—what it *is* all for. Am I safe? And if I am, what do I do? Where do I go? What do I say?

I'm still shaking so hard that my knees keep almost giving way, bending me over and making me flail about for blind balance. I can smell the sea, which should be impossible because I'm still covered in petrol and Wendy's blood—but I can smell it all the same. I can even hear the crash of waves out on the Sands.

He comes out through the back door. It doesn't bang or creak open. It shuts with a tiny snick that I still hear. Over the wind, the waves, the shaking chatter of my teeth, the stutter of my breath.

I imagine eyes looking at me in the darkness again. I imagine that darkness sucking close until nothing else is left between us. I push my sore tongue against my incisor.

A hand grabs at my wrist, bringing it up in front of my chest. Fingers prise mine open and something crinkles inside my palm. When my fingers are forced shut, the round feel of it scratches at my skin.

I feel a breath that isn't a breath. A chuckle that isn't a chuckle. A threat that isn't even a whispered word. And then my fist is let go—dropped like a stone against my sore thigh.

I close my eyes because they won't stop watering. I take one breath and then another.

"Go away." But I don't think I say it. And no one is there to hear me even if I do.

He's gone.

I stand in the middle of Brooklands for a long time. Long enough for clouds to move inland, first spitting against my skin, and then beating down hard enough to echo inside the Red Lion's ribs and against steel shutters.

The sound wakes me up a bit. Or maybe it's because the worst of the petrol is washing away in the rain. I lift up my fist and let my fingers fall open. The paper doesn't crinkle so much now it's wet. I think of playing rock, paper, scissors with Old Western on the front porch as I peel it away from the rounder thing beneath.

I know what that thing is, of course. I let my numb fingers slide over its slick, bumpy surface for a second or two, and then I push it into my jeans pocket. I don't know why. Maybe because it belonged to Mick.

The paper is wet and getting wetter. I try to smooth it out, but I don't know why I'm bothering. I can't see it any more than I can see anything else. And I know what it says—I can *guess* what it says.

21 BROOKLANDS: NEXT TO OLD WESTERN,

OPPOSITE THE BURNT OUT RED LION

I screw it into a ball between my palms, and my skin is now numb enough that it doesn't hurt at all. I throw it into the dark.

And I start walking back towards Julie's bit.

UNKINDLY GIRLS

HAILEY PIPER

Hailey Piper is the Bram Stoker Award–winning author of *Queen of Teeth, A Light Most Hateful, The Worm and His Kings*, and other books of dark fiction. She's also the author of over one hundred short stories appearing in *Weird Tales, Pseudopod, Cosmic Horror Monthly*, and many other publications. She lives with her wife in Maryland, where their occult rituals are secret. Find Hailey at www.haileypiper.com.

On the third morning at Cherry Point, Morgan met the unkindly girls. Dawn had hardly touched the beach, giving the sand a grayish tone. Red rocks dotted the stone path from their small white beach house down to the water. Up the shore, a fishing boat cast off.

Morgan wore the ugliest swimsuit. Dad's decision—a one-piece, dull maroon abomination with sleeves and shorts. She'd never been allowed to wear a bikini, but in the past her swimsuits had looked presentable. The designer must've thought the faintest hint of shoulders and butt would draw too many wandering eyes.

Dad probably agreed. "You're still my baby girl," he'd said when Morgan complained. Six years old versus sixteen made little difference to him. He would scoff when he saw women and girls wear more revealing swimsuits. He'd call them unkindly—one of his favorite words, as if to look appealing meant flipping him off.

But Morgan had spent her life at his side and had seen him lick those chastising lips. She was not to become an unkindly girl. Never.

"You wouldn't do that to dear old Dad, Morgie," he'd say.

She'd come out early to dip into the water, but with so few people wandering the beach, she had her pick of seashells. The more colorful, the better. Hunting for them used to be a treat. Dad would only let her keep three per trip. He said to take too many would damage the ecosystem or something, but the hunt was the fun part.

Now, every shell that sparkled on the beach turned dull in her hands. She let them tumble back to the sand, one by one. A lot had changed at home since last summer. Try as she might to leave it behind, the change had followed her to Cherry Point.

"That is the ugliest thing I've ever seen."

Morgan dropped her last lackluster seashell and looked down the beach, where two girls her age walked the damp sand. One's face was all angles and wreathed in dark hair. The other flashed a soft smile; white stripes patterned her red hair where she'd bleached it. They wore dark, baggy pants and loose-fitting blouses that bared their chests.

Unkindly. The word popped unwanted into Morgan's head. She'd never glanced at other girls' chests the previous summers, but now Dad's eyes dominated hers.

"Like wearing blood," said the pointy-faced girl, still fixated on the swimsuit. "Sickening."

"Isn't it?" Morgan asked, tugging one stunted sleeve. "That's what the tag says. Ugliest Swimsuit, one size fits none."

The two girls giggled, and then the pointy-faced one beckoned Morgan. "I'm Blue, and the redhead's Clown. Follow us. We'll fix you up."

Morgan smiled to herself and obeyed. This wasn't unusual for summer vacation. Somehow, she always made at least one friend.

Neighbor houses squatted a couple hundred feet from each other, but closer to the wet sand stood a dull wooden shop. Water damage darkened its lower walls, and the discoloration gave the shop a sea-worn feel.

Blue and Clown led Morgan inside. Plastic shovels and pails dangled from nails, snorkels lined a metal tray, and bathing suits hung on a circular clothing rack. Plus, there were shelves of the usual gift shop garbage. A tacky ceramic crab clutching a flag in its claw read, "Ain't Life a Beach?"

The shopkeeper, a balding man with a scraggly goatee, let his eyes wander up and down the other girls' bodies. Morgan thought of Dad and how he'd never be so obvious. His shame always forced him to avert his gaze.

Fabric swatted her arm, tearing her gaze from the shopkeeper. Clown shook a plastic hanger, dangling an aquamarine two-piece swimsuit with navy-blue striping. Shiny sequins lay trapped between layers in the trim. They looked almost like scales and made Morgan think of mermaids.

"Lovely, yes?" Blue asked. Her smile was all teeth.

Morgan shrugged, but Blue was right. It was gorgeous.

Blue guided the bikini to Morgan's front. "On you. To die for, yes?"

Exactly Morgan's thinking. Dad would kill her.

Morgan stepped back, letting the two-piece dangle again. "It's pretty, but I don't have money."

"We'll spot you," Blue said, taking the hanger from Clown. "In return, you hang with us tonight on the beach. Agreed?"

Morgan shrank inside. If only it weren't so easy to make friends, Dad would have no one to chastise, and these would be peaceful vacations, nothing more.

Blue laid the swimsuit on the counter. The shopkeeper didn't look at her now, his eyes sharply focused on the cash register. Clown reached inside her blouse and pulled out a black purse. Dollar coins thudded on the checkout counter. Morgan couldn't see their faces, but they made her think of pirate doubloons.

Blue pressed the swimsuit into Morgan's arms. "At the beach, just before sunset." She marched past, and Clown trailed her.

Morgan began to follow them out.

The shopkeeper cleared his throat. "Watch out for them two."

Morgan turned to him. "What?"

He ran his fingernails from temple to goatee, scratching an itch he couldn't catch. "Every summer, they come to Cherry Point and sell dope up and down the beach. Don't get caught in their mess." He began to fiddle with a coin, but his eyes focused on Blue and Clown as they sauntered out the door.

Vacationers, not locals.

They were just the kind of girls who'd make Dad avert his eyes.

If they would stop going to the beach each summer, maybe he wouldn't have to see any unkindly girls. Sometimes he saw them at the pool in Syracuse, but nothing would come of that. Too close to home.

When Morgan was little, she'd thought their beach trips were a fun way to spend each summer together after Mom died. Cape Cod, Miami Beach, La Jolla. Different coasts, different kinds of beaches, but always full of sand castles, ice cream, and splashing in the shallows, though never past the sea shelf where the undertow might suck her into the deep. Safety first was one of Dad's rules.

At each beach, Morgan made a friend. She never meant to. They would stumble into each other, or Morgan would see the other girl wearing something pretty. A day would pass, Dad would disappear for a night, and then they would head home.

Morgan tiptoed through the beach house and into her room, where she stashed the aquamarine bikini beneath her sagging mattress. Cool salty air swept through an open window and across her arms. She stripped out of her maroon one-piece and dressed in a tank and shorts. She'd meant to swim, but now a grimmer outlook haunted her thoughts.

She would have to tell Dad about the girls. Since Mom was gone, she'd told him everything, even after she realized he hadn't been telling her everything in return.

Utensils clinked in the kitchen. He was awake.

She stared at her window, thinking about sneaking out, but Cherry Point lay hundreds of miles from Syracuse. If she ran away, she'd just have to come back. He would think her unkindly for worrying him, and he might then worry that she knew his secret.

She traipsed into the kitchen. Dad loomed over the stovetop, his thick yet dexterous fingers sliding an egg from bowl to rim to pan. He wore a blue-and-white Hawaiian shirt, khaki shorts, and white sandals. Harmless middle-class vacation father—his best costume.

"Morning, Morgie," he said. "Out early?"

"I wanted to swim while it was cool," she said, plopping down on a stool by the kitchen island. The pedestal creaked around a loose screw.

"Your hair's dry." Dad didn't look at her. Somehow he just knew these things. Another egg cracked and sizzled.

"I didn't get a chance. I made a friend."

Dad focused hard on his hands as he slid his graceful spatula beneath the omelet. It flipped and hissed against the pan. "That's nice."

"A couple friends, actually." The cold marble countertop felt soothing under Morgan's palms. If she kept them there, could she keep from getting blood on her hands?

Dad picked up a knife. Its blade slid around the omelet, sawing off brown arms of crust. "Staying safe, right?" he asked, working magic with pepper and cheese. "Staying kindly?"

Dad laid a plate on the countertop. The omelet was perfect, Dad having cut off all signs of burning and crust without losing any of the cheesy yellow center.

Morgan swallowed before biting. "Yes, Daddy. Always."

He would watch her leave tonight. He would see Blue and Clown, and then lick his chastising lips.

Morgan didn't say goodbye in the evening. They wouldn't really be apart, after all, though only she would approach the beach, where the unkindly girls sat around a small fire just outside the tide's reach. Coastal winds batted at the flames. A storm was coming.

"Now what are you wearing?" Blue asked. She and Clown had not changed out of loose-fitting blouses.

Morgan wore baggy jeans and a hoodie. She'd told Dad that it was going to be chilly this close to the water tonight.

"Where's your swimsuit?"

"Under my clothes, same as yours," Morgan said. The girls tittered, and she realized their cleavage was still on display, no hint of bikini tops underneath.

Clown tugged a large brown bottle from the sand beside her feet, took a swig, and passed it around the fire, first to Blue and then to Morgan. There was no label. Brine clung to the bottom, as if the glass had been trapped in a shipwreck for a hundred years.

She thought of Dad and passed the bottle back to Clown. "Anything fresher?"

"We'll have something fresher after sunset," Blue said. She and Clown tittered again, the only sound Clown seemed to make. Her hair caught the firelight; its shadows twitched this way and that, as if alive.

As red and purple dusk gave way to black, cloud-covered night, the small fire became an island of light on the beach. Windows glowed down the beach, except at Morgan's house, but the rest of the world was dark. She wondered exactly where Dad was holed up. He could be anywhere the light didn't touch while the campfire illuminated the girls for him.

She'd figured things out after last summer. It wasn't like in the movies where he might've accidentally left out some crucial clue that grabbed her attention or a serendipitous news article happened to link their past vacation locales. She was older now and getting attention from boys at school. The way they looked at her wasn't so different from her father. They were just too juvenile to feel shame. Then there were his comments, his averted eyes, and the nights he'd go out before they left their vacation spots for home. Her brain had linked the chains.

Now she wrapped those chains around her legs. She wondered what heavy thing she'd tether them to and throw into the ocean to drag her down.

"The night's ready, girls," Blue said, standing up and turning to Morgan. "Fancy a swim?" She didn't wait for an answer, just tromped toward the water and expected the others to follow.

They did. Where the tide lapped at their feet, Clown spun around and held out a fist to Morgan. She took the offering, a coarse square that reminded her of dehydrated fruit.

"Ever been swimming high?" Blue asked. "Unforgettable."

And unkindly. Morgan made to pass the square back, but Clown was already running into the tide.

The light was gone. Dad would never know, same as he'd never know about the sequined bikini. Morgan lifted her palm to her mouth, and her lips closed around the square.

"Melts on your tongue," Blue said. She was already knee-deep, the tide drenching her clothes.

Morgan stripped and followed. Salt spray stung her nose. Her mouth filled with the static that blew from Dad's radio when he let her switch between stations. The other girls bobbed, dark driftwood on black waves.

Vague warnings slid beneath Morgan's thoughts. "The shelf. The undertow."

Thunder and waves drowned her out. The girls drifted farther. Morgan meant to follow. Only the thought of Dad anchored her to land. She wasn't an unkindly girl. Never.

Waves rolled toward her. She took a deep breath, stinking of seawater, and plunged beneath the surface. She couldn't see underneath, but somehow she knew that Blue and Clown were diving, too. The ocean became less an undulating wave, more a hand that grabbed Morgan and yanked her deep.

She floated beneath the creaking hull of an aging ship, its underside as glassy and coated in barnacles as the bottle passed between Blue and Clown. Inside, pirates dragged helpless hook hands against smooth walls. Their glass prison was filled with seawater and beer, and their pockets were so loaded with doubloons that they couldn't swim away.

Blue and Clown beckoned Morgan to the surface, their scaly turquoise and orange tails flapping. Neither mermaid seemed unkindly. They just wanted to see selfish men die.

An enormous golden tail rocked the drowning ship. The black sky flickered alive with lightning, painting the silhouette of an enormous woman against the clouds. If Blue and Clown were guppies, she was a shark. Plains of kelp matted her scaly head, and coral coated her arms. One gargantuan hand grabbed the bottle by the neck and slung it at the sky. It shattered in thunder, and its shards sliced every pirate to pieces. Their lungs flopped atop the water's surface, helpless as fish on land.

"Unforgettable," Blue said.

Morgan dug her hands into wet sand and hauled herself onto the beach. The tide splashed across her back, spraying saltwater into her mouth, but her muscles felt too worn to move another inch. Rain pattered the sand. The storm that swirled out on the water had almost reached Cherry Point. Whatever drug Clown had given to Morgan, it seemed to be losing its effect.

Lightning forked overhead, illuminating a smoking mound where the campfire once burned. Morgan thought she saw other shapes closer to the water. She stared hard at black-on-black outlines until the sky lit in another blue flicker.

Two naked bodies lay in the surf, red and white hair swirled around one's head. A bulky figure kneeled beside them. The flicker faded as he turned to Morgan, and he stared until lightning again tore across the sky. Its flash lit his familiar eyes and made his chastising lips glisten.

"I'm sorry, Morgie, but they were unkindly," Dad said. Thunder rumbled, and he paused for it to pass. "You know, don't you? I thought you knew when you told me about them." He started toward her.

Morgan's chest ached against the sand. She wanted to slither back into the water. She felt the lightning coming, the sky's tattling forked tongue, and the beach glowed as blue as her swimsuit. He could see her clear as day.

She lifted her head. "Dad—"

"What are you wearing, Morgie?" he asked, but he didn't say it like a question. He sounded the same as when she was six, the day he told her Mom wasn't coming home. Thoughts of him had shriveled out on the water, but now he was here and real, and he dwarfed every fantastical ocean.

"I-I-I—" Morgan tried to stand, but her legs felt waterlogged. She wondered if that was the drug's doing. She managed to sit up and wrap her gooseflesh-covered arms around her chest.

"It was only a matter of time, wasn't it?" He sounded calm, almost peaceful. He squatted down, drew her into his firm arms, and scooped her up against his chest. Fire beat inside in time to the spitting rain. "You had to grow up someday."

Morgan closed her eyes and tried to forget everything she'd realized since last summer. Dad used to be a good man, or at least that's what she'd believed. She could believe it again, couldn't she? If he just held her like this and warmed her bones against every chilly seaborne wind, she would believe anything he wanted.

"Daddy, carry me home," she said. Lightning flickered past her eyelids. "It can be like it was." She felt him walking, but he hadn't turned around.

"It can't," he said.

Water slopped at her dangling feet. She opened her eyes. The world lay dark between lightning flickers, but she made out frothing waves that encircled them, churned ugly by harsh wind. Dad was walking into the sea.

"Why?" she asked.

"Because I can't feel the way I feel about unkindly girls for you!" he shouted, loud as thunder. "Not my baby girl. Never."

She squirmed, but she'd exhausted herself, and he held her tight. Rain and sea crashed across her, plastering her swimsuit against her skin. He didn't look at her, averting his eyes for when lightning next lit the coast.

He didn't have to avert them for long. Chest-deep in the water, he plunged her under. One hand grasped her shoulder; the other shoved hard against her head. She clawed at his unyielding wrists and kicked at his legs and groin, but her feet were heavy, the water weighing them down. Lightning reflected in Dad's eyes. The storm would watch her die.

Was this how he'd killed the other girls, every summer vacation past? Had he held them first so that they might know a loving embrace before drowning them? Always far from home, those unkindly girls. They were vacationers who might've met anyone on the beach, but instead they'd met Morgan and her father. Dead summer friends were coming to collect. She had been his accomplice, knowing or not, and she would join them beneath the sea. He hadn't been caught for murdering them; would someone wonder why he returned to Syracuse alone this time? Would neighbors ask if Morgan died kindly?

He would tell them so. Someone would come to collect him, and he'd say his daughter died still his baby girl. Always.

Morgan stopped fighting. Her lungs screamed to keep thrashing, but she had to catch his gaze. She stared up at him, bubbles slipping from her lips. The sea calmed for a moment, as if anticipating a mighty wave. Dad glanced down at her.

Lightning flashed. She slipped her fingers beneath the lower rim of her bikini top and yanked it up.

Had he waited, the lightning would have faded and he wouldn't have seen, but even a glimpse seemed too much. His body shuddered backward. He turned his head, eyelids squeezed shut, the sight threatening to drive nails through his eyeballs.

The tide crashed across them, shoving him back and taking her under. It bought her time to break from the shallows. She dove under the next wave. Thunder crashed, but it came warped and uncertain underwater. She thought she might be swimming over the sea shelf by now. Her skin stung with cold as she surfaced.

"Morgie!"

Dad swam against the waves. His drenched clothing tugged at him, but she'd been fighting the ocean for an unknown time, whereas he had a fresh start. He could manage. His fingers snatched her ankle.

If he tried to drown her this far from shore, he'd probably kill them both. Would keeping her kindly be worth the sacrifice?

She looked out to sea for the miracle she'd seen earlier, but there was no static in her mouth, only her tongue. The drug had worn off. No mermaid was coming to save her, same as no one had saved her summer friends in every year past.

She let Dad draw her close and wrapped both arms around his trunk. He embraced her, too. He might've thought she was trying to hug him, one last desperate grasp for sympathy.

She sucked in a deep breath and thrust downward hard as she could. Flexing her legs, she kicked herself and Dad into the next wave, where the undertow pulled them under. He was stronger and larger, but freed of land, she could move him.

He shoved at her face. Lightning revealed his flailing limbs—he must've missed the chance to take a breath before submerging.

She didn't let go. Her lungs burned again, still faint from the first attempted drowning. She promised them this would be the last. Fighting him wasn't just about Blue and Clown. It was about all the unkindly girls he had already killed and all the ones who might die yet. No more.

Burning faded from her chest, her lungs at last giving out. The surface seemed far away, and she was tired. Ghostly cold ate through her muscles. One more unkindly girl drowned in the deep.

Lightning burned in ferocious flashes, the sky playing catch between two clouds, and the world flickered black and blue. An ocean of fish and seaweed appeared. Vanished. Returned full of faces. Morgan might've believed they belonged to mermaids or dead pirates, but when the next lightning flash brought them closer, she recognized them.

They were easy to remember; none had aged since she'd last seen them. Little girls, adolescents, teens, Blue and Clown among them. All her summer friends.

And there were strangers who crowded beyond, more than Dad should've murdered in the ten years he'd been taking Morgan on summer vacation, more unkindly girls than years in her life. Some were women who might've been Mom's age. Others he must've met when he was younger.

He had been finding unkindly girls for a long time. Noticing them and averting his gaze, he poured his strength into unlatching Morgan's legs. He didn't seem to realize she was good as dead.

The ocean formed hands in the uncertain darkness between lightning flashes. They hugged him, hugged her. The undertow, the dead—she couldn't tell what helped her hold him anymore. The difference mattered little to an almost-ghost. No more breathing, eating, or sleeping. No more distracting life functions. She could focus now, all secrets bare, and bend her will and body to one last purpose.

The dead wanted him, and she wouldn't let go.

A LOVELY BUNCH OF COCONUTS

CHARLES BIRKIN

Sir Charles Lloyd Birkin, 5th Baronet (1907–1985), was an English writer of horror short stories and the editor of the Creeps Library of anthologies. Typically working under the pseudonym Charles Lloyd, Birkin's tales tended towards the conte cruels rather than supernatural fiction, although he did write some ghost stories.

THE HEAT OF THE DAY was beginning to subside and an intermittent breeze had sprung up, stirring the pale dust coating the baked earth into ever-changing patterns.

In one corner of the compound, behind the Officers' Mess, a coconut shy had been set up, shielded from the setting sun by a faded awning, and positioned a few yards from a trio of parched linden trees. It was an evening in late August and the year was nineteen hundred and forty-three.

A wire trash basket, supported on trestles and half filled with weighty balls of tarnished steel, stood at a distance of twenty feet from the hollowed-out stands of the targets. These, however, were not the usual bearded nuts, but a row of dummies twice their size, like Aunt Sallys, nesting in the cups, their faces caricatured in primary colours, and labelled in thick black lettering so that there might be no mistake as to their intended identities. Their features were all female and each was surmounted by a tattered scarf tied into a bow; but the models from which these grotesques had been taken had obviously been male. Thus, "Miss England" bore the cherubic lineaments of Winston Churchill,

"Miss America" those of President Roosevelt, "Miss Russia" was a demonic Stalin, while the Misses "Poland" and "Free France" bore distorted resemblances to the one-time leaders of those countries.

To one side, and seeking the shade of the trees, were lined up five men wearing the striped cotton uniforms of the doomed. They were slumped in apathy, and had no idea as to why they might have been selected from the "appell," or roll-call parade, and marched away. They had, they fully realized, been fortunate in the fact that they had bypassed not only the crematoriums, known among themselves as "the bakehouses," but also the hospital which had come to be accepted as the point of no return.

Of the men who waited three were little more than skeletons, their eyes grown enormous in their sunken faces, their arms and legs diminished to barely covered bones.

David Cohn, the youngest and biggest of the prisoners, looked 'round him furtively with a speculative curiosity. He retained still some flesh and muscle on his once powerful frame and, as a result, appeared to be of a different species from the rest of his emaciated companions.

Four camp guards, fully armed, lounged with their NCO, Feldfebel Braun, sprawling at a wooden table which had been strategically placed to obtain the best view of the sideshow. It was early yet, and although they had been ordered to report with their prisoners at twenty hundred hours, Herr Major Beyer was not renowned for his punctuality and there was no knowing when he might choose to appear.

Cohn could not make up his mind what the reason could be for their summons. The Feldfebel had accompanied Leutnant Hering to where they were being paraded and had shouted out five names and numbers. Besides his own there had been those of Aaron Blumenthal, Jacob Mendel, Joseph Ullmann, and Samuel Wolf, and then they had been marched away immediately to the forbidden side of the electrified fence where they now found themselves, and which lay at the back of the Officers' Mess, territory unknown to them as the surface of the planet Venus. They had been waiting for God knows how long; they had not dared to ask for information.

Cohn found it hard to believe that only ten months had passed since they had been detained at that bleak siding. It had been his second such experience. The previous one had happened at the end of nineteen forty-one when, together with his wife, Lise, they had been rounded up with a score of other Jewish families and sent to a forced labour camp some sixty miles from Stuttgart. It had taken the cattle trucks into which they had been crammed a whole day to complete the journey.

He could still picture Lise at the station carrying an overnight bag and dressed as smartly as if she had been starting out on an ordinary expedition, for no one had known what was waiting for them at their destination. On the platform he had caught a glimpse of Hans Vogel hurrying, as usual, to his office, briefcase in hand, but pink with embarrassment he had refused to acknowledge his presence and murmured greeting, although their shoulders had almost touched.

It had come as a shock to him that none of the travellers, as they went about their normal business, had evinced the slightest pity, compassion, or even concern at what must have become an accepted sight.

By the time the day had ended Lise's head had been shaved and she had been dressed, in common with all the others, in a striped shift, straight off the back of some dead woman. But all of that had been in the forced-labour camp. The concentration camp had been still to come. He remembered that at the gates they had been divided into groups, men being sent to the right and women and children to the left, and later subdivided again into those who were capable of work and those too old or young or ill to be of use. He had not seen Lise since, but she had fortitude and was courageous and must surely have survived.

Through the open windows of the Officers' quarters drifted the music of a gramophone record—a Strauss waltz, one to which he and Lise used to dance during the months of their courtship, in the time when he had been a free citizen possessing human rights.

Life had been good in those days while he had been busy establishing his reputation as an architect and had, after work, rowed and boxed and played tennis on the courts in the public parks for relaxation. After the anti-Jewish demonstrations had begun he had thought recurrently of emigrating to America, had talked over the possibility at length with Lise, but she had been unwilling to leave her parents behind, and he to abandon his mother, and the chance had slipped by them. He thanked God that they had had no children.

An orderly walked along from the kitchen, swill buckets swinging from his hands which he proceeded to empty into a garbage bin of corrugated iron. Cohn looked away. To a certain degree he had been able to discipline himself to ignore the dreadful hunger that consumed them all.

There was the sound of laughter and voices, and the music stopped. They were coming out now, a little procession of officers wearing the black uniform and silver flashes of the SS, followed by a straggle of mess waiters, one of whom carried a tray on which were set out glasses and a bottle of cognac. Due to the heat the officers' tunics were unbuttoned and they wore no belts. Their faces were flushed. They were all of them there, save for a few of the Leutnants who must be on duty.

Feldfebel Braun and the escort at once sprang to their feet. "Atten-shun! Present arms!" There was much stamping and slapping of wood or metal.

Herr Oberst Albrecht walked slowly forward, his hands clasped behind his back. He raised one arm in a languid salute.

"Heil Hitler!"

"Heil Hitler!"

"At ease, Feldfebel."

Cohn studied them from the corner of his eye. The standard of this elite Corps had deteriorated, he thought, during recent months. It was a pointer of hope, the only item of uncensored news as to the progress of the war which had not been bellowed at them morning and evening through the loudspeakers that listed the Third Reich's victories on land and at sea and in the air.

Major Beyer was the lone representative of the Senior Staff of a year ago, and he was florid, handsome, a burly giant of a man. He was joking with Oberst Albrecht as they walked out together, Albrecht paunchy and bald, with the wicked expression of an angry boar, watchful, yet filmed with suspicious stupidity.

Then there were the newcomers, Oberleutnant Dorsch and Hauptmann Fochtmann, unconcealed sadists and as vicious as hell with their megalomania of extreme power over the defenseless. They were both of them in their late thirties. Finally, there was Leutnant Hering. Cohn had often wondered how he had contrived to get into the SS, and, having done so, why he had kept on, or consented to remain. He seemed so temperamentally unsuited. Karl Hering was timid and gentle, totally ineffectual and, if left to himself, quite incapable of inflicting pain. He seemed scared of his own shadow, and detested the harsh measures which he had to enforce.

It was rumoured that he was much closer to the Herr Major than duty or rank demanded. Beyer's homosexual tastes were no secret, and many of the younger men and boys from the camp had been taken on by him for temporary terms of light employment. None of them had been sent back to the camp. And an order to report to the Herr Major had come to be regarded as a shortcut to "the bakehouse." But such had become increasingly rare after Leutnant Hering's posting.

Conrad Beyer actually ran the camp, Oberst being virtually a figurehead who was seldom there, and whose main duties consisted of receiving and conducting parties from Berlin on their periodic tours of inspection, and dealing with a vast amount of reports and paperwork which were kept for his signature.

The Oberst liked Beyer. He was also impressed by him, for he had learned that on his mother's side he came from a good family, and since Albrecht himself could lay no claim to similar exaltation, he was flattered by, and rather in awe of, him. Sigmund Albrecht was a "dug out" from the First World War, and to him such things were important.

The Herr Oberst settled himself behind the table between Beyer and Hering. Oberleutnant Dorsch and the Hauptmann taking the outside chairs. All of them with the exception of Hering were smoking cigars. The orderlies were bunched together, within call, at the back door of the mess, and were waiting to see what was to happen.

Beyer gave an order to the NCO, who came smartly to attention. In his turn the Feldfebel barked a command, and Cohn and his companions executed a left turn which brought them round to face the seated officers.

Beyer glanced enquiringly at Oberst Albrecht, who nodded, and then he got up from his chair, resting his hands on the table top. He did not trouble to remove the cigar from his mouth.

"You have been brought here," he began, and his voice was easy, even affable, "you have been brought here to take part in what is really a kind of game . . . a competition. We have decided to put four of you from the camp on mess duty. Well, perhaps 'mess' is an exaggeration," he qualified, "since mainly it involves cleaning our latrines." He gave a friendly grin. "So maybe it is not such a misnomer! But it involves also disposal of the garbage from the kitchens, a task which will have, as I feel it is hardly necessary to point out, enormous advantages so far as you are concerned. Not only for you yourselves," he went on with a smile, "but also for your womenfolk over in their section." He paused. "I take it that most of you are married? Doubtless you will be able to find a way," he continued, "of getting the odd potato, or fish head, or any other delicacy, across to your dear ones." A murmur of laughter from around the table greeted this surmise. "On occasion a blind eye can be turned where a good and willing worker is involved—even here. You will notice that I am not offering you cheese or sausages, or roast goose, but I take it that any addition to your Spartan diet, however simple, will not come amiss." He removed the cigar from his lips and balanced it carefully on a glass ashtray. "As I have said," he continued, "we can make use of four of you; but there are five." He contrived to sound put out and vexed by this discrepancy. "The nature of the competition is this: the row of Aunt Sallys . . . quite a beauty chorus, by the way, aren't they? . . . are, you will observe, clearly numbered. Each one of you will now also be given a number, and then will have twenty shots at the target corresponding with the numeral allotted to you. I doubt if any of you will be successful in actually dislodging one of the frauleins, as they have been securely tied on, but should you be able to do so you will be awarded an additional ten points. So heave hearty! We will keep a tally of your efforts, and all but the man with the lowest score will be transferred to his new duties as from tomorrow. The loser will be returned to his former employment, which I am told is somewhat arduous. Naturally, the highest count of points will receive preferential treatment and undoubtedly a chance of a greater share of the perquisites." He glanced down at his watch. "You may take your time. There is no hurry—and Number One will start."

Beyer sat down after this speech, while the Feldfebel distributed the slips of paper to the prisoners, on which had been written a figure. Cohn stared down at his, which showed the numeral three, which corresponded with that nailed to the peg of "Miss Russia." He was puzzled. What was the catch, he wondered, or were the swine just bored?

He looked at the assemblage of black uniforms, relaxed and anticipatory, like an audience at a theatre waiting for the rise of the curtain. The officers had pushed back the chairs on which they were seated, and the gleaming leather of the jackboots on their crossed, sturdy legs shone like columns of polished jet.

In a low voice Karl Hering asked Major Beyer incredulously: "They are really going to work for us? Is that wise?"

Conrad Beyer thrust out his lower lip and his eyes twinkled. "My dear fellow! Those diseased scarecrows! Have you taken leave of your senses?"

"Then why . . . ?"

The Herr Major laced his fingers across his wide chest. "It is the principle of the carrot and the donkey, my dear Karl. Incentive. What human beings can, and will, do, given strong enough incentive is sometimes fantastic. As you will see! These men are scarcely in a condition to compete in the Olympic Games!"

An orderly came forward to fill their brandy glasses and when he had retired Major Beyer said: "They may begin, Feldfebel Braun. We are quite ready."

Aaron Blumenthal was the first. Cohn had known him all his life. He was a few years older than himself, and had managed a highly successful jeweller's shop in Stuttgart. Then he had been a stout, benign little man, with a wife by the name of Grete, whom he had worshipped. Now he could weigh no more than ninety pounds. He was trembling so much that he could barely grasp the heavy steel ball which the guard handed to him. His first three shots, with the sum of his small strength behind them, went wide, and Cohn saw angry and desperate tears start to his eyes. The fourth struck "Miss England," at which he was aiming, lightly on the painted cheek.

"Take your time," prompted Major Beyer's voice mildly. "There's absolutely no hurry." The Feldfebel made a mark on a piece of paper.

Aaron Blumenthal rested gratefully. There was so much at stake. Extra food, which would mean added life, even a possibility of survival for himself and for Grete, for someday the war must come to an end, the Allies must be the conquerors, and then those who had still managed to cling to life would be liberated. He knew that the same thought was also uppermost in the minds of his friends. And yet one of them must be the loser, and the rations in the camp were in themselves a death sentence. So far as the question of health and strength came into it the odd man out would in all probability be either himself or Samuel Wolf, who was by far the oldest man among them, almost of a different generation.

Aaron took careful aim, and the Feldfebel made another mark on his card. After the final shot had been made he had been successful in gaining for himself a score of thirteen. He stepped back exhausted. From a great height in the sky came the drone of many aircraft heading northeast.

Next to play was Josef Ullmann, who had once been a scientist. Only yesterday the camp "underground" had reported that his wife, Hilde, had either died or else been liquidated during the previous week, but there had been no mention of his daughter, Herta, in the rumoured list of casualties. Herta had just passed her seventeenth birthday and so should have greater resistance, and it was for her sake that he should be among the winners. He had heard, too, that she was with child, presumably by one of the SS guards. He began to play what he deemed to be the most important and grisly game of his life.

Sixteen was Josef Ullmann's total.

David Cohn took up his position, weighing the steel ball in his right hand. He had been a good athlete and so was not nervous. He threw overarm and smacked the ball straight into "Miss Russia's" face. A burst of clapping and cries of encouragement came from the watching officers. Smack. Smack. Smack. The painted effigy rocked on its support with the force of the impact. At last, he thought, there was something he could do for Lise, some small protection which he could give to her. He was getting into the rhythm of the thing. The steel balls made a dull thwack as they crashed into their target, and Cohn wondered with what the masks could have been stuffed, whether it was sand or earth or sawdust.

He was beginning to feel the glow of achievement, and the thought of his responsibilities gave him added strength. If only he could but topple that vacuous grotesque from its stand and gain those precious bonus points and the privileges that would go with them. The steel sphere whirled through the air with all of his will behind it, but the added force was at the expense of accuracy, and the ball flew high and to one side, parting the hair that framed the crudely painted face.

The scorer looked towards Major Beyer who shook his head. Cohn felt rattled, and the next shot went wide also before he was able to pull himself together and finish with eighty percent of the possible maximum.

"Not bad!" he heard Oberst Albrecht exclaim. "Not bad at all!"

A pair of blackbirds came to rest in the drooping leaves of the linden trees, skirmishing there and calling to one another.

Cohn was followed by Wolf, and it was a case of comedy following drama, of the clown the hero. "In life" Samuel Wolf had been a theatrical producer and had remained in Berlin during those dangerous years when he could have left Germany and followed his career in any country of his choice. Despite the pleas of his friends he lingered on, like so many others, until all doors of escape had been closed, and now not only himself but Louise, his French wife of thirty years, were having to pay the price of misguided loyalty.

The elderly man's first four attempts were complete misses, which was not astonishing since without his spectacles, which upon his arrival had been removed from him for the sake of their gold frames, he was extremely short-sighted.

He heard the mockery from the spectators. "You must do better than that, Grandfather Moses. Pretend to yourself it's Jesus on the Cross at which you are aiming. Or our beloved Führer. Put some guts behind it!" The advice came from Oberleutnant Dorsch who had risen to his feet to get a better view. His head was flung back in amusement, his hands were splayed out on his hips, jackboots straddled. With mock severity Herr Oberst Albrecht frowned at him to be silent. Such barracking was undignified.

Louise must have a chance. It was disastrous for her that he was myopic. He must give her a hope of survival, however remote. He was swaying with weakness. He changed his tactics, narrowing his eyes in an attempt to focus and lobbing the ball towards the indistinctly observed outline of "Miss Poland," but hitting instead the adjoining target.

"Left . . . to the left," called the Oberleutnant.

He endeavoured to close his ears to the comments of the officers, who had rightly ignored the Herr Oberst's token caution, so that he might concentrate, and waited anxiously after his last effort for the result to be read out.

"Thirteen," announced the Feldfebel.

The old producer was scarcely able to stand. He must not let them see how near the end he was.

The final contestant was Jacob Mendel. He was the second youngest of the competitors and, after Cohn, the one in the best trim. He scored sixteen and, with one lucky swipe, nearly succeeded in dislodging "Miss Free France," causing her to tilt back on her support at a rakish angle, as if savouring some riotous peasant joke.

Mendel was unfortunate in his appearance, which for propaganda purposes would have delighted Streicher; but he had a double spur to urge him on: Ingeborg, his gay and feather-brained wife, who had proved herself so unexpected tough in adversity—and young Michael.

"Bravo!" called Oberst Albrecht. "It is the same in play as it is in war. It is our enemies who receive the biggest knocks!" Beyer leaned across and whispered something to him, causing him to nod in agreement. "There is a draw," he announced, "for the bottom place. So we will have a play-off. Numbers one and four, is it not Feldfebel?"

"Yes, Herr Oberst."

The bye was played out in tense silence, Aaron Blumenthal emerging the loser. Their scores were seven and eight. Blumenthal stood quite still, the tears coursing down his sunken cheeks. He blamed himself for having given way to panic. Wolf was holding on to the rope from which they had been throwing, out on his feet.

Oberst Albrecht got up. "Feldfebel," he said, "we have witnessed a remarkable display of athletic prowess. It is time for you to distribute the prizes to the competitors. Yes, Number One shall have his also. It will be in the nature of a consolation." He raised his arm in the salute and all the officers leaped up, "Heil Hitler!"

"Heil Hitler!" came the ragged response.

The Feldfebel and one of the guards marched down the alley to untie the targets. At the same moment Karl Hering turned on his heel and began to walk quickly away towards the Officers' Mess. His face was ashen and his mouth tightly compressed. Major Beyer watched his slim figure with amusement. He allowed him to cover half of the distance before he spoke. "Leutnant Hering," he called softly, "come back. Come back and sit down next to me. The show is not quite over and I do not wish you to miss any of it." His mouth curved in a pleasant smile, but his blue eyes were icy.

The young Leutnant faced him with a set jaw. "I have duties to attend to, Herr Major," he said, speaking with difficulty.

"They can wait. Come back and sit down beside me," repeated Beyer. "I am sure that you have the Herr Oberst's permission to do so."

Karl Hering saluted. "Herr Major!" He returned to the seat which he had just vacated, but his fists were clenched, and there was sick loathing in his heart.

Silence fell once more, a silence curiously significant and intent. The faces of the officers were expressionless as carvings. The highspot of their evening was about to come.

The Feldfebel had finished distributing the trophies among the prisoners and now stood to one side, his gun tucked under his arm. Major Beyer addressed himself to the waiting men. "You may open your bundles before being returned to camp," he told them graciously, "and you may take the contents back with you, should you so desire."

They began plucking clumsily with their fumbling fingers at the string which was tied to, and also treaded through, the canvas masks.

David Cohn succeeded in getting the wrappings undone, while the others were still struggling to disentangle the tight knots. The straw hair glued to the daubed and stained canvas slipped to the ground, and "Miss Russia's" sly countenance gazed up from the dust into which it had been dropped at the evening sky from which all colour was draining. The noise of many bombers, bound for England, was heard once more.

There was an expectant hush from the group behind the table. The mess waiters were thronging the doorway, and one of them winked at another. The blackbirds flew up from their tree and winged away over the wire fences, skimming the serried rows of huts that housed thousands of cadaverous wretches, and off into the freedom of the woods that lay outside. A tic began to work at the corner of Leutnant Hering's mouth as he sat rigid at the table with his eyes closed.

The prisoners did not look at one another, as each was occupied with his own task, now nearing completion. David Cohn was staring down at what he was holding in his hands. It was a human head—a woman's, with its features smashed and discoloured, the teeth broken, one eye crushed to a pulp. The hair had been shaved close to the skull, and the skin oozed blood, but he came to realize slowly that what he was cradling in his arms was the head of his wife Lise.

From his left there came a moan, inhuman in its abject misery, as Jacob Mendel regarded what he, too, was grasping.

Old Samuel Wolf appeared to be unseeing, turning what he held over and over, like an automaton, until he broke into an idiot's titter, spittle flecking his mouth and dribbling down over his chin and matted beard. An ululation, which might have issued from a beast in agony, came from Josef Ullmann as he recognized in the nearly unmarked face the identity of his daughter, Herta. His appearance was waxen, and he held the object as gently as if it had been made of fragile crystal.

The officers were moving, preparing to go back to the Mess. Oberleutnant Dorsch clicked his heels together. "A delightful entertainment, Herr Oberst." He made a stiff bow. "Herr Major! So very original!" He glanced at the line of prisoners and shrugged his neatly tailored shoulders in disgust. "The Wailing Wall!" he said. "They are so very unattractive. How they sicken one!"

David Cohn swung back his arms and hurled the ruined head which he was holding straight at Major Beyer, who stepped quickly to one side. At the same instant the Feldfebel opened fire, the gun stuttering in short bursts. He aimed at Cohn's lower abdomen and crotch, and the range was short.

Cohn sagged down into the dust, writhing and clutching at his stomach and genitals, making patterns of blood with the arching of his body, weaving like some giant and mutilated caterpillar on the cracked surface of the ground. The officers did not give him a second look.

The guards had circled the rest of the prisoners, guns at the ready. The Feldfebel barked: "Fall in. Right turn. Quick march."

Still carrying their burdens the men moved to the gate in the barbed wire that led back to the camp. "You will throw your trash into the dustbins as you go by," ordered the Feldfebel curtly.

Behind them, under the linden trees, and watched only with detached interest by a couple of orderlies, Cohn still twitched and jerked around spasmodically, which he was fated to continue to do with ever decreasing vigorousness for a long, long time.

The windows of the Officers' Mess sprang to light and emphasized the gathering dusk, and again waltz music softly filled the compound.

In the dusk outside Cohn had slowly dragged himself as far as the nearest linden tree.

A prick-eared police dog belonging to Karl Hering trotted out into the dust from the direction of the kitchens and stopped to sniff inquisitively at a blood-stained object which lay on the dried-up earth behind the abandoned table, but finding it insufficiently enticing padded on.

Leutnant Hering went over to collect the belts of the Herr Major and himself from where they were lying across the back of a sofa. It was a nightly ritual. He buttoned up his tunic and buckled on his belt as he re-crossed the room, and stood patiently waiting behind the older man's chair. Major Beyer finished his beer. He bowed to the Oberst. "It has been a long day, sir. I am permitted to retire?"

"Yes, Major."

"You appear to be fatigued also," said Beyer to Karl Hering. "Come." All except Oberst rose as they left the Mess.

On their way down the corridor they heard the sound of prolonged firing from beyond the wire fencing.

"Yes, it is!" Beyer answered in reply to his companion's unspoken question. "And the types from tonight have been included. We have a further consignment arriving tomorrow—and the ranks must be thinned. Also," he added drily, "we do not want gossip."

Halfway down the passage they passed an open door through which the moth-haloed bulb above their heads sent a shaft of illumination across the compound, at the end of which was the hunched taut figure of Cohn. He sat motionless hugging his knees, his head leant forward over his chest.

Leutnant Hering's hand caressed the revolver holster at his belt as he turned towards the doorway, but Herr Major Beyer made a gesture of dissent. "No, Karl." He strode across to where the young man was standing. "He will die eventually, and there is no point in wasting a good bullet." His arm lightly encircled Hering's shoulders, his large ring with its elaborately wrought coat of arms bright against the black stuff. "For that, my dear boy," he said, "is not the way in which wars are won!"

TEETH

STEPHEN GRAHAM JONES

Stephen Graham Jones is the *New York Times* bestselling author of thirty or thirty-five books. Most recent are *Earthdivers* and *Don't Fear the Reaper*. Coming soon are *The Angel of Indian Lake* and *I Was a Teenage Slasher*. Stephen lives and teaches in Boulder, Colorado.

THERE WAS A WOMAN waiting for him just outside his office. Kupier nodded to her, opened his door, and shrugged out of his jacket. Tuesday, it was Tuesday. He had to say it like that until noon sometimes to get it to stick.

The woman was now standing in the door he hadn't closed behind him.

"Well," Kupier said, easing into his chair, looking across his desk at her, "don't make me start guessing, here."

The woman entered, timid.

"Detective," she said.

Kupier spread his fingers and pressed his open hands onto all the manila folders on his desk, like he was trying to keep them down against something—the shuffle of the nine o'clock shift-change the woman was letting in, maybe—but then cocked his elbows, straightened his arms, pushing himself up. Because she seemed like the kind of woman who was used to that.

"Sit down," he said, offering her a chair.

She was wearing a denim skirt, her hair fixed close to her head. Sixty-five, give or take.

"I didn't know who else to tell," she said, then flashed her eyes out the open door, at the station house. "They told me to wait . . . that you—"

"They're real comedians at eight in the morning," Kupier said. "I think it's the donuts, something in the sprinkles."

The woman hid her eyes and clenched her chin into a prune.

"You have to understand," she said. "I started out just watching birds—"

"Ms. . . . ?" Kupier led off, his pencil ready.

"Lambert," she said. "I'm married."

Kupier wrote into his notebook *Tuesday.*

"Now," he said, leaning forward like he was interested, "birds?"

Mrs. Lambert nodded, wrung her hands in her lap. They were already red and chapped from it. The bench outside Kupier's office was wallowed out like a church pew.

"It's a logical progression," Mrs. Lambert said. "You start out just wanting to know the name of one you think has unusual coloring, a unique call, and then every time you see that bird, you say its name inside and it feels good, Detective, familiar, but now the rest of the birds in the park have names too, so you learn them too, and then it's trees, what kind of trees the birds are in. It makes the world more . . . more *alive*, Detective. Instead of birds and trees, you have elms and chinaberries and grackles and thrushes and—and—"

Kupier nodded, knew not to interrupt.

"And then, one day, one day you . . . you see it."

"It?"

Mrs. Lambert tightened her mouth, embarrassed, but amused with herself too, it seemed. "Maybe I shouldn't have—"

Kupier said it again, though: "It?"

"Them," Mrs. Lambert corrected, then started to say whatever she'd come to say but stood to go instead, suddenly unsure how to hold her purse.

Kupier let her get almost to the door. "*It,* Mrs. Lambert?"

Mrs. Lambert stopped, a mouse.

Kupier smiled, could almost hear her eyelids falling in defeat.

"Pellets," she said. "Owl pellets. Detective."

Kupier tapped the eraser of his pencil on a file before him, the James one, and tried to place it, attach it to the right dead body. But there were so many. "Owl droppings?" he said.

Mrs. Lambert settled back into her chair. She shook her head no. "*Pellets*, Detective." She sounded like a piano teacher. "When an owl catches the smaller rodents, it sometimes, it doesn't chew them. But that doesn't mean it can digest them whole, either. So it, it spits the undigestibles back up a few hours later. The hair, the bones, teeth."

Kupier pictured it. "Think I've collared a few of those," he said.

It was supposed to be a joke.

Mrs. Lambert nodded. "It's the only way we can see them, Detective. The owls, I mean."

"Because the park after dark is no place for a young woman."

The blood seeped up to Mrs. Lambert's cheeks.

"Tuesday," he said aloud.

"Detective?"

Kupier waved it off, asked her about these owls, then. She corrected: the *pellets*. He'd been playing this game for twenty-five years, now.

"I don't want you to think I'm . . ." Mrs. Lambert started, stopped, finished: ". . . that I eat cat food or anything. Just because I collect—"

"It's underrated," Kupier said. "Cat food."

Mrs. Lambert finally smiled, God bless her.

"After you collect the *specimen*," she said, "you soak it in a pie tin of water, Detective. And you can see the little animal that was there." She held her hands up under her jaw, in imitation, and probably wasn't even aware she was doing it.

Kupier didn't look away. "Okay," he said, dragging each syllable, leaning forward to make this thing easy for her. "But you're not here because of the little animals, Mrs. Lambert. That's a different division."

Mrs. Lambert nodded, looked down, then reached into her purse. For a moment Kupier had no control of, he wondered if she'd made it back here with a gun somehow—the mother of some years-ago collar—but then it wasn't a gun she laid on the table, but a plastic sandwich container. It sloshed after she set it down.

"I don't think this was an owl, Detective," she said, patting near the container instead of the container's lid. It was something to note.

"You saved the water," he said back.

"Forensic evidence," she said. "I watch the shows."

Kupier smiled. Of course she did.

In the silted water in the container was a human finger bone. That someone had thrown up in the park.

Tuesday, Kupier said to himself again. Tuesday. By lunch he had it down, but he wasn't hungry anymore either.

That afternoon he walked alone to the park, to the place near the dying elm by the two benches that Mrs. Lambert had explained for him. He'd looked it up after she was gone, *Lambert*. It meant gray, featureless. Kupier pictured her husband in his easy chair with the remote control, his wife ten feet away under the kitchen light, watching the fragile bones of mice and voles resolve in a disposable pan.

The scene was two days old already. There was nothing, just a bird Kupier didn't have a name for.

"See anything?" he asked it.

It flew away.

The lab came back two days later, that it had been human saliva in the water, not canine.

Kupier got out another manila folder.

There were still three years until retirement. The rest of Homicide-Robbery was leaving him alone for it, mostly. Since the cancer.

On the tab of the folder he wrote Gray Owl. It sounded like a comic book name though, or an Indian, so he changed it to Finger, R. Ring: J Doe. They didn't know if it was male or female, just that it was adult. And bitten off. A specialist was supposed to be making a cast of the teeth; he was working off striations in the bone. Kupier told his captain this wasn't a trophy-thing, he didn't think. Maybe self-defense.

"Go home, Koop," his captain told him. "It's six o'clock, man."

The next morning Kupier was watching the steam roll off his coffee and waiting for Animal Control to pick up their phone. Their number had been on his door when he'd walked up; the note was stamped with two other precincts already. It had taken a while to find him.

"Yeah," the voice on the other end said. There were all manner of dogs in the background. Or maybe a lot of the same dog, but all saying different things.

"This is Detective Kupier," Kupier said. "You called about a finger."

The man on the other end paused, paused, then told Kupier yeah, yeah, the finger. What took them so damn long?

"How long's it been?" Kupier asked. A door closed somewhere far away and the steam of his coffee eddied back down into the cup.

"Three days," Animal Control said. "She's going to die, maybe."

Kupier switched the phone to his other ear, held it closer.

"Say again," he said.

"Penny," the man said, being attacked by a cat, it sounded like. "You don't know anything, do you?"

Kupier didn't answer, just got the address from the front desk, went down to motorpool to check out a car.

"Thought you just went out on Tuesdays?" the officer at the window said, and Kupier signed his name, took the keys from the drawer, walked through the garage, didn't answer.

Animal Control was a loud place. There was no one at the front desk, just a list of animals that had been run over and collected over the last two weeks. There was one column for dogs, one for cats, with tight, ten-word descriptions of each. Someone had gone through with a pencil and circled all the Labrador-type dogs, but missed one in the second row.

Behind the front desk in a cage was a green parrot. It didn't say anything. Finally Kupier walked around the desk, past the bird—nodding to it because maybe it understood more than just words—and into the tombs, or catacombs, or bestiary, or whatever they called it down here.

It was full of animals, anyway.

The man he found was in a wheelchair, spraying out cement kennels with a high-pressure hose, the water running back under him to the drain. The floor sloped down to it.

"This is about Penny," Kupier said.

The man winked at him, shot him with his finger gun, and said to follow him. His tires left thin wet trails; Kupier walked between them deeper into the place. Far off, someone was whistling.

They stopped at a stainless steel examination room.

"Not the owner, right?"

Kupier shook his head no.

"Just making sure," the man said, and did a wheelie-turn to a bank of files. On the wall behind him was the memo for their mandatory sensitivity training. It had just been last week.

What he pulled out was the temporary file on the Penny dog. She was a copper-colored Irish setter, and she was dying. The man held her film up, getting the light behind them, and nodded.

"This is her," he said.

Kupier took the X-Ray, held it up too, closer to the light. It was the color of motor oil.

Lodged in Penny's stomach was the radiation shadow of another finger.

"This common?" Kupier asked.

"Maybe," the man said. "We don't shoot film on them all."

"Why this one, then?"

"*Her.*"

"The dog," Kupier said.

The man shrugged, reached into Penny's cage. She nosed into his sleeve and he buried his fingers in her red hair, came up with a silver, bone-shaped tag with hearts engraved into the corners.

Kupier nodded: somebody might actually come get this dog. At least for the collar.

"You say she's dying?" he said.

"Wouldn't you if you had that in there like that?" the man said, cocking his own finger against his stomach.

"Well," Kupier said. "Is *she* going to?"

"Without surgery, yeah, maybe," the man said.

"I thought somebody was coming to get her," Kupier said.

The man shrugged. "X-rays are sixty bucks," he said. "And her owner's machine says they're skiing. They say it all at once, together, the whole family."

"Must have taken them awhile to get it right," Kupier said.

The man nodded, had somewhere else to be now.

Kupier stared down at Penny. "We need that finger," he said.

"You could just," the man said, "y'know. *Wait.*"

Kupier nodded. Both his hands were in his pockets.

"We need it now," he said, and turned directly to the man. "Can that be arranged?"

The man leaned back in his wheelchair, in thought, then shrugged what the hell, fingershot Kupier again. Kupier took the invisible bullet like he'd taken all the rest.

"You okay?" the man said, leading Kupier back to the waiting room, and Kupier just watched the missing dogs smear by on either side and wondered what it was like here at night. Whether they left the lights on or off.

Two nights later Kupier was eating alone at the Amyl River. It wasn't a cop place, just a bar. The preliminaries on the finger bone from Animal Control was that it was an index finger, not a ring like the one from the park. So it could still be from one person. Kupier crumbled his cornbread into the glass of milk he'd ordered. It was dessert; his wife had always only let him have it on Sundays. He left the spoon in his mouth too long. It wasn't Tuesday anymore, just Thursday or Friday or some other day. Behind him a dart thumped into its board, money changed hands, a woman met a man. Kupier stared into his glass.

Earlier in the day he'd looked up Mrs. Lambert's record. She was clean, and her kids were clean, and her husband was clean. Kupier was glad for them. He was already calling them the Gray family, picturing them standing in order from tallest to shortest. He was glad for them.

The dinner crowd left to the patter of falling coins, and Kupier moved from milk and cornbread to rye and water. It was all the detectives drank in the movies. He didn't want to have a taste for it, but he did, and that was that.

In the pocket of his jacket was the plaster cast of teeth the department had contracted out for. *Teeth*, Kupier kept saying to himself. It was the first case of his career that had to do with bite patterns. They were useless, though—a glass slipper he couldn't ask anybody to try on. All they told him was that whoever they belonged to wasn't missing any from the front. The real trick now would be to see if they fit into the bone from Animal Control. Kupier looked at his own finger, rotated it in the half light.

"So we know it's not you," a man whispered over Kupier's shoulder.

It was Stevenson. The transplant from Narcotics.

Kupier shrugged. Stevenson sat down anyway. "So this is where the old guard hangs," he said. "You on stakeout for the rat squad or what, man?"

"What are you doing here?" Kupier asked. They were both carrying their pistols in their shoulder holsters, the only two men at the bar with their jackets still on.

Stevenson lit a clove. The bartender scowled over.

"You know this guy?" he asked, nodding at Stevenson.

"We're buddies," Stevenson said. It was the precinct joke. He was already drunk, maybe more. He whispered to the bartender that they were on stakeout, too. Kupier stared at the bottles lined up before him, watching in the mirror as the bartender calmly removed the clove from Stevenson's lips, doused it in the dregs of an abandoned beer.

"Thought this was a cop place," Stevenson said.

"It is," Kupier said.

Stevenson laughed through his nose at the insult. They drank and stared and stared and drank, and then, deeper into the night, Stevenson smiled, tugged at the elbow of Kupier's jacket.

It was a man at the other end of the bar. He'd just walked in. One of his sleeves was empty. It made him carry his shoulders different.

"Your one-armed man," Stevenson said.

Kupier looked away. He should have stayed at the office, or gone home. Or to the park again.

At ten o'clock Stevenson left suddenly, like he'd just realized he was missing something. Kupier followed him out with his eyes. As he passed the one-armed man he turned to Kupier, pointed down at the man, his gestures drunk and overdone. Kupier nodded just to have it done with, and the one-armed man nodded back, raised his beer.

Instead of walking, Kupier took a cab. He wasn't committed to going back to the office yet, but wasn't going home either, and was two blocks away from the Amyl River before he recognized the one-armed man, lodged in his head. Goddamn Stevenson. He didn't even dress like a homicide detective, didn't walk like he had a shoebox full of crime scene photos tucked away in the top of his closet for his grandchildren to find someday.

Kupier stood on a corner trying to figure it all out, what he was thinking—the fingers, the one-armed man—and then a bus hissed up for him, unfolded its doors. Three gaunt faces looked down at Kupier from three separate windows.

Kupier recognized one of them from somewhere, the way the teeth fit into the mouth, or didn't. Kupier wanted to give him a cigarette for some reason, even touching his chest pocket for where they would have been, but then the bus driver had his hands off the wheel in impatience and Kupier waved him on.

Eric, his name was Eric.

Kupier said it to himself as he walked—*Er-ic*, *Er-ic*, *Er-ic*—and the easy rhythm of it almost hid his beeper, thrumming at his belt. He palmed it, aimed it at his eyes, called Dispatch back. This time it was the eight tiny bones of the wrist. They'd been found in a public toilet, floating in a latex glove that had passed through a body. Kupier looked from the phone booth back in the direction of the Amyl River, and then he got it, what he'd been thinking: this was only the beginning.

He stepped out of the cab a block down from the bar with the unflushed public toilet. So he could walk up, compose himself. Pretend he had less alcohol in him than he did. The wind was supposed to be bracing.

Forensics was already there, crowded into the stall with their tweezers and microscopes. The sign on the restroom door said Place Your Ordure Here. Kupier felt like Mrs. Lambert must have felt: untethered from any recognizable decade. Cannibalism? Kupier said it to himself now so that no one could catch him off guard with it later.

He stayed there questioning regulars until last call, but nobody'd seen anything.

Kupier called his captain, told him that they should pull the liquor license at that place, because they were serving bad alcohol. It was blinding the clientele. The captain didn't laugh. Tomorrow was Saturday; it was three in the morning.

Kupier escorted the wrist bones to the lab, walked with them from table to table then woke suddenly in his office at noon. What he was picturing now was a museum skeleton, where they stain all the missing bones black for display. Only this skeleton wasn't from the Pleistocene, or whenever.

The next day Kupier went to church, sat in the back rolling and unrolling a newspaper. There was nothing in it about a hand surfacing bone by bone from under the city, reaching up like it was drowning.

On Monday they had a briefing about it, Homicide-Robbery. The table was small and Kupier sat with his back to the window. It made Stevenson have to stare into the sun with his already-red eyes.

The lab had rushed the bones overnight for two nights. They went together, more or less. It was supposed to be a male, now.

"A *one*-armed male," Stevenson said.

Kupier leaned forward, out of the sun.

"This is my case, right?" he said to the captain.

The captain nodded, said of course, of course.

"Thought you had chemo on these days," McNeel said, making a show of squinting, as if not believing his eyes that this could be Kupier, here, alive.

"No," Kupier said, instead of *Tuesday*.

McNeel held his hands up in apology.

The rest of the briefing was the usual parade of forensic pathologists and criminal psychologists. At one point someone clapped ponderously.

Two weeks later it was an ulna.

Kupier didn't tell his two grandchildren about it. His daughter had left them there with him for the afternoon. They were Rita and Thomas; Thomas was named after Kupier. He took them to the park, bought ice cream all around. They called him Grandpa K. The other Grandfather was Grandpa M, probably, for Marsten. Thomas was ten, two years older than Rita. Grandchild R and Grandchild T. Kupier kept both of them in sight at all times.

"Do you know about owl pellets?" he asked them.

They looked up at him.

He sat them down and had to explain first about owls at night, and then about mice, scurrying, their whiskers sensitive to the least shift in the air, and then about the owls stumbling out of the sky, vomiting bones into the wet grass.

Thomas looked up into the four o'clock sky when Kupier was done.

Rita asked about Mrs. Lambert.

They were standing by the dying elm.

"I don't know," Kupier said.

The last time he'd seen Rita and Thomas had been in the hospital, before remission, and they'd had goodbye cards for him, drawn with pictures of him and Grandma K in heaven. They'd never met her, though, so she was just a woman with white hair and glasses. He still had the pictures.

"More ice cream?" Thomas said.

They knew they were at Grandpa K's.

He ushered them through the line again, watched the sidewalk for their mother. She was late, her body full of bones. There was no message from her on the machine, either. Just Stevenson, asking if he should say this on the recorder then just saying it anyway, that the high end of the ulna had been a green fracture, which doesn't happen so much with dead—

The tape ran out there. Rita and Thomas were standing at Kupier's legs.

"Like with trees," Thomas said, using his interlaced fingers to show the way a limb will break when it's alive.

Kupier turned on cartoons for them and stood at the window. He could hear the children's teeth rotting, and wanted to lead them into the bathroom, stand there while they brushed.

"Where is she?" Rita asked.

Kupier turned back to her and said their mom had probably just stopped for dinner. It wasn't the first time. Rita asked where. Kupier looked past her to his beeper, by his keys on the counter. It was dancing across the Formica.

It was McNeel, calling from the bullpen.

"I can't," Kupier said.

In the cartoon, a tall robot was shooting flame from his hand at a column of water. It steamed away.

"Who *can*?" McNeel said back.

There was a tibia at the fair.

Kupier stood at the phone for a long time, his finger on the plunger, the dial tone in his ear, and then shrugged into his jacket. No gun, though. Not with the children.

They took a cab out past the city limits, and the neon Ferris wheel rose out of the horizon, spreading the children's mouths into grins. They were sitting on the other side of the car from Kupier, because he'd stood on the curb behind them, guiding them in, making sure the door was closed.

"How many tickets can we have?" Thomas asked.

"As many as you want," Kupier said.

The cabdriver was humming something ethnic.

The sanitation engineer was waiting for them at security booth. "This way," he said, studying the children, then just led the way to the long bank of porta-potties. Trash was blowing from blade of grass to blade of grass, strands of cotton candy drifting through the air. A clown stepped out of the fifth of the plastic outhouses, his red hair frayed up into the night, thin, vertical diamonds of greasepaint bisecting his eyes. The engineer pointed two down from him, to the third. It was cordoned off, out of service.

"Usually it's just vitamins and coins and the odd pair of glasses," he said. "But this . . ."

In the fiberglass collection tub under the floor was a human tibia.

The skeleton in Kupier's mind got less black.

"He had to carry it here," Kupier said.

"It wasn't there before," the engineer said. He was holding his hat on, curling it around his temples. They were upwind.

"I'll send them to get it," Kupier said.

"Take the whole thing if you want," the engineer said, indicating an iron hoop at the apex of the outhouse, and then looked over Kupier's shoulder at something. Kupier turned. It was the fair. Thomas rode the Ferris wheel six times in a row while Kupier stood holding Rita's hand at the gate. Kupier wondered if they'd learned tibias yet in the second grade, or third.

They took another cab back to the city, both children falling asleep, their lips stained blue.

Waiting on the stoop was Ellen.

"Where were you?" Kupier asked.

"Where was *I*?" she asked back.

One of the buttons on her blouse was still undone.

After she was gone, two twenties stuffed into her hand, Kupier sat in the living room. The cartoons were still on, muted. He dialed in the number from the photocopy of Penny the dog's tag, but didn't get the machine like he wanted, the voices all in sing-song unison.

"Yes?" the father said. "Hello?"

In the cartoon one character was whirling another over his head like helicopter blades.

"Penny," Kupier said, unsure.

"Who is this?" the father asked, his voice cupped into the phone, away from whatever living room or dinner table he was standing over.

"Just checking," Kupier said, eyes closed, and hung up.

What kept him awake some nights were the bones they weren't finding, that they were supposed to have found. Because if they didn't have a humerus or clavicle or zygomatic arch to fit into their skeleton, maybe the killer would have to supply them with one. With another one, one they could find.

Stevenson said it wasn't like that, that there was just one victim, tied up in a cellar. He explained how the gauchos in the nineteenth century used to carve steaks from the cattle they were working, then rub a poultice into the wound, slap the cow back into the herd. He was slouched in Kupier's doorway, a cigarette threaded behind his ear.

"That all?" Kupier said.

Stevenson shook his head.

"You should at least pretend to try," he said, clapping his palm on the metal doorjamb in something that was probably supposed to look like restraint. "Set a good example for us rookie types."

"Because you're taking notes, right?" Kupier said.

Then the labs came back.

The blood type from Mrs. Lambert's pie tin, mixed in with the saliva, was O positive, another glass slipper—good in court but useless until then—but the fragments of genetic markers from the two fingerbones and the wrist bones and the ulna and the preliminaries on the tibia, they seemed to share more than they didn't. Which was statistically unlikely, narrowing the victim profile to an ethnic subgroup maybe, or an extended family. Kupier sat in his office the rest of the afternoon. It was Tuesday again. Kupier was still saying *Eric* in his head, tapping his pencil with it, and then he got it: Eric from Group.

He'd been the only one in Cancer Support who still smoked. In public at least. They'd made him sit by the door because of it, even. Kupier had always watched him sitting there and thought of scuba divers from television, how they sat the same way on the edges of boats before they rolled out: knees together, hands on their thighs.

At first, Kupier had watched him because he wanted to go with him, into the picture Rita and Thomas had drawn of heaven, but then he'd lost the drawing for a few frantic days, and when he finally found it again, the James case had been open—a woman poisoned in her own kitchen—and he couldn't just leave it, her, so he didn't.

The tibia had striations, of course. Like the ulna. Gnaw marks. And, because it was the fair, the public, the newspapers got hold of it. Kupier had three years left, and a cast of teeth in his pocket. At the airport earlier, dropping Ellen and the kids off for a weekend trip to see their father, the teeth showed up in security as dentures. The guards were too young to know any different.

Kupier checked the car out every day now, drove the street for bones.

He drank rye and water at the Amyl River and waited for the one-armed man.

He read the news before dawn. On the third day he was named in the C-section, second page, and the next day there was the picture he'd had in his head, of the blacked-out skeleton. That afternoon Dispatch fielded one hundred and twenty-two calls about bones. They were in rain gutters, bird nests, untended lots. All but four were bogus, and one of those turned out to be another finger joint, only this one was from a funeral urn, the ashes all blown away. Kupier walked away from it to the other three. It took eight days, total. It was a twelve-year-old boy with a cardboard box and an encyclopedia set. He'd reconstructed the bones he'd found over three weeks into a fibula, a calcaneus, and most of the bones of the foot. He said ants had eaten the rest. Kupier asked him where, and the boy pointed four lots down and two weeks back, to before a foundation had been poured for a new house. Kupier stood in the frame of what was going to be a kitchen. It smelled like pine. In the trunk of his car, caulked together into the shape of a lower leg just like the illustration in the encyclopedia, were the bones. The boy's mother said she'd thought he was just gluing animal bones together to look like a foot, or a leg, or whatever.

Kupier ran the boy's nonexistent sheet too, and everyone on the block, and none of them came up as registered cannibals or former serial killers.

Stevenson sent him a copy of a page from a book, about a man who, over the course of a year, had eaten a bus, piece by piece.

Kupier wrote *pelvis* into his notebook.

The next morning was his six-month checkup. He was clean, still, but didn't feel like it.

"You sure?" he asked the oncologist.

The oncologist stopped on his way back into the hall. "Alright," he said. "Not supposed to lie to the police, right?" He smiled, his eyes golf balls, his voice going mock-solemn. "You've got seventy-two hours, Thomas."

Kupier's hands played along, trembling on the buttons of his shirt.

The oncologist looked at his watch when he passed Kupier, walking out through Emergency. It was too loud to do anything else. Kupier smiled with the outside corners of his eyes, stepped out the double doors, and then the world flashed silver and his hand fell to his gun, and he had it out before he could stop himself, even when he knew it was a photographer.

"You're Detective Cooper, right?" the photographer asked. "Working on the Maneater case?" He was wearing running shoes.

Kupier lowered his weapon.

Behind the photographer, a pair of paramedics were holding a patient on a stretcher, the aluminum gurney rolling away behind them, down the slope to the parked cars. The patient wasn't moving. Still thought he was being saved, maybe. That this was that kind of world.

"Detective?" the photographer was still asking.

Kupier turned back to him. "Maneater?" he asked.

The photographer shrugged, disappeared.

The following morning, Kupier just sat in his office, waiting to get thrown up against his own door. He didn't have to wait long. His captain unrolled the paper on his desk, smoothing it with deliberate strokes. In the picture, Kupier was an old, frightened man. With a gun.

That night he went back to Group for the first time in months. The poster someone had brought and taped up on the wall over the coffee machine read (re)MISSION, and the shadow the uppercase letters cast was a cross. Kupier wasn't sure what it meant. The people in the group smiled sidelong smiles at him but didn't approach. Because he might run off again, huddle around the memory of chemo in his apartment alone. He didn't ask where the other missing people were. Of the new people, one was on crutches, her sweatpants tied up at the middle of her missing thigh. Kupier held his breath and eased out the door, into the Amyl River.

"Where's your friend?" the bartender asked.

Kupier pretended to cast around for Stevenson, then looked at his watch and did the math: sixty-one hours left until the doctor's joke could be funny. He tried to say *remission* the way it had been on the poster, with a cross behind it, and when he finally got the door open to his house—sure that a great, gray owl was gliding soundless down the street for him—he found Rita and Thomas sleeping on his couch, their mouths stained red from popsicles. The television wasn't on, which meant they'd been carried in already in their blankets. Kupier wrote *Cooper* into his notebook and slept in the chair, his gun nosed down into the cushions.

Ellen didn't come back for the children until noon. Kupier didn't say anything, just listed what they'd eaten, what they hadn't.

"You're working on that investigation in the papers," she said.

Kupier nodded as little as possible.

"You were named for your mother," he told her.

She looked away, blinked.

"You going to find him?" she asked.

"Eventually."

He didn't get to the station house until three thirty. There was a package on his desk, all the labels printed on a printer. The brown paper was grease paper, and it was tied with brittle twine. He opened it with a pair of pliers, expecting hair matted with blood, a sternum, a scapula, but it was just a twenty-five year plaque with his name on it, and a handful of Styrofoam peanuts. He asked his captain about it.

His captain held his head in his hands and stared down at his desk calendar.

"That wasn't supposed to come to *you*," he said. "It was *for* you, but not *to* you, see?"

"Surprise," Stevenson said, suddenly in the room.

Kupier didn't know what to do with it.

His teeth were still powdery from the children's toothpaste the children had said he had to use if they had to. It was like plaster, like he had the cast in his mouth. He brought it up from his pocket and looked at it. Nobody had asked him for it because it was already no good—not fitted for the ulna, the tibia.

The assumption was that the soft tissue was getting digested.

Stevenson had sent another memo, too. This one was an entry on hyenas. The passage highlighted was about how the hyena didn't have an MO like a lion or a leopard—teeth to the throat, the skull—but that it simply ate its victims until they were dead. Which could take awhile, Kupier thought. If you did it right.

After the day shift was gone, Kupier thumbed through Stevenson's personnel file, but he was clean too. No proclivities for human flesh, anyway. He almost laughed: next he'd be running his own sheet.

Night came, and with it another package.

It was the second set of labs Kupier had requested. They were in an oversized brown envelope. He sat on the pew outside his office and read them and then read them again: the DNA from the blood from the saliva from that first fingerbone matched the genetic workup of the bones themselves.

Kupier leaned back. Across the room from him, on the board, was a diagram of a human skeleton. The bones they'd found so far were blacked out, and the ones that were missing were grey, presumed missing, just not found yet. The tacks stuck into the blacked-out bones were color-coded to the map alongside the skeleton—where they'd been found—and there was yarn trailing from two of the tacks, from where McNeel or somebody had tried to luck into a pattern, a pentagram or arrow or happy face or something. The drop sites were random, though, all over the city. But Kupier was looking at the skeleton, again. It was one person now. No longer a body the killer was building, but one he was taking apart. All the blacked-out bones were from the right side, too.

Kupier looked down at his own hand in a new way, spread his fingers so that the tendons pushed against the skin.

Twenty-five years, Kupier said to himself.

That night it was another homicide, unrelated. It was in a sprawling parking lot; there were witnesses, even. Evidence to bag. Kupier stood in the middle of it all and surveyed the endless series of trash cans. They were spaced twenty parking slots from each other, staggered every third row. In one of them there would be more evidence.

A uniform approached, asking what Kupier wanted him to do.

Kupier shrugged, his hands in his pockets.

He gave them McNeel's home number.

In the park later he walked until the dead elm was silhouetted against a streetlight, and then he drew his shoulders together once, twice, and on the third time his dinner came up. He leaned forward, walked his hands down his legs to the ground. Was this how it was with the killer?

When the tree shifted with the wind, the streetlight pushed through, and Kupier's hands were spattered with blood. His mouth, his lips. Like before. He started laughing around the eyes and then convulsed with it, and when he stood there was a figure watching him across the grass. Thin, gaunt—at first he thought it was the woman from the parking lot, risen to accuse him, then it was Mrs. Lambert, a pie tin in her hand for his vomit, but then it was neither of them. Just somebody with a cigarette. Eric. From group. He inhaled his cigarette and the end glowed ashen red, and then he breathed in again, deeper, and Kupier could feel it in his own chest.

Eric turned, flicking the cigarette away, and Kupier followed.

It was too late for the Amyl River, so they went to one of the all-night cafeterias instead. They sat across from each other.

"So," Kupier said.

"Why are you following me?" Eric asked. His hands were balled in the pockets of his jacket.

"I'm not," Kupier said.

Eric looked away. "I wasn't at Group," he said. "I saw you go in, though."

Kupier wiped his mouth: no blood.

Eric smiled.

"You too?" he said.

"What?" Kupier said back.

"Re-lapse . . ." Eric said, drawing it out, making it into a happy, benign song.

Kupier shook his head no.

Eric shrugged, said he didn't go anymore because Group was for people who needed support—people who needed to deal with having *had* cancer. It wasn't for people who were having it again.

"What were you doing in the park?" Kupier asked.

"It's a public place."

Kupier leaned back. "Do you need anything, then?" he asked.

Eric smiled, raised his eyebrows. "A pancreas," he said, "yeah. You?"

"I told you," Kupier said. "They got it the first time."

Eric shrugged whatever.

"I was meeting somebody," he said.

Kupier didn't bite on this like he knew he was supposed to. Instead he laid a twenty down for their two coffees, stood into the fluorescent light. He called for the waitress to give Eric the change. Eric shrugged.

"Still using?" Kupier asked.

"Asking as a cop?" Eric asked.

Kupier just stared down at him.

"Tell me why I shouldn't," Eric said.

Kupier went home to his living room and sat, going through his own file this time. He didn't throw up anymore, but he wasn't moving either, just sitting there. When his beeper shook he thumbed it off, and when his alarm clock rang he walked upstairs, killed it too, then called Natty at the front desk, told her he wouldn't be in today. He had thirty-two hours of the joke left. He saw the oncologist's golf ball receding into the sky. He ate tomato soup so that when it came back up, if there was blood in it, he wouldn't have to know.

The next time he opened his front door it was Stevenson on the stoop.

"Two days, hoss," Stevenson said.

"It's Cooper," Kupier said. "Don't you read the papers?"

Stevenson wormed his way in. He had two coffees in the crook of his arm, both sloshing over the rim, and a bagful of grease that was supposed to be breakfast.

"Captain said to hand-deliver this," he said.

It was Kupier's Finger, R. Ring: J Doe file.

"You went in my office?" Kupier said, taking in the manila folder.

"Not me," Stevenson said around his cup. "But look."

Kupier did: there was a third lab report now.

"Our first soft tissue," Stevenson said, widening his eyes with how important this was.

Kupier scanned for a location, but it looked like a misprint. "The park?" he said.

"Nearly the same-ass exact spot," Stevenson said. He'd been saving it. "And here—" He flipped the page back to a black-and-white photograph of a cast of a footprint.

"Who found this?" Kupier asked.

Stevenson shrugged, looked away, his off-hand pointing at himself from the back of the couch.

It was Kupier's footprint, Kupier's blood. Farther out, past the edge of the crime scene, would be another footprint. Eric's, if Eric had even been real.

"Anything else?" he asked.

"Just that he's sick or something," Stevenson said. "His blood-tox came back but loaded, man. I mean, it's like I'm working Narc again all over. Oh, oh, and this guy's not O positive anymore, either, going by the puke. Know what I think?"

Kupier looked at the food soaking into his coffee table.

Stevenson rolled on: "—That this nutjob's like *feeding* the vics to each other, man. See?"

Kupier pushed his lower lip out with his tongue.

"Got a car here?" he asked.

Stevenson nodded.

Kupier went upstairs and got dressed. The only thing different from every other day was his shoes.

"You okay?" Stevenson asked, slumped in the driver's seat.

Kupier was looking away from whatever pill Stevenson thought he was getting away with palming into his mouth. It was yellow. In his office, the second lab report was face down right where he'd left it. Kupier read it again, then slid it under the veneer surface of his desk, pushed the glue down around it with his elbows and held his head with his hands. The only other choice was telling Stevenson it had been him in the park, that he was sick again. But then he'd be pulled off the case, have to take another extended sick leave.

Now he was the only one who knew, though. Meaning he was the one responsible for cleaning up—stopping it all.

"What now?" Stevenson asked from the door.

Kupier stared at him for long seconds, deciding. It was obvious, though. There was only one thing. "It's a cycle," he said. "We stake out the rest of the drops, wait for him."

The next morning it hit the papers, the bloody sputum in the park.

Mrs. Lambert was waiting on line one for him.

"Is it him?" she asked.

Kupier closed his eyes.

"Yes," he said, "yes."

The next lab report identified the particulate soft tissue as the malignant bronchial matter of a lifetime smoker. Which gave them a range of ages, from forty to maybe sixty, just because sixty was the oldest active pattern killer to date. And the spectrum of pharmaceuticals in the bloody sputum from the park broke down in the lab's pie tin as medicines for medicine—chemotherapy.

"He's dying," Stevenson said, another joke.

Kupier got in his car and drove the streets for bones, until Ellen showed up one night bruised around the face, silent, Kupier's hand dropping to the gun he didn't wear to bed.

"Ellen," he said.

She laid her head against his chest and moved in, moved out again a week later.

"Still working on that Maneater thing?" she asked when she came back for a dress from her old closet. The kids were standing in the living room waiting for the television to warm up.

"That's just what the paper calls it," Kupier said.

Sometime after that—a week, a month, no bones, the stakeouts all dry, abandoned—Kupier saw Eric again, at the bus stop on the east side of the park. The bus came, lowered itself onto its forelegs, then stood up again, left. Eric was still there.

That he was waiting for something illegal was obvious. He had that nervous stance, moving gravel around with his toes.

Kupier eased into the diner half a block down, sat by the plate glass. When it finally happened, the drop, Kupier wished he wasn't there: it was Stevenson. He walked out into the grass with Eric, away from the streetlight. Kupier left a ten on the table and followed them, arcing wide to come up out of the darkness. They were talking low when he stepped in with them.

"K—Harold . . ." Stevenson said, stuffing both hands into his pockets.

Kupier looked away. To Eric.

"What do you want?" Eric said.

Kupier pursed his lips.

"*Harold*," Stevenson was saying. "A little late, aren't we?"

"Just saw you here," Kupier said back, still watching Eric.

"Well here I am," Stevenson said, holding his empty hands up.

There was nothing to do, really, so Kupier rubbed his eyes, left.

The next morning Stevenson was in his office door again. "Eric Waynes," he was saying.

"I'm not—" Kupier started to say.

"It's not what you think," Stevenson was already saying, "not what I know you're thinking."

Kupier looked up. "What is it, then?" he said.

Stevenson blew a pink bubble of gum, collapsed it. "He's a . . . contact. From the old days. We've got kind of a system worked out."

"This isn't Narcotics," Kupier said.

"I know it's not Narc," Stevenson said. "I tell myself that every day, man. But listen. This guy, this Eric Waynes, he says he was in the park the other night. That he could maybe give us a description of the Maneater."

Kupier breathed in, made himself exhale.

"In trade?" he led.

Stevenson shrugged, did something with his lips.

"I don't want to know," Kupier said then, "do I?"

Stevenson shook his head no, just once, in a way that Kupier knew he used to have long, greasy bangs.

That night Kupier called Eric. He still had the number from the list they'd made at group, passed around from left to right, the pen tied onto the top of the tablet with kite string.

"What do you want?" Kupier asked.

"Relax, man," Eric said. "I'm not going to tell him anything."

Kupier laughed through his nose, hung up.

That night, drinking coffee at the cafeteria, Kupier threw up again, spilling red out onto the table.

The waitress backed away.

This was what the Maneater was in all the papers for.

Kupier made himself breathe, breathe, then rose calmly for a wet dish towel.

The night shift was all gathered around, watching him.

"You don't have to . . ." one of them said—clean it up—but Kupier did. He took the towel with him too, after wiping his cup down with it, and the seat, and the napkin holder, and the door. They knew who he was, though. If anybody came around asking.

Kupier quit going to Group again, because he thought they could see it in him, eating him, then sat in the parking lot of the clinic for as long as his nine-month checkup would have lasted.

It had been two more weeks now, and still no bones.

"He's dead," Stevenson pronounced. "Choked on a kneecap or something . . ."

But then he showed up with a sketch. It was in Eric's anonymous hand. It was Kupier in the park, a silhouette lurching from tree to tree, all in black except for the lungs, which were red C's, facing each other.

"What was he on when he drew that?" McNeel said.

"All-points bulletin," Stevenson said, covering the smile on his face with the CB he didn't have.

That night Kupier called his captain at three in the morning again, after the Amyl River had closed, and asked about early retirement. His captain outlined what was involved like he was reading from an index card, like he'd had this all ready for some time now, and Kupier leaned into the phone booth and pretended he could hear the captain's wife in the bedsheets on the other end, listening to all this with her eyes closed. She was beautiful. She was there.

Next he called Eric, and asked him in another voice if he had it?

"Thought you did," Eric said, using another voice too.

Kupier drove, drove, parked in front of Penny the dog's house. Twenty-five years. His gun was on the dash. Penny was a crown of reddish hair jumping for the top of the fence every four seconds.

When the security floodlights over the garage glowed on, he pulled away.

He wrote *Rita* in his notebook. And *Thomas.*

Finger, R. Ring: J Doe was the only case he had that was still open. Kupier did the one thing he could: he drove to Ellen's, knocked on the door.

"Dad," she said.

"Just wondering if the kids—" he said.

She was clutching her robe at her neck.

"What's that in your mouth?" she said, quieter.

Kupier pulled his lips over the plaster teeth.

"You alright?" she asked. "It's late."

Kupier nodded. It was.

Thomas appeared in the doorway off the living room, dragging an old ski jacket of his mother's he'd been sleeping in. It scratched across the carpet, one arm trailing. Kupier thought of the black-and-white photograph of the James woman looking up from behind her washing machine.

"Just wanted to see if they wanted to stay with Grandpa tonight," Kupier finally got out.

It was too late, though. All the other excuses.

In her complex's parking lot, Kupier held the wheel with both hands. It was for the best. What he had been going to get them to do was open Penny's gate for him.

He found Stevenson instead.

Kupier rolled his car alongside, unlocked the passenger door.

"On the job," Stevenson said, after he'd climbed in. Both hands in his pocket. He smelled like sweat.

"Talked to Eric Waynes?" Kupier asked, pulling away from the curb.

The corners of Stevenson's eyes crinkled. He shook his head no as if this was the funniest question he'd had all week. "You?" he asked back.

Kupier drove. "That blood in the park," he said.

Stevenson looked at him, patted the dashboard above the radio for some reason.

"Blood?" he said.

Stevenson's hand was trembling, yellowed.

Kupier nodded.

Stevenson watched him from his side of the car.

They rolled to a stop behind Penny the dog's house.

"Should I ask?" Stevenson said.

"Personal," Kupier said back. He hooked his chin at the gate. "Just open it," he said.

Stevenson snorted. "That all?"

"I need to be in the car."

Stevenson shrugged, rolled out into the alley, leading with his shoulders. The dome light didn't come on because Kupier had already disabled it. He watched Stevenson over the hood—hunching toward the gate, his long, careless steps eating up the gravel and the weeds.

He looked back to Kupier once before he did it, to be sure, and then flipped the handle with the belt of his jacket. To leave no prints, if this was coming to that. The door swung in and a metallic flash of red exploded from the tails of Stevenson's jacket.

He smiled, held his hands up, and Kupier gunned the car.

Stevenson chased behind for a few steps, filling the rearview, then slapped the trunk bye, stood there trying to breathe.

Kupier kept Penny at the leading edge of his headlights, and, for a moment, couldn't remember if she'd lived through the surgery or not—couldn't remember what he was chasing, where she was leading him. He coasted to a stop at the end of the alley.

Minutes later, Stevenson leaned down by his side mirror.

"Let me guess," he was saying. "Ex-wife got the dog in the divorce, and you—"

Kupier looked over at him. Stevenson. Who always had morning breath in the middle of the afternoon.

He showed Stevenson the drawing of his wife Thomas or Rita had done. It was creased from his wallet.

"I'm sorry," Stevenson said.

"Where do you want to go?" Kupier said.

Stevenson stood, staring past the hood. "To hell, now," he said.

Kupier smiled, blinked. "Get in," he said.

On Tuesday, Kupier started canvassing the houses downstreet from Penny's. In the direction she'd run without thinking. Police work. It took a week, up one street, down another, his notebook clammy in his palm. He wrote down the numbers of the houses that he didn't know about—where no one answered the door—and then he came back after five thirty, got them crossed off the list. Except for eight. Out of seventy-two. It was just him doing it.

He watched the houses at night, then. Off the clock, out of radio contact. Nobody was calling him anymore anyway. Not since the fast draw at the hospital. It was supposed to be a kindness—not opening any more files he wouldn't be able to close—but it wasn't. It gave him too much time to think.

At work on a Thursday morning he pulled the reverse directory, attached names to the eight houses in Terranova where no one was ever home. He ran their sheets. Nothing. One had various handicap privileges, so he marked him off. Another was an international something or the other. Kupier had the front desk call his employer, see if he'd been out of the country at any of the right times. He had. So had two more of the people. Which left five. Kupier crossed the woman off, got it down to four, then crossed the two married men off. So now it was two. He alternated nights, watching one then the other, until he knew Terranova's schedule, which kids would explode from which door, when. It was like being part of it.

But then his beeper interrupted.

It was another drop, an old one. Just a finger.

McNeel took multiple pictures of which way it was pointing, like it had been arranged in the grass after being vomited up.

Kupier left the two men remaining on his list to themselves, visited Penny at Animal Control.

"They know she's here?" he asked the man in the wheelchair.

The man nodded, disappointed.

"Anything show up lately?" Kupier asked.

"Like what," the man said, wheeling back in jest, "a *skull*?"

After two weeks, Kupier paid the twenty-eight dollars to have Penny spayed, then delivered her to Rita and Thomas.

"I'm sorry," he said to Ellen.

"No," she said, watching the kids, the dog. "They need something just like this."

There was a thin scar on Penny's belly. It was like a little ridge, like she'd been cut in half, glued back together.

"She's good with kids," Kupier said.

He didn't know what he was doing anymore. He could feel a tiny homunculus of bones in his stomach—himself—waiting to be thrown up. His notebook was full of words he didn't remember writing down. He had to mark them out each morning.

After Halloween—Rita and Thomas dressed up as a race car driver and a zombie cowboy—Kupier met his replacement. It was another transplant from Narcotics. Like they were taking over. He looked around Kupier's office, leaning back on his heels, both hands buried deep in the pockets of his oversize, probably stylish slacks.

All Kupier's stuff was in boxes around the desk.

"Maneater," the transplant said, in appreciation.

Kupier nodded. The skeleton was still on the wall, but tacked over now with other cases, other dead people.

"Merry Christmas," the transplant said, to himself it seemed—taking in the office—then caught Stevenson flashing by, palmed his shoulder like a bike messenger will a truck, let himself be pulled down the hall.

Kupier had four days left. Early retirement. Rat off a sinking ship,

McNeel said in the mornings, smiling. Kupier smiled too. The line in his toilet at home that had been sterile blue for years now—accumulated crystals you could scratch off—was red now. From the tomato soup.

Kupier clenched his fists.

For retirement someone had already left him an aluminum walker. It still had its Evidence tag wired onto it. Alone in his office at night Kupier leaned on it, tried it out, and fell over the front, crashing into the filing cabinets.

He thought of Mrs. Lambert. He pictured the man in the wheelchair at Animal Control. A dog he'd seen on television that didn't have any back legs, just a pair of strap-on wheels. And then the handicapped man in Terranova.

Kupier breathed hard, suddenly aware of the dusty smells of the floor, the light seeping in under the door, a moth flailing in his trash can.

Of course.

He took a bus to Terranova and walked up the driveway of 2285 Rolling Vista, jack-o'-lanterns smiling behind him. The garage was open. For a cat, evidently, the litter box up on the dryer in the corner.

The car was fitted so that all the controls were on the left side of the wheel—accelerator, brake, blinkers, horn, quadrant, lights, everything. It bristled with levers. Kupier opened the door. The key was in the ignition. He advanced it to Accessory, turned the blinker for a right signal.

The wall of the garage before him glowed yellow for three intervals, then the fourth was dimmer, the fifth dimmer, and the sixth just a sound, the battery only strong enough to push the relay, not the bulb.

The car hadn't gone anywhere for months. Since the drops stopped, probably.

Kupier loosed his gun, closed the garage door. It was so loud, so heavy. But he went in, no warrant, walking slow for his eyes to adjust, feeling for the kitchen counters which were lower than usual—custom—and at last he stepped into the living room.

Leaned against the brick hearth was a man without either of his legs, and with only a left arm. He was chewing the meat of his right shoulder, strings of red connecting him to himself.

Kupier sat down across from him.

They watched each other. The man swallowed. Kupier did too.

The air of the house was fetid, rotting.

The man was eating himself.

Kupier withdrew his gun, laid the cool side of the barrel against his forehead, then closed his eyes, felt for the garage again. The plug-in battery charger. It took all of four hours, but there was still enough time before dawn for Kupier to cradle the man in his arms, place him in the back seat, then drive the one-handed car to the curb in front of his own house. He unloaded the man, locked the door behind him—the phone already disabled—then took the car back, wiped the house down of himself.

In oversize freezer bags in the guest bathroom were other body parts, and a cooler full of gauze and antibiotic and morphine.

Kupier took it all.

By the middle of December, another Narc had seeped into Homicide-Robbery. Kupier heard about it through McNeel. He was the only one who still called. In his living room, the cardboard boxes he'd brought home from his office. The boxes were still packed with cases. He didn't want to look in them anymore.

"Didn't they give you a plaque or something?" Ellen had asked, dropping them off.

Kupier nodded.

After they left, he called the station house to ask what McNeel was already supposed to be finding out: if Eric Waynes was still listed as a criminal informant. But then Stevenson answered the phone.

The plaque was balanced on the mantel.

"Looking for Len," Kupier said.

"Detective McNeel . . ." Stevenson dragged out, then grinned through the phone somehow, hushed his voice: "I think—yeah, I think somebody spilled some Worcestershire sauce or something on him, K, then like just left him in the park, man. Real tragedy."

"Tell him I called," Kupier said.

Upstairs, Martin Roche was watching cartoons. Kupier had found a mannequin in an alley, taped the legs and the left arm to Martin, then put him in his own old clothes. It was like dressing a doll. The blond wig he already had leftover in a closet; it just needed cutting into a man's hairstyle. The sunglasses were because Martin's eyes were always going everywhere. It made Kupier nervous.

For Thanksgiving, Kupier had cut Martin's turkey up for him into small portions then pressed down on it with his fork until the meat came up between the tines in a festive paste.

Here, here.

His tongue was gone, of course, chewed off. Probably the first thing, really—the closest. When he talked it was with his tablet, the pen he kept tucked in the back of the leather glove of his one good hand. Sometimes, walking to the store for a paper or some more gauze, Kupier would think about the litter box in the garage of 2285 Rolling Vista, and apologize to the cat. But it was just a cat. No matter what kind of eyes Martin drew it with.

Christmas Eve, after the more dutiful of Homicide-Robbery had knocked on his door, caroling, guns at their hips, Ellen showed up with the kids. The presents were under the tree for them already. Kupier sat in his chair watching them. It was a sea of wrapping paper. Ellen got him a small portable television. She'd already put batteries in it. Kupier turned it over and over in his lap.

"You look good," Ellen said.

Kupier shrugged. His cancer was upstairs in the laundry corner of his bedroom, the brakes of his wheelchair clamped down.

Rita and Thomas were spitting up bows by now. Rita paused, looked at Kupier and then back, and asked her mother what was that in Grandpa K's teeth?

"Ketchup," Kupier said, pulling it in. "Tomato soup."

Penny was there, her leash hooked under the andirons of the cold fireplace so she wouldn't go upstairs.

Before bedtime, Kupier got Rita and Thomas to singsong a greeting into his answering machine, then immediately started picturing unnecessary trips to the corner store, dialing his number from the pay phone, talking to Martin through the speaker.

This is remission, he might say. *This is retirement.*

He was in the upstairs bathroom dry heaving when the andirons clunked out of the fireplace, chipping the tile. Penny was loose now, not up the stairs though—Kupier knew every sound after thirty-two years—but at the front door.

Kupier stood, steadying himself on the towel rack, and walked down the hall as if in a dream, looked down onto his lawn.

Looking back up at him, pointing grudgingly up *at* him, a strung-out Eric Waynes.

Idling at the curb, smiling behind his hand, Stevenson.

Merry Christmas.

The way Kupier looked down the stairs at Ellen made her run up to him, a kid under each arm, her eyes full.

"Who is it?" she whispered.

Kupier pushed her into his bedroom.

"Close it," he said, about the door.

She did, twisting the deadbolt into the jamb.

Kupier nodded. There was blood still on his chin, from throwing up.

Ellen picked up the phone but Kupier guided it back down.

"What?" she said. "Who is it? Is it *him*?"

The Maneater.

Kupier closed his eyes, then opened them back. Looked over at Thomas. He was just staring at him, at Grandpa K, his mouth and chin bloody.

"You're him, aren't you?" Thomas said, his voice full of wonder, and in answer Kupier held his arm out along his side in the shape of a grandson. Thomas didn't step into it.

"A misunderstanding," Kupier said, starting to cough, spattering the wall red, "she said it was just an owl . . ." and then was just concentrating on trying to breathe *air* when Rita crossed the room to gather something, one of her mother's porcelain figurines maybe, that she hadn't seen for years now. Whatever it was, it made her lead with her hand, the expression on her face the kind you have in a dream: wonder. Until an arm reached up for her from the laundry, pulled her into its lap, and for the next twenty minutes, as long as Stevenson made Eric stand there knocking, the arm drew pictures for Rita and Thomas on a notebook, sketches of all of them up in heaven now, already—Grandma and Grandpa K, Rita and Thomas as bunny rabbits holding hands, Ellen hunched over on the other side of the room screaming, her fists balled at the sides of her head, her toes pigeoned together, knees knocked.

Kupier put his hand on her shoulder and told her not to worry, that this was going to work out, and for an instant saw himself as Mrs. Lambert, gaunt at the edge of some great light, and he smiled inside, so deep that he crumbled away altogether, everything but the teeth, and the legend he was about to become.

About Ellen Datlow

Ellen Datlow has been editing science fiction, fantasy, and horror short fiction for forty years as fiction editor of *Omni* magazine and editor of *Event Horizon* and *Sci Fiction*. She currently acquires short stories and novellas for Tor.com. In addition, she has edited about one hundred science fiction, fantasy, and horror anthologies, including *The Best Horror of the Year* series, and most recently *Body Shocks: Extreme Tales of Body Horror*, *When Things Get Dark: Stories Inspired by Shirley Jackson*, and *Christmas and Other Horrors*.

She's won multiple World Fantasy Awards, Locus Awards, Hugo Awards, Bram Stoker Awards, International Horror Guild Awards, Shirley Jackson Awards, and the 2012 Il Posto Nero Black Spot Award for Excellence as Best Foreign Editor. Datlow was named recipient of the 2007 Karl Edward Wagner Award, given at FantasyCon for "outstanding contribution to the genre," was honored with the Life Achievement Award by the Horror Writers Association, in acknowledgment of superior achievement over an entire career, and honored with the World Fantasy Life Achievement Award at the 2014 World Fantasy Convention.

She lives in New York and co-hosts the monthly Fantastic Fiction reading series at KGB Bar. More information on Ellen Datlow can be found at www.datlow.com, on Facebook, and on Twitter as @EllenDatlow. She's owned by two cats.